Queen of The Unveiled Path

Case File: TDG-512B

The Time Bureau Files

Book 2

Table of Contents

Map of Vaelthara

"The world is a chord the gods once struck; every forest, sea, and mountain is the echo of that first, eternal note." — *Aetherholt Prologue Tablet, Line 3*

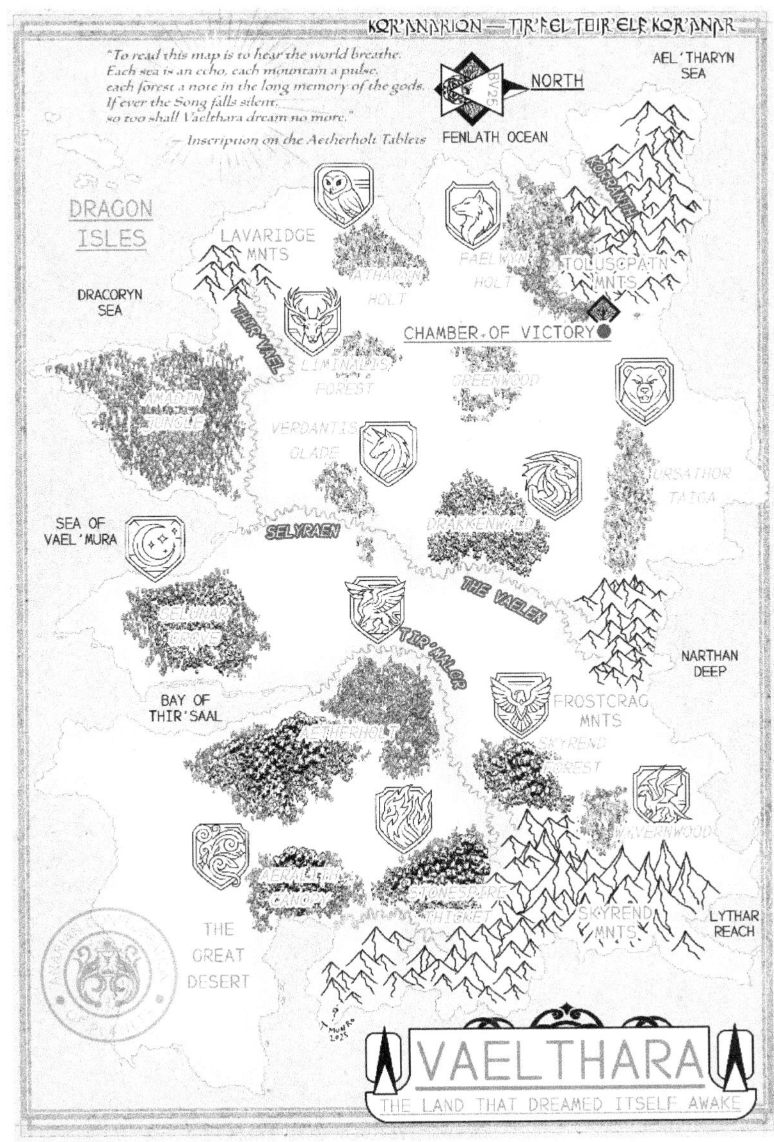

"Where the wind's song falters and the sands begin to dream, the fate of the world hangs upon a single breath." — *Aeralith Border Inscription*

Author's Preface

There is comfort in believing that progress supplants what came before—that each discovery renders older truths obsolete and that knowledge once abandoned was never truly needed. Science teaches us how the world works. It does not always explain why certain powers endure after belief has faded.

History remembers moments when dismissed forces returned without permission—when truths dismissed as superstition proved real and dangerous. What was lost was never the power itself, but the understanding of how to recognize, restrain, or survive its return.

The Time Bureau Files began as a story of time travel and lost civilizations. Following Kellyn Windstream and the refugees of the Anari Confederation carried it into something deeper. Fleeing their future, they brought science and memory into a forgotten age—only to discover that reason alone would not preserve them. Some truths do not vanish when abandoned. They wait.

Book 2 offers a narrow window into who the ancient Anari truly were. It is told through the traditions, beliefs, and limits of the Sylph Clan—masters of the Aeralith Canopy—but theirs is only one understanding of a far older and broader civilization. Beyond their histories and assumptions lies a deeper, more fractured truth that no single clan fully remembers.

Old rivalries sharpen. Fractures spread among the twelve clans. Beyond the forest, the Osiri—ancient, hostile, and patient—begin to stir. The Anari's struggle is no longer about escape but about unification in a world that resists it at every turn.

Throughout this volume, the oldest Anari legends resurface—tales of gods, forgotten races, and forces that shaped the world before history learned to deny them. What once seemed symbolic presses uncomfortably close, as the boundary between myth, memory, and belief begins to fail.

The pages ahead are not a rejection of science, but a warning about certainty. Leaving the past behind carries a cost. Sometimes that cost is paid generations later, when what was forgotten comes back to haunt.

Enter knowing this is not a complete history.
It is a reckoning with what has been lost—and with what still waits beyond belief.

— Kurt Hausheer
The Time Bureau Files

Foreword

Readers may judge me harshly for what follows.
I accept that judgment.

I was trained in the halls of the Sylvancrest Time Bureau,
where every oath binds us to preserve the integrity of the
timeline above all else. We are taught that extinction is
preferable to interference and that the river of time must flow
unbroken, even when it leads into darkness.

I am Anari.
I watched my people die to a power beyond what the most
advanced science could counter.
I will not watch it happen again.

The records you hold were never meant to exist. They
originate from a timeline that should have ended in silence.
Instead, through a catastrophic convergence of resonance,
collapsing gates, and decisions history will not forgive, they
were carried back to us—into this distant past.

The Anari you will encounter here are not the people I knew.
They are not the distant descendants who built starports of
living wood and cities that sang with light. We did not merely
explore the stars. We colonized them.

These are our ancestors.
A people alien even to us.
Rougher. Wilder. More terrifying. Beautiful.
Able to command magic with a gesture, a breath, or a note.

Each clan is a fragment of a civilization that had not yet
learned unity but had already mastered its own truths. Each

forest is a kingdom. Each enemy—especially the Osiri—
guards secrets the future Anari never suspected.

In this era, we are strangers among our own kind.

Kellyn Windstream—once known to me only as a linguist
and investigator—is becoming something far greater. In her,
the old world and the new converge. Her divination reveals
patterns no chronoscope can resolve and futures no model
can contain. The clans will give her many names before this is
done.

But one title shall endure:

The Queen of the Unveiled Path.

She sees what others refuse to acknowledge. She walks where
others will not. She creates a way forward where none should
exist.

As for me, I am a scientist in a world still learning what
science is.
A time agent bound to a timeline that no longer exists.
A dark mage moving through the oldest shadows of my
ancestors' gods.

I do not know whether we will survive what lies ahead. I
cannot say whether changing the past will save us—or merely
change the manner of our destruction.

But I know this:

If the Anari have any future at all, it begins here—in
forgotten paths. This is both a record and a warning.

— Ellendyl Felhart
Sylvancrest Time Bureau

Prologue – The Twelve-Floored Tavern

Case File Addendum TDG-512B-00
The following myth appears across multiple Anari cultural layers. Its symbolic connections to recorded historical events justify its inclusion for interpretive context.

The best way to explain this saga is with a story.

Once, in an era before memory, there was a magnificent tavern at the edge of the world. It rose twelve storeys high, each level adorned with carved stone columns, banners of races long forgotten, lantern-light warm as hearthfire, and walls covered by paintings of every people that had ever lived. The aroma of countless meals drifted through its halls; its cellars stored wines never tasted twice.

After ages of tending the tavern, the owner decided at last to sell it.

One evening, Twelve Gods entered.
One human, one dwarf-bred Gravhal, one giant-sized Thraekar, one scale-skinned Sza-thir, one forest-born Anari, and others of stranger form — horn-crowned, veiled, radiant, or marked by powers the world no longer recalls.
The owner poured each their favorite drink. As they surveyed the great hall, every one of them said:

"I want to buy this tavern."

The owner smiled patiently.
"I can sell it only to the one who will care for it best."

Uneasy glances passed among the gods.

"How will you decide?" one asked.

The owner tapped a finger thoughtfully on the bar.

"My tavern has twelve floors. Each of you may shape twelve champions of your kind. One champion claims one floor. When the struggle ends, the race that controls all twelve floors shall be the winner."

A reptilian god flicked his tongue.

"May we interferesss… or aid our children?"

"No," said the owner.
"You must leave. My staff and I must leave as well. No one may interfere."

A gnome god with an oversized nose leaned forward.

"And how shall we know the contest is done?"

The owner withdrew a simple brass bell, polishing it until it gleamed like a star.

"When only one race remains, the last survivor may ring this bell. It will summon the winner's god. I will re-enter with them. Together, we shall confirm that they stand alone. Only then may the victor attempt to purchase my tavern."

A cold voice—the god of the undead—asked:

"What dost thou mean by attempt?"

The owner chuckled. Then the tavern changed.

His skin turned black as midnight obsidian. Horns curled from his brow. Wings of shadow unfurled behind him. His barkeeps twisted into towering horrors, armor blooming across their forms like calcified bone.

"Oh," said the owner pleasantly, now tall enough to brush the rafters, I never sell a tavern without testing the buyer."

His voice rolled like distant thunder. "When your twelve races have finished their war, the surviving race must then face me—and my staff. If they defeat us, the tavern is theirs."

The gods fell silent.

The owner placed the bell upon the counter with a final, soft chime.

"Go to your floors. Forge your champions. When you are done, leave this place. Tell your creations not to touch this bell unless they stand alone."

The gods climbed the twelve staircases. On each floor, they shaped twelve perfect beings—champions of stormlight and shadow, will and fury.

When the shaping was done, the gods departed.

The owner and his monstrous staff sealed the tavern doors and stood outside, with the doors beneath the quiet sky.

"You may watch from here," the owner said.
"But do not enter until the bell rings."

Only then did the first distant cry echo from a window.

A thud. A roar. A crash of battle.

The Tavern of Twelve Floors had begun its brutal contest.

That is how the Chamber of Victory was born.
Its bell has not rung in an age.

Chapter 1 – Time Exodus

Planet: Sylos IV
Capital: Calystron Spire
Aelthrys Temporal Directorate
FY 3553 — Year of the Malloch Breach

Sylos IV was one of the Confederation's far-flung jewels—an outer colony planet founded not for convenience, but survival. Beneath its emerald highlands ran the richest known deposits of Harmonic-Grade Rare Earths: the metals that powered reactors, star-gates, and resonant technologies. An entire civilization leaned on one world.

From the Director's vantage atop Calystron Spire, life rarely seemed fragile. He remembered standing here with his wife—before death took her—watching copper ridgelines blaze beneath the orbital rings.

Beauty. Order. Abundance.

The first alarm shattered all of it.

It wasn't sound.

It was a harmonic vibration—alive, wrong—rippling beneath his boots. The lights flickered. The Spire inhaled sharply, as if bracing.

"Run a diagnostic on the harmonic grid."

Another tremor. Sharper. Discordant.

"Not internal," an analyst whispered. "Signature is external."

The central holomap flared red.
Nine worlds pulsed in synchronized distress.

INTERSTELLAR ANOMALY — CASCADE BREACH
DETECTED

A cascade.
Not random.
Targeted.

"Sylvaranth is transmitting a breach distress!"

"Put it through."

The feed crackled into life—alarms, rushing researchers, walls
shaking from an unseen force.

"Grid collapsing—attempting evac to—BV—24—"

On the map, white glyphs blinked over their destination.

BV 24.
Before Victory.
Before the end of the War of the Twelve Races on the
homeworld.

Felhart's forbidden temporal anchor.
The codematrix that condemned her research and led to her
disappearance still operated, buried within the gate systems.
Her fingerprints were the only remaining trace of her survival.
The death sentence pronounced on her lingered.

Static surged.
Sylvaranth's marker blinked twice—and then disappeared.

A hollow voice:
"They're gone."

"Korrin's Reach incoming!"

Director Maelyn emerged from the fireglare and distortion, burned and trembling—but still holding on.

"Breach expanding—two hundred thousand evacuated—cycle your gate."

Her eyes locked with his across collapsing channels.

"See you in the past, Sylos IV."

The feed died to white snow.

For a heartbeat, the command deck fell silent. He remembered her laughing with him over bad coffee and gate-stability projections, two directors discussing crisis scenarios that never felt real.

Red strobes flashed across the map.

"Distance: 0.14 AU!"
"We're targeted!"

"Begin evacuation. Put families first."

Officers ran.

"Southern barrens miners?"
"Cleared."

A chime sounded.

"Ping from Korrin's Reach—wave confirmed."
"Destination: Vaelthara. BV 24."

One world saved.

More feeds arrived—fragmented, flickering, fading.

"Aelthrys—breach accelerating—gate cycling—"

Golden entropy tore through the transmission, revealing a silhouette like living sunlight.

"God-signature—Galath—"

Static.

A violet marker flickered on the map.

Two worlds saved.

"Korrin's Reach—orbital platforms gone—breach swallowing everything—gate at ninety percent—"

"Your wave is clear," he said. "Safe travels."

"If we make it…" Someone coughed. "Drinks are on us."

Eight worlds dropped out in rapid succession.

"This is surgical…" a technician whispered.
"They know exactly where every world is."

The Spire shattered itself apart.

"Local breach amplitude rising!"
"Entropy tendrils in high orbit!"
"Spiral signature confirmed!"

A spiral.
Intentional. Precise.

"This world is next," the Director murmured.

Hearthfall Refuge cut in:

"Evac underway—gate stability ninety-six—"

Light split the ceiling. The deck lurched.

"See you—BV 24—"

Static.

Three worlds saved.
Everything else is gone.

The Spire tilting sideways, alarms wailing—

"Harmonic stabilizers failing!"
"Temporal pylons destabilizing!"
"The breach is brushing the outer ring!"

"Move civilians into the gate."

"But sir—"

"Now."

Reality unraveled under pressure.

"Gate at one hundred twenty percent load!"
"It's going to tear—"

"It will hold."

He didn't understand why he believed it. Only that something
inside him did.

Then came the stillness.

Not cold.
Not absence.
Older.

Shadows pooled on the broken balcony, forming deliberate
shapes.

At first, he thought it was harmonic distortion.
But distortions do not pick their forms.

A man stood there.

Tall, cloaked in shadows that flowed like willow rather than fabric. Bone-pale light slid over him but never settled, as if the universe itself refused to touch him. His presence bent the air—as if the room remembered
what it meant to fear.

A Malloch tendril punched through the ceiling, shrieking recognition.
The void recoiled from him.

Static-hunger-noise poured through the chamber—
unintelligible to mortal ears.

But the figure understood.

"You… are Silence.
Join.
Unmake."

He raised his head slowly, eyes soft and ancient, unbearably weary and inevitable.

"I am not Silence."

Bone-white radiance unfurled.

"I am Closure."

The shadows at his feet ripped loose like a tide.

"And you shall have none."

The Malloch shrieked—pure terror.
Anti-reality tendrils recoiled as if burned.

He extended his hand.
The shadows he wielded were not chaos.
They were pure.

Final.
True ending.

Reality buckled.
The breach recoiled—panicked.

"Go!" the Director shouted, forcing movement back into his bones.

He drove civilians into the vortex. Technicians followed.

"What about you?!"

Closure walked forward, shadows bracing the failing chamber like invisible pillars.

"Run, child." His voice was soft. Almost kind.
"This ending is mine."

The Director sprinted across the cracking walkway and hurled himself into the temporal vortex—

He did not look back.
If he did, he would see copper mesas shattering like glass, the orbital rings tearing apart, the sky of his childhood unmade.

—as Sylos IV died behind him.

In the silence of his exit, one ancient story whispered up from memory: twelve floors, twelve races fighting in isolation, the Chamber of Victory born in blood.

Their contest had begun again.

Thalorin facing the Malloch on Sylos IV.

Chapter 2 - The Final Transmission

Timestream Interlude — Between FY 3553 → BV 24

Darkness wrapped around him.

Not falling.
Not flying.
Only drifting—weightless, breathless—through a river of
fractured time.

The Director plunged through the vortex, surrounded by
streaks of collapsing histories. The timestream carried him
like a leaf in a cosmic tide, each pulse a reminder of all that
had just died.

Somewhere, he sensed the others—the refugees of Sylos
IV—scattered across the stream like sparks in the void.

Then a shape appeared before him.

Not physical.
Not real.
A creation of memory and emergency code.

A hologram.

Its voice was cold, mechanical, and fraying at the edges of
existence.

Final Transmission Initiated.
Bureau Archive // Interstellar Network Node: Sigma-Nine.

A holographic star map unfolded—impossibly intact,
perfectly whole.
He almost couldn't bear to look at it.

THE FALL OF THE WORLD-NET

The map pulsed. One by one, worlds dimmed and changed:

TERMINATED — CONFIRMED LOSSES

- Aegros — Polar anomaly collapse

- Draventhis — Forge mantle rupture

- Sylvaranth — Crystal lattice implosion

- Faelwyn — Forest ignition cascade

- Torvalis — Oceanic fortress dissolution

- Calenwynd — Harmonic canopy failure

- Eloweth — Song-veil rupture

- Veylthar — Agricultural mantle collapse

- Thaloryn — Necropolis overrun

- Caeranthys — Tundra breach spread

- Carinth III — Colonial grid failure

- Eryndor Beta — Provisional arc collapse

- Selen Rift — Rift-storm ignition

- Narthan Outpost — Relay annihilated

- Lirien Prime Station — Lost post-evac

- Vaelthara Prime — Homeworld extinguished

Sixteen worlds gone.
Billions lost.
The weight settled in his chest like a stone.

The map pulsed again.

DEPARTED — TEMPORAL EVACUATION CONFIRMED

Lirien — Stabilized. Aetherholt evac complete.
Korrin's Reach — Drydock evac confirmed.
Hearthfall — Refuge wave verified.

Three violet markers.
Three fragile stars in the dark.

"Good," he whispered. "Good… that's good."

The map updated once more.

LOST — PLANETARY COLLAPSE IMMINENT

Partial Evacuation: 647,792 confirmed
Last Interference: Unidentified Harmonic Presence — active at severance

He swallowed hard.

He had left a being once called Thalorin—the god of Death—holding the breach with shadow and willpower.

Refugees verified: 647,792.
A fraction of a fraction.
Yet nearly 650,000 lives swept into the past—
enough to rebuild something, if the past had allowed it.

UNKNOWN — FINAL TRACE

One last icon flickered.
Not stable.
Not readable.
Just… echoing.

Vaelthara — FINAL SIGNATURE RECORDED
Unidentified harmonic resonance detected during collapse
Malloch interference overwhelming

A single heartbeat of light.
Then silence.

He reached toward the dissolving icon.

"Whoever was left… I hope they didn't die alone."

The map broke apart.

NETWORK SHUTDOWN

Text scrolled past in cold, clinical lines:

Primary Species Index: Anari — BIOSIGNAL NULL
Classification: EXTINCT

Confederation Network Offline.
All channels terminated.

Good luck.
See you in the past.

The star map shattered into shards of blue-white light,
scattering like dying embers into the timestream.

Darkness folded around him once more.
Weightless.
Alone.

Then new code sparked—twelve blue spirals unfurling like frozen flowers.

[AUTOMATED LAUNCH SEQUENCE // BLACK ARCHIVE CODE 512]
Directive: Maintain Temporal and Genetic Continuity
Status: Collapse Confirmed

Light flared.

From the dying ruins of Sylos IV, twelve deep-space buoys launched, each carrying:

- an archive

- a harmonic memory

- a fragment of the civilization that had been

- and the encoded song of a world that no longer existed

They streaked outward in twelve perfect lines—
each a memory of the gods,
each a shard of the worlds that fell.
One for each echo of the people they once were.

Twelve streaks of harmonic memory piercing the dark.

Ellendyl once called them the mirror that remembers.

And at the end of all things, the mirror awoke.

As the final buoy vanished into endless night, a gentle green pulse rippled outward.

A single note.
A promise that not everything had been erased.

Then the light was gone.

The timestream convulsed.
A sudden gravitational pull locked onto him.

Destination Locked: Vaelthara — BV 24.
Re-entry Imminent.

The timestream tore open.

A burst of light engulfed him.
The past reached out like a living hand—

and everything turned white.

Two Anari leaving their future extinction….

Chapter 3 - The Forest That Should Not Exist

Planet: Vaelthara — BV 24
Region: Faelwyn Holt (Predicted: Uncertain)
Time Since Arrival: 00:00:14

Light collapsed inward.

Sound vanished.

The Director fell—and then stopped—then existed all at once.

He dropped to one knee, drawing in a ragged breath. The ground beneath him was soft and wet, thick with living moss. The scent of sap and loam filled his lungs, grounding him after the nothingness of the timestream.

His hand sank into the moss. He forced himself to breathe.

He was still young by Anari standards—under 30—but the timestream had marked him. His once-auburn hair now streaked with ember strands, his sharp features hollowed by exhaustion, his freckles stark against pale, shaken skin.

He blinked hard.

Not now.
Not yet.
People needed him standing.

Around him rose a forest the Confederation had never cataloged.

Trees spiraled upward like living towers, their trunks braided with glowing veins of bioluminescent moss. Warm spores drifted like embers. The air hummed with life so dense it felt like a physical presence against his skin.

Behind him, refugees tumbled from the timestream—hundreds, then thousands—collapsing to their knees, sobbing, gasping, and clinging to anything solid.

The weight of their terror settled on his shoulders.

"Status check!" he barked, his voice hoarse.

Wardens scrambled to gather survivors, pulling them into clusters and taking counts. The last flickers of the collapsed vortex shimmered behind them.

A warden jogged up, breathless. "Most are alive, sir. Still counting."

He nodded, relief sharp enough to hurt. He had watched an empire die in a heartbeat.

They were alive.

But the forest around them was wrong.

The trunks were too smooth, too thick, too intentional, as if carved rather than grown. The canopy didn't sway in the wind.

It swayed as if listening.

A cold thread of dread curled along his spine.

"Set up an internal perimeter," he said quietly. "No one wanders. No one gets separated."

"Yes, Director."

But it was already too late.

A strange silence fell—not an absence of sound, but a presence. A listening.
The kind that made every hair on his arms stand on end.

He sensed it first.
The forest watched.

Not hostile.
Not welcoming.
Assessing.

"Movement on the western ridge!" a warden called.

He turned sharply—like a man conditioned by catastrophe.

Three riders emerged from the fog, mounted on tall, four-legged creatures the refugees had seen only in historical archives.

Horses.

The riders wore leather and wool, primitive and rugged. One lifted a wooden staff. Their hoods shadowed their eyes, yet he saw them glint—sharp, wary, ancient.

The Director raised a hand. He kept the tremor from his voice by sheer will.

"Hello! We've arrived because of an emergency displacement. Are you—Anari?"

The riders didn't answer.
Didn't move.
Didn't help.

They *watched*.

Then the lead rider leaned toward the others and
whispered—too softly to hear.
Not quite a language.
Not quite a song.

The three riders turned and slipped silently back into the
trees, swallowed by green shadows.

A wave of unease rippled through the refugees.

"What language was that?" someone whispered.

It didn't sound like anything recorded in their databases.

The Director's throat tightened.

Because something else was wrong.

The canopy above them moved.

Not with wind—
with intention.

A scream tore through the clearing.

He spun around—but saw only drifting spores and a swirl of
glowing embers where a child had stood just seconds earlier.

"Where is she?!" a mother screamed. "Where's my
daughter?!"

Wardens tore through the moss, searching—roots, logs,
vines.

Nothing.
No prints.
No drag marks.
No sound.

Only a soft, melodic hum threading through the trees.

A warden stiffened. "Sir. That sound… it's harmonic."

Not technology.
Not song.

Something older.

Another scream.
Farther away.
Then another.

"Director!"

Refugees pointed at the treeline, faces bone-white with terror.

"They're going into the trees!"

"What does that mean?!" he demanded.

"The trees are taking them!"

He ran.

He reached an enormous trunk just as the bark split open—a giant wooden mouth blooming with amber light.

A young man walked toward it, eyes vacant.

"Stop him!" the Director shouted.

Two Wardens lunged—

—and froze.

Women stood between them and the youth.

Women of living wood.

Skin like polished bark.
Hair flowing like rivers of leaves.
Eyes glowing amber.

They sang.

A soft, tender melody that wrapped around the mind like warm sleep.

The youth stepped willingly into the open trunk.

The bark closed gently—almost lovingly—and he vanished.

A single leaf drifted down.

Wardens staggered backward.

"My gods…" one whispered. "They're taking them."

Another trunk opened.
And another.
And another.

Dozens.
Then hundreds.

Woodland beings emerged everywhere, singing that gentle, irresistible harmony.

Refugees drifted forward in mesmerized waves.

"NO—STOP!" Wardens yelled, dragging people back.

A woman brushed a woodland being's wrist—
her eyes glazed—
and she walked into the tree without resistance.

Scores vanished.

Hundreds more followed.

"CLOSE RANKS!" the Director shouted, voice cracking.
"PULL THEM BACK!"

Wardens forced the remaining survivors into a tight circle, bodies pressed shoulder to shoulder.

The Director stepped forward, fury and fear burning behind his eyes.

"STOP!" he shouted at the creatures singing from the trees. "We don't want to hurt anyone! Release them!"

The forest answered.

Their song changed—ancient, mournful, resolute.

It pressed meaning into his bones.

Too many.
Too hungry.
The forest must feed.
We take what the forest claims.

His throat closed.

"Why?" he whispered.

The leaves shivered.

The dryadic beings withdrew.
The trunks sealed.
Silence fell—a silence heavy with absence.

Hundreds were gone.

Alive?
Dead?
Absorbed into something older than their science could comprehend?

He didn't know.

But he knew one thing:

This forest was not passive.
Not safe.
Not theirs.

He exhaled shakily. His voice wavered only once.

"Everyone… stay close. This place is hostile."

He walked to the transmitter the technicians had pulled through the gate.
His hands shook only slightly as he activated it.

"This is the Time Director of Sylos IV, Aelthrys Temporal Directorate. We have arrived. No sign of our ancestors." He swept the forest with his ocular scanner, then transmitted the data. "Report your status if you survived FY 3553."

He turned to his team.

"Set up solar chargers for all systems—then arm the pulse rifles."

The forest watched.
And waited.

Chapter 4 – Council of the High Druid

Planet: Vaelthara
Location: Drakkenwyld Forest — The Living Hall
BV 24.003

"I'll change my mind… once the mountain does."
— *Bromdur Ironshoulder (Gravhal)*

FILE TDG-512B — FRAGMENT 02 / Ellendyl Felhart —
Personal Log

Confirmed refugee enclaves: Drakkenwyld, Wyvernwood,
Northern Thickets. Fourth enclave unaccounted for; long-
range scans indicate siege conditions in Faelwyn Holt.
Enemy activity coordinated—Aeryndai, Minos, and Osiri.
Dryad behavior anomalous; multiple future-born have been
absorbed into root-networks.
Urgent Assembly recommended. End log.

The High Druid's Tree was alive.

Not merely ancient.
Not simply immense.

Alive the way a symphony is alive.
Alive like something that remembered creation.

Amber-glass roots rippled across the ground, branching
upward into halls that curved like the ribs of a sleeping god.
The air thrummed with harmonic tension—warning,
welcome, heartbeat—all at once.

Kellyn felt it in her feet when she stepped onto the living floor.

Her breath hitched. Not from awe. From memory.

She was lithe and long-limbed by Anari standards—more suited to laboratories and linguistics chambers than to sanctums carved from living roots. Her bronze-toned skin looked dull from stress, and the faint constellations of freckles across her nose stood out beneath the Hall's amber glow. Her auburn hair, usually tied in a precise linguist's braid, spilled loose around her shoulders—days of collapse, flight, and terror tearing her discipline apart.

Her eyes, sharp and crystal blue, never stopped scanning. Even here, even now, she was cataloging, analyzing, and translating the Tree's heartbeat into meaning.

Her fingers twitched toward the side-tool at her hip, seeking something rational in a world that defied logic. The tremor in her hands took effort to mask; she clasped them behind her back, straightening her posture as if preparing for an academy review.

But this wasn't a lecture hall.

It was myth made real.

The same subtle vibration she'd felt in Faelwyn Holt was present—just before the roots split open and swallowed screaming refugees. The Tree's law hummed through the chamber.

Break peace here, and the Tree will bind you forever.

A child stood on the root-dais.

Nine years old. Barefoot. Golden-eyed.
Every breath he took glowed faintly beneath his ribs.

Brun Dreamweaver.
High Druid of Drakkenwyld.

He didn't look like the High Druid.
But when he spoke, the forest listened.

Roots spiraled upward, forming twelve living thrones as the clans took their places. Wood creaked softly, reshaping itself to bear the weight—and the conflicts—of its occupants.

The Twelve

Lady Nadja — Dragon Clan
Storm-lit gauntlets, jaw clenched with fresh grief.

Lord Sylveron Windstream — Griffyn Clan
Silver feathers braided through a mantle of stormlight.

Lord Kalmir Aeralion — Eagle Clan
Wingtips rimed with frost; judgment in every blink.

Lord Lowsm Thalosmyr — Owl Clan
Robes of dusk-light; voice like a memory echoing.

Lord Corbys Elaryaen — Unicorn Clan
Movements measured as geometry, as precise as starlight.

Lord Perris Moon'Sael — Moon Clan
Tidal silver circlet glowing faintly with lunar rhythm.

Lord Tans Bjorn — Bear Clan
Half armor, half scars; pine-scented and unmovable.

Lord Flans Felhart — Felhart Clan
Still as carved stone; eyes amber-sharp.

Lady Vyrna Faelorwyn — Wolf Clan
Cloak entwined with thorn and mourning-sap.

Lord Thalos Hart'Thorne — White Hart Clan
Winter made flesh; serene, solemn.

Lady Vaelwyndra Dravokh — Sylph Clan
Edges wavering like heat-haze; half wind, half flesh.

Lord Maerwyn Wyvernaeg — Wyvern Clan
Ash-smeared, ambitious, never trusted.

One seat remained empty.

Sahn Moonspear—Dragon Clan's greatest warrior—was
missing.

Brun raised his small hand.
The Tree inhaled.

"The Hall is sworn. Be seated."

Saplight dimmed. Silence settled.

And immediately shattered.

The Sylph in the Room

As the lords composed themselves, several stole glances at
Lady Dravokh.

Her presence was… difficult to ignore.

Light curved around her.
The air bent near her skin.
Her hair rippled like moonlit smoke in a wind no one else
could feel.

Kalmir tried not to stare. Failed.
Corbys inhaled sharply.

Maerwyn blinked three times—predatory focus.
Even Lowsm's owl-calm façade cracked.

Dravokh ignored them entirely.

Brun narrowed his golden eyes.

"Attend."

One word.
Like a root striking stone.

Twelve clan leaders snapped their gazes forward like
chastened apprentices.

Dravokh's lips curved slightly.

Kellyn's Summons

Brun stepped onto the living floor.

"One seat remains unfilled," he said.
"By fire, by vision, by the oldest root—
it is hers."

He spoke the name in triple harmony—three tones woven
together like a chord.

"Kellyn Windstream."

The sound struck Kellyn's bones like a memory.
Her chin lifted involuntarily.
The amber glow caught her hair as she stepped forward,
casting her in warm light that made her feel exposed—as if
every buried fear glowed with her.

The Tree breathed toward her, tasting her name.
Kellyn, it's rings whispered.

She swallowed hard.

Dravokh's voice drifted like a cold wind.
"She heareth the third wind. Rare, little one."

Rare.
Dangerous.
A problem, Sylveron's tight jaw seemed to say.

Kellyn steadied her voice.

"Someone with whom I am familiar is among the new
arrivals," she said. "Refugees from my time are scattered.
Some were taken into the roots, while others fled toward
familiar names."

She tapped the implant behind her ear.
A sphere of light flared from the dais—her stored
transmission.

The Director's voice, strained, frantic:

"Gray trees—hollow—armed bipeds—they're hunting us—
anyone hear—Windstream—scatter—."

Static shredded the image.

The Tree itself recoiled.

Vyrna's hands tightened around her throne.
"Gray trees," she said, her voice breaking. "That is Faelwyn
Holt. My home forest."

The word carried memory—wolf-song, snow-lit branches,
and a forest that once embraced its children.

And now devoured them.

Sylveron rose, feathers rustling like thunder.
"Would the Wolf claim these refugees' souls beneath the

mask of grief?" he snapped. "Human steel took your Holt, and now you seek future-born warriors as payment?"

Old wounds cracked open like brittle bark.

Dravokh vanished into mist—then reappeared behind him. Her breath brushed his ear.

"Marvelous, Sylveron," she murmured, her voice sharp as broken moonlight. "That thou speakest of kin, who cast thine own brood to wander untethered."

Sylveron flinched, his feathers flaring.
He swung at her—striking only air.

She was already seated, looking bored.

"Show yourself when you speak!" he snarled.

Kellyn's heart whispered treacherously:
… I like her.

She forced her expression into neutrality.
Too late; Sylveron had seen the flicker of admiration.

Dravokh smiled—moonlight on shattered glass.

The council erupted.

Tans slammed a fist into the Tree's wood.
Kalmir bristled with frost.
Maer's smirk sharpened.
Flans Felhart murmured casualty projections under his breath.
Nadja cursed in Dragon-tongue, making the sap hiss.
Vyrna's eyes burned with grief.

"The Holt has turned its face," she said. "It takes the future-born first."

Kellyn saw the memories in her eyes: the trees opening, the dryads singing, and the forest choosing its prey.

Brun struck the floor twice with his staff.
The Tree trembled.

Silence.

"We do not shatter here," he said.
"The roots hear. The Holt hears. Speak only oaths you can bear to have carried on the wind for a thousand years."

He looked at them—one by one.

"First, we bring our kin to safety," he declared.
"Then we choose their homes."

Kellyn's pulse hammered.
Sylos IV burned behind her eyes.
Her brother's voice echoed from the broken holo.

She stepped forward.
Her knees trembled; her back did not.

"Send me."

The Tree listened.
It always listened.

Froster moved beside her, jaw tight.
Khandyl, silent as snowfall, stepped forward as well.

"I was born in Faelwyn Holt," Khandyl said. "Before its fall. I know its true paths… and where they shift when watched."

Kalmir blinked.
"The Holt moves?"

"It always has," Khandyl replied. "You noticed only when it turned on you."

Nadja leaned forward.
"Can you get them out?"

Khandyl hesitated.
It hurt.

"I can try," she said. "If they still breathe above the roots."

"And those beneath?" Flans murmured.

Silence.

Brun lifted his staff.
Roots wrapped around his ankles, glowing with decree-light.

"So bound," he intoned.
"Kellyn Windstream.
Lady Vyrna.
Froster.
Khandyl.
And all Wolf who will answer the call—go to the Holt.
Bring out the lost. If the Holt will yield them."

The oath carved itself into the Tree, glowing like living law.

Root to root.
Leaf to leaf.
Branch to branch.

Carried out into the waiting night.

The solemn tension cracked as the meeting dissolved.

Children rushed to Brun instantly.

"Brun! Make the tree glow again!"
"Show the sap trick!"
"Let's play roots-and-rivers!"

The High Druid abandoned dignity without hesitation.

"Aye! But only if Perrin quits making the river cheat!"

"I DO NOT CHEAT!" a small Moon Clan child yelled.

Laughter rippled.
Even Tans rumbled his approval.
Kalmir muttered, "By the stars…"
Nadja sighed. "By the flame… we are ruled by a child."

Flans, watching Brun, murmured,
"A child with ten thousand years of memory."

Tans said, "Let him be a child while he can."

No one argued.

Dravokh drifted past; Kalmir intercepted her.

"Lady Vaelwyndra," he began, wings half-spread, "might a
courtier of frost seek—"

Corbys cut in too quickly.
"Or perhaps a Unicorn lord could discuss ward geometry—"

Dravokh hardened like moonlit stone.

"Nay. My vows are older than your ambitions."
She passed through them like mist.

Both men looked like scolded apprentices.

Children swarmed the other lords.
Even Lowsm let a girl try on his owl feathers.

Sylph warriors flickered near Dravokh—half-seen.
Their skull-helmed, silent riders drew no children near.

Kellyn started toward Myrrathis's grove.

But Sylveron blocked her.

"Windstream blood is not unbound," he said quietly. "Your relative—will they bow to ancestors they have never met?"

It was typical of him—turning rescue into legacy.

Kellyn met his gaze, chin lifting.

"This isn't about Windstream legacy," she said. "It's about family."

She walked past him.

His feathers rustled.
Old winds shifted.

Departure

Brun paused mid-game as Kellyn, Froster, and Khandyl approached the exit.

"Kellyn," he called softly.

She turned.

"The Holt remembers the singing wolves," he said. "Remind them of what they sound like."

Vyrna bowed her head, shoulders trembling once.

Kellyn nodded.

The Tree carried her vow outward:

Root to root.
Leaf to leaf.
Branch to branch.

Until even the gray trunks of Faelwyn Holt could hear it.

The War of Twelve Races would not begin in vengeance.

It would begin with a rescue attempt.

Chapter 5 - When the Forest Sang

Planet: Vaelthara
Location: Faelwyn Holt — Southern Ash Vales
BV 24.004

"The forest remembers every step, even the ones we wish we hadn't taken." — *Lirael Moondrift (Anari)*

[COLONY FIELD LOG // FILE TDG-512B — FRAGMENT 03-01]
Hostile contact confirmed: native-human forces, pre-industrial yet rapidly adapting.
Weapons: black-powder matchlocks, iron cannon, primitive steam-powered armor construct ("tank"), horse cavalry.
Estimated enemy strength: $\approx$ 400,000.
Refugee contingent: $\approx$ 600,000 (combat-capable: < 25%).
Environmental interference: canopy smoke, 91% humidity, airborne ash, and blocked low-orbit sensors.
Current status: holding line; failure projected within 3–5 hours without relief.
— Anonymous, Aelthrys Temporal Directorate

They arrived as the forest was burning.

Not the crisp burn of controlled demolition, nor the cold blue hue of directed energy, but filthy, chaotic fire—black, oily smoke billowing into the canopy like a second sky.

Humanoid figures roughly Anari-sized had been lurking at the edges of the refugee encampment for days. Now, hundreds of thousands of legendary hostile beings had arrived, armed and aggressive. Some called them humans. Others called them Anari ancestors. The Director of the Aelthrys Temporal Directorate identified them as a threat.

The Director crouched behind a shattered trunk, pressing his pulse rifle against its scorched bark. His suit's impact mesh had hardened three times—each time a musket ball struck, flattened, and fell away like a spent tooth.

"Status?" he snapped over the short-range comm, his freckles shifting in clusters as he spoke.

Ocular overlays flickered across his vision:

LEFT FLANK: Holding.
CENTER: Breached twice, re-sealed.
RIGHT FLANK: Cavalry pressure is extreme.
CIVILIAN CLUSTERS: Displaced and unstable.
AMMO: 31% (pulse packs), 12% (heavy charges).

He muttered quietly, not about the numbers—about the banners cutting through the smoke.

Red sun. Split by twin blades.

They were called humans. What he didn't know was that they were known as the Red Sun Kingdom. Creatures of myth, now native to this world. Pale, with rounded ears and bright eyes filled with fanatic certainty. Their armor was made of layered leather and iron. Their doctrine was based on relentless attrition.

"Line Two, adjust five degrees east!" the Director shouted. "Concentrate fire on the banner-bearers. Lower their morale."

Refugee rifle teams—miners, engineers, med-techs—shifted into position with hesitant obedience. Their pulse rifles were centuries ahead of the battlefield around them, bright lines of coherent light slicing through the powder smoke, yet they were not trained for combat. Each shot tore through multiple men at once, and each disciplined volley created gaps in the advancing gray ranks.

It didn't seem to matter.

For each line that collapsed, another pressed forward. Kneel. Fire. Rise. Reload. Advance. Repeat.

"Commander!" Governor Reen of Sylos IV ducked into cover beside him, his armor scraped, his cheeks streaked with soot. "They're still coming. Their tech curve is off, sir. These people shouldn't have that many cannons yet."

A cannonball screamed overhead, tearing through branches. Somewhere behind them, half a dozen voices fell abruptly silent.

The Director clenched his teeth. "Accelerated cultural development. Highly unlikely for them to be this advanced. Gunpowder. We knew this scenario was possible, though improbable."

"Knowing doesn't help much when you're up against four hundred thousand zealots armed with black powder, sir," said Reen.

"Hopefully, we can also keep stray shots from hitting the supplies and gear we brought along," the Director replied.

"That's why we brought tools they don't have," muttered Reen.

The Director triggered a command gesture.

Heavy emplacements—roughly assembled from dropship parts, barricade plating, and repurposed kinetic coils—activated along the ridge. Crackling orbs of compressed energy struck the enemy artillery line, flipping cannons end over end and turning crews into silhouettes of light and ash.

The refugees cheered weakly.

The humans did not break.

Drums thundered as priests moved through the ranks—robes as gray as the soldiers' and staves topped with symbols of the red sun. They chanted in a harsh, clipped language the Director's suit only partly understood.

TRANSLATION APPROX: *"Sun devours, sun divides, sun remakes…"*

The first enemy cavalry wave hit.

Horses screamed as they crashed into a wall of shielded bodies and concentrated fire. Pulse bolts punched through armor; impact-resistant suits deflected blades and projectiles. Refugees fell, but fewer than expected.

The refugee guards were outnumbered…

… but they were not outgunned.

"Hold them back!" the Director shouted, rifle barking. "You've survived the Malloch! You can survive this!"

The name Malloch hit the refugees like a slap. Their shots grew more intense. Fear turned into anger.

For a moment, the line held.

Then the steam tank came into view.

[FIELD ANOMALY NOTE // APPENDIX A-17]
Object: Human steam-armor construct (designation: "Tank-01")
Description: riveted iron hull, rotary cannon, primitive boiler & piston drivetrain.
Threat level: disproportionate vs local tech baseline.
Probable origin: assisted design from external emissary (Twelve-Race interference).

It moved through the smoke like a crawling furnace—iron plates riveted to a blunt, snub-nosed beast, chimney spewing white steam. Its front plate bore the red sun sigil, now painted over with a stylized dragon skull.

Its main gun roared.

The ground in front of the refugee line erupted. Armor-hardened suits or not, nothing could fully absorb that blast. Bodies flew. The Director's HUD flashed red across the center of the formation.

"Tank? They built a tank?" Reen gasped. "Here?"

The Director's heart pounded. "Someone helped them."

The machine jerked forward—steam pistons wheezing, treads grinding broken roots into pulp. Matchlock musket fire sparked harmlessly against its armor.

Every time the gun fired, another section of the refugee wall disintegrated.

"Target that thing!" the Director roared. "Heavy packs only!"

Lines of blue-white energy struck the tank's front. Iron burned red, then white—but the armor held. Someone inside cheered.

"Sir," Reen said hoarsely, "that hull metal—"

"Yeah. Not local. Or not yet local." The Director's jaw clenched. "We've just seen the first page of their next century."

The tank ground forward, barrel tracking. It aimed at the densest cluster of refugees—medical tents and non-combatants huddled under a burned hill.

The Director didn't have time to conquer his fear.

"ALL UNITS—"

He never finished.

The forest answered first.

[BATTLEFIELD REPORT // FILE TDG-512B — FRAGMENT 03-02]
External forces detected:
• Forest cavalry (antlered mounts; harmonic resonance confirmed)
• Airborne cavalry (Griffyn Clan)
• Draconic entities (2): one Verdant Flame aspect, one Life aspect
Magical resonance: Class Omega.
Observed doctrine: sound-structured warfare ("Songs").
Outcome: enemy cohesion collapses within 19 minutes.
— The Director

It began as pressure in the bones.

Not a tremor. Not shell shock.

A note—so faint he sensed it before he heard it. Soil vibrated beneath his boots. Charred trunks quivered, shedding ash like old skin.

"Seismic?" Reen choked.

The Director shook his head slowly. "No. That's… not the ground."

The sound swelled—a three-tone chord, each layer distinct yet intertwined. The air thickened; breathing grew harder, yet the air itself felt cleaner than it had in hours. His HUD overlay flickered with interference.

UNKNOWN HARMONIC PATTERN.
SOURCE: ENVIRONMENTAL.
STATUS: NON-LETHAL.

"Sir," a comm-tech stammered, "signal looks like… like a song."

The first of the stag riders burst through the smoke.

They erupted from the treeline in a wedge—massive forest stags with antlers like living crowns, hooves thudding softly on moss. Their riders wore armor grown and woven from living fibers—fungal plates and root-laced leather, with faint blue-green glyphs pulsing across the surface.

Wolf Clan. Anari.

The Director didn't know the name, but he saw who they were attacking.

Each rider sang.

Not like soldiers. Like battle-priests. Their three-part harmony wove the same chord he felt pulsing through his bones.

"Are those humans, too?" the Director asked. "They don't use gunpowder. Why are they attacking the same enemy we are?"

Arrows of cold blue light arced from their bows, curving around refugees and striking officers, banners, and priests. Wherever they struck, enemy lines crumbled—shields shattered, gun crews staggered back as if shoved by invisible beasts.

"Sound as fire control," the Director murmured into his comm, half to himself. "They're aiming with music."

"They're attacking a gunpowder-equipped army with bows and arrows," Reen said. "Foolish. Brave as hell, but still foolish."

The stag cavalry crashed into the human flank. Horses panicked, rearing at the antlered giants. Wolf Clan riders cut down the gun crews behind the matchlock lines with precise, efficient strikes. The steam tank pivoted, its turret grinding, oblivious to the chaos forming around it.

A deeper note joined the song.

The sky darkened.

Something enormous roared, freezing rifles on both sides mid-motion.

A shadow swept over the burning Holt.

The Director looked up.

The dragon descended like a verdict.

Its scales were emerald and bronze, veined with molten gold. Wings like a living forest canopy beat back the smoke. Fire wreathed its jaws—not red or orange, but green, the color of new growth and furnace heat combined.

Its roar hit the soul before the ears.

"Pinch me," Reen whispered. "Because this can't be real."

"Real it is, Governor," the Director said softly. "Grandmother's stories were right, after all."

"Someone's riding it. How do they manage not to fall off?" Reen muttered. "I think its rider is Anari too."

"Why do you think that?" the Director asked. "How can you tell?"

Reen shrugged. "It just looks that way. Feels like a memory. I can't explain."

The dragon dove, its rider curled low.

Green fire surged over the human artillery line. Cannons sagged as iron melted like wax. Powder stores erupted in soundless emerald blooms. Men shouted and vanished into the light.

The dragon did not touch the trees.

Flame flowed around roots and trunks like a tide around stone, leaving bark unburned, leaves intact.

"Selective energy shaping…" the Director muttered helplessly. "Like a godsdamned miracle."

The dragon pulled up and circled. On its back, an armored rider stood in the stirrups, blade raised. Her armor bore shifting sigils—gold, jade, and white—that made his HUD glitch and stutter.

Her visor was mirrored, her helmet disturbingly reminiscent of a corporate security guard's from FY 3553. When she spoke, her voice carried across the battlefield with the same measured rhythm as the Wolf Song below.

"We saw… something like this on Sylos IV," the Director said quietly. "A being the Malloch feared. Maybe these are the same kind of… whatever he was."

He still couldn't understand the rider's words, but his implants caught the underlying structure.

Three-note harmony. Always three. A chord of three notes.

The rider aimed her sword at the human steam tank.

Myrrathis—though the Director didn't yet know his name—folded his wings and dove.

The tank couldn't elevate its gun high enough. It lumbered, trying to angle for a shot.

The rider's blade carved a sharp downward arc. Green fire erupted from the dragon's jaws, a focused torrent slamming into the tank's front armor.

This time, the metal broke.

Iron glowed white. Rivets popped and ricocheted. Steam screamed from ruptured pipes. The tank sagged, then folded in on itself like a melting candle, its barrel curling in defeat.

"That," the Director said faintly, "was our future problem. Solved. By bows, arrows—and dragons."

"And stag riders," Reen added. "Don't forget those. Devastating on impact."

A second roar answered the first.

Human matchlock lines, pikemen, even some refugees, paused and looked up.

Another dragon descended beside the first—smaller, silver-green, with wings veined like vines. Where the first had burned, this one bloomed: roots broke through ash, moss spread over blackened stone, and shattered bodies were gently overgrown with bioluminescent lichen.

"Look at that one!" Reen shouted, pointing. "It's different from the other. Wait—so this is the past on our homeworld? I must have slept through history lessons."

"This wasn't taught in history class," the Director replied. "This lived in myth and fairy tale."

A woman without a visor sat at the life-dragon's neck, her cloak of living leaves flowing behind her. She held a staff aloft.

Her eyes shone like emeralds.

Where her staff pointed, wounds closed. Refugees who'd been bleeding out a moment earlier gasped and sat up, staring at unbroken skin.

"Life-healing energy," the Director whispered. "Actual… living-field reconstruction."

Reen tried to hold himself together but failed. Tears streaked his soot-stained face. "We're dead, Director," he choked. "This is the afterlife."

"I wonder if she knew…" the Director murmured.

"Knew what?" Reen asked. "Who are you talking about?"

The Director shook his head. "Nothing. No one."

The sky filled with shadows.

The Griffyn riders arrived after the dragons—feathered wings edged in metal, beaks snapping at matchlock barrels. Silver-armored knights led them, blades carving arcs that mirrored the harmonic pulses below.

"There's more—and they're different," Reen said.

"Griffyns," the Director answered.

"Is that what they're called? How do you even know that?" Reen asked.

"Part of my family crest," said the Director. "And my grandmother's stories, too."

One rider laughed aloud as he dove, his griffyn tearing through a cavalry banner. The Director's HUD pinged, tagging the rider with biometric data:

HARVEY OAKENSTRIDE — VAELTHARA, SYLVARA PRIME (ANOMALOUS ORIGIN)

"That rider is from the future," the Director said. "From our time. Harvey Oakenstride."

Of course, Harvey would be laughing.

"Riding a griffyn does seem quite exhilarating," Reen muttered.

The human army broke.

Commanders fell to light-blue Queen's Kiss arrows loosed by Wolf Clan archers. Priests scattered beneath griffyn claws.

The steam tank lay shattered and cooling, green fire still crawling over its hull like stubborn vines. The perfect machine of faith and gunpowder unraveled into chaos—men throwing down their weapons, horses bolting, formations dissolving.

The Song did not relent. Stag riders swept after fleeing humans, cutting them down. The forest itself seemed to slow the panicked humans while making the Anari swifter and deadlier.

Wolf. Griffyn. Dragons. And something vaster moving through root and leaf—the Holt itself—pushed outward until the last coherent human line shattered.

Gunfire sputtered, then stopped.

The only sounds left were the echo of the Song, the soft hiss of cooling metal, and ragged breathing.

The Director slung his rifle.

His hands were shaking.

"They sang as they fought," he said. "It was like they sang the math into battle."

[CONTACT LOG // FILE TDG-512B — FRAGMENT 03-03]
Post-battle contact with local Anari subspecies (Proto-Anari). Observed:
- Forest cavalry (giant stags; harmonic archery)
- Griffyn-riding airborne knights
- Two draconic entities with Verdant Flame and Life harmonic patterns
- Organized doctrine based on Song-structured combat and

divine resonance

Immediate emotional impact among refugees: fear →
reverence → dependence.

The battlefield exhaled.

Ash drifted down like exhausted snow. Dragon-fire green
faded to a gentler mossy glow where the worst burns had
been. Refugees moved among the fallen—their own and the
enemy's—checking pulses and sealing wounds with med-gel
and unfamiliar green light.

Wolf Clan warriors patrolled the perimeter, their stag hooves
leaving no mark where they stepped. Their amber, luminous
eyes calmly searched for survivors and threats.

"Those warriors are Anari," Reen muttered.

Near the smashed tank, the two dragons settled.

The life-dragon—Sylthara, though the Director didn't yet
know her name—folded her wings with a rustle like living
leaf litter. Her rider slid to the ground, boots touching ash
that turned to moss with each step.

Elowen.

The Director didn't recognize her, but his chest tightened
anyway. She moved among the wounded with effortless
grace—staff lowered, green light spilling, broken bones
knitting under her touch.

"Director," Reen whispered, "if that's magic, do you think
she's single?"

"Get in line," the Director muttered—and flinched as his ribs
tingled, pain fading. He glanced down; a blackened scorch

mark on his suit brightened, then flaked away like char, revealing undamaged material beneath.

Elowen hadn't even looked at him. Her power had just… brushed past him.

He watched her go, his mind scrambling for vocabulary.

Life-field? Biomantic resonance? Divine parasympathetic override?

Nothing fit.

A shadow loomed over him.

He turned.

A griffyn landed nearby, claws gouging the dirt. Its rider dismounted—a tall Anari in a silver-feathered cloak, with a face so eerily familiar that the Director's stomach clenched.

The man's gaze fell to the signet ring on the Director's hand. The Director saw the same ring on the stranger's hand.

A spiral. The mark of Windstream.

The stranger's eyes widened.

He spoke in a language the implants only partially understood—Old Anari, older than any dialect in the Director's databanks.

Harvey Oakenstride arrived a heartbeat late, boots kicking up ash. He dismounted and joined them.

"By the Song… Windstream blood?" Sylveron asked in the Old Tongue.

Harvey translated for the Director and explained to Sylveron that these people did not speak Old Tongue.

Then Harvey grinned at the Director, switching to Confederation Standard. "He wants to know where you stole that ring, sir. You're refugees from the future, right?"

"I didn't steal it," the Director said, dazed. "It's my family crest. I am Director Corlyn Windstream of the Aelthrys Temporal Directorate on Sylos IV Colony. And you are Harvey Oakenstride, unless my HUD is lying. Who is he?"

Harvey's grin softened. "Correct, I'm Harvey Oakenstride. And this gentleman is Sylveron Windstream, Lord of the Griffyn Clan. Your great-many-times-grandfather."

Sylveron stepped forward, eyes locked on Corlyn.

He set a gauntleted hand on Corlyn's shoulder—firm, warm, utterly confident.

His Old Anari words came slowly, deliberately.

"You. Are. Kin. Windstream does not abandon its own. Welcome home."

Harvey translated lazily; Corlyn barely heard him.

Home.

On a planet thousands of light-years away, nearly four thousand years from where he'd been born.

His throat closed.

A nearby griffyn rider removed her helm—Nyssara Windstream, Sylveron's daughter. Suspicion softened into cautious wonder as she took in Corlyn's freckles and signet ring.

"Who is she?" Corlyn asked Harvey quietly.

"She's Nyssara Windstream," Harvey said. "Sylveron's daughter."

"So, the song loops back," Nyssara murmured in Old Anari. "Storm-born blood returns to its root."

"Director… Corlyn," Reen whispered over a private channel, "is this… could this be an aftereffect of time-travel?"

Corlyn smiled shakily. "If it's a hallucination, it's the most structurally consistent one I've ever had. Reen, I wore the mantle to bring us here and hold this line. Now it's your turn to handle the politics."

A shadow moved at the edge of his vision.

The Verdant dragon—Myrrathis—shifted back, just beyond the tank's crater. His rider slid from the saddle, boots crunching softly on cooling slag.

She wore scorched armor etched with shifting sigils. Her visor reflected the wreckage, hiding her face. She moved with a tight, confident stance that made his combat instincts prickle.

Something in her shoulders tugged at him.

Sylveron's voice dropped, suddenly formal and rough-edged. "The Queen of Swords," he said. "The Storm-Queen. The Pretender."

Corlyn's heart slammed against his ribs.

"She can't— I mean, we lost—"

The dragon rider approached, the visor reflecting ash, antlers, griffon wings, wolf banners, and stunned refugees.

She stopped three paces away.

For a long moment, she stood there.

Then her gauntleted hands rose.

She unfastened the helmet and lifted it free.

Bronze hair spilled out, damp and tangled. Freckles dotted her cheeks in the same constellation he saw in his own reflection.

Her blue eyes were bright despite exhaustion, scanning him as she once dissected ancient texts—quickly, meticulously, with a trace of accusation. A loose strand fell across her cheek; she pushed it back behind her ear with the same impatient gesture he remembered.

"Hey, little brother," Kellyn said, voice trembling. "Where have you been these past five years?"

Corlyn's signature disappeared from the Confederation lattice the day his shuttle vanished into deep space five years ago.

The world vanished.

Kellyn punched him in the chest, then yanked him into a tight, overwhelming hug. He clung back just as fiercely.

"Kellyn," Corlyn breathed. "You've been here a while, haven't you? You look… good."

Kellyn glared at him, eyes bright. "Why the hell didn't you tell us you were okay over the past five years? Mom, Dad, all of us—beyond worried about you, you knothead!"

Sylveron whispered, "Yes. No doubt. They are family."

"Well," Corlyn said, breathless, "I kind of got lost. Then we found Sylos IV, and… you're right. I'm sorry, sis."

Kellyn pressed her forehead to his. "Raife… our older brother—"

Harvey quietly continued translating for Sylveron and Nyssara.

Her voice shook. "Raife was last heard fleeing to the Outer Rim. Malloch ships were chasing the last of the Homeworld Fleet. We never confirmed he made it out."

She swallowed. "And Mom and Dad… they defended the Windstream homestead with the neighbors. They sent a final goodbye message."

Her eyes brimmed. "They were thinking of you, Corlyn, even after you disappeared five years ago." Her breath hitched. "We're the last…"

Before she could break, Sylveron stepped forward and laid a steady hand on her shoulder. Nyssara mirrored him, resting her hand on Corlyn's arm.

"No," Sylveron said softly, voice deep as stormwood. "You're not the last. You are with us now… even though you do not wear a signet."

Then they converged—armor clanging, helmets nearly colliding—arms wrapping around each other like storm anchors.

Refugees watched in silence.

Wolf riders observed with unreadable eyes.

Sylveron's mouth settled into a complex expression—pride, grief, and relief mingled.

Nyssara exhaled softly. "So you are Windstream, after all."

Kellyn held Corlyn as if she could drag him physically out of death's grip.

"You're late," he murmured into her shoulder, because anything else might make him cry.

"I had to stop and borrow a dragon along the way," she murmured back.

He laughed, and a half-sob slipped through.

Over his shoulder, Kellyn caught Elowen's eye as the Life Mage approached, the staff dimming now that the bleeding had slowed. Something passed between them—recognition, gratitude, an unspoken later.

Harvey cleared his throat. "Not to ruin the reunion, but we should move these people before the humans arrive with another invention."

Vyrna Faelorwyn rode up on her great stag, her mourning cloak torn and ash-streaked, her eyes still raw from the Holt's wounds.

She surveyed the sea of shell-shocked refugees beneath the trees.

"These Anari are mine by right of soil," she said in Old Anari. "Faelwyn Holt-born by fate, if not by blood. I will not see them die here."

Harvey translated.

Kellyn loosened her grip on Corlyn but kept a hand on his arm.

"Then let's get them out," she said. "All of them we can."

Sylveron nodded once. "Drakkenwyld will take those unable to march. Aetherholt can shelter more. We will speak at the council about how to divide them."

Elowen brushed her fingertips along Corlyn's shoulder. A faint green light flickered there.

"You will live," she said in a lilting accent that the translator stumbled over. "That is enough for today."

Corlyn looked from her to Kellyn, then toward the dragons, the stag-riders, and the griffyns circling overhead. Bruise-pain from musket impacts ebbed from his ribs.

"Thanks, um…" he started, and the name stuck in his throat.

Reen stepped forward and offered his hand to Nyssara. "Hi. I'm Reen."

Nyssara stared, uncomprehending, until Harvey translated.

Nyssara smiled faintly. "Greetings, Reen. I am Nyssara Windstream."

Science and myth stared at each other across scorched earth and new moss. Refugees and the ancient Anari began to mingle, hands tracing gestures, voices testing words.

Corlyn swallowed. "I have so many questions, Kel," he whispered. "When are we?"

Kellyn squeezed his shoulder. "Welcome to BV 24, little brother. My team arrived a year ago."

Harvey added, "It's a time-travel thing, but on the same planet. I'm no time analyst, but how did you cross over and land right here? Ellendyl's going to want to dissect that. Politely. With diagrams."

"Well, yes. Of course," Corlyn said. "I've got a lot to explain—and even more to ask."

"Try staying alive long enough to ask them all," Kellyn replied.

Above, Myrrathis beat his vast wings once. Emerald pollen-fire drifted upward, settling over the ash like a newborn constellation. The Holt sighed—wounded yet breathing.

Far beyond the burned trees, other fires burned steadily.

The War of the Twelve Races crept back into memory.

And somewhere beneath a distant desert sun, the Osiri listened.

As the clan lords began to disperse to ready their people, Faelwyn Holt sighed again—a low, melodic breath. Kellyn touched Corlyn's arm, guiding him forward.

"Come on," she whispered. "They need to see us."

Together, they stepped forward—four Windstreams walking side by side: Kellyn, Corlyn, Sylveron, and Nyssara. Refugees parted gently, recognizing a legacy returned.

Nyssara paused, then faced Kellyn. "I was wrong," she said quietly. "We were cautious. Others have falsely claimed Windstream blood. I doubted you. I am... sorry."

Kellyn hugged her. Sylveron rested a hand on both their shoulders. Corlyn watched, baffled and moved.

"Mom and Dad took my signet when I left the family business," Kellyn said. "I'll explain later. For now, we need to get these people to safety."

As they looked out over the tide of refugees beneath the Holt, Corlyn added quietly, "You know, every one of these six hundred thousand refugees is related to the Anari of this time."

Kellyn and Corlyn's reunion.

Chapter 6 — Ash, Song, and Shelter

Planet: Vaelthara
Location: Faelwyn Holt
BV 24.004

"A single wing is useless; the swarm is the wind."
— *Chirr-Tala (Krikk'ar)*

The firestorm had passed, but the silence that followed carried its own heavy weight.

Refugees moved through the smoke-filled clearing in exhausted groups—bloodied but alive. Wolf Clan riders guided them with gentle yet firm instructions, their stags snorting mist from broad nostrils. Griffyn knights patrolled overhead like silver hawks.

Two hours ago, the Holt had screamed.
Now it merely breathed.
And every living soul could feel the difference.

Kellyn sat on a broken root, helmet in her lap, trying to steady her racing heart. Corlyn leaned against her shoulder—armor scorched, freckles shining through soot. Beside him stood a thin, olive-skinned man in a soot-stained suit jacket, datapad in hand, trembling under the weight of a task no one had prepared him for.

Governor Reen Halcyra, the Confederation-appointed administrator of Sylos IV.

No soldiers, no staff, no ruling government but him—and even that seemed ceremonial in the ancient forest.

"You look like death," Kellyn murmured.

Corlyn offered a faint smile. "You look like someone who rides a dragon through cannon fire."

"Which is worse?" Reen muttered, staring up at Myrrathis circling high above. "You ride... that? That thing? Does it need a flight license?"

Kellyn blinked. "A what?"

He waved the question away. "Never mind."

Elowen approached, her life-staff now dimmed as triage had paused. Sylthara coiled protectively around the wounded nearby, vines sprouting wherever her claws touched the ground.

"The injured are stable," Elowen said softly. "The Holt is regrowing enough to shelter them."

Corlyn watched the vines creep over a burned root. "This place heals itself?"

Kellyn translated. Elowen smiled faintly.

"Only when someone asks nicely."

Harvey jogged toward them, his two-handed sword strapped on his back, sporting a tired but still present grin. Froster followed, already approached by three different refugees seeking translation help.

"Council runners are coming," Harvey said. "Sylveron wants you all ready for the meeting."

Then he leaned in. "Also—Vyrna is claiming a hundred thousand refugees to rebuild the Wolf Clan."

Kellyn nodded. "She said that."

Corlyn stiffened. "On what authority? These people are Sylos IV citizens, not… feudal subjects."

Reen took a sharp breath. "Governor's authority supersedes clan claims. Forced relocation violates every Confederation charter—"

Kellyn sighed. The Confederation had died with Sylos IV, but she didn't want to tell him yet; he needed to understand. "Governor, the Confederation is gone. New ways to learn."

"Governor," Harvey interrupted softly, "they can't understand you unless one of us translates."

And instantly, 20 people rushed toward them.

Voices overlapped:

"Ask them what the stag-warrior wants!"
"Where do we sleep?"
"Is there food?"
"My wife—please, she's hurt, they don't understand me—"
"What did that owl-looking man say?"
"Where's medical? Where's water?"
"My son is missing—please help!"

Three translators.
Six hundred thousand refugees.
Twelve foreign clan cultures. No structure.

Froster's eyes widened. Harvey stepped in front of him, barking orders like a battlefield sergeant. Kellyn tried to interpret for three families simultaneously. Reen attempted to assert control—

"Everyone, please stay calm—these people are trying to—"

—only more refugees to spiral into him, shouting questions.

Chaos swelled.

Then—

A flash of silver light.

Sylveron descended like a storm, taking shape, Griffyn warriors forming a perimeter with military precision.

"Peace!" he commanded in Old Tongue.

The clearing froze over.

Kellyn translated swiftly. The refugees gradually stepped back.

Sylveron's voice gentled. "You fought well."

Kellyn smirked. "You missed the human steam tank."

"I saw the aftermath. The world didn't explode. Adequate."

He turned to Corlyn, then to Reen.

"And this one?" Sylveron asked.

Kellyn translated.

"This," Corlyn said, "is Governor Reen Halcyra. He represents all Sylos IV citizens."

Reen straightened, sweating but dignified.

"I need to speak to your ruling body," he said. "There are governance issues that must be addressed immediately."

Kellyn translated.

Sylveron's eyebrows lifted. "My people saved your people's lives today. These 'governance issues' can wait."

Reen bristled. "With respect, Lord Sylveron, the refugees are free citizens. They have the right to choose where and how they live. They cannot be divided by force."

Kellyn translated slowly, then raised her eyebrows at Reen and said, "Governor, understand their ways first. This world isn't suited to what you came from."

Sylveron's feathers rustled.
"Clans are not… merely families. We are ancient sovereign forests. You cannot 'form your own' clan any more than you can declare yourself the sea."

Reen sputtered. "That comparison doesn't even—what does that mean?"

Kellyn translated.
Reen buried his face in his hands.

Behind Sylveron, Nyssara tried not to stare at Harvey. Both realized the other was watching and looked away instantly.

Kellyn shot Harvey a warning look. "Don't."

"She looks like she wants to kill me."

"She's Griffyn," Kellyn said. "Which means she wants to kill you, marry you, or both."

Harvey turned pale.

Nadja emerged next, bark-plates still smoking.

"The humans left scorch-lines deeper than we thought," she reported. "Their tank weapon will not be the last."

Kellyn straightened. "They'll build more."

"They innovate quickly," Nadja said. "Someone is pushing them."

"Osiri or Sza'thir?" Elowen asked.

Harvey shook his head. "It doesn't match the technology of the ancient Anari battlefield doctrine. It seems like off-world intervention."

Reen stared. "Off-world? From who? Humans don't have spaceflight here."

Kellyn placed a hand on his shoulder. "Reen... this world is at war with 11 other races."

He blinked. "I… I'm sorry?"

Kellyn sighed. "Long story. Corlyn, were you able to bring any time travel equipment here?"

Corlyn shook his head. "None. We're stuck here unless we can advance technology by 3000 years. We don't have the power source or the expertise to build one."

Before more could be said, Vyrna stepped forward, with Wolf warriors spreading out behind her.

"Speculation later," she commanded. "The Holt cannot shield these many souls. We move now."

She looked at Kellyn.

"Storm-Queen. Will you ride with us?"

Kellyn hesitated—thinking of Sahn, the Amadin Jungle, and of the Song she hadn't heard in a year.

Hundreds of thousands of people were watching her.

"Yes," she said quietly. "We march."

At dawn, the trees opened for them.

Wolf riders flanked the refugees, with stags moving lightly as if the forest bent around their hooves. Griffyn knights circled above. Sylthara flew low to heal the wounded; Myrrathis soared high to watch for enemy banners.

Children whispered in awe, holding tiny glow-wolves and moss-rabbits that nuzzled their hands.

Corlyn walked beside Kellyn.

"You ride dragons now?"

Kellyn smiled. "Dragons ride themselves. Sometimes they let you come along."

Corlyn exhaled. "My whole worldview is shattered."

Ahead, Elowen moved through the crowd, humming a soft healing tune. Vines curled around her like affectionate pets.

"That one," Corlyn murmured, "is dangerous."

Kellyn laughed. "That's why I keep her close."

Reen walked nearby, flanked by two Sylos IV security officers who had survived the Malloch. He clutched a datapad that had long since lost its satellite connection.

He kept glancing at the trees.

"They're… moving," he said quietly. "Are they watching us?"

Kellyn nodded. "Yes."

"Oh."

By dusk, the forest became denser, darker, and more aged. Bridges made of intertwined live vines descended as if bowing. Nadja encountered them.

"The council meets tomorrow."

Sylveron frowned. "Already?"

"The forest spoke," Nadja said. "It told us to hurry."

Harvey translated for Corlyn and Reen.

Reen stared. Corlyn snorted.
"The forest… told you?"

Nadja tilted her head. "Yes."

Reen whispered to Corlyn, "I am profoundly unqualified for this world."

Corlyn patted his shoulder. "Welcome to the club."

As dragons curled around redwood trunks and tents rose beneath the ancient canopy, Kellyn stood at the forest's edge, gazing south toward where the humans had fled.

She whispered: "Sahn… if you still live… guide us."

A breeze stirred. A direction whispered. A storm-memory flickered.

Kellyn touched her sword hilt.

Tomorrow, we face the council.
The day after… we begin searching for Sahn.

Myrrathis rumbled behind her.

Far across the sands, the Osiri Sun-Chains shimmered—waiting.

Chapter 7 — Terms of Peace, Seeds of War

Planet: Vaelthara (Pre-Confederation)
Location: Drakkenwyld Forest — The Living Hall
BV 24.004

"Still water hides the quiet hunter; loud water feeds the bold fool." — *Sskevros (Sza'thir)*

The Living Hall glowed with a soft, golden ache—light pulsing like a wounded heart beneath layers of sapglass and braided roots. The great Tree seemed tired tonight, burdened by the weight of too many dead and too many yet unspoken fears. Lantern-fruit flickered above like constellations mourning their fallen stars.

Brun Dreamweaver stood barefoot on the root-dais. Saplight shimmered beneath his skin, each pulse reflecting the memory of thousands he carried. He looked older—strained, hollowed, yet unbroken.

When he spoke, the Tree listened.

"The hall is sworn."

Roots tightened beneath the Twelve Thrones as clan lords and ladies took their seats—scarred from battle, cloaked in ash, eyes hard with grief.

Kellyn stood among her companions: Harvey, Elowen, Froster, Khandyl, Loka, Witmar, and Aafje.
Corlyn remained just behind them, shoulders straight, expression neutral but intent.

Beside him waited Governor Reen Halcyra—the final, faint remnant of the Sylos IV Republic. His suit was torn, datapad scorched, but his sense of duty had survived the end of a world.

Ellendyl watched from the shadows near the Living Bark, her darkmage implants glowing faintly.

Outside, dragons scraped claws against bark. Griffyns tightened formation overhead.
The Tree braced for truth.

Brun lifted his staff. Amber gathered at its tip.

"First," he said softly, "we speak of those who live."

Nadja of Drak'Nest—Dragon Clan—stepped forward, soot still clinging to her gauntlets.

"Faelwyn Holt sent the refugees to us," she said. "We cannot shelter and feed so many."

Vyrna Faelorwyn rose sharply, mourning cloak rustling like thorns, "My Holt burned. My people died. A hundred thousand survivors have accepted the Wolf Claim. They are Wolf now. That is my right."

Kalmir Aeralion unfurled his wings, feathers rippling like stormclouds.
"You rebuild a clan with strangers from another age?"

"Not strangers," Vyrna snapped. "Kin of those who bled beside us."

Behind Kellyn, refugees muttered anxiously:

"They're dividing us?"
"This isn't our government!"

"We're a republic!"
"Translate! Someone translate!"

Kellyn, Harvey, and Froster scrambled to translate multiple conversations at once.

Governor Reen pushed forward, trembling with frustrated authority.

"As governor of Sylos IV," he said, "I object. These people are citizens of a republic. They have the right to choose where they live. You cannot assign them like property or soldiers—"

Kellyn translated carefully, then shot Reen a glare.

Clan leaders stared at Reen as if he had spoken freezing iron.

Vaelwyndra Dravokh stepped forward, voice like frost. "What is this 'right' thou namest? A leaf declaring the river must obey it?"

Reen pressed on. "They may form their own Sylosian community if they choose. No ancient law overrides that."

Sylveron rose, stormlight rippling across his plumage.

"You speak of rights as if they are trinkets one may simply pick up. Here, rights are bound to forests, blood, and song. A people cannot invent a clan. The land decides such things."

Reen faltered.

Corlyn moved beside him—steady, calm.
"Governor… this world does not follow our frameworks. We must learn before we challenge."

Reen said, "Silence now implies acquiescence."

Kellyn translated, and tension eased a fraction.

Brun tapped his staff. Roots beneath the hall shifted into glowing lines.

"We share the burden," Brun said softly. "Not the people."

Nadja placed a hand on the bark.
"The Tree can open root-paths to every clan. Families may choose their home. Sky for Griffyn. Quiet for White Hart. Hearth for Wolf. Choice by will—never decree."

Reen exhaled."That… aligns with free migration in our colony systems. People will balance themselves by opportunity, not force."

Kellyn translated.

The refugees calmed.
The clans nodded.

The Tree sealed the decision with a pulse of amber light.

Brun's gaze lifted toward Ellendyl.

"Now," he said, "we speak of those who rejected peace."

Ellendyl stepped into the center. Her shadow curled around her feet like ink.

Ellendyl spoke with the weight of someone who knew how timelines collapsed. "In the days since the fall of Lirien," she began, "emissaries of the other races have awakened— descendants from nearly four thousand years ahead of my future. They felt the harmonic shock when the Chamber opened. They came to negotiate. Observe. Prepare."

Kalmir frowned. "To sharpen spears while pretending to sheathe them."

"Yes," Ellendyl said.

Nadja crossed her arms. "And the twelfth race?"

Ellendyl's voice hardened.

"The Osiri Sun-Chain Pantheon."

Growls. Hisses. Feathers rising.

"They refused peace," Ellendyl said. "They believe their chained sun-god gives them dominion over power, including Malloch entropy. They claim to bind lesser Malloch fragments beneath their temples."

The hall recoiled.

"They think they can command dissolution," she continued. "They cannot. It will devour them."

"And their emissary?" Sylveron pressed.

"He knows the timeline has changed," Ellendyl said. "And he believes this is the era when the Osiri rise over us."

Vyrna snarled. "Then war walks north."

Ellendyl did not deny it.

"There is more," she said softly. "From a stolen temple-memory, my mentor Ahsin recovered."

She lifted a black shard. It pulsed with shadow.

"A codex," she said. "Older than every clan.
The Necrodemicon."

The Tree dimmed.

"It manipulates the boundary between life, death, and Malloch entropy," Ellendyl said. "In my timeline, we never found it. But here—now—it lies beneath the Great Desert, in the tomb of Amenemapet."

Nadja slammed her gauntlet. "If the Osiri claim it—"

"They will weaponize death," Ellendyl said, "and burn your forests with shadows."

Arguments erupted:

Tans: "Burn the desert first!"
Corbys: "Impossible undertaking."
Nadja: "Humans innovate too quickly."
Sylveron: "If it offers a counter to entropy, we must seek it."
Lowsm Thalos: "A tool of death to defend life? Madness."
Another murmur: "Necessary wickedness."

Ellendyl's voice sliced through the chaos.

"In my timeline, we debated. We hesitated.
And we died.
Not again."

Dravokh's whisper slid like a knife:

"Send a blade. Not a council."

Her gaze found Kellyn.

Brun lifted his staff.

"Kellyn Windstream," he said.

Kellyn stepped forward.

"You have crossed worlds. You have seen the Malloch and lived. You carry storm, fire, and unyielding will."

Behind her stood:

Harvey
Elowen
Froster

Khandyl
Loka
Witmar
Aafje
Corlyn

Brun lowered his staff.

"A blade is more than steel. It is the heart that guides it."

He tapped the dais.

"As divinely appointed Speaker of the Tree, I task you,
Kellyn Windstream, and your company to enter the sands of
the Great Desert.
Find the Necrodemicon.
If it can save us, return it.
If it cannot—destroy it."

Nadja bowed. "Rootguard will open a path close to the
desert."
Dravokh offered whisper-thread armor.
Sylveron pledged sky and steel.
Vyrna gave her blessing.

Harvey muttered, "Either legendary or incredibly stupid."
Kellyn smirked. "Ellendyl, you're too valuable to risk going.
Remain here, work with my brother, Corlyn. He's a Time
Bureau Director, or was."
Elowen: "We go where we're needed."
Froster: "Does anyone know how hot deserts *actually* are?"
Aafje: "Hot enough to hide sins."
Loka: "Death sleeps under sand."
Witmar: "We move."

Governor Reen approached, pale.

"You're volunteering… for a death-temple… to retrieve a book that manipulates entropy?"

Kellyn nodded.

Reen swallowed. "Then don't die. Please."

Corlyn stepped forward.

"If this codex can stop the Malloch, our future depends on you. If it corrupts you…"

He hesitated.

"…then we depend on you to end it."

Kellyn met his eyes. "I won't let it touch me."

Worry lingered, but he nodded.

Ellendyl came last.

"The Time Bureau would forbid this," Kellyn said.

"The Time Bureau let us burn," Ellendyl whispered. "I won't."

She placed a hand on Kellyn's shoulder.

"The Necrodemicon isn't a tool. It's a question. Every answer costs something."

Kellyn nodded. "Then I won't answer alone."

Ellendyl looked at Corlyn and Reen, "Were you able to bring back any time travel gate parts or means to build one?"

Corlyn shook his head, "No. We are all trapped in this time."

Ellendyl replied, "If we win this war, then we are armed only with magic to fight the Malloch, instead of science and magic in the future."

Brun lowered his staff. Saplight dimmed.

"The Hall remembers your vow," he said.
"May the Song know your names when this age ends."

The lords departed.
Dragons shifted.
Griffyns unfurled their wings.
Stags stamped the moss.

Kellyn stepped toward the edge of the hall, staring south.

Harvey called, "Kel! The stew is edible—mostly. Also, Vyrna wants Khandyl to help choose Wolf crest colors, and Sylveron's already trying to recruit Corlyn."

Kellyn groaned. "Of course he is."

Elowen approached, staff glowing softly.

"You're thinking about the desert," she said.

Kellyn nodded. "We leave soon."

Elowen smiled. "Then I'll learn to make cacti like me."

Kellyn finally laughed.

They walked toward the fire together.

Far to the south, beneath moon and sand, the Necrodemicon turned a page—as if sensing its hunters.

Chapter 8 – The Sun Feels a Tremor

Planet: Kaht-Surath (Osiri name for Vaelthara)
The Great Desert of Shattered Mirrors
Temple-City of Reforging, Below the Solar Gate
Chronometric Overlap: BV 24.004

"He who prepares three exits will never need to flee…
quickly." — *Zurmik Softstep (Zagg'rin)*

The desert was silent.
It listened.

Every grain of scorched sand glimmered like a tiny shard of
Ra-Khepra's chained sun, each particle a mirror reflecting
obedience. On lesser worlds, deserts produced heat and wind
and storms.

Kaht-Surath produced only heat, silence, and the distant echo
of chains grinding beneath the earth.

Far beneath the largest pyramid, deep within the Vault of
Birth-Fire, the Sun-Chain Emissary Ma'at-Khenu knelt alone.

Nine feet tall.
Muscles carved like obsidian blades.
A jackal's skull-visage, carved into perfect predatory angles.

His golden eyes did not shine—they pressed outward, like the
sun itself forced to bow.

Crucibles pulsed around him like molten hearts.

He waited.
He listened.

Beneath even this chamber—

Something shifted.

A long stone sleeping… turning once.
A breath… but not from lungs.
A pressure… but not from motion.

Ma'at-Khenu lifted his head slightly.

Something ancient acknowledged him.
Something patient.
Something waiting.

He tapped one claw against the stone.

Clink.
Clink.
Clink.

The heat in the floor answered with a dull, resonant pulse—
as if the desert remembered an old command.

Then the tremor faded.

But Ma'at-Khenu's ears twitched.

"The deep places listen," he murmured.
"They have heard the trespass."

Across the Great Desert, the sun flickered—just once, like a
heartbeat interrupted.

Ma'at-Khenu inhaled sharply.
A tremor ran through him, shaking bone and chain alike.
The links across his chest writhed like serpents hungry for
memory.

He rose.

"The desert hears a theft."

The words rumbled out of him in three voices layered into
one—

a harmonized snarl of judgment, shadow, and fire.

Glyphs exploded to life along the chamber walls.

A thousand miniature visions of Amenemapet's tomb
unfolded, projected directly from the sun. Symbols crawled
like golden insects toward new configurations.

Beneath the tomb-glyphs…

Older sigils awakened.

Curved pathways.
Tunnels spiraling beneath continents.
Nodes glowing beneath foreign forests.

The Khem-Duat—the deep empire beneath the living
world—was responding.

Ma'at-Khenu's voice was soft but cutting:

"Someone seeks the Book of Bound Shadows."

A figure emerged from the far side of the chamber.

Tall.
Masked.
Feminine.

Nema-Hra the Pure, First Priestess of the Solar Gate.

Her golden mask bore a flawless, emotionless serenity. Her
silver eyes glimmered through the slits like moons caught in
judgment.

Her voice was the cold underside of flame.

"Which lesser race dares touch the Necrodemicon?"

Ma'at-Khenu turned.

"Anari."

Her pupils contracted behind the mask.

"The forest-worshipping wood-elves?"
A scoff.
"They cling to roots and pretend they understand power."

"Roots crack stone," Ma'at-Khenu replied. "If left to spread."

Nema-Hra paused at that.

He gestured toward the living glyph wall.
A glowing line traced beneath a towering forest canopy,
ending at a pulsing node carved with sun-runes.

It brightened.

Then brightened again.

Nema-Hra stiffened.

"The Aeralith Canopy," she whispered.

Ma'at-Khenu snarled softly.
"Their forest. Their arrogance. Their refusal to kneel."

"They have blocked three surface incursions already—"

"Surface," he repeated, disdain dripping from the word.

He tapped a claw on a sigil depicting a long, winding
subterranean path.

"The Khem-Duat does not travel the surface."

"The tunnels aren't complete—"

"They are ancient," he corrected. "Older than Amenemapet.
Older than our line. We merely reclaimed them."

The glyphs pulsed again.
A warning.
A threat.
A promise.

"The forest-born believe roots hide them," he said.
"But the desert has roots beneath them as well."

Nema-Hra swallowed.
Even masked, the motion was visible.

Ma'at-Khenu turned toward the crucibles.

Hundreds of unborn Sun-Children floated in golden amniotic
light—limbs weightless, eyes closed, faces serene.

He extended both hands.

The chains across his chest sank deeper into his flesh,
glowing like metal plunged into a forge.

"Wake," he commanded.
"Wake, my children."

Light flared—then roared.

One by one, eyes opened.
Reflecting only:

Mirror-fire.
Obedience.
Silence.

Nema-Hra whispered: "Emissary… if we send them through the deep roads now—"

"They will reach the forests unnoticed," he said.
"The Anari do not know the Khem-Duat breathes again."

The crucibles opened.
Golden fluid spilled like liquefied dawn.

The Sun-Children stepped forward.

Ma'at-Khenu placed a clawed hand on the nearest one's head.

"Go."
"Walk the Hidden Sun Road."
"Enter the roots of the forest."
"Burn those who defy the chain."

Eight pillars of solar flame erupted upward—
drilling through stone,
cutting through sand,
rising toward the sky.

Ma'at-Khenu watched them vanish.

His golden eyes narrowed.

"Anari," he murmured, "you may walk the winds and whisper to trees…"

His claws tapped slowly.

"… but beneath your sacred groves, our footsteps are already waiting."

Chapter 9 — The Maw of Stone

Planet: Vaelthara
Western Ocean → Dragon Isles
BV 24.007

"The sea remembers every trespass. The stone chooses which ones to forgive."
— *Old Dragon Clan Proverb*

The sea had finally ceased screaming.

An hour ago, the horizon had looked like a graveyard of moonlit sails—ghost ships swirling around the stolen Sza'thir serpent vessel, dragging chains of bone and kelp across the waves. Necrotic runes burned like diseased stars across their cracked hulls. The storm had shredded the sky. Malloch-tainted winds had tried to tear the serpent-ship apart.

And they had fought through all of it.

Now…

Silence.

The storm had not ended.
It had been *dismissed*.

Kellyn stood at the rail, armor soaked, hair clinging to her face, sword still faintly humming with harmonic charge. The waves had settled into unnatural stillness, as if something vast no longer permitted chaos.

Harvey leaned beside her, rubbing his shoulder.

"Well," he muttered, "I've fought undead. I've fought the weather. Pretty sure I've never fought both at once while stealing a lizard-man battleship."

"We didn't steal it," Aafje corrected.

"We liberated it," Froster added helpfully.

"Temporarily," Witmar said.

"Without permission," Harvey finished.

Kellyn wiped grime from her cheek. "Sahn's city was gone— we had to follow the Sza'thir trail south. These ships were the only way."

"And look where that led us," Loka murmured. "The storm didn't stop. Something ended it."

Elowen rested a hand on the railing. "The Lifewind is calming. The sea recognizes something ahead."

Kellyn squinted at the horizon as the mists parted.

Jagged volcanic stone rose from the water like the teeth of a sleeping leviathan—black cliffs streaked with obsidian sheen, crowned with veils of white waterfalls. Mist clung to the heights. A deep harmonic resonance thrummed through the serpent-ship's hull.

Her heart caught.

"The Dragon Isles," she whispered.

Myrrathis roared above, a sound that vibrated in bone.

Harvey whistled. "So Sahn ran here?"

"He never runs," Kellyn murmured. "He repositions."

"Repositioned very far," Froster said.

Elowen closed her eyes. "The cliffs aren't just stone. They were shaped. Taught."

"Harmonics," Aafje said.

Kellyn nodded. "Then this is where he went."

She turned to the others.

"Prepare yourselves. We're going in."

A dark river-mouth appeared ahead—a vast carved tunnel, like a throat in the cliff.

Harvey gripped the wheel. "Hold on. This is going to be stupid."

The serpent-ship surged forward as the current seized it.

The hull shuddered as the sea funneled violently inward.

"Angle 30 degrees—NOW!" Harvey barked.

Witmar angled the tiller and shouted back, "Just because you were in the Navy doesn't mean you can shout orders at me, little brother!"

Harvey's focus didn't waver as he peered into the tunnel.

Waves crashed against obsidian teeth jutting from the walls. Spray burst upward like white fire. But the narrow gap ahead held subtle order—deliberate resonance cutting a safe channel through chaos.

"This is no natural tunnel," Kellyn said.

"No," Elowen murmured. "Someone taught the mountain to sing."

The serpent-ship crossed an unseen threshold.

Darkness swallowed them.

Then—

The walls erupted in blue light.

Veins of bioluminescent fungus traced flowing calligraphy across the basalt and jutting crystals pulsed with alternating tones, creating a layered symphony of ancient sound.

The cave *sang*.

Myrrathis dove alongside them, its scales shimmering with reflected light. Sylthara followed, their harmonics blending—and the tunnel shifted pitch to greet them.

Froster stared. "This is… an ancient resonance-map. Older than any written Anari memory."

"No," Kellyn whispered, brushing her fingers along a rune. "Dragon Clan work. From before Draknest fell."

More runes appeared along the walls, glowing faintly:

Sanctuary. Vigil. Exile. Fire sleeps but does not die.

The current accelerated. Waterfall spray blinded them for a moment—

—then the tunnel opened into light.

They burst into a colossal lagoon encircled by black cliffs. Dozens of waterfalls thundered into the basin. Terraces carved into the cliff faces held platforms, docks, and roosts large enough for dragons.

Dragons perched at different heights—emerald, bronze, storm-gray—watching with smoking nostrils.

Horn blasts echoed across the cliffs.

Harvey winced. "Friendly?"

"Uncertain," Froster said.

Kellyn stepped to the bow, raising her hands.

"We come in peace!"

Elowen sent up a soft halo of seed-light.

On a high terrace, a figure raised a hand. Horns ceased. A rope was dropped.

Harvey tied them in.

They had arrived.

The Dragon Isles breathed around them, ancient and watchful.

Kellyn leapt onto the stone landing.

Footsteps echoed above.

Someone was coming.

The first figure to descend the stairs nearly tripped over his own boots. A wild haired figure with a staff paused and stared.

Kellyn blinked. "… Krack?"

Kracklenut of Draknest froze.

"By Galather's incandescent backside," he whispered. "You're alive!"

Kellyn laughed. "And you're still on fire."

"Only in the appropriate ways," he sniffed, gesturing to the serpent-ship. "This is somewhere between genius theft, war crime, and heroic salvage."

Harvey leaned over the rail. "Heroic salvage."

"And you," Kracklenut squinted, "are the storm-prayer boy. Miracles *do* happen."

Harvey groaned.

A heavier tread echoed above.

Kellyn inhaled sharply.

Sahn Moonspear appeared—broad-shouldered, battle-scarred, carrying a wrapped spear, eyes as storm-gray as she remembered.

He froze at the sight of her.

"Kellyn."

Her breath hitched. "Sahn."

He descended the last steps and offered his forearm.

She grabbed it. He squeezed once—grounding, familiar.

"I felt you in the storm," he murmured.

"And we followed your trail," she said. "Through jungle and sea."

He nodded. "We lost Amadin. We built this."

He gestured to the fortress carved into the cliffs.

"Come. There's much to explain."

Inside the mountain, Emberhold spread out in vaulted caverns lit by molten glass lanterns and bioluminescent vines. Forgeries glowed deep within. Dragon roosts lined the upper ledges.

Dragon Clan warriors watched silently, many scarred.

Kellyn felt the loss in the walls themselves.

Sahn saw her reaction.

"We're ten thousand now," he said quietly. "That's all."

Kellyn's heart twisted. "We can help."

Harvey stepped forward. "Sahn, we have eight hundred thousand refugees. You can shelter twenty-five thousand if they choose to come."

Sahn's tone sharpened. "No more. Any more and we starve. This place is a fortress, not a farm."

Kellyn interjected, "Fishing. The sea is full of life."

Harvey added, "And our people bring knowledge. We've colonized alien worlds before. We can make this place thrive."

Sahn paused—then nodded.

"Elowen."

Elowen bowed her head. "If you let me anchor a tree here, I can open a gate to Draknest. The roots remember."

Sahn placed a hand on the ancient tree sprouting from basalt.

"Then I will send two dragon flights with you," he said. "To guard your sky."

Myrrathis and Sylthara rumbled approval.

Kellyn exhaled. "That's more than enough."

Sahn stepped closer.

"I will join later. There is more to rebuild—and vengeance to set in motion."

Kellyn nodded. "We'll return for you."

Something passed quietly between them.

Kracklenut ruined the moment.

"RIGHT! Packing time! Please avoid touching anything that glows, hisses, sings, vibrates, or looks at you funny. That's about eighty percent of the island."

Harvey sighed. "We're going to die."

"Not today," Kellyn replied.

Elowen placed her hand on the ancient tree.

"Ready?" she asked.

Kellyn nodded. "Let's go home."

The tree's light flared.

Dragons roared.

The world folded.

Return to Draknest

Planet: Vaelthara
Location: The Dragon Caves — Draknest
BV 24.007 (Later That Night)

They stepped out of the tree-gate into a cavern the size of a buried sky.

Roots thicker than towers hung from the ceiling. Lichen glowed in soft golds and greens. Platforms spiraled down into a massive empty roost—waiting for life again.

Harvey staggered. "That was worse than the storm."

Two Emberhold dragons burst through after them—a storm-gray male with bronze streaks and a young emerald-scaled flyer—shaking off the teleport with irritated rumbling.

Moments later, Myrrathis emerged in a flash of bronze light, followed by Sylthara, whose healing chords calmed the cavern.

Then—

The refugees began arriving.

In waves and bursts, as the forest allowed: families, wounded soldiers, children clutching stone toys, future-born Anari blinking at ancient architecture.

Governor Reen stared upward. "This… this could house cities."

"It did," Kellyn murmured. "Before the meteor swarm of FY 2041 buried it."

Footsteps echoed.

Griffyn guards appeared first.

Followed by:

- Sylveron Windstream

- Nyssara

- Nadja, Rootguard Commander of Dragon Clan

- Vyrna of Faelwyn Holt

- Other representatives

They stopped dead at the sight: dragons, refugees, and Kellyn's weather-beaten company.

Sylveron bowed—just slightly.

"You have done what was asked," he said. "And more than we believed possible."

Vyrna stepped forward. "You truly found Sahn Moonspear?"

Kellyn nodded. "He's rebuilding. He can shelter twenty-five thousand."

Nadja inhaled sharply. "That is a gift beyond measure."

Kellyn continued, "Two dragon flights will follow the sky once the coastal paths are safe."

Respect flickered across the clan leaders' faces.

Kellyn turned to Corlyn.

"We're building something new," she said. "A future these refugees can survive."

Corlyn's voice softened. "This can be a home."

Above, Myrrathis lifted his head and sang a long, low harmonic note.

Sylthara echoed.

The two Emberhold dragons added their voices.

The cavern resonated in answer.

Far across the sea, Sahn stood atop the Dragon Isles and felt it.

He exhaled. "She made it."

Kracklenut jogged up. "Feel that earthquake of good news?"

Sahn placed a hand on the cliff. "When the time comes… we join the Song."

Thunder rolled far away.

In Draknest, Kellyn gazed up, sensing the storm-call across distance.

She smiled.

Refugees settled. Moss dimmed. Dragons curled high on perches like living statues.

Kellyn stood on a ledge overlooking it all.

Harvey approached quietly.

"Long day," he said.

"Long month," she replied.

He stood beside her—close, but not touching.

"You held everyone together," he murmured. "Corlyn. Reen. Sylveron. The clans. All of them."

"I didn't do it alone."

"No," Harvey said gently. "But you're the only one who didn't break."

Below, a child laughed as Sylthara's glowing tail drifted by.

Kellyn lowered her head. "When we were in the storm… and the ghost-ships closed… I thought I wouldn't see you again."

Harvey froze—not from fear, but from the honesty in her voice.

"I wasn't afraid of dying," she whispered. "Just the things left unsaid."

Harvey took her hand lightly. "And what things are those?"

Kellyn turned to him fully. "I care for you. More than I should."

Harvey swallowed. "I crossed that line long ago," he said. "I didn't know how to tell you."

Their fingers intertwined.

He leaned his forehead to hers. "You don't have to be the Queen of Swords tonight," he whispered.

Kellyn exhaled, steady and real.

"No," she said softly. "Tonight, I just want to be myself."

He brushed a strand of hair behind her ear. "Stay with me."

She nodded.

Hand in hand, they slipped into the upper tunnels, glowing moss lighting their path.

The doorstone slid shut.

No words followed. Only the warm hush
of a night when two warriors
finally breathed freely.

Chapter 10 - Wings Gathered in Shadow

Planet: Vaelthara
Location: The Dragon Isles — Hidden Lagoon
Chronometric Stamp: BV 24

"The sky favors those who leap before they doubt."
— *Serale Windplume (Aeryndai)*

[FIELD LOG // TDG-512B — FRAGMENT 08]

Recovered personnel: Sahn Moonspear, Kracklenut of
Draknest, 239 Dragon Clan survivors.
Recovered assets: 5 dragons, 9 half-finished vessels, 1
operational shipyard.
Threats: Osiri–Sza'thir hybrid forces; unknown biological
corruption events.
Status: Negotiation complete. Alliance secured.
— Acting Commander Kellyn Windstream

The landing platform glistened beneath a thin curtain of sea-
mist, each stone smoothed by centuries of dragon claws and
Anari feet. The lagoon echoed with dragon calls and the roar
of waterfalls—sound so vast it swallowed breath and thought
alike.

Sahn let go of Kellyn's hand and stepped back. His gaze
studied her—equal parts commander, comrade, and
something brotherly.

"You're looking comfortable leading," he said.

Kellyn tried not to smile. "It's beginning to feel… less like work."

Kracklenut snorted. "She stands taller. You grew more insufferable. Balance of the universe restored."

Sahn shot him a flat look. "Balance will be restored when you're sealed in a barrel and rolled off a cliff."

Kracklenut brightened. "Ah. Then we truly *are* back to normal."

Myrrathis swooped low, landing with an armored thump. The dragon lowered his head toward Sahn, who pressed a hand to the scaled brow.

"You kept her alive," Sahn murmured.

Myrrathis exhaled warm steam.

"Good. I will require that again."

They ascended the carved stairway. The misted lagoon spread below—dragons drifting through the air like living shadows, the skeletal ribs of unfinished ships jutting from the shallows.

Kracklenut tromped beside her.

"We've been out here since the fall of Aeradnor," he said. "Two dozen ships escaped before the Sza'thir swarmed the harbor. The rest…"
He grimaced. "Let's just say the fish have armor plates now."

"And the dragons?" Kellyn asked.

"Scattered and wounded," Kracklenut said. "Some found mates. Some went missing. Verdess's nest was torn apart."

Kellyn's breath caught. "Verdess lives. The dryads healed him at Amadin's edge."

Sahn halted mid-step.

"He lives?" His voice was low, almost reverent. "Then he waits for me. And I will not fail him."

Kellyn exhaled. "Sahn… how were the Osiri and Sza'thir reaching you? No roads. No rivers…"

Sahn's expression darkened.

"We never learned. They appeared from the immovable stone. No tracks. No warning. Scouts found nothing—and then war-bands would be *present*."

A chill rippled through the group.

Kracklenut muttered, "Always where our sentries weren't looking."

"It felt…" Sahn searched for the word. "… designed. As if someone cut the map and slid warriors through the gap."

Kellyn frowned. "Magic?"

"Not Anari," Sahn said. "Not anything the forest could sense. Even the dragons felt nothing until their arrows fell."

He turned west toward the jagged silhouette of the Isles.

"That is why we left. Not from defeat—but from losing the ability to understand our enemy's path."

The upper terrace opened before them—a half-circle of basalt with a firepit at its center. Around it stood the survivors: lean Dragon Clan warriors, each marked by jungle scars and exhaustion.

Conversation halted the instant Kellyn stepped onto the terrace.

They bowed first to Sahn—rightfully so.

Then slowly, unexpectedly… to her.

Kracklenut lifted his hands theatrically:

"Commander Kellyn Windstream, breaker of hive-queens, rider of forest flame, slayer of—"

Sahn elbowed him hard.

"She knows what she's done."

Kellyn cleared her throat. "I'm open to hearing it later."

"Wonderful," Kracklenut replied. "I'll produce a longer edition."

Elowen approached the fire, her palms open. Soft green light flickered from her fingertips, weary but alive. A young bronze dragon nudged her gently, drawn to the resonance.

A Dragon Clan warrior whispered, awed, "A Verdant Caller…"

Elowen blushed.

Sahn motioned for silence.

"The Sza'thir were not alone," he said. "When they destroyed Aeradnor, they carried Osiri glyphs woven into their resin."

He tossed a shard of hardened black material into the fire. Red-gold chain glyphs flickered along its surface.

Elowen recoiled.
Loka hissed.
Harvey muttered a curse.

"That," Sahn said, "is demon-binding script. Produced by Osiri hand. And something worse."

He lifted his gaze.

"They are altering creatures. Binding Malloch taint with solar chain-runes. And they appear through stone. Through nowhere."

Kellyn's voice hardened. "Teleportation."

Sahn nodded grimly.

"It appears primitive… but intentional."

Kracklenut spat into the flames. "Abominations welded together. They're going to break the world."

"They want something," Sahn continued. "Prisoners we captured mentioned the Necro—"

He stopped.

Kellyn whispered, "Necrodemicon."

Sahn's head snapped toward her. "How do you know that name?"

"Ellendyl," Kellyn said. "She learned it from Ahsin's stolen memories."

Sahn's expression darkened. "Ahsin Blackvein… the vampire of the Veydrath? I thought the White Hart clan had him in chains. This age grows stranger by the hour."

Kellyn nodded. "We have peace with ten races. Only the Osiri make war. The Sylph clan is taking the brunt of it."

Sahn exhaled slowly.

War was coming.

The young bronze dragon nudged Elowen again. She rested a hand on its snout.

"He likes you," Kracklenut said. "Which means the Isles like you. Which means Sahn will work you twice as hard."

Elowen looked uncertain.

Kellyn placed a hand on her shoulder. "You're becoming something new."

Elowen whispered, "Something that frightens me."

"Good," Sahn said. "Only fools feel no fear at the edge of becoming."

He rose, spear gleaming faintly.

"You didn't come here by accident, Kellyn Windstream."

He faced the dragons roosting along the terrace.

"Two wings will return with you to Drakkenwyld. Four dragons to guard the forests. Four to stand with the council. Mated pairs—all eight. The caves of Draknest will no longer be empty."

Myrrathis rumbled deep approval.

Kracklenut leaned toward Kellyn. "That means we're going home-ish."

"You are," Sahn corrected softly. "I am not."

Kellyn's eyes widened. "Why?"

He pointed toward the volcanic ridge.

"The Sza'thir fleet fled northwest. Something calls to them. Something old. I must find it before it reaches our shores."

"You can't go alone," Kellyn said.

"I won't. Two dragons. Four warriors. Enough to see what stalks us."

"And if you find something you cannot survive?"

Sahn smiled faintly. "Then you will find only my echo."

Myrrathis growled. Sylthara hissed in warning.

Kellyn's voice shook. "Sahn—"

He placed a hand on her shoulder.

"You will lead where I cannot. Drakkenwyld must be fortified. The refugees will need training in language, song, ritual, and craft. Your people will change the world simply by living here."

Kracklenut sighed loudly. "Gods help us. Two dramatic leaders. Perfect."

Sahn lifted his spear skyward.

His voice shifted into full triple-harmonic:

"Kellyn Windstream, High Daughter of Storm and Steel— the Dragon Isles stand with you."

A tremor shivered through her bones.

Kellyn bowed.

"And my storm stands with you."

Elowen paused beside a twisted cliff-root jutting from the volcanic stone.
It had no business growing here — yet its bark pulsed faintly, as if it remembered rain from a forest far away.

Kellyn glanced at Sahn. "Can we use this?"

Sahn nodded once.
"One of our druids planted the seedling when we arrived. It does not remember the Drakkenwyld, but the roots beneath the isles remember *being* part of it. They were one forest once, before the sea rose."

Elowen knelt, laying both palms upon the bark.
A faint green pulse answered her touch.

"I believe I can awaken it to Draknest as a portal," she whispered. "The Draknest tree knows me. It knows my Song. If this one listens… I can bridge them."

Kracklenut leaned in over her shoulder, whispering loudly: "If we end up halfway underground, I claim zero responsibility. Tree-gates have moods."

Sahn ignored him.
He stepped forward and placed a steadying hand on Kellyn's arm.

"My road takes me elsewhere," he said quietly. "But the path you walk must begin with certainty. Go — take the dragons, take the future-born. Build what we cannot yet reach."

Kellyn squeezed his forearm once, the old Dragon Clan greeting of equals.

"We'll return," she said.

"And when you do," Sahn answered, "Emberhold will stand."

Elowen inhaled, drew the Life-Song up through her chest, and pressed her fingertips deeper into the bark.
Green fire spiraled through the root like veins awakening.

The air rippled — a tunnel of living light opening within the tree's heart, stretching outward toward a distant memory of home.

"Elowen?" Kellyn asked softly.

Elowen nodded.
"The path is open."

Myrrathis roared approval.
Sylthara answered, wings flaring with silver-green resonance.
Two brood-partner dragons stepped forward, talons gripping stone.

Kellyn looked over the assembled survivors — her company, the dragons, the ten thousand future-born preparing to return.

"Everyone through," she commanded.
"This is the fastest way home."

They stepped into the spiraling green light.

The last thing Kellyn saw before the world folded was Sahn standing on the terrace edge, the mist curling around him like a crown of storm.

He raised his spear in silent promise.

Then the tree-gate closed, and Emberhold vanished behind them.

Chapter 11 - Council of Returning Storms

Planet: Vaelthara
Location: Drakkenwyld — Heartwood Chamber
Chronometric Stamp: BV 24

"The sun reveals all truths—usually sooner than we are ready for." — *Amenhet Serapis (Osiri)*

[FIELD LOG // TDG-512B — FRAGMENT 09]

Returned from Dragon Isles.
Four dragons deployed to Draknest.
Sahn Moonspear pursuing Sza'thir fleet west.
Council summoned urgently.
— *Commander Kellyn Windstream*

The wind carried the scent of moss, rain-soaked earth, and faint wildfire as Kellyn entered the Heartwood glade. The living paths parted for her—roots shifting aside, guided by the silent will of the forest.

She had barely crossed the threshold when a warm voice called:

"Kellyn!"

Sylveron strode toward her—tall, bronze-skinned, wearing the storm-gray and green of Windstream. His face held equal measures of relief and strain. He swept her into a brief embrace; one he had clearly been holding in for days.

"I feared your Song had gone silent," he whispered.

"Not today," she replied.

Above them, Myrrathis roared—not in challenge, but in greeting—his flame-bronze wings shaking the canopy. Sylthara's silver-green wings glimmered beside him.

Sylveron raked his hand through his hair. "The others will want explanations. Preferably ones that don't begin with: 'We rode into a hurricane and punched undead off a ghost ship.'"

Harvey perked up. "Okay, but that was *one* skeleton I punched."

Froster elbowed him. "You kicked it."

Harvey spread his hands. "Look, it *fell*, didn't it?"

Kellyn sighed. "Both of you... hush."

The Heartwood doors—living bark that folded back like petals—opened. Drakkenwyld guards stepped aside as Kellyn and her companions entered the council chamber.

The chamber thrummed with quiet tension.

Eleven clan thrones were filled.

One remained empty: Sahn's.

Kellyn's chest tightened.

Brun Dreamweaver sat upon the living dais—bare feet dangling inches above glowing rootwood. He held his staff upright, trying fiercely to look stern despite being nine years old. His crown of woven sprigs glittered faintly with dew.

To his right: Nadja of Drak'nest, arms crossed, expression carved from granite.

To his left: Lady Dravokh of the Sylph Clan, quiet as drifting smoke—silver eyes reflecting the chamber's living light.

The roots pulsed beneath the chamber floor, threads of life weaving like veins under skin.

Brun tapped his staff. The pulse deepened.

"Be welcome," he said. "The storm returns home."

Kellyn bowed. "We bring news from the Dragon Isles."

Nadja's voice cut across the chamber. "You brought dragon wings."

Kellyn nodded. "Four—two for the forest, two for the council. A new clutch will rise from Draknest."

A ripple of relief passed through the room like a breath held too long.

Kalmir Aeralion leaned forward. "And Sahn? Why does he not return?"

Kellyn answered, "The Sza'thir raiders—and ghost ships— plague the waters around the Isles. Sahn is pursuing them west. None will escape with knowledge of his settlement's location."

A low murmur spread.

Dravokh murmured, "The desert sings too loudly this season."

Brun's staff struck once. "Tell us all."

Kellyn recounted everything:

The fall of Aeradnor.
The hive-corrupted nests.

The Osiri glyphs woven into Sza'thir resin.
The serpent-ships fleeing west.
The dragons gathering in the Isles.
New ships being built.
Verdess still alive.

Brun exhaled—half childish relief, half High Druid gravity. "Good," he whispered.

Then his brow furrowed. Something older moved behind his young eyes.

"Windstream," Brun asked softly. "Why did Sahn abandon the Amadin Jungle? Why yield his city?"

Kellyn drew a long breath.

"Because the Osiri were appearing behind his defenses. From nowhere. No roads. No rivers. No trails. Not called by fire or ritual. Simply… present."

The chamber stilled.

"No tracks at all?" Kalmir asked quietly.

"None," Kellyn said. "It seemed like… teleportation. Primitive. But intentional."

Roots coiled under the council floor—an instinctive reaction of the Heartwood itself.

Dravokh's voice slid like cold mist. "They have begun appearing in our Sylph Canopy as well. In glades untouched for centuries."

Nadja's jaw clenched. "Impossible."

"Impossible," Dravokh repeated, "and yet it occurs."

Brun lowered his gaze. "And so Sahn left."

Kellyn nodded. "The Isles are ringed in stone—basalt and obsidian. No roots to twist through. No tunnels to cut. Nowhere for unseen armies to appear. He trusted the dragons. And he believed Drakkenwyld could fall the same way the Amadin Jungle did."

The silence deepened until even the roots seemed to hold their breath.

"A wise choice," Brun said at last. "Danger beneath the roots… unseen, unheard."

Vyrna leaned forward. "And the future-born?"

Kellyn nodded toward Sylveron.

He stepped beside her, voice steady but cracked at the edges.

"They hold the line near Aetherholt. Many have never seen a forest. Many…" He swallowed. "Many lost their world days ago."

He continued.

"They are dispersed among the clans. Food and shelter are the primary challenges. They learn quickly. But they know firearms, not spears. Their implants confuse our ley-lines. They do not understand song."

Nadja folded her arms. "We will teach them. Or they will die."

"Some already have," Sylveron whispered. "Dryads snatch up those who wander."

A hush fell. Even Dravokh bowed her head.

Brun lifted his staff.

"Harvey Oakenstride. Step forward."

Harvey jolted. "Uh—me?"

Kellyn nudged him. "Go."

Harvey approached awkwardly, trying to stand straighter without looking like he was trying.

Brun studied him as though reading past lives etched on his skin.

"Lord Sylveron reports you showed unusual Green magic during battle," Brun said. "Wild, uncontrolled. Strong."

Harvey puffed a breath. "I didn't mean to. It was—well—it just kind of… happened."

Brun touched his staff to the floor.
The roots brightened around Harvey's feet.

"Magic finds those who must wield it. But it will change you. And if you wake the Wild Hunt wrongly… it will devour you."

Harvey forced a crooked smile. "Right. No pressure. Wait, Wild Hunt?"

Brun closed his eyes and spoke with a rhythm of one of the line of high druids before him,

"The Green Knight shall walk where none may live.
The dead shall burn at his passing,
ash upon the moss,
and the Greenwood shall not take him.

He alone may sound the Horn that calls the Hunt awake
and break the god's prison beneath the roots.
Then giants shall fall,
the curse shall remember its ending,
and the Crone's forest shall learn fear again."

Kellyn squeezed his shoulder. "He won't face it alone."

Harvey grinned—lighter, brighter, still the Harvey she knew.

Brun opened his eyes again and said, "Oh, but he must."

The doors creaked again. Harvey shifted and turned to the doors.

Ellendyl Felhart entered—pale, exhausted, every inch of her lined with the residue of dark magic. Shadows clung to her like something freshly born.

Even the roots shifted subtly away from her steps.

She bowed to Brun. "High Druid. I bring intelligence."

"Speak," Brun said.

Harvey moved to the edge of the room.

Ellendyl placed a crystalline slate upon the dais. Shimmering sigils swirled—memories ripped from Ahsin's captured mind.

"The Sza'thir do not act alone," she said.
"They serve the Osiri."

The sigils rearranged into a jackal-headed figure wrapped in burning chains.

Nadja hissed. "Sun-Chain heresy."

Ellendyl continued, "They experiment on captured races. Sza'thir, Serpentes, possibly humans. They use Malloch taint—stabilized through solar chain-runes. They are building something."

"Stronger," Dravokh finished.

Ellendyl tapped the slate again.

A single word filled the chamber:

NECRODEMICΩN

The temperature dropped.

Kalmir whispered, "A legend."

"No," Ellendyl said quietly.
"It is beneath the Great Desert. Amenemapet's tomb. And
the Osiri know."

Kellyn felt her pulse hammer. "So do we."

Ellendyl bowed. "The council must send someone. Quickly."

Dravokh's silver eyes fell on Kellyn.
"The Queen of Swords will bear a sharper burden than she
knows."

Silence answered her.

Deep. Rooted. Ancient.

Brun rose—small, slight, but suddenly vast.
The roots around the dais bent toward him, bowing.

"Kellyn Windstream."

She stepped forward.

"You found Sahn. You saved the refugees. You returned
dragons to our sky."

He placed his tiny hand on her wrist—soft, warm, trembling
with centuries of memory.

"I now ask you to save us from what stirs beneath the
desert."

His voice shifted into a rising triple-harmonic:

"I name you Bearer of the Western Quest."

The roots shivered.

"Gather your companions, including Loka Meadows. His
mind is needed.
Go to the Aeralith Canopy.
Seek the Sylph.
Take what gifts they allow.
Then descend into Amenemapet's crypt.
Return with the book that may save our world…"

His voice softened.

"… or destroy one."

The weight settled like prophecy and iron.

Kellyn bowed her head.
"As the wind commands."

As the lords dispersed, Dravokh stepped silently beside
Kellyn—no sound, no rustle—only the faint scent of storm-
wet leaves.

"Journey to the western Aeralith border," she whispered. "A
great grove awaits. You will be met. Then… sent south."

Her fingers brushed Kellyn's shoulder—cool, feather-light,
dangerous.

"The Osiri move exactly as Sahn warned. They appear behind
our scouts. Where no path leads. In glades untouched since
before the First Songs."

Kellyn swallowed. "No tracks?"

"No movement. No warning."

Dravokh's pupils narrowed, silver burning like a blade. "They enter our forests as though the world itself delivers them there."

She stepped backward into the darkness beneath the roots—and vanished.

Harvey exhaled shakily. "She terrifies me."

Kellyn murmured, "She terrifies everyone."

Sylveron approached. "The Sylph Canopy… are you ready for it?"

"No," Kellyn admitted. "But I'll go anyway."

Pride softened his features. "Then you are Windstream. When you return… we should talk. About the family. And your place in it."

She stepped out into the glade.

The wind rose around her—warm, restless, urgent.

Dragons circled overhead.
Refugees trained in the clearing.
Ancient races plotted the Anari downfall.
The desert stirred.
The Necrodemicon waited.

A quest had been set in her hands.

Kellyn Windstream drew one long, steady breath.

Her path led west.
To the Sylph.
To Amenemapet.
To the sleeping heart of the desert.

And nothing—nothing—would ever be the same again.

Chapter 12 – The Aeralith Whispers

Planet: Vaelthara
Location: Verge of the Aeralith Canopy
Chronometric Stamp: BV 24.01

"Eternity is wasted on those who lack purpose."
— *Countess Vyralithe Noctworn (Veydrath)*

[FIELD LOG // TDG-512B — FRAGMENT 10]

Aeralith perimeter reached.
Forest readings: anomalous triple-harmonics.
Visual contact: none.
Audio contact: all.
RECOMMENDATION: Proceed with care.
— Commander Kellyn Windstream

The Aeralith Canopy did not rise so much as *unfurl*—a wall of silver twilight where the outer trunks pulsed with soft cyan light. Leaves drifted in spirals without wind. The air hummed with a resonance that felt like the forest breathing.

Even Harvey stopped talking for once.

"Feels like the dead are whispering," Loka murmured.

"They probably are," Froster said. "Sylph bind honored spirits into the root-skin."

Khandyl grimaced. "Comforting."

Kellyn stepped forward—
and the moment her foot crossed from the ordinary woodlands into Aeralith soil—

A harmonic chord struck through her bones.

Three tones.
Layered precisely.
Not meant for mortal ears.

Seris was formerly a security guard for the Sylvancrest Time Bureau. She exhaled. Of all of them, she had the deepest ties to the Sylph now—reborn in Dravokh's Ritual, carrying a trace of the forest in her very blood. Light bent faintly around her edges.

Kellyn frowned. "Seris… you're glowing again."

"I'm not glowing," Seris whispered.

"She is," Froster said. "And humming."

Harvey squinted. "That's humming? Sounds like my stomach."

Aafje rolled her eyes. "Your stomach has never reached triple harmony."

Witmar grinned. "Give it time."

Seris laid her palm on a glowing root.
Her outline blurred—soft, translucent, like she was half-stepping into another layer of reality.

Khandyl hissed, "She's disappearing!"

"No," Kellyn said softly. "She's resonating."

Seris drew back, trembling. "The forest remembers me. From the Ritual."

Her gaze glimmered—not fear, but longing.
"It sees me."

Kellyn touched her back gently. "You're safe."

"No," Seris whispered.
"You are not."

Before Kellyn could reply—

The air shifted.

Not wind.
Not motion.
But *attention*.

The canopy leaves all tilted toward a single direction, as if listening to a voice deeper in the heart of the forest.

"That's never good," Harvey muttered.

"No," Aafje said softly. "That is a summons."

The shadows thickened around them. Aafje flinched— hearing faint syllables in a whispered language she had read once in a forbidden book before her grandmother burned it.

They pressed deeper.

The forest grew colder.
Then warmer.
Then weightless—
as if they walked through overlapping worlds.

The ground felt like moss. Then stone. Then a sigh.
Elowen's brow furrowed.

"This forest is layered," she murmured. "Harmonic territories overlapping."

Kellyn whispered, "How many?"

Elowen's eyes flicked around the canopy. "Six. At least."

"It's Fae-built," Loka said. "Mortals don't design forests that move."

"They're not moving," Aafje murmured.
"They are *choosing*."

"Choosing what?" Witmar asked.

"Whether we belong."

Harvey swallowed. "Wonderful."

Khandyl froze. "Movement."

The word barely left her lips—

A shimmer.
A ripple of moonlit distortion—

And a woman stepped out of a tree trunk as if the wood were just a curtain.

She was slender, silver-haired, bronze-skinned—
wearing translucent Sylph armor woven from living vines.
Her leaf-green eyes glowed faintly.

She lifted a hand—not in warning—

In urgency.

"Be still," she whispered, her voice thin as a wind-thread.
"The Clan-Lady stands in peril."

Kellyn stepped forward instantly. "What danger?"

The Sylph woman answered without hesitation.

"Osiri. An entire war-band."

Shock snapped through the group.

Harvey's hand flew to his weapon. "A whole war-band? Inside the canopy?"

Witmar shook his head. "Impossible."

Aafje's voice was a tremor:
"The Osiri cannot tree-walk. They have no Life-Song. Teleportation demands familiarity with the target. They should not reach this place."

"Unless they learned a new trick," Loka muttered.
"And the Osiri excel at tricks."

The Sylph woman's gaze swept the group—measuring skill, magic, resolve.

"I am Thiriel Saelwyn," she said.
"Life-mage of Aeralith. The Osiri breach our southern undergroves. We fall back… too slowly."

Her voice cracked—only slightly.

"They brought fire. And something else."
She shivered.
"Something that walks without sound."

Seris paled.

Kellyn stepped forward. "Take us."

"You cannot reach it on foot," Thiriel warned.
"The undergroves shift. The forest denies haste."

"Then we go through the roots," Kellyn said.

Thiriel hesitated only long enough to weigh their resolve.
Then nodded.

"For Dravokh's sake—yes."

She pressed both palms against a luminous tree.

Its bark pulsed with ancient life.

"Gather close," she whispered.

They pressed inward—Kellyn, Harvey, Froster, Khandyl,
Loka, Witmar, Aafje, Seris, Elowen—
a single knot of breath inside a living god's ribcage.

Thiriel began to sing.

Not words.
Not melody.
A harmonic breath woven from root and wind.

The tree softened—
glowed—
opened.

A spinning corridor of green luminescence unfurled.

Harvey grabbed Witmar's sleeve. "If this kills us—"

"It won't," Aafje said.

"It won't," Loka echoed, "but you'll scream anyway."

Thiriel stepped backward into the light.
"Come."

The forest pulled them in—

Light bending
Roots twisting
Shadows flowing

And then—

Smoke.

Blood.

Burning bark.

Screams.

The Sylph were fighting for their lives.

Kellyn drew her sword in a single, sharp motion.

"MOVE!"

And the battle swallowed them whole.

Chapter 13 – The Shaken Canopy

Planet: Vael'thara
Location: Aeralith Canopy
BV 24

The first tremor was small — no more than a sigh beneath the living bridges of Aeralith.

But the Sylph did not mistake it.

To another clan, it would have meant nothing.
To them, it was a *voice gone wrong*.

Daaren Leafstride, Warden of the Second Layer's eastern span, froze mid-step. The Whisper-Vines along the rail recoiled, tightening inwards, their hollow resonance fibers trembling with a warning hum. Birds burst upward from the canopy in arcs of silver-green wings.

Daaren whispered, "Fael'tharyn… something stirs below."

He placed his palm to a branch.

It throbbed once.

Not heartbeat.
Not wind.
An *echo* — returning upward from the deep earth. Wind should not move upward through roots.

Wind did not travel like that unless something *pushed it*.

Daaren spun and sprinted across the bridge toward the inner platforms. All around him the canopy shifted in uneasy synchrony — leaves twisting to catch a wind that did not exist, Whisper-Vines tightening like muscles bracing for impact, the very breath of the forest halting for a single unnatural instant.

By the time he reached the Heart-Platform, Lady Dravokh Mistshaper was already there.

She stood at the center of the crescent deck, still as carved moonstone, green-gray cloak hanging unmoving despite the restless winds. Her braided silver hair draped over one shoulder, amber eyes fixed far below the canopy as if watching the earth itself breathe.

"Report," she said without turning.

"We felt a reversal in the wind-line," Daaren said. "Air being pulled downward. Hard. Like something inhaled beneath the roots."

Only then did Dravokh face him. "Again?"

"Yes," Daaren said softly. "And stronger."

Other wardens arrived, each pale, each having felt it.

A muted thrum rippled beneath their feet — a harmonic gone wrong.
Not natural.
Not forest-born.

Dravokh closed her eyes, listening. "Once is chance," she murmured. "Twice is omen. Three times is intrusion."

"Osiri?" Daaren asked.

"No," Dravokh said. "This is deeper. Older. Something moving beneath the Osiri's feet as well as ours."

She stepped to the railing, staring down through spiraling layers of living branches.

"Something climbs upward from the deep stones," she said. "Something that has never touched our forest before."

A faint metallic chime sounded behind her.

Maaren Faelwind, cloaked in blue-green, stepped forward. Whisper-Vine leaves curled around his wrists like living sigils.

"We traced the reverberation," Maaren said. "It is not a natural wind shift. It is… harmonic tunneling."

Dravokh's eyes narrowed. "That is not possible."

Maaren shook his head. "We thought the same."

Daaren swallowed. "What does that mean?"

Maaren knelt by the platform's edge and pressed a Whisper-Vine to his cheek. The vine coiled tighter, as if sharing memory.

"It means," Maaren said slowly, "that something is carving resonant channels through the bedrock far below us. Tunnels grown—or forced—by harmonics not of this forest."

Dravokh's amber gaze sharpened.

"Roots cannot be opened with foreign harmonic patterns," she said. "Not unless something understands their language."

Maaren nodded grimly.
"That is what frightens me. This intrusion… is not blind. It is *searching.*"

The wind changed — warm, dry, tasting faintly of stone and sun.

Not a forest wind.
A desert wind.

Daaren whispered the old line:

"The forest breathes out… and something breathes in."

The second tremor hit.
Harder.

It rattled the Whisper-Vines, sent ripples across the bridges, and made the whole Heart-Platform shudder.

Dravokh steadied herself.

"That is no storm," she said.
"That is pressure from below. Something testing the boundaries."

An older warden whispered, "If it reaches the lower roots—"

"It won't," Dravokh snapped. Then, quieter: "Not yet. Not while we feel its every breath."

Maaren stepped to her side.

"This pattern grows clearer," he said. "The intrusion is deliberate. Methodical. Like scouts pressing upward, studying the layers."

Dravokh inhaled slowly, exhaling a faint Catal'ri breath, a warrior-mage habit born of centuries of near-silent battles.

She faced the wardens. "Double patrols," she commanded. "Along every root-layer. No light. No spoken word. Move as shadows. If you sense anything with the scent of stone-heat or desert wind…"

Her eyes hardened, "… you do not attack. You vanish. And you watch."

Maaren bowed, "The unseen will move as well."

Two male silhouettes detached from the shadows — indistinct, cloaked in deep-shadow windweave. Even seasoned wardens startled at their appearance.

"We will not let anything reach our core," Maaren said.

Dravokh touched the Whisper-Vine railing again. Its tremor pulsed like a warning heartbeat. "No," she whispered. "But something is trying."

A third tremor struck — deeper than the others, resonant enough to quiver every suspended bridge.

Dravokh's head lifted sharply. "Three times," she said. "The door has been tried."

Her voice softened into the wind, "Now we wait… for what seeks to enter."

The canopy fell silent. Utterly, unnervingly silent.

As if the entire forest leaned in to listen.

And far below, through layers of living root and ancient stone, something continued digging upward — precise, patient, relentless.

.

Chapter 14 — The Battle for the Under-Groves

Planet: Vaelthara
Location: Aeralith Canopy — Southern Under-Groves
Chronometric Stamp: BV 24.01

"A plan lasts until breakfast; courage lasts until the end." —
Marek Holt (Human)

[FIELD LOG // TDG-512B — FRAGMENT 11]
Engaged Osiri raiding force inside Aeralith territory.
Origin of hostile incursion: UNKNOWN.
Sylph forces engaged, heavy losses.
Clan-Lady Dravokh surrounded.
Assistance rendered.
— *Commander Kellyn Windstream*

The world snapped back into existence in fire and screaming.

Kellyn hit the ground mid-step, sword rising on instinct. Heat blasted her face. The undergrowth burned in violet and gold flames. Trees that should have sung with the forest's breath trembled like wounded animals. The air reeked of burning vine-sap and Osiri alchemical smoke.

Sylph warriors fought in fragmented, ghostlike motions— silver silhouettes vanishing between roots, blades flickering like cold moons.

And towering over them—

Osiri.

Jackal-helmed giants, bronze-skinned, nine feet tall, desert sigils burning along their arms. War-spears. Chain-runes. Eyes like molten judgment.

Harvey inhaled sharply.
"Okay—seriously—how the hell are they *here*?"

"No teleportation," Aafje murmured. "No tree-magic. No leyline displacement. Nothing about this should be possible."

"Well," Loka said, pointing at the burning bark, "apparently someone forgot to tell them the rules."

Witmar nudged Harvey with his elbow.
"First to ten Osiri buys dinner."

"You don't eat dinner," Harvey snapped.

"Then I'll buy yours."

Aafje groaned. "Focus, children."

Seris was trembling. The forest's pain thrummed across her skin like a fever.
"They're strangling the root-light," she whispered. "The canopy is… hurting."

Kellyn touched her shoulder.
"We stop them."

She stepped forward.

"MYRRATHIS—NOW!"

A roar ripped through the canopy.
Myrrathis dove, emerald fire streaking past the branches—burning Osiri, but not a single leaf.

Sylthara followed, vines blooming in her wake to smother the fire-pits.

The Osiri formation buckled—

For a heartbeat.

Then something massive stepped through the smoke.

A Sun-Child.

Eight feet tall.
A jackal-headed juggernaut.
Burning with molten-gold fire.
Eyes blank with obedience.

Loka blanched. "A Sun-Child. Osiri war-forged. Born to burn worlds."

Harvey cracked his neck.
"Born to get punched."

"It has fangs," Witmar noted.

"Then I'll punch the fangs."

Kellyn didn't wait. The screams in the grove's center sharpened—
Dravokh.

Kellyn sprinted toward the heart of the battle.

Lady Dravokh stood alone.

She moved like mist and razorwind—appearing behind an Osiri, blade at its throat, then dissolving again. But her cloak was torn, her arm bleeding heavily.

"Kellyn!" Dravokh cried—just as an Osiri spear plunged toward her heart.

Kellyn didn't think.

She leapt.

Her sword shattered the spearshaft. She landed between Dravokh and the attackers.

"Kneel!" Kellyn barked.

Dravokh obeyed instantly, dropping to the roots.

Kellyn swept her blade in a fierce Dragon-Clan arc—
a Vor'Shar stroke Sahn himself had drilled into her bones.

A thunderclap of Dominion erupted.

Three Osiri flew backward, crushed by an invisible force.

Behind her—

Harvey slammed into the Sun-Child.
Loka unleashed necro-inversion flares.
Aafje dissolved into shadow and reappeared behind Osiri throats.
Froster hammered harmonic shockwaves.
Witmar hurled knives of shadow, laughing manically.
Seris knelt, singing in terror—
and the forest answered, vines ripping through Osiri legs like living spears.

The Sun-Child hurled Harvey into a tree.

Witmar shouted, "Harvey!"

Harvey wheezed, "I'm—fine—just—winded—"

Kellyn pivoted.
"Loka—NOW!"

Loka carved a corruption-sink rune in the air.
The Sun-Child staggered—fire guttering—

Harvey lunged back in, blade driving through the creature's chest.

A blast of green radiance.
The Sun-Child dissolved into molten dust.

Harvey collapsed to his knees.
"My kill," he gasped.

"Take it," Witmar said. "It smelled terrible."

The battle tipped sharply.
Sylph assassins struck from nowhere—appearing behind Osiri necks, vanishing before the bodies fell.

Fifty Osiri broke and fled.

Their screams echoed for 30 seconds, then fell silent.

Witmar squinted into the shadows.
"That wasn't us."

Kellyn scanned the bodies. "So… those *were* Osiri."

Silence fell.

Uneasy.
Heavy.
Wrong.

Dravokh rose slowly, pressing her hand to her bleeding shoulder. Her amber eyes swept the devastation with cold fury.

Kellyn approached.
"Are you hurt?"

"No more than the forest," Dravokh answered.

Harvey stepped forward.
"Where did the rest go? They were everywhere."

Witmar pointed toward the deeper glades.
"Something killed the runners. Fast. Clean. No footprints. No bodies left behind."

Aafje knelt by the roots.
"No scorch marks. No ley-distortion. No tether lines."

She frowned deeply.
"This wasn't teleportation."

"How do you know?" Loka asked.

Aafje's fingers shimmered with illusion-light.
"Teleportation leaves harmonic shearing. The forest would scream from it. There is none."

Harvey blinked.
"Then what—did they just walk away?"

"No," Aafje whispered.
"They *vanished* without leaving a magical signature at all."

"That's… worse," Witmar muttered. "Harvey, get your camera. Oh, wait—no power. Shame. Paranormal Pursuits: Osiri Edition would've been great."

"Not ghosts," Aafje snapped.
"But something we don't understand."

Seris trembled.
"They should not be here. They cannot be here."

Kellyn nodded grimly.
"They're hundreds of miles south. They couldn't have marched here unnoticed."

Aafje hesitated.
"There is… one possibility. But it should be impossible."

Harvey groaned.
"Just say it."

Aafje's voice lowered.
"Stone-travel."

Harvey blinked. "Like dwarv—like Gravhal?"

Witmar shrugged. "Basically dwarves."

Kellyn shook her head.
"Osiri don't have that magic…do they?"

"Correct," Aafje said.
"That's why I said it *should* be impossible."

Witmar said, "Unless they've learned something new."

"Their emissary from the future," Kellyn finished.

Dravokh stiffened—
not with anger.
With fear.

"This is the third intrusion this moon," she whispered.

"Our scouts watch every southern path. Our magi guard every ley-thread. And yet… they appear."

Her gaze locked with Kellyn's.

"The Osiri walked into our forest today as though the world itself had opened a curtain just for them."

Kellyn felt a cold spike of dread.
"They shouldn't know the canopy this well."

"No," Dravokh agreed.
"And that is what troubles me."

She straightened, gathering her poise like armor.

"You saved the under-groves," she said.
"You saved me."

The Sylph warriors knelt in a crescent around Kellyn's group—silent, reverent.

Dravokh raised her hand.

"The Hidden City awaits you.
You have earned entry."

Seris inhaled sharply—wonder and fear entwined.

Witmar whispered to Harvey,
"Are we sure this is a reward?"

Harvey whispered back, "No idea."

Dravokh's silver hair caught the dim light as she turned.

"Follow. The forest has judged you worthy."

The Aeralith roots twisted open—forming a living path downward.

And somewhere deep in the green darkness—the Hidden City waited.

Chapter 15 - The Hidden City of Aeralith

Planet: Vaelthara
Location: Aeralith Canopy — Threshold of the Veiled Paths
Chronometric Stamp: BV 24.01

"We don't get lost. We simply discover better paths."
— *Thaliryn Leafstride (Anari)*

[FIELD LOG // TDG-512B — FRAGMENT 12]
Entered Sylph territory beyond surface pathways.
Spatial geometry distorted; harmonic fields unstable.
Sylph city is located across shifting arrays of light, illusion,
and root-architecture.
Recommend extreme caution.
— *Commander Kellyn Windstream*

The smoke of battle still clung to Kellyn's clothes as Lady
Dravokh moved ahead of them—
not walking,
not drifting,
but gliding like moonlight that had decided to take a shape.

"Stay close," Dravokh said without looking back.
"The forest rearranges itself for outsiders."

Froster whispered, "Rearranges? As in *moves*?"

Khandyl muttered, "You have no idea."

Dravokh lifted one slender hand.

"Silence."

The forest obeyed.

Leaves stilled mid-rustle.
Even the wind paused, as if kneeling.

They followed her beneath boughs glowing with soft inner radiance, the roots curling upward like cathedral stone. The ground seemed to breathe—firmer one step, softer the next—never quite the same twice.

Witmar drifted too far left—

And vanished.

"WITMAR?!" Harvey yelped.

Aafje raised her hands to invoke a shadow-pull, but Dravokh didn't turn.

"He is safe."

A heartbeat later, Witmar stumbled back into view from an entirely different direction, pale and sweating.

"I was up there—then sideways—then—"

Dravokh glanced at him, amused.
"The forest tests orientation in those of lesser blood."

Witmar sputtered. "It thinks I'm disoriented?"

"Are you not?"

"… I mean—yes, but—"

"Then it is correct."

Harvey sighed. "Wit, you walked into a tree last week."

"It moved!"

"It didn't."

"It *did!*"

Aafje pinched the bridge of her nose. "By the shadows, please stop."

They reached a grove with no entrance—just a wall of gently shifting silver leaves.

Dravokh stepped forward.

The leaves recoiled.

A doorway of void opened where foliage had been.

Loka breathed, "That is not an illusion."

"No." Dravokh's voice thinned to a whisper. "It is the forest recalling a wound."

Kellyn frowned. "A wound?"

But Dravokh did not explain.
She stepped through.

Kellyn followed—and the world changed around her.

It was not a city.
It was a vertical dream.

Platforms spiraled up colossal silverwood trunks that glowed with their own twilight.
Bioluminescent vines spilled like waterfalls of cold fire.
Walkways intertwined like woven moonlight.
Homes rippled subtly—alive, aware—breathing with the rhythm of the canopy.

A thousand Sylph eyes watched them.

All women.
All sharp-boned and beautiful as obsidian blades.
None hostile.
None welcoming.
Simply assessing.

Seris inhaled sharply.
"Home," she whispered—and the word nearly broke.

Dravokh led them onto a root-lift: a circular platform shaped from living wood.
When she placed a bare foot on it, the entire structure rose like a tide-lifted raft.

Harvey gripped the railing. "I hate this."

"It's safe," Aafje said.

"You fell off one once," Witmar noted.

"It *tested* me."

"So, it was right."

Aafje looked ready to throw him off the platform.

Kellyn cleared her throat. "Enough."

They ascended through drifting lights and quiet Sylph choruses until the lift settled atop a broad silverwood platform.

Dravokh turned to them.
"The Clan-Lady welcomes you."

Kellyn blinked. "You're the Clan-Lady."

A flicker crossed Dravokh's face—pride mixed with fatigue.
"I am one voice. The forest speaks through many."

She gestured to a tall archway braided from roots and shimmering light.

"Enter."

Sound died the moment they crossed the threshold.

Not quiet.
Absence.

Sylph warriors lined the perimeter, motionless as carved moonlight.
A glowing circular platform pulsed gently at the center.

Dravokh stepped onto it.

"Kellyn Windstream," she said, her voice echoing with faint harmonic layering.
"You have saved my life.
You have saved the undergroves.
You may stand upon sacred ground."

Kellyn stepped onto the platform.

The wood brightened beneath her boots.

Witmar whispered, "This feels—festively ominous."

"Shh," Aafje hissed. "It's listening."

It was.

The walls vibrated with slow pulses.
Roots curled like veins.
Leaves whispered in languages older than speech.

Kellyn swallowed. "What does the forest want?"

Dravokh stepped closer, eyes luminous.

"To know," she breathed,
"whether the storm you carry brings mercy…

… or doom."

The platform resonated—a rising tri-tone that felt like it was peeling back the world.

Shadows bent inward.
Roots tightened.
Air thinned.

A voice—not Dravokh's—uncoiled in Kellyn's mind:

You carry the break in the world.
You will choose what lives…
or what dies.

Kellyn staggered—but Dravokh held up a hand, stopping Seris from rushing to her.

"This is her path."

The glow faded.
Kellyn steadied herself.
The forest released a long exhale.

"You are accepted," Dravokh said.

Kellyn rasped, "Accepted as what?"

Dravokh's smile was sharp.
"As a guest. Nothing more."

For now.

The next chamber was cathedral-vast, shaped from living silverwood ribs. Sylph elders stood in a shifting spiral, no two at identical distance or angle.

Witmar whispered to Harvey, "Why does their seating look like it wants me to fail geometry?"

Aafje elbowed him. "Sacred formation logic. Try not to insult it."

"I'm not insulting it. I'm saying it hates me."

Harvey said, "Everything hates you, Wit."

"That's not—okay, maybe."

Dravokh raised a hand.

Silence fell again.

"Lunethryn acknowledges the debt owed," she said. "Your blades spared the forest blood it could not lose."

Kellyn bowed. "We only did what was right. We are all Anari."

Murmurs rippled—respect, skepticism, old grudges.

An elder stepped forward.
"Courage is not trust."

Dravokh lifted her chin.
"They request permission to undergo the Whisper-Vine Armor Rite."

Half the elders inhaled sharply—shock in perfect synchrony.

"A Griffyn who moves like a Dragon wrapped in our wind-shadow?"
"The forest remembers old feuds."
"Can such a one bear Windwoven armor?"

Before the argument could grow—the air behind Dravokh changed.

A presence.

Not a person.
A pressure.

Leaves shifted subtly, as if brushing an unseen body.
Harvey flinched.
Witmar froze.
Seris trembled.

Dravokh tilted her head—listening to words no one else could hear.

"My husband speaks," she announced.

Witmar mouthed, *She has a husband?*

"No," Aafje whispered. "She has a wind-walker. They're not the same."

Kellyn forced herself still.
"What does he say?"

Dravokh's voice softened.
"He says: *The wind owes its life to the storm-born blade.*"

Murmurs—startled, reverent.

"Aye," Dravokh declared. "The first vote."

One by one, more elders stepped forward.

"Aye."
"Aye."
"Aye."

Then the last approached.

Veil-shrouded, feet not touching the ground.

Her gaze swept over Kellyn… then Harvey… then Seris.

"Three threads walk with you," she whispered. "Storm. Veil. Hunt."

Her eyes were fixed on Harvey.

"Green Knight."

Harvey blanched. "Me? No. Absolutely not. I'm barely good with a sword."

"Yet you killed undead warriors," Aafje murmured.

"That was luck."

"It was power."

Harvey groaned. "I refuse to be mythical."

The elder did not bend.

"Seeds do not choose whether they grow."

Harvey muttered, "This seed wants a refund."

Witmar clapped his shoulder. "Heroes rarely get refunds."

"Shut up, Wit."

The elder lifted her hand.

"The final vote… Aye."

Light surged.

Dravokh stepped forward.

"The Whisper-Vine ritual begins at moonrise. Your armor will be woven according to Sylph law."

Her tone hardened.

"The forest will judge you each time you walk beneath it."

Kellyn bowed. "We accept."

Harvey muttered, "I accept the armor, not the Green Knight thing."

Seris tried not to laugh.
Aafje didn't bother.

As the council dispersed in drifting silver shadows, Kellyn noticed the air behind Dravokh shift again—her unseen husband departing, or simply fading.

"Will we meet him?" Kellyn asked quietly.

Dravokh's answer was soft.

"No. Men do not walk where he walks."

"Why not?"

"The wind does not carry them back."

Then she turned, silver hair catching the bioluminescent glow.

"Prepare yourselves.
Moonrise comes swiftly."

Chapter 16 – The Council of Leaves

Planet: Vael'thara
Location: Aeralith Canopy
BV 24

The Heart-Platform of Aeralith had never held so many voices.

Living branches arched overhead like silver ribs, Whisper-Vines hanging in gentle green curtains. Lantern-fruits glowed above the gathered council: clan-mothers, hunt-mistresses, bindweavers, singers, druids—and, in their reserved crescent of muted blue and gray, the male Sylph mages.

Beyond the railing, the Aeralith Canopy stretched into layered green infinity. Far to the south, a scattering of pale canvas and campfires marked the refugee encampment—a strange, angular wound at the forest's edge.

Fifty thousand refugees.
Fifty thousand future-born Anari who did not grow up beneath trees… and who had arrived on Sylph soil without warning.

Lady Dravokh Mistshaper stood at the center of the platform, her hands resting lightly on the Whisper-Vine rail. The vine hummed faintly beneath her touch, still carrying tremors from the deep roots.

She let the murmurs rise and fall for 30 slow breaths.

Then she spoke.

"We have three problems."

Silence spread in ripples. Even the lantern-fruits dimmed slightly.

Dravokh continued:

"First: something is digging toward us. We felt testing shocks two nights ago.
We will feel more."

Uneasy rustles traveled through the gathered elders. Maaren Faelwind—foremost of the visible male mages—bowed his head, confirming her words.

Dravokh's eyes narrowed.

"We do not yet know what lies beneath us… but the pattern is deliberate. Something is searching."

A sharper ripple of unease.

"Second," she said, "the forest strains. The Whisper-Vine is unsettled. The lower roots complain. Aeralith knows something approaches."

She let that settle before delivering the third blow.

"And the third: we have inherited fifty thousand of our own people from a future not yet written.
We did not ask for them. We will not abandon them.
But we cannot pretend they are nothing."

She gestured southward, toward the campfires.

"They are everything. For good or ill."

A bindweaver elder stepped forward, leaning on her dried-vine staff.

"Lady Dravokh, we lack the threads for this. Whisper-Vine takes years to grow. Bark-thread and storm-hide take seasons. If we arm and clothe fifty thousand at once, we will strip half the canopy bare."

A hunt-mistress snapped her fingers.
"Scatter them. Twenty here, 30 there—let them vanish among us. The forest will teach them quietly."

Murmurs of agreement—and sharp dissent.

"They walk like stone pillars."
"They flinch at root-shifts."
"They carry Malloch shadows in their bones."
"They are Anari—lost and wounded."

Dravokh listened without interrupting, weighing every fear.

From the male-mage crescent, Maaren spoke softly:

"If we scatter them, we weaken every bough."

An elder scoffed. "And what do you suggest, Faelwind? Gather them into one branch and hope they don't break it?"

Maaren lifted his chin.

"Yes."

The council stirred.

Dravokh raised her hand. "Explain."

Maaren stepped into the light, his cloak whispering like woven breeze.

"They are a storm," he said.
"We can let that storm tear at every leaf… or give it a valley to roar in, and shape it."

He pointed south.

"We will build a quarter for them. Close enough to feel our Songs. Far enough not to crush our roots. We feed them, shelter them—and we train them. Over time, we bring them in until the Quarter is empty."

Dravokh murmured, "A Windborne Quarter…"

Maaren nodded.

The bindweaver elder shook her head.
"We do not have enough armor. Enough cloaks. Enough anything."

"Then we teach them to weave," Maaren said.
"Not full Whisper-Vine. But leaf-cloth, bark-thread, storm-hides. They will learn by hand. They will mend what they wear."

A younger huntress spoke.
"And who teaches them to fight? Half move like stones, the other half startle at branch-creaks."

"The women," Hunt-Mistress Laeryn said firmly.
"Our bladesisters and archers will train them. The male warriors remain unseen. They do not stand before outsiders."

Assent rippled through the huntresses.

Dravokh's peripheral vision caught a flicker—a form half-seen in the shadows beyond the lantern-fruit glow. Not invisible, but intentionally forgettable.

One of the Hidden Host.
Watching. Listening.

She continued.

"Sacred flora will bind the quarter," Dravokh said.
"Whisper-Vine to learn their sound.
Driftsong Moss to soften their steps.
Dreamwillow for the mind.
Skybloom Resin for those who cannot yet see the third wind."

"Lady—those are sacred plants," someone protested.

Dravokh's voice sharpened.

"So are they."

"And their training?" asked a druid, tattoos winding like dark roots along her arms.

"We begin with preparation," Dravokh said. "But eventually—"

The druid finished for her.

"The Ritual of Discovery."

Uneasy shifts among the elders.

"That ritual was made for young Sylph," one murmured. "Not war-broken travelers."

"Then we soften its teeth," the druid said. "But they must learn the forest. To walk it, read it, feed themselves. If they are to live under Aeralith, they must learn Aeralith."

Dravokh nodded once.

"When their time comes, the Singing Tree will test them. Those with magic will be trained. Those without will still serve—scouts, crafters, ward-tenders."

Laeryn said, "We will need schools. Instructors. Watch-lines."

"And new mistakes," Vaeryn Shadecaller murmured from the mage crescent.
"They bring memories of sky-fire and machines that split worlds. If we do not shape those memories, those memories will shape us."

The platform quieted.

Dravokh rested her palm on the Whisper-Vine.

"Every instructor we assign to the refugees is one less watching the borders.
Every bindweaver who teaches leaf-cloth isn't mending our armor.
Every druid who guides their dreams is one less listening to the deep roots."

She met every eye.

"We thin our defenses."

Heavy silence.

Maaren's voice, soft:
"And if we turn them away?"

Dravokh looked toward the distant campfires.

"Then the future dies in the desert," she said quietly.
"And we betray everything Sylvara and Lyra taught us."

A wind gust rolled across the platform, stirring every leaf and setting the Whisper-Vines thrumming in a single low chord.

Dravokh straightened.

"The Windborne Quarter is established."

She continued, voice clear:

- "We commit instructors, bindweavers, healers."

- "Combat training begins with female warriors only."

- "Male warriors remain unseen unless a refugee survives the Ritual of Discovery."

- "Male mages will oversee magical testing and first Songs."

- "The forest will test each refugee's steps. Those who walk true, we keep. Those who do not…"

She didn't have to finish.

Laeryn struck her fist to her heart. "Sylph stand."

One by one, every councilor echoed:

"Sylph stand."

The wind settled.

Below, the forest edge glowed with new fires—refugees cooking, building, arguing softly in a dialect born in a future no one here would ever live to see.

The Windborne Quarter was beginning—not in platforms or vines yet, but in decisions.

Dravokh turned to Maaren.

"Send word to the Hidden City," she said. "Tell Vaelkorh the Windstep Vanguard will have many new eyes to watch."

She paused—and allowed herself a thin, humorless smile.

"Tell him," she added, "the future has moved into our front yard."

Maaren bowed, cloak whispering like a quiet wind.
"The future," he said, "is about to discover how narrow our paths truly are."

He vanished down the spiraling ramp.

Above them, the Aeralith Canopy rustled like a living lung drawing breath—preparing for the weight of fifty thousand new souls.

And beneath them—far below the roots—something continued digging upward, one wrong note at a time.

Chapter 17 - The Windveil Rite

Planet: Vaelthara
Location: Aeralith Canopy — Lunethryn, The Hidden Heart
Chronometric Stamp: BV 24.01

"I'll change my mind… once the mountain does."
— *Bromdur Ironshoulder (Gravhal)*

[FIELD LOG // TDG-512B — FRAGMENT 13]
Subjected to Sylph Windveil Rite.
Whisper-Vine integration: partial symbiotic weave with fungal armor.
Result: limited photoadaptive concealment + vibration damping.
Note: Sylph males remain unseen; local harmonic signatures suggest additional observers.
— Commander Kellyn Windstream

The Sylph did not call for the Rite.

They arrived.

Kellyn woke to the soft rustle of leaves and the presence of three Sylph matrons standing at the edge of the guest lodge. Their silver hair glowed even in the false-dawn twilight, eyes reflecting the canopy's soft blue luminescence.

Lady Dravokh stood at the center, composed as a blade held upright.

"It is time," she said.

No explanation. No ceremony. Only inevitability.

Kellyn tightened her armor straps. Around her, the others stirred awake:

- Harvey blinking sleep from his eyes

- Witmar sprawled half off his sleeping roll

- Aafje already cross-legged, watching

- Froster groaning for nonexistent coffee

- Seris standing still as a whisper

- Khandyl stretching her bow arm

- Loka quietly fastening his gauntlets

- Elowen waiting near the door, calm as morning wind

They followed Dravokh along a spiral walkway deeper into Lunethryn's upper canopy. Leaves folded behind them as though sealing the world away.

At last, they reached the Rite Glade—a floating platform braided from silverwood roots suspended between three ancient trunks. Bioluminescent vines flowed around it like waterfalls of green fire. Coiled masses of Whisper-Vine lay in the center, humming with soft resonance.

Seris inhaled sharply.

"I remember this," she whispered.

"Only as an initiate. Never as… whatever this is."

Harvey whispered, "What exactly *is* this?"

Witmar murmured back, "Probably something we regret later."

Aafje elbowed him. "Hush. The forest is listening."

Dravokh glided to the center of the platform. The air tightened, as though the entire glade held its breath.

"This is the Fael'tharyn Luneth—the Windveil Rite," she said.

"You have spilled blood for our roots and saved our under-groves.

You bear blades the wind itself watches."

Her gaze lingered on Kellyn.

"And some of you bear storms older than memory."

Harvey opened his mouth. A matron raised one finger, and he closed it silently.

Dravokh continued:

"The Windveil will cloak you—

But it demands a price."

Loka exhaled. "The Necrodemicon copy."

All Sylph eyes turned.

"You wish to handle a book that should never have survived," he said.

"We wish to understand the weapon our enemy seeks," Dravokh answered. "Your book will not be yours alone for long. Let us prepare for the day it escapes your grasp."

Kellyn watched Loka struggle with a grief that had no words.

At last, he said, quietly:

"I agree. With conditions."
And he listed them—no binding replication, copying only in their presence, stopping on command.

Dravokh listened.
Weighing.
Judging.

"The forest accepts," she said.

The vines rustled in approving whisper.

The matrons began a slow Vael'Shar circle—feet tracing spirals, hands brushing vine coils. Every harvested thread glowed, pulsed once, and regrew anew.

Seris whispered reverently, "They prune with consent."

Then the matrons approached.

"Strip to your armor," one said.

Froster sighed, "Can I at least pretend I'm awake for this?"

Dravokh ignored him.

Whisper-Vine threads were lifted, warm and living. They wrapped around each person differently, adjusting to breath, stance, magic, bloodline.

Kellyn felt the first touch at her collarbone.
A hum vibrated down her spine.
Her breath synced with an unfamiliar wind-pattern.

The vine wound around her shoulders, linking to the plates of her armor, whispering against scars she didn't know she had.

She wobbled—once.
The vine corrected her posture back into the Syl'phyr alignment: wind-flow stance.

"Feel that?" Seris murmured. "It's teaching you."

Harvey flinched when the vine touched his gauntlets.
"It's cold—no, warm—no, alive—no—this is wrong—"

"It's right," Witmar said, watching his own vines tighten around his forearms. "Or at least, it's happening."

Aafje's shadow twitched around her ankles as the vine touched it.
"That's not supposed to react," she muttered.

A matron replied, "Shadow hides. Wind hides differently. Now the two will argue."

Khandyl felt her bow arm grow lighter, steadier—as though wind adjusted her aim.

Froster discovered his vibration-shockwave strikes hummed smoother, cleaner.

Elowen watched quietly; the vine did not wrap her fully— only wove into her sleeves and around her hips.

"You resist it," Dravokh murmured to her.

"I heal living things, Clan-Lady. These vines… don't want me inside them."

"That is wisdom," Dravokh replied.

Loka's turn came last.

The vine hesitated at his wrists—sensing necromantic residue.
Then, split around his palms and wove tighter along his arms.

Loka swallowed.
"It's… protecting itself from me."

"Correct," Dravokh said.

Dravokh lifted both hands.

"Repeat after me."

Soft wind shaped each syllable of the Whispering Oath.

"By leaf, by breath, by wind unseen—"

They echoed her.

"I walk the paths between the worlds."

"I walk the paths between the worlds."

"Let no shadow claim me, let no storm unmake me."

"Let no storm unmake me."

Then Dravokh paused for the final line.

"You do not say the oath of the Sylph-born," she said. "You are not Sylph."

The forest agreed—leaves rustling lightly.

Instead she offered a new line:

"Let the wind know me, if not call me its own."

They spoke it together.

The glade brightened.

Kellyn inhaled—

—and the world shifted.

Harmonic threads shimmered in the air.

Three tones. Perfectly stacked.

She felt—beneath her feet—a tremor.

A distant vibration in the ground.

A wrong note in the earth.

She froze.

She could sense directional harmonic distortion—something moving beneath the world.

"Kellyn Windstream," Dravokh said softly, "the triple-harmonic hears you. Rare. Dangerous. Useful."

Harvey lifted his sword.

The vine responded:
his stance aligned, balance shifting subtly, his Griffyn form gaining one instinctive perfect counterstrike—usable only when still and grounded.

Harvey blinked, "That wasn't me."

"It was," Aafje murmured. "Now."

Witmar tested his throwing-knife grip—light bent a little around his outline.

Partial concealment.
A flicker-dodge.

He grinned.
"I love this forest."

Her shadow curled tighter, thinner—now able to blend into the Windveil, granting stationary invisibility while casting.

"I feel seen," she muttered.

"You are," a matron replied dryly.

His spellcasting aura dimmed—
his necromantic resonance masked, softened.
Still him.
But quieter.

"Invisibility while still," he said, amazed. "Useful."

Her bowstring hummed—arrows would fly truer in the wind.

His harmonic shockwaves condensed—
less wind lost, more force retained.
Storm-punching perfected.

The vine wrapped her lightly—
her healing field became silent, no glow unless she willed it.

A stealth healer.

As the vibrations faded, Dravokh stepped closer to Kellyn.

Her voice softened so only Kellyn heard:

"We have kept the Windveil for ourselves for thousands of years and hidden it. Guarded it. But hiding has not saved us."

"If other clans wear our Windveil…
perhaps we will not stand alone when the desert rises."

"Perhaps unity begins with the sharing of a garment."

Kellyn swallowed.

Dravokh continued: "A Griffyn carries Sylph vine.
A shadow mage weaves with wind.
A necromancer learns to go unseen by breath."

"One day, all Anari may walk each other's paths."

Then, with something like tired hope:

"Perhaps the future you came from died because we failed to
do this sooner."

"The Windveil will guide you," Dravokh said louder,
returning to ritual tone.
"But understand: it is not a true Windveil.
It will falter if you panic, run, shout, or lose breath."

Witmar: "So… don't be Harvey."
Harvey: "I *heard* that."

Dravokh continued: "You have two days to master it. Then
you go south—
to our deeper canopy scouts.
They will arm you with maps.
Beyond that, the desert owns you."

Kellyn nodded.

Dravokh's eyes flicked upward to where unseen feet shifted above the vines.

"The forest approves," she said softly.

Though her eyes told Kellyn she was withholding a deeper truth.

Female Sylph Clan female warrior.

Chapter 18 – Strain on the Boughs

Planet: Vael'thara
Location: Aeralith Canopy
BV 24

Dawn crept reluctantly across the southern Aeralith Canopy, as though even the sun hesitated to shine on what had changed beneath its branches.

From above, the new Windborne Quarter looked like a foreign scar pressed against the ancient forest. Canvas roofs. Rope lines. Cooking fires. Straight, inflexible walkpaths carved by feet untrained in the flowing geometry of living wood.

Smoke spiraled upward in pale columns, bending the wind in ways the Sylph had not allowed for generations.

Dravokh Mistshaper watched from an upper bough, her expression carved from quiet calculation.

Below her, refugees hacked stubbornly at roots, hammered tent-stakes into bark that protested, misstepped across tension-lines that had held perfect wind balance for centuries.

Laeryn, the hunt-mistress, settled beside her like a shadow descending from a higher branch.

"The forest groans under them," Laeryn murmured. "It's like placing stoneweights on a bird's wings."

"It will adjust," Dravokh replied. "Or they will."

"Preferably the latter," Laeryn muttered.

Dravokh's gaze shifted toward a clearing where 20 future-born struggled through their first wind-step lesson with Shaela Windblossom.

Shaela danced the opening pattern of the First Gale Path—light, effortless, a pattern drawn from the breath of storms themselves.

Not one refugee matched her.

A young man tripped. Another stumbled sideways. A third stepped on a Whisper-Vine.

The Whisper-Vine snapped upward and struck him across the face with a sharp *crack*.

The man yelped.

Shaela did not stop moving.

"You stepped without listening," she said calmly. "The vine corrected you."

"It hit me!"

"It will again," Shaela said. "Until you stop moving like a frightened goat."

Laeryn snorted. "How did these people survive five thousand years?"

"Machines walked for them," Dravokh murmured. "Now the forest must remind them they have legs."

A ripple of tension drew Dravokh's attention farther south.

Maaren Faelwind knelt beside a row of Singing Sprigs—silver-toned stems used only for pre-screening magic potential. Refugees lined up before them, each waiting to touch a sprig and hear its reaction.

A woman reached out.
The sprig chimed a soft rising third.

"Life school," Maaren nodded. "To the healer's hollow."

A hard-eyed man touched the next sprig.
It shrieked a discordant tone like shattered glass.

The man recoiled. "What does that mean?"

"Shadow, or trauma," Maaren said gently. "Both can hide power. You'll train until we know."

Another refugee stepped forward.
He touched his sprig—

—and was blasted backward by an eruption of black spores.

The sprig wilted.

Maaren inhaled sharply. "Dark school. And unstable. Keep him from Dreamwillow."

One of the mages leaned closer. "We do not have enough sprigs. Or testers. At this pace, the forest itself will wither before we screen them."

Maaren's lips tightened. "Then we work through night and dawn. Five millennia of silence ends now."

A wooden tent-frame collapsed nearby—a tangle of canvas and shouting.

A Sylph archer descended in a blur of movement.

"Not this root!" she snapped. "It feeds the moss-glen. You would starve three groves."

"We're trying!" the refugee protested. "None of this makes sense."

"Because you are not listening," the archer replied. "The forest speaks. You must learn its language."

Her voice softened.

"You will learn. Or it will continue beating you."

Dravokh allowed herself the smallest sigh.

At least someone speaks plainly.

Here and there, promise flickered:

- A young man finally shifted his weight correctly and completed a wind-step without falling.

- A woman braided bark-thread into a proper spiral pattern without snapping the fibers.

- Another sensed a Whisper-Vine twitch and moved out of its path instinctively.

Tiny triumphs.

Seeds of what could become a future.

But then—

A scream tore the clearing.

A refugee lay on the ground, arm wrapped in a tightening coil of Dreamwillow.

Maaren reached him quickly, placing two fingers on the tendril.

One soft Catal'ri note.
The Dreamwillow released.

"You tried to *force* calm," Maaren murmured, inspecting the bruising. "Dreamwillow cannot be bullied. It remembers."

Laeryn approached Dravokh again. "Forty-three injuries today. None serious. But the forest is losing patience."

"The forest is teaching," Dravokh replied. "Teaching often looks like punishment."

Then the wind shifted across the northern quarter.

The first group of refugees—those whose breathlines aligned with the Singing Sprigs—were escorted deeper into a cordoned section of thick boughs.

There, for the first time, they saw them:

Male Sylph warriors.

Not mages.
Not ritualists.
Warriors.

Tall. Silent. Armor woven of whispering leaf-metal.
Faces veiled. Eyes sharp as starlight.
Their movements bent the air—not vanishing, not invisible, but always *where the wind intended them to be.*

The refugees stopped dead.

Some stared.
Some backed away.
One whispered, "I thought Sylph only had female warriors…"

No one answered.

The Hidden Host simply turned as one and melted into the branches.

Dravokh's throat tightened with equal parts pride and dread.

"It was time," she said.

Laeryn nodded. "Only the ones who are ready. The rest would break under their eyes."

As dusk bled into the canopy, a scout sprinted across the wind-path.

"Lady Mistshaper!"

Dravokh turned.

"Ward-lines along the southeastern roots dimmed for nearly an hour. Possibly five—maybe six—failures. We can't confirm."

Laeryn stiffened. "The Osiri?"

"Or whatever claws upward beneath them," Dravokh murmured.

The scout swallowed hard. "One vine-seer reported… echoes. Harmonic echoes. Like someone carving the stone under the secondary roots."

A hush spread like frost.

Laeryn whispered, "They're getting closer."

"They're accelerating," Dravokh corrected.

She straightened.

"Gather the Hidden Host," she said quietly. "Send them into the tunnels."

"And if they find something?" Laeryn asked.

Dravokh's amber eyes sharpened.

"If they find something," she said,
"they will cut it down before it can scream."

As darkness settled:

- Lantern-fruits glowed across the Windborne Quarter.

- Refugees slept in exhausted heaps.

- Sylph instructors watched with cautious nods.

- Maaren's mages reset the sprigs for another night of testing.

- Far north, male Sylph warriors slipped into the undershadows toward the deep tunnels—
silent as falling leaves.

Dravokh stood alone on her upper perch, listening to the forest breathe.

The branches groaned with strain.
The roots whispered warnings.
The wind tasted faintly of heat and distant sand.

"The strain becomes fracture," she murmured.

Her fingers tightened on the Whisper-Vine railing.

"But before the forest breaks… the desert will bleed."

Chapter 19 - The Call to the Desert

Location: Aeralith Canopy — The Trade Grove
Chronometric Stamp: BV 24.016

"Relax! It's only exploded twice." — *Tinkletop Gearwisp (Nimvrel)*

Morning filtered through the Aeralith in slender beams of pale jade and blue, the air thick with dew that glimmered like suspended stars. The Trade Grove lay too quiet. Too peaceful. Kellyn's stomach twisted with the sense of a world holding its breath.

The whisper-woven Sylph armor around her ribs shimmered faintly as she tightened its buckles. The Whisperthread plates shifted with her breath—never fully opaque, never entirely gone. The Windveil Rite still hummed along her bones, its subtle bend of light and sound adjusting to her still-awkward motion.

Harvey stared openly.
"Why do you look like a ghost halfway through a bad magic trick?"

"Because," Khandyl said, adjusting her bowstring, "she passed the trial. You did not."

Harvey scowled. "I didn't even get to duel anyone."

Froster tugged at his own Whisperthread bracers. "Be glad. We might need her to walk through a wall before this is over."

Kellyn smiled despite herself—small, wary, but real. Yet beneath it she felt something else: the desert. Dry heat.

Endless sand. And the crawling unease of an enemy watching from beyond the horizon.

Elowen joined her at the grove's edge, Sylthara circling high above like a river of emerald fire.
"The sands are unkind," she murmured. "And the Osiri do not miss what crosses them."

"That's why we leave before dawn," Kellyn answered.

"No," came a voice like sliding wind, "it is why you leave now."

Lady Dravokh Mistshaper stepped from a hanging veil of branches. Her form coalesced with the ease of a leaf choosing to be solid. Her gray-teal eyes locked on Kellyn—measured, wary, and softened by a flicker of something dangerously close to respect.

"You have lingered long enough. The desert pushes against our southern roots. The Osiri dig beneath dunes that should never be breached."

Kellyn tightened the strap on her swordbelt. "You said they wouldn't march so far north."

"I said they *should not*," Dravokh replied. "The Osiri do not respect 'should'."

Harvey cleared his throat. "So, what exactly are they after?"

Dravokh's expression hardened—her outline sharpening until the air seemed to brace around her.
"They seek that which was never meant to be found."

A single silver leaf drifted down, humming with faint runes. It landed in Kellyn's palm, and Ellendyl's voice rippled through it—distorted, urgent.

"Kellyn. They know.
The emissary has marked you.
The Osiri march toward Amenemapet's crypt."

Static cracked like tearing silk.

"Ahsin was not wrong.
The Necrodemicon is real."

The leaf burned into silver ash.

Silence swallowed the grove.

"… That's bad," Harvey whispered.

Dravokh stepped closer, her presence suddenly heavy—fully visible, fully solid. Among the Sylph, it was the closest thing to a battle stance.

"Listen well, Kellyn Windstream. The Osiri do not conquer. They remake. Their priests unbind the soul. Their Sun-Children hollow the land. And their god watches every dune like an unblinking furnace."

She traced a circle in the air. Leaves vibrated in sympathetic resonance.

"They come to unseal what sleeps beneath the desert."

Elowen's face paled. "How large a force?"

"A battalion—perhaps more. Their outriders are already near."
Her gaze drifted over Kellyn's shoulder, deep into the trees.

A low tremor rolled through the grove.

Harvey froze.
"… Please tell me that was thunder."

"It was not," Dravokh said.

Seris stood utterly still, her hands clasped, eyes unfocused—listening to something none of the others could hear.

Dravokh approached her gently.
"You will go with them. Your training is unfinished. But unfinished wind still blows hardest."

Seris bowed her head, though her gaze remained fixed on the empty air between two old silverwoods.
As though someone stood there.

Kellyn followed her line of sight.

Nothing.

Yet the Windveil along her shoulders pulsed once—recognizing… something.

Dravokh retrieved a small pouch from her belt, woven from silver leaves and pale thread.
"The last Whisperthread Cloak of this season. It scatters presence, confuses heat signatures, and blinds Osiri watch-scribes. Wear it when the desert tries to erase you."

Kellyn accepted it with a bow. "Thank you."

Dravokh's mouth curved into a sly, almost affectionate smile. "Use it well, Queen of Swords. And—for once—do not stride like thunder through sacred places."

Kellyn flushed. "I do not—"

Harvey snorted behind her.
Khandyl nodded vigorously.
Elowen pretended not to hear.

"… Fine," Kellyn muttered. "Sometimes."

Dravokh laughed—a Sylph laugh—air dancing through leaves, light turning warm at its edges. The forest itself shimmered in response.

Then the dragons descended.

Myrrathis.
Sylthara.

Their weight shifted the branches, but the Windveil held firm, silver threads tightening to support them. Scales like liquid emerald. Wings that warped the wind.

Sylph warriors gathered at the grove's rim, awe and apprehension in equal measure. None had seen dragons within Aeralith in generations.

Dravokh leaned close to Kellyn—the wind between them suddenly still.
"When you return," she whispered, "bring me the head of the one who chains the sun."

Kellyn blinked. "…Is that a request or an order?"

"Both."

Then Dravokh dissolved into wind and vanished without bending a single branch.

Harvey exhaled shakily. "She is terrifying."

Kellyn shrugged. "She likes you."

"How can you possibly tell?"

"She didn't threaten to push you off the canopy."

Harvey considered this. "I'll take that as a win."

The dragons crouched low, letting the party climb aboard. They launched upward with a force that scattered leaves in spiraling arcs.

The first part of the journey would be by air—until the forest thinned and the Aeralith gave way to broken scrub. After that, the dragons must remain behind. The desert killed storms that tried to enter it.

Kellyn looked back once.

Sylph warriors stood in a crescent.
Dravokh watched from a high bough.
And Seris… Seris stared into the leaves with a sorrow that did not belong to her alone.

Kellyn moved closer. "Seris?"

Seris brushed away a tear. "The Aeralith is beautiful. I will miss it."

But her eyes lifted again.

Toward that same empty space in the canopy.

A shadow shifted.
Or a memory.
Or a guardian no longer meant to be seen.

"We'll come back," Kellyn promised. "All of us."

The dragons banked south, wind ripping away the last hints of forest-song.

Behind them, the Aeralith faded into a veil of green.
Ahead—the desert waited. And beneath it, the Osiri.

Chapter 20 - The Great Desert: Storms & Mirages

Location: Border of the Aeralith Canopy → The First Dunes
Chronometric Stamp: BV 24.017

"Patience is the calm before the stomp." — *Urmak Storm-Walker (Thraekar)*

The forest ended too abruptly.

One moment there was canopy—cool green shadow, leaflight filtering in shifting patterns, the quiet murmur of Sylph Songs moving through living wood.

The next—

Heat.

Sky.

A wind like sandpaper across the tongue.

Kellyn stepped out of the last fringe of silverwood and felt the Aeralith fall away behind her like the edge of a continent. Before them, the desert stretched in endless waves of gold and white, dunes catching the sun in blinding crescents.

The air smelled of hot stone and old dust. No sap. No leaf. No forest.

Just absence.

Elowen came up beside her, drawing her green cloak tighter despite the rising heat.
"The desert has no Life-Song," she said quietly. "Only bone-songs. And memory."

"Whose memory?" Harvey asked.

Elowen didn't answer.

Behind them, Myrrathis and Sylthara landed on the last strip of scrub and broken rock, talons digging furrows in the earth. They were already breathing harder than they should for such a short flight.

Myrrathis lowered his head so Kellyn could rest a hand on his brow. Heat radiated off his scales—not just from the sun, but from the reflected furnace of sand ahead.

"Here," he rumbled in Dragon tongue, "the sky-song breaks. The air… twists."

Kellyn's throat tightened. "You can't go farther south. We will be moving into halls and tunnels too small for you."

"Indeed." A low growl rolled in his chest. "We would thirst and starve beneath the sun. The desert does not suffer dragons."

Sylthara huffed in sharp agreement, tail lashing once.

Elowen pressed her forehead to Sylthara's muzzle. "Wait for us in the Aeralith. If we do not return…"

Sylthara exhaled, a warm gust that ruffled Elowen's hair.

"You will," the dragon whispered into her mind. "Or the desert will burn for it."

They parted with reluctance that felt like tearing a thread. The dragons turned north again, wings beating hard as they climbed back toward the sheltering green. In moments, they were specks against the sky—then gone.

Only then did Kellyn step into the desert proper.

Sand shifted beneath her boots with a dry hiss. Wind tugged at her Whisperthread cloak; the Sylph-woven fibers flickered in the corners of her eyes, bending light, muting the crunch of her steps.

"Feels like walking on a graveyard," Froster muttered.

"That's because it is," Loka said. He knelt briefly, scooping a handful of sand. It poured through his fingers like powdered bone. "Deserts like this are layers of endings."

Harvey grimaced. "Fantastic. Bone-dust. Great vacation spot."

Serithyl and Vaelinnae moved with them in silence, stepping neither ahead nor behind, always just slightly off where Kellyn expected her to be. The Sylph warrior's outline blurred occasionally as the Windveil took her, her form slipping into the wind's intention rather than the eye's expectation.

"The desert watches," Serithyl murmured. "Do not give it more attention than it deserves. It will grow arrogant."

"Can land be arrogant?" Harvey whispered to Witmar.

Witmar replied under his breath, "This one can."

By midmorning, the heat pressed on them like a hand. Sweat slid down Kellyn's spine, trapped under mail and Sylph armor. The sun made shadows sharp and mean.

The first oddities came after the second ridge of dunes.

Not mirages in the usual sense—no shimmering pools of phantom water or distant, wavering cities.

Instead, *structures* surfaced briefly in the glare—broken pillars, ribs of stone, what might have been the fragment of an obelisk—appearing for a breath's span and then gone.

Froster squinted and pointed. "There. On that ridge. Tell me you see that."

Kellyn shaded her eyes. A jagged silhouette rose from the sand—a half-buried archway etched with faint markings.

She blinked.

It was gone.

Harvey swore. "Okay. Nope. That actually *was* there."

Khandyl's jaw clenched. "The desert is pulling memories to the surface… then hiding them again."

"Or something wants us to know we're being watched," Aafje said.

The Windveil along Kellyn's shoulders pulsed once—almost a flinch—like the Sylph threads themselves disliked this landscape.

They made camp under the thin shelter of a broken sandstone outcrop when the sun climbed too high to fight. The rock gave minimal shade, but it was something.

Seris stood at the edge of their makeshift shelter, staring south. Her hair clung to her cheeks in the heat, eyes half-closed, as though listening to a tune no one else could hear.

Kellyn joined her. "You're quiet. Even for you."

Seris didn't look away from the dunes. "There's something beneath us."

Kellyn's hand went to her sword. "Alive?"

"No." Seris shivered. "But aware."

Loka stepped forward, dropping to one knee. He pressed his palm flat to the sand and immediately sucked in a sharp breath.

"Not life. Not death." His voice had gone thin. "It feels like necromancy written into the land itself. Layers and layers of it. Old."

"Then stop touching it," Harvey hissed. "In fact, let's all stop touching it. Let's go home. This place is cursed."

"I am listening," Loka said quietly. "Because it is… calling."

Kellyn's stomach sank. "Calling for what?"

Loka swallowed. "… To rise."

The warning came as a sound—low and grinding, like stone being crushed into powder.

Serithyl's head snapped up. "Storm."

Vaelinnae stood.

"Form up!" Kellyn ordered.

Wind changed direction in a heartbeat, slamming into them from the southeast. A towering column of sand twisted up from the horizon, building toward them with unnatural speed.

At first Kellyn thought sandstorm.

Then she saw the glint.

The air ahead was full of glittering dust—not just sand, but razor-thin shards of glass. They chimed softly as they collided, like a thousand tiny bells in a furnace.

Harvey threw an arm over his face. "Why is the air *sharpened?*"

"Desert firestorms," Elowen shouted. "Heat enough to melt sand—then break it again."

Seris's gaze tightened. "Not just heat. Something burned it on purpose."

The storm hit.

They braced behind the rock as the wind screamed. Glass-shards sliced across the dune faces, scoring lines into stone and skin. Kellyn felt a dozen tiny cuts open along her exposed forearms before the Whisperthread cloak blurred, bending the slicing gusts just enough to turn lethal lines into stinging grazes.

Froster swore as a shard buried itself in the sand beside him. The sliver was long, curved—

—and carved.

Kellyn plucked it out carefully.

A sun with chains around it gleamed along its surface, etched in molten gold.

The Osiri's chained sun.

Her breath left in a hiss. "Message received."

As quickly as it had formed, the storm thinned. Glass settled. The wind dropped to a hot, whispering rasp.

The dunes around them were scarred—marked with slashes and faintly glowing runes burned into the sand where lightning or ritual had struck.

"Their patrols are close," Khandyl murmured, crouched near one of the branded symbols. "This one's fresh."

"Closer than we wanted them to be," Witmar added.

Seris turned, slow and tense, gaze shifting north, then east, then south.
"No," she whispered. "They're not just close. They're around us."

Kellyn was about to ask where when the chanting began.

It started as a vibration.
A low, bone-deep hum beneath their boots.

Then sound.

Distant. Rhythmic. Like a stone being taught to sing.

"Osiri battle-priests," Elowen said quietly. "Their rites ride the air."

"Their magic uses sound as a net," Aafje added. "If we can hear it this clearly, we're already in its reach."

A thin crack split the fused crust of glass-sand behind them.

Grains spilled down.

Something rose from beneath.

Harvey yelped and scrambled backward, nearly tripping over Froster. Kellyn swung her sword up instinctively—then froze.

The figure that pulled himself from the desert looked wrong in too many ways.

Tall and lean, his cloak was a tatter of once-black fabric bleached to gray, edges melted and torn by heat and sand. A cracked Osiri bone-plate fused into the flesh of one shoulder, as armor half-melted into its wearer.

His skin was the color of old marble—stretched tight over sharp bones, cracked in small, branching lines as if the desert had tried to dry him into dust and failed. His ears were Anari-shaped.

His eyes were the worst.

Copper once.

Now they burned like heated metal, just shy of collapse.

For a terrifying instant, she thought the desert itself had learned to mimic a man.

"Ahsin, I presume," Kellyn breathed.

He lifted one clawed hand, palm out—not in attack, but in warning.

"Be still," he rasped. His voice sounded like gravel dragged down a tomb wall. "Or they will hear you."

The chanting shifted, somewhere beyond the nearest dune. The rhythm altered, searching.

Witmar's jaw clenched. "You shouldn't be alive."

Ahsin's mouth pulled into a thin smile. "I'm not," he replied. "That's rather the problem."

Elowen moved closer to Kellyn, keeping her tone even. "Why appear now?"

"Because Amenemapet stirs," Ahsin said. "Because the desert is restless. And because you are walking a straight line into annihilation."

Froster muttered, "Good, straightforward annihilation. Nice to have clarity."

Ahsin ignored him. The desert wind played with the torn edges of his cloak as he studied their positions, their armor, the faint flicker of Windveil around them.

He looked… impressed. And worried.

"Osiri outposts lattice this region," he said. "The next ridge is watched. You cannot see them. They see you."

Kellyn's grip tightened on her sword. "Then show us where to walk."

A new sound rolled across the dunes—heavier than chanting—a slow, deliberate crunch of boots on sand.

Ahsin's head snapped toward the north. His voice dropped. "Down. Now."

He moved with sudden, predatory precision, slipping into a narrow slit between two dune slopes that had been nothing but shadows until he stepped into it.

Kellyn didn't hesitate. "Move!"

They followed in quick order: Khandyl first, then Serithyl and Vaelinnae, then Aafje, Witmar dragging an incredulous Harvey by the collar, Loka and Froster close behind, and Elowen and Seris last.

The crevice cut into the dune at an angle, like a knife wound. Inside, the air was cooler, still as held breath—yellow light slit in from above.

Ahsin pressed his back to the sandstone wall, eyes gone flat. "Hide your breath if you can. The rest is the Windveil's work."

Kellyn pressed into the shadow beside him. The Whisperthread along her armor tingled, threads pulling tight, muting the tiny grinding sounds of her armor against stone. When she forced herself still, her own outline fuzzed at the edges.

Above, something vast stepped into view.

A jackal-headed Osiri warrior strode along the ravine's lip. Nearly nine feet tall, skin obsidian-black, its body etched with pulsing sun-sigils that glowed molten gold beneath layered armor. Each step sank deep into the dune.

It raised a staff crowned with a bronze sun-disk.

The disk rotated once.

Light spilled out in a thin, flat sheet, sweeping across the dunes like a scanning blade.

Every muscle in Kellyn's body locked.

The light passed over the ravine mouth—hesitated—then continued.

"Do not move," Ahsin whispered. "It hunts motion and breath-heat."

Beside the sentinel walked another Osiri in ornate armor, khopesh of fused glass and bone resting across one shoulder. Chains of miniature suns looped from pauldron to belt. This one moved with a commander's unhurried confidence.

The two murmured in their harsh desert tongue.

Ahsin's jaw tightened. "They smell magic."

Sand trickled down near Seris. A single grain landed on her nose.

She did not flinch.

The light-sheet swept back.

Harvey's eyes watered. Kellyn could feel his urge to blink, to sneeze, to *do anything*. She laid her hand on his arm, just enough pressure to anchor him.

The Windveil pulsed in time with her heartbeat. For an instant she had the surreal impression of seeing herself from outside—blurred, dimmed, just another shadow in a fold of stone.

The sentinel paused directly above their hiding place.

It sniffed the air.

Chanted a phrase that made the ravine walls resonate.

Elowen's lips barely moved. "…Binding-perception rite. It's tasting for anomalies."

"Terrific," Witmar mouthed.

Time stretched thin as glass.

Then another Osiri called from farther along the ridge—a barked command.

The sentinel's ears flicked.

It turned away.

The light-sheet faded as they walked on, their silhouettes shrinking against the blinding sky until they vanished beyond the next dune. One of the dune slopes was shaped like a face.

Silence fell like a dropped curtain.

Harvey collapsed backward into the sand, sucking in air. "I think my soul just tried to leave my body."

Witmar tapped his forehead. "If it did, it changed its mind."

Ahsin stepped away from the wall, tension still tight in his frame. "That was a Sun-Chain Sentinel. Elite. They should not be this far north."

"Yet they are," Kellyn said. Her voice came out steadier than she felt. "Because of the crypt."

"Because of whatever is waking beneath it," Ahsin corrected. He looked south, toward the invisible heart of the desert. "They fear someone will tamper with the seal."

His gaze returned to Kellyn.

"And they are right to be afraid."

They retreated deeper into the ravine's shadow to regroup. The air held a different kind of weight here—not heat, but anticipation, as if the rock itself remembered old footsteps. Along the wall were a small set of inscribed glyphs that faded when focused on.

Elowen moved to Kellyn's side and frowned at a thin line of blood beading along her forearm where a glass shard had cut through.

"It's nothing," Kellyn said automatically.

"In this heat, every cut bleeds water," Elowen replied. "We cannot waste either."

Kellyn opened her mouth to argue.

Elowen didn't wait. She laid two fingers along the abrasion and murmured a soft, clean note. Life-Song flowed through the touch—quiet, efficient. The cut sealed, leaving only a faint warmth behind.

Kellyn exhaled. "I still don't understand how your magic works in this era."

"Understanding isn't the same as belonging," Elowen said gently. "You belong here, whether you understand it or not."

Kellyn met her eyes.

For a heartbeat, the desert around them felt less empty.

Then Ahsin's voice cut through the quiet.

"Enough rest." He turned, cloak fluttering in the still air as if stirred by some private wind. "Follow exactly where I step. The desert is listening, and we are already late."

Kellyn adjusted her grip on her sword, the Windveil whispering against her armor.

"All right," she said. "Show us the road that doesn't want to be walked."

The ravine opened southward like a throat.

They walked into it.

The heat-warp of air sometimes bent sound into hollow rattles — like bone chimes.

And behind them, beneath meters of sand and stone, something old shifted—just enough to notice.

Just enough to dream of rising.

Chapter 21 - The Chant That Should Not Be Heard

Location: The Broken Dunes of Khet-Ra
Chronometric Stamp: BV 24.019

"If the water bubbles, lunch is coming."
— *Ssilvar Yex (Sza'thir)*

The silence after the Osiri patrol withdrew was brittle—thin as heat-fused glass.

Only when the last boot-fall faded into the dunes did Ahsin exhale. His cracked skin caught the sunlight like fractured porcelain.

"They've extended their perimeter farther north," he said quietly. "This hunting net belongs to Outpost Four. We are too close."

Kellyn glanced south. "Outpost Four is the first fortress between here and Amenemapet."

"One of them," Ahsin replied. "And not the most merciful."

Harvey made a quiet strangled noise. "There's a less merciful one?"

Ahsin didn't answer.
He slipped deeper into the ravine, moving with an eerie, light-footed silence. The rest of them followed, grateful for the cooling walls.

The ravine twisted like something clawed through stone. Heat faded, but the ground trembled now and then, as if something ancient shifted far below.

Kellyn ran a hand across the rock. "River erosion?"

Ahsin shook his head. "Older teeth than rivers."

Elowen walked near the back, eyes not on the stone… but on Ahsin.

There it was again.
Barely a hum.
A rhythm in his breath and step.
A subtle combat-cadence woven into movement.

Every Anari warrior carried harmonic geometry through their form.
Twelve sanctioned root keys — seven major, five minor — the sacred scaffolding of the Codex Harmonica.

But the pitch threading Ahsin's gait lay outside them.

A minor key.
Dark, unresolved.

C minor.

A tone steeped in sorrow.

Elowen's breath caught.
"We do not craft in C minor," she whispered to Aafje.
"It isn't in the Harmonica."

Aafje's voice tightened with reverence — and fear.
"The lost key. To the clan that fell."

Harvey blinked. "The what?"

Aafje's reply was barely sound at all:
"Lynx."

Even the desert wind held still.

"Their death is the deepest cut in our histories," Elowen murmured.
"Their phantoms are said to run the Horn forever. We do not speak their name under open sky."

Harvey swallowed. "And you think he—"

Ahsin's hum vanished.

He offered no denial.
No truth.

Only silence.

And that silence felt older than the dunes.

The ravine bent sharply.
Below lay a wide basin — pale, powder-fine, almost luminous under the sun.

Not sand.
Bone.

Fragments so small they moved like drifting ash.

Loka knelt, breath catching. "A trench ossuary. Centuries of dead."

Ahsin traced runes half-buried beneath the bone-dust. "Boundary markers. The Osiri do not cross this trench. Their seers claim the ground remembers what was done here."

Harvey shuddered. "Why are deserts always full of bones?"

"Because deserts are where memory can't rot," Khandyl said softly.

They climbed to the ridge and peered over.

Outpost Four broke the dunes in a jagged scar:
Black-glass jackal statues.
Sun-etched fangs.
Spiral braziers.
Bone-priests pounding sigils into sand until the dunes trembled.

Osiri warriors — tall, jackal-headed, molten sigils glowing under armor — marched in precise lattice patterns.

Elowen whispered, "They're weaving a sound-net."

"For anything approaching Amenemapet's seal," Ahsin confirmed. "Something — or someone—who could break old bindings."

Kellyn pointed to the cleft west of the outpost. "How far to the pyramid?"

When Ahsin answered, his voice was flat:

"Three weeks of open desert. No rivers. No shade."

Harvey sagged. "And water?"

"Ra Oasis lies 12 to 15 days south," Ahsin said. "It is the only mercy between this outpost and the tomb."

"And beyond the oasis?" Witmar asked.

Ahsin pointed.

A half-buried triangle pierced the edge of the horizon — black stone swallowed by dunes.

"Amenemapet's pyramid waits two weeks beyond that, if the dunes show favor."

No one spoke.

The desert's silence became a weight on their ribs.

They turned toward the fissure.

And that dissonant hum returned — soft as regret.

C minor.
A forbidden resonance.
The harmonic fingerprint of something the Anari no longer named.

Elowen's voice was almost a prayer:

"The clan that used that key died. The Harmonica shut their tone away when the Greenwood fell. Their forms were lost."

Aafje breathed the word again, as if afraid of awakening something:

"Lynx. Based in dark magic."

Ahsin's stride faltered for only a heartbeat.

He remained silent about everything else.

And kept walking.

At the fissure mouth, Kellyn blocked his way.

"You're coming with us," she said.

The desert wind clung to the torn threads of Ahsin's cloak. His eyes reflected an age none of them could measure.

"You think the pyramid is what I fear," he said softly. "But my dread is older than its stones."

Harvey didn't tell a joke.
Even he could sense this wasn't the time for noise.

"When the Greenwood died," Ahsin murmured, "the Lynx did not pass on. Their souls were caught — claimed by the Horn of the Wild Hunt, chasing forever through Aelrindel's dreaming cage."

Elowen's hand rose to her mouth.

"I refused that fate," he continued.
"I went to veiled Vecha-los. I begged for enough time in flesh to free them.
She gave survival… not life.
I rose half-dead, still Anari in shape, nothing Anari in fate."

His gaze went to the dunes — distant, haunted.

"In that half-existence, I thought another who walked death might understand. I found others like me — revenants who had bargained for breath or risen from the Crone's touch. Together, we sought Amenemapet. Arch-Lich. Pharaoh of sun-bound tombs."

He paused. Jaw tight.

"He saw us as possessions. Tools. When we refused him, he slaughtered nearly all the vampires. Only I and a few others escaped. We forged the Veydgrath from refusal and ash. Our first law was simple: no master but our own night."

Silence devoured the fissure.

Then:

Ahsin's voice softened, almost breaking:

"I still hear the harmonics of my people in dreams.
C minor, dying on a breath that will never end."

It hurt to hear—because none of them knew how to answer something that ancient.

Kellyn swallowed.

"Then walk with us," she said. "Not ahead. Not behind. With."

Ahsin searched her face — searching for deception, pity, motive.

Finding none.

A tension finally eased from his shoulders.

He moved into the shadow beside them.

Not leading.
Not following.

With.

The wind shifted.

A low hum rolled across the dunes — not natural wind, not mirage. Chanting. Rhythmic. Bone-deep.

Outpost Four had resumed its sound-net.
Only now the cadence was probing — hunting for dissonance.

Hunting for the 13th key.

Elowen shivered.

And somewhere beneath meters of sand and stone, something old heard that forbidden tone — and listened.

Chapter 22 – The First Cracks Beneath Us

Planet: Vael'thara
Location: Aeralith Canopy
BV 24

Night in the Aeralith Canopy was usually a soothing lullaby—soft leaf-breath, warm glow of lantern-fruit, wind humming through spiral-branches in gentle resonant tones.

But not tonight.

Tonight, the forest listened.

Tonight, the forest feared.

Dravokh Mistshaper descended the spiral staircase of woven roots leading to the Lower Green, a platform so close to the forest floor that the air smelled of damp earth. Rarely did Sylph leaders walk this deep; the lower boughs were the domain of druids, root-seers, and the shadow-watch.

But after last night's report—after the whisper that the earth itself was crawling upward—Dravokh knew she needed to see it with her own eyes.

Laeryn awaited her at the platform's edge, bow in hand.

"They found something," the hunt-mistress said.

Dravokh nodded once. "Show me."

Laeryn led her along a narrow branch path that coiled close to the ground. The trees here were twisted—old enough that their bark swirled like muscle fiber, holding memories in their rings. Whisper-Vines hung limp, drained of resonance, as if the wind had been pulled out of them.

That alone set Dravokh on edge.

Whisper-Vines never fell silent unless something had overwritten their Song.

They reached a small clearing where three wardens knelt in a circle around a body.

Dravokh approached quietly.

The fallen Sylph woman lay on her side, eyes open, mouth relaxed, with no signs of struggle. No bruise. No wound. No poison-blackness. Her skin was pale—drained, emptied, as if her breath had simply… gone elsewhere.

Dravokh crouched beside her, brushing fingers over the woman's cheek.

Cold. Not like night-cold.
Cold from within.

"Laeryn," Dravokh said quietly, "what killed her?"

"We don't know," the hunt-mistress whispered. "There was no fight. Her partner found her like this."

Dravokh closed her eyes and reached with her senses.

A faint tremor—like a plucked string, snapped.
Not the forest's Song.
Not life.
Not shadow.

Harmonic, but twisted.
A resonance that did not belong in trees or wind.

"Osiri magic," Dravokh murmured.

Laeryn grimaced. "A draining spell. Desert rite?"

"No," Dravokh said slowly. "Related, perhaps. But this pulse came from below. Beneath the roots."

A grinding sound rumbled near the arch-root — faint stone-on-stone.

Dravokh and Laeryn moved closer. Beneath an ancient root, soil sagged inward, forming a deepening hollow. Fine dust streamed through hairline cracks.

Dravokh touched the soil.

It vibrated.

Not randomly.
Not like shifting earth.

Pulse.
Pause.
Pulse-pulse.
Pause.

Khem-Duat cadence.
Osiri ritual pattern.

But folded into it was a spiraled undertone — Gravhal tunneling logic.

"Someone merged techniques," Dravokh whispered. "Osiri sigilcraft riding Gravhal resonance-mapping, or…yes, these appear to be carved by elementals of the earth."

Laeryn went pale. "This far southwest of the mountains? Did you say earth elementals? I thought only Gravhal summoned them."

"Which means their spies learned something they should not, or their emissary taught them something he shouldn't."

Three male Sylph emerged from the shadows, cloaks whispering like wind made visible.

Vaelkorh, commander of the Hidden Host, bowed, as did the other two males, Shyr and Laeryn.

"Lady Mistshaper. We traced five branch-line distortions. They converge here."

He looked toward the dead woman. "This is only the beginning."

Lady Dravokh gestured toward the soil. "Hear the pattern?"

Vaelkorh crouched, palm brushing dust. Something sharp flickered in his eyes.

"They're not digging," he whispered. "They're decoding. Mapping the root structures, harmonic ley-lines, maybe even anchor points. They're moving through the earth nearly half as fast as we move on the surface."

Laeryn stiffened. "Mapping our forest?"

"Or scouting for something beneath it," Vaelkorh said. "Trying to bypass canopy protections. Perhaps even reach the hidden city."

All three warriors tensed.

"That will not happen," Vaelkorh said. "But we must know how far they've reached."

Shyr signaled softly from near another root cluster.

"You should see this."

Carved into the underside of a thick root—hidden until bark was peeled away—was an Osiri glyph. Angular. Harsh. Missing curves and harmonic strokes, as if carved by hands that only half understood what they shaped.

Dravokh hissed. "Fyra's harp."

Laeryn frowned. "Osiri military mark?"

"No." Dravokh traced the edges. "Priesthood sigil. Near-pharaonic. This isn't soldiers — this is Amenemapet's doctrine."

The soil pulsed again.
Harder.

"Tunnel's expanding," Shyr whispered. "Fast."

Dravokh straightened. "We collapse it."

"And quietly," Vaelkorh added. "They must not realize we're listening to their frequencies."

"What do we do?" Laeryn asked.

Dravokh stared at the trembling root.

"The cracks have begun. The war reached us before the armies have."

She looked to Vaelkorh. "Mobilize the Hidden Host. Silent teams at all five breaches. Collapse every passage — substitute root-growth barriers if you have to."

"They'll tighten their net if they notice," Laeryn warned.

"They will not," Dravokh said. "Not while our Song holds faster than theirs."

She looked down once more.

The earth shuddered.
And this time, the tremor felt… responsive.
Warning.
Trusting.

"Lady…" Laeryn whispered. "The forest is frightened."

"Yes," Dravokh said softly. "And for the first time in a generation… so am I."

Her cloak whispered as she turned back toward the branches above.

"But fear is only a signal. And we answer signals with action. Prepare the Windborne Quarter. Accelerate the Ritual of Discovery. Every Sylph who shows even the faintest spark — we awaken them faster."

Laeryn hesitated. "Harder? They can barely stand after one day."

"They must," Dravokh said. "Because Amenemapet is stirring. And the Osiri are already beneath us."

She placed her hand once more on the trembling root.

"We hear you. We are not blind. We will not leave you to old enemies."

Behind her, the Hidden Host moved — silent as storm-breath before lightning.

The forest listened.

And hoped.

Chapter 23 - The Desert's Edge

Planet: Vaelthara
Location: Southern Fringe of the Aeralith Canopy
Chronometric Stamp: BV 24.14

"Individuality is overrated. I tried it once—awful experience."
— *Kritt-Kritt (Krikk'ar)*

[FIELD LOG // TDG-512B — FRAGMENT 17]
Left Sylph territory.
Ahsin confirms Osiri Outpost Four grid overlaps the
expected route.
Surface conditions: unbearable heat, zero shade, shifting
dunes with intermittent mirage distortions.
Primary threat: detection.
Secondary threat: dehydration.
— Commander Kellyn Windstream

The forest had vanished long ago, swallowed by dunes that
stretched like an unbroken sea of gold.
Sometimes Kellyn caught a trace of the Aeralith on her cloak
— resin scent and the ghost-memory of silver leaves — but
the green world was now only a dream against the scorched
horizon.

"It still feels wrong to have left it behind," she murmured.

Seris nodded, voice distant. "Forests don't understand
endings. They assume every story grows new roots."

Khandyl planted her spear deeper into sand that flowed like
dry water. "This isn't growth. This is crossing a scar."

Aafje scanned the horizon. "How do the Osiri survive out here?"

Harvey shrugged. "They also try to live in our forests. Apparently they like stealing shade."

Witmar nudged him. "Try not to insult ancient desert empires while standing in their front yard."

"No promises."

Loka squinted southward. "Wind's blowing the wrong direction. Air is streaming toward the deep desert, not away from it."

"That shouldn't be possible," Kellyn said.

"It is," Seris whispered, "if something is drawing breath."

The sand shifted underfoot.

No wind.
No tremor.
Just a faint inhalation — as though the dunes tasted the air.

Froster crouched, pressing a palm into the sand. "Warm under the surface. Not solar heat. Something internal."

"A hearth?" Harvey guessed.

"A furnace," Froster replied.

Aafje grimaced. "Lovely."

A gust swept the dunes — dry and hollow — like exhalation from a skull. Instinctively, blades, bows, and magics tightened in their hands.

Kellyn steadied herself. "We keep moving."

They pressed deeper into the valley of dunes, the Aeralith shrinking behind them until even memory struggled to hold its shape. Every step sank too deeply, erasing prints faster than they could be made. Loka counted heads too often, as if expecting one to disappear between blinks.

Shadows pooled wrong — darker than noon should allow, angles bending slightly against the sun. The press of the desert felt alive.

Harvey muttered, "Feels like something's watching and waiting."

Witmar added, "If something wants to kill me, it could at least introduce itself first. Professional courtesy."

Aafje flicked fingers, conjuring a small shadow shimmer. It vanished instantly, as though swallowed.

"Not Osiri suppression," she murmured. "Older."

A deep vibration thrummed through their boots.

Seris inhaled sharply. "You feel that?"

Kellyn nodded. "Yes. Not sound. Pressure."

A low pulse.
Slow.
Ancient.
Like a heartbeat buried under miles of sand.

Khandyl bristled. "Something sleeps down there."

"And something else wants it awake," Froster replied.

Harvey started a laugh. It died halfway. "Wonderful."

Sand twisted 30 paces ahead — not blowing, but assembling.

Loka whispered, "Sand-devil?"

"No," Aafje said. "Look inside."

A figure stood within the swirl — still, tall — until the sand sloughed away.

Bronze skin.
Jackal-like ears.
Golden eyes like molten metal cooling.

Osiri.

But no soldier's posture.
No priest's chant.

Something other.

He raised one hand. Not hostile. Not welcoming.

Harvey instinctively stepped in front of Witmar.

Kellyn drew her blade but held position. "Identify yourself."

The Osiri studied her like a monument, deciding whether to bury her or spare her.

"You walk toward a place forbidden to the living," he said, his voice an empty-hall echo.
"Turn back."

Kellyn's jaw tightened. "We can't."

Sorrow flickered in the Osiri's eyes. Not hatred. Not threat. Grief.

"Then be consumed."

His body unraveled into dust — real dust, not magic — swallowed by wind.

Silence crashed over the dunes.

Aafje whispered, "That wasn't a warning. That was pity."

Loka exhaled. "They know we're coming."

Kellyn slid her sword away. "And we go anyway."

They marched on, tension wrapped tight around every footfall.

After a long stretch of silence, Witmar spoke, eyes on Ahsin:

"You said something before. About the Hunt. Faelor is Night Hunt. But Aelrindel… how's his different?"

Ahsin did not answer quickly. When he did, his voice was sand rasping on stone.

"Faelor hunts life in respect. His hunt is a moonlit ritual. A predator who remembers the balance."

He looked south, as if the dunes carried memory.

"Aelrindel is the master of the hunt, who hunts the worthy. His quarry are equals — those who refuse to kneel or flee. He hunts to understand. To test the edge of spirit."

Witmar frowned. "So why imprison him?"

Ahsin's eyes dimmed — haunted.

"He hunted what he should not. A winter-being sacred to the Frost Thraekers. They followed him from the frozen wastes to the Greenwood and dragged him down. The Crone aided the Thraekers, as she bore enmity for Aelrindel. What happened afterward turned the Greenwood into a dimension of death to the living."

Kellyn's voice softened. "The Greenwood curse."

Ahsin nodded. "Vecha-los sealed it after the Thraeker rite. A cradle became a prison — and the Horn of the Wild Hunt caught every Lynx soul in its echo."

Seris whispered, "You… had a family?"

Ahsin was silent long enough that even the sand seemed to pause.

"A mate," he said finally. "Two children. I remember their voices more than their faces."

Nothing in the desert comforted him.

Harvey swallowed. "I thought the Veydgrath formed because of Amenemapet."

"They did," Ahsin murmured. "But their roots began in tragedy. Greenwood survivors. Necropolis wanderers. Spirits who couldn't die properly. We went to Amenemapet believing an arch-lich would understand."

His voice hardened.

"He tried to bind us. Make us part of his sun-dead armies. When we refused, he slaughtered nearly every vampire he could find. Only a few escaped. We forged the Veydgrath out of refusal and ash."

He looked across the dunes as if measuring them against old battlefields.

"Our first law was simple: no master but our own night."

Kellyn's voice was quiet. "If Aelrindel is imprisoned still… and the Horn remains…"

Ahsin's gaze found hers.

"Then the Hunt is incomplete. If freed, the song that died would breathe again. And the Lynx might finally rest."

A pulse throbbed faintly underfoot, and Kellyn felt the dunes respond — as though whatever slept beneath them recognized the C-minor resonance in Ahsin's voice.

Seris murmured, "I feel spirits here that are like you."

Ahsin's smile was thin, cracked.

"Yes. The desert holds prisoners. Buried gods. Broken rites. Memories not permitted to die."

He looked south.

"You will meet them if we keep walking."

They advanced, boots sinking into a land that seemed almost alive.

The dunes whispered beneath every step.

Something waited there.
Something old.
Something that remembered the Lynx, the Huntsman, and those who defied a Pharaoh.

And with every step, the heat pressed closer, like the breath of a patient predator.

[FIELD LOG // TDG-512B — FRAGMENT 18]

Sgt. Mirren "Froster" — Sylvancrest Time Bureau Security

Subject: Ahsin — probable Anari origin; hostile-environment survival intelligence
Timestamp: BV 24.141 – Desert Fringe

• Confirmed that Ahsin is not originally Osiri.
Physical cues: pointed ears; Anari cranial structure; bronze skin tone consistent with Greenwood lineage.
Speech and movement patterns match harmonic-based combat forms (Anari origin).

• Identified clan markers consistent with extinct Lynx Clan.
Key indicator: his base resonance hum aligns to C-minor harmonic register.
(Cross-reference with Codex Harmonica: no clan presently uses that key as a dominant form.)

• Extraction: Lynx Clan did not vanish to war or exile.
Per Ahsin: clan destroyed by a curse linked to the Greenwood.
Curse origin: imprisonment of Aelrindel (Anari Huntsman deity).
Force involved: Frost Thraekers.
Unclear motive except violation of sacred hunt boundaries and Thraeker pantheon protection laws.

• Surviving Lynx spirits are reportedly bound to the Horn of the Wild Hunt.
Suggests harmonic or metaphysical servitude, not spiritual dissipation.
Implies Horn remains active, calibrated to C-minor resonance.

• Ahsin survived by petitioning Vecha-los (Crone).
Outcome: vampiric half-state.
Not standard necromantic undeath — no typical consumption cycle or rot.
The state seems engineered to bypass the effects of the Greenwood curse.
Key info: daylight resilience and cognitive retention intact.

• Early Veydgrath formation linked to refugees from the Greenwood tragedy.
Ahsin and others originally approached Amenemapet for an alliance due to their shared undead condition.
Amenemapet attempted forced binding.
Result: mass execution event ("Sun-Purges").
Survivors formed Veydgrath as a sovereign undead faction.
Operational doctrine: no master but their own night.

• Ahsin still displays combat reflexes consistent with Anari harmonic formwork.
However, cadence and motion are offset — dissonant, non-aligned to any existing Codex mode.
Suspect post-transformation sub-harmonic adaptation.
Record for Codex review.

• Ahsin expresses ongoing auditory memory of Lynx choir in C minor.
Phrase: "Dying on a breath that will never end."
Possible psychic linkage to Horn-bound spirits.

Assessment:
Ahsin is a high-value lore and navigation asset with critical knowledge of Osiri perimeter networks and crypt-sites.
Psychological profile indicates trauma from the Greenwood collapse and Amenemapet betrayal, but cooperative intent confirmed.

Risk Analysis:
The presence of a Lynx-key harmonic signature may attract entities tied to Hunt or crypt seals.
If Horn or imprisoned Aelrindel is encountered, expect a harmonic resonance cascade affecting Ahsin first.

Recommendation:
Maintain protective posture around the subject.

Monitor for spontaneous C-minor pulse events.

Record harmonic fluctuations for the Codex database.

If Horn is discovered, consult Elowen and Khandyl before activation.

Do not allow Osiri to capture Ahsin alive — risk of re-binding or ritual inversion too high.

— Froster

Chapter 24 - The Long Crossing

Planet: Vaelthara
Location: The Great Desert of the Osiri
Chronometric Stamp: BV 24.041

"The best pranks reveal themselves after you leave the room." — *Krizzle Snaptooth (Zagg'rin)*

[FIELD LOG // TDG-512B — FRAGMENT 18]
Surface temperature: lethal during midday hours.
Visual distortion: severe.

Water supply: inadequate for the expected duration.
Enemy activity: nearly continuous, primarily auditory or mirage-phase.
Team cohesion: stable. Fatigue: increasing. — *Commander Kellyn Windstream*

The desert changed.

Not slowly.

Not naturally.

But as if someone turned a page in reality.

One moment, the wind howled.

The next—total stillness.

Sand hung in the air, motionless, grains suspended like sparks caught in amber.

Froster slammed into Kellyn's back.

"Uh—did the world just… lock up?"

Everyone felt it.

Aafje shivered. "Shadow magic. But not mine."
She stared across the still horizon. "…Something older."

Heat vanished.
The sand beneath them shuddered.

Something was rising.

Harvey instinctively stepped in front of Kellyn, his sword half-raised. His terror was obvious, but he didn't retreat. The Hunt-mark within him flickered—faint emerald along the edges of his veins, as if sensing dead things.

Loka knelt, touching the sand.
"Tracks. Bare feet. Deep. But—" he swallowed. "They stop right here. As if the walker sank straight down."

Seris stiffened. "Stone-travel?"

Aafje shook her head. "Impossible. They have no life-song, no Gravhal resonance, no root-step. If something is doing this…"
Her eyes narrowed, "…then it isn't ours."

The tremor intensified.

A crack split across the dune—long, jagged, widening.

"BACK!" Kellyn shouted.

They scattered just as skeletal hands burst upward—five, ten, 20—their armor half-fused with sun-resin. Osiri corpses dragged themselves into the light, eye sockets full of molten glow.

Harvey whispered, horrified, "They're all dead."

One lunged at him.

He swung blindly—no stance, no form—just instinct.

And something ancient answered.

FWOOOOOM—

Emerald-white fire roared outward, harmonic shock radiating as a bell struck beneath the earth.
Where the blade connected, dawn-bright patterns sang along the strike—four notes, minor key, crisp and unmistakable.

C-minor.
The lost Lynx key.

The undead disintegrated to ash mid-motion, vanishing before their bones hit sand.

Silence.

Even Harvey stared at his own hands.

Froster pointed weakly. "Uh… that. That was new."

Harvey blinked hard. "I don't know why or how yet."

Kellyn stood beside him, voice gentling. "You don't have to mean it."

Ahsin's reaction came slowly and utterly unguarded.

He stared at Harvey—truly stared—like the boy had cracked open a grave in the cold stone of his soul. His fingers curled inward, knuckles bone-white beneath cracked skin. For the first time since they stepped into the sands, Ahsin took a half-step back.

Not fear of Harvey.
Fear of memory.
Fear of something old that should have remained buried.

Before Harvey could speak, the sand fissure widened—

—and something emerged.

A towering figure, taller than any Anari.
Gold and obsidian resin armor.
Jackal helm.
Eyes burning sun-fire bright.

An Osiri Sun-Warrior.

When it spoke, its voice thundered like a tomb opening:

"The Green Knight walks."

Harvey croaked, "I—I'm uh, what?"

The warrior pressed fist to chestplate in a ritual vow older than kingdoms, blade held close in reverence — a stance still carved on the walls of forgotten tombs.

"Ender of Death's Dominion," it intoned.
"Breaker of the Silent Sun."

Then it lifted its blade.

Sand thundered beneath its steps.

Kellyn slid into Dragon stance — Anar'thyr, the Immutable Axis.
Her spine aligned perfectly vertical, elbows tucked, blade forming an unbroken line of Dominion.

"Aafje! Loka! Eyes up!"

The warrior lunged.

Kellyn met him head-on.
Her strike followed the Straight Axis — Dominion's Line — every vector absolute, every angle a law: not suggestion, not threat, but declaration.

The impact shuddered through her teeth.

This thing was strong.

Her foresight flashed — half-second windows, just enough to live.

She pivoted on sand-locked heels, flowing into the Pillar Path, Lýren'thal — perpendicular footwork and angle-cut geometry shaping the rhythm of reality around her.

The Osiri swung, faster, too fast — she ducked but still felt steel kiss her cheek, blood warm against the heat.

Aafje hurled twilight-flame.
The warrior adjusted.

Loka shouted, "Kellyn — right side incoming!"

Kellyn locked back to Dominion's Line — vertical, pure — and struck.

The warrior caught her blade with one hand.

"You cannot declare law to the dead."

He flung her like dust.

Sand erupted around her as she skidded down a dune.

Harvey charged in.

Kellyn saw the future — all of them — Harvey dying in a dozen possible angles.

She moved.

Dragon Breathlock.

Not a strike.
A declaration.

Her blade thrust forward to halt the rhythm of the world itself.

For a single heartbeat —
the universe slowed.

Harvey dove aside.
The killing blow passed him by inches.

The moment broke.

Kellyn staggered upright.
Breath ragged.
Vision tunneling at the edges — white rings sparking in her sight.

Dominion always demanded a toll.
Law did not shape reality without taking a piece of the one who spoke it.

The Sun-Warrior regarded her with curiosity, testing her limits.

Kellyn inhaled.

"Vael'Shar — Final Edict."

Her blade rose.

Reality held its breath.

Her alignment formed perfect Dragon geometry: a centered axis, heel line locked, elbows angled in a sacred ratio — the shape of Absolute Decree.

She struck.

The Osiri raised to parry — too late.

The law had already been spoken.

Her blade split the helm, skull, and the burning light beneath.

The warrior collapsed into drifting ashes.

Silence.

Harvey swallowed. "You… killed him."

Kellyn nodded faintly. "So did you."

Harvey shook. "No. That wasn't me. Something in me — something I don't know —"

Aafje laid a hand on him. "It saved your life."

He whispered, "I don't want it."

Kellyn murmured, "No one ever does."

Far across the dunes, wind ripped back into motion like the desert had been holding its breath for judgment.

Kellyn steadied herself.

If the past demands a price, I will pay it.

Loka scanned the horizon.
"More will come. Or worse. We need to keep crossing."

Kellyn sheathed her blade.
"Stay close. Eyes sharp. This crossing isn't finished."

After the winds finally died, Kellyn found Elowen sitting alone on the dune, faint green flickering around her fingers.

"Your magic's still settling?" Kellyn asked, sitting nearby.

Elowen nodded.
"Amenemapet showed me a future where I traded everything I am for knowledge. For a moment… I believed I could live with that."

Kellyn looked up at the hard, sharp stars.
"You don't have to choose between pieces of yourself. Not here. Not with us."

Elowen's breath trembled.
"And you? What would you choose, Kellyn?"

Kellyn pulled her mantle tighter against the night.
"I thought understanding our ancestors would make me strong. Instead… it just made me feel small."

Elowen smiled faintly.
"Small things still shape the world."

And from the dunes' edge: Ahsin watched the two women, silent and still as carved stone.
His gaze lingered longest on Harvey.

Around Ahsin, the sand faintly thrummed — the old binding spell echoing the emerald key that could unmake him.

His voice cracked as he whispered into the dark:

"Green Knight."

Not in hatred.
But in dread.
And in recognition.

A faint wind slid past, carrying a whisper so old no tongue owned it:

"Do not wake what sleeps beneath."

Chapter 25 - Ra Oasis (The Water That Lies)

Planet: Vaelthara
Location: Ra Oasis (Outer Pool)
Chronometric Stamp: BV 24.025

"I don't have anger issues. I have anger solutions."
— *Thalgar Redhorn (Minos)*

[FIELD LOG // TDG-512B — FRAGMENT 19]
Reached water source. Detected necrotic resonance patterns below sand strata.
Single reanimated guardian encountered.
Subject: unusual—partially sentient.
Harvey displayed an unprecedented cleansing harmonic burst.
Recommend reevaluation of Green Knight historical parameters.
— *Commander Kellyn Windstream*

The oasis seemed like a blessing.

Palm shadows flickered over a dark pool. Reeds whispered along its banks as though offering solace. Dunes curved inward, creating a green refuge locked inside the white.

Kellyn exhaled. The tension in her shoulders loosened for the first time since they entered the dunes.

Elowen knelt and drank. Froster practically fell face-first into the pool. Seris tested its flow and magic.

Harvey arrived last, pale from sun and exhaustion. Witmar wet a cloth, pressing it to his mouth and cheeks.

Ahsin did not drink.

He stood still as carved obsidian, head tilted, nostrils flaring almost imperceptibly.

"Be cautious," he murmured. "The desert does not give freely."

Harvey wiped sweat from his brow.
"We're dying out here. I think the desert can spare—"

Sand whispered.

Kellyn's voice hardened instantly.
"Witmar. Don't move."

Witmar blinked—and skeletal fingers burst from the sand, clamping onto his ankle.

He went down with a cry as the corpse hauled itself upward. Its bones were lacquered with resin, spine twisted, sockets burning faintly blue.

Necrosis spread where its hand touched flesh.

Harvey didn't think.

Green erupted.

His blade ignited in brilliant emerald fire and cut once.

ASH.
Instantaneous. Silent. Complete.

Wind scattered the remains.

Even the oasis stilled.

Witmar gasped, clutching his ankle.
"What—what just happened?!"

Harvey stared at the glow crawling along his blade.
"I don't know. I… react to undead."

Elowen pressed glowing fingertips to Witmar's skin, lifting the sickness away like peeling dark frost.

"It tried to drink me," Witmar muttered.

Khandyl surveyed the ground.
"Why did it come alone?"

Seris spoke without looking up.
"It didn't."

Kellyn followed her gaze.

Stone pillars ringed the oasis—half buried, carved with weather-worn Osiri glyphs. The arrangement was too intentional to be random.

Ahsin paced toward one, his voice thin with dread.

"A guardian circle. Ritual-binding. Older than the dynasties."

Kellyn frowned.
"Then why only one corpse?"

"The bindings are damaged."
Ahsin traced the dust where it rose.
"Only fragments of their dead can answer the call."

But his gaze wasn't on the bones.

It was on Harvey.

His voice lowered—quiet and shaken.
"Harvey Oakenstride… what did you do?"

Harvey held his sword awkwardly.
"It's just Green Knight magic, right?"

Ahsin's head shook very slowly.
"No. I have lived long enough to see three Green Knights—chosen, proven, sanctified. None could undo the dead. Not like that."

Harvey swallowed.
"I'm not special."

Ahsin stepped back a fraction—instinct, not choice.

"Whatever you are… is not something this world has seen."

Silence crept in with the desert wind.

Kellyn broke it.
"Refill flasks. Carefully. Quickly."

Later, as water settled and the circle's hum faded, the group gathered near the pillars.

Ahsin crouched, studying an inscription worn nearly flat: a stylized sun pierced by spears.

Elowen's voice was soft but unable to hide awe.
"Ahsin… you said you've seen Green Knights before. Then you lived before the Chamber of Victory?"

Ahsin didn't answer immediately.

Something fragile entered his posture—as if memory hurt more than sun or sand.

Finally:

"Yes. I walked the world when gods still wore flesh. When they taught rather than hid. When we prepared to face the Malloch openly."

Aafje's breath caught.

"That era is myth to us. We know of the Lynx only through ruin-songs and genealogy charts."

She hesitated.

"Did you… know them? The Lynx?"

Ahsin's jaw shifted.

"I knew them."

Elowen glanced sharply at his ear shape, the undertones of bronze in his skin, the lean angles of old Anari lineage.

"Your fighting stance," she whispered. "It resonates wrong. Outside the Twelve Songs. Minor harmonic key—C-minor, if I had to name it. That key belonged to the Lynx Clan."

Ahsin didn't confirm.

Didn't deny.

He merely said:

"The dark school of Anari magic blends with my fighting style. No other schools of magic have been blended with an Anari fighting style."

Witmar blinked.

"Wait. You taught Ellendyl, so Ellendyl knows this style?"

Kellyn's gaze sharpened.

"Ellendyl knows this style, then. So, the Lynx style is not lost."

Ahsin exhaled slowly, eyes sinking toward a past too large for language.

"Indeed. Ellendyl is my student. She knows all of the magic but continues her work to master it."

"Why did the Crone hate Aelrindel enough to betray him?" Aafje asked.

"Aelrindel sought to destroy the Malloch. The Crone believed that the world should never be reduced to one race to free the Malloch. She was the lone voice against the gods, advocating peace to keep the Malloch forever banished."

Kellyn asked quietly,
"And you saw him walk the forests?"

Ahsin nodded once.

"He shaped the Lynx. The Crone bound him after our clan followed too far. The Frost Thraekers hunted him from the northern wastes for killing a sacred spirit of their pantheon. When they shattered him and the Crone laid curse upon curse, the Greenwood warped. My people… vanished into its roots."

Elowen's breath trembled.
"What happened to the Lynx after that?"

Ahsin stared at the pillar's chipped glyphs.

"We became memory. And the Greenwood became a prison."

Seris spoke gently.
"And you? How did you survive when all others fell?"

He didn't answer for several seconds.

"I and a few others bargained with the Crone. In that moment, the Greenwood tried to devour me. She offered survival. I chose it."

Aafje whispered, "That would make you—"

Ahsin cut her off.

"Old."

Witmar tried again.
"What of the other gods? Before the Chamber? What were they *like*?"

That question hit differently.

Ahsin froze.

His voice came low, distant.

"Anaridin was the morning sun, warm until you defied him. Sylvara laughed like rainfall. Lireal judged with silence until the truth weighed too heavy. And Aelrindel… walked between breaths."

The desert wind stilled.

Kellyn waited for more.

Something shuttered behind Ahsin's eyes—grief sealed in iron.

He stood.

"Enough. No more questions. Memory is weight. And dawn brings worse things."

He turned toward the dunes.

The quiet that followed felt like a tomb slowly closing.

Kellyn's voice remained steady.
"We refill our waterskins, then move on. The pyramid is still waiting."

The group dispersed in silence.

Harvey watched Ahsin the longest—how he stared at the horizon not like a predator, but like someone remembering a house long burned.

When Kellyn spoke again, she did not raise her voice.

"It knows we're coming."

And the wind, too cold for a desert night, whispered agreement.

Chapter 26 - Windborne Quarter At Readiness

Planet: Vael'thara
Location: Windborne Quarter
BV 24

The Windborne Quarter had grown over four days from a chaotic jumble of tents into something that resembled a living creature—dense, humming, unpredictable, and stubbornly out of sync with the Aeralith forest.

The trees barely tolerated it.

From the high branches above, Dravokh Mistshaper watched as the first full day of training officially began.

Lantern-fruits flickered awake. Dreamwillow bristled with irritated silver hairs. Whisper-Vines curled inward like children hiding from noise.

And on the clearing floor below—
Fifty thousand refugees struggled to learn how to breathe like a Sylph.

A piercing, sharp whistle sliced through the morning air.

Hunt-Mistress Laeryn walked through the training glen, her bow on her back and twin wind-blades at her hips.

"All trainees—circle!" she barked.

Refugees scrambled, half-falling and half-lurching into an uneven crescent. Some still struggled to balance on knots of root or angled bark. Others clung to borrowed Sylph staves like crutches.

Laeryn didn't slow.

"You walk like stone," she said. "You breathe like sand. You hold your weight like broken Osiri statues. This ends now."

A few refugees exchanged glances—wary, defensive.

Laeryn smiled thinly. "You're not here to become Sylph in a day. You're here to stop being a danger to yourselves and everyone around you in our forest."

She gestured toward Shaela Windblossom, who stepped forward.

Shaela took a shallow breath, and the Whisper-Vines around the glen responded by lifting and spiraling slowly. Leaves rustled like pages turning. Branches gently bent as if bowing.

"This," Shaela said, "is how the forest breathes."

She began the First Gale Path—barefoot and graceful, each step bending wind-lines without disturbing them. The movement was both a prayer and a warning.

Refugees watched in awed silence.

Then Shaela paused and pointed at a middle-aged man with a stubborn jawline.

"You first."

He blinked. "Me?"

"Yes. Copy."

He tried.

He failed.

Catastrophically.

His first step sent a cloud of leaf litter flying. His second step disrupted the wind pressure in the wrong way, triggering a Whisper-Vine backlash. The vine swung up and struck him directly in the ear.

He yelped. The refugees flinched. Shaela tilted her head.

"Better," she said. "Again."

Farther into the glen, bindweavers sat with groups of refugees, teaching them to twist bark-thread into spiral patterns to make basic Sylph fabrics.

"It's like rope," one refugee insisted.

"No," the bindweaver corrected. "It's alive."

He tugged the thread tighter. It snapped, recoiling like a severed tendon.

The bindweaver didn't even react. "And now it's angry."

The broken bark-thread wriggled, then curled around his wrist like a punishing snake. He hissed in pain.

"You pulled. It responds to guidance, not force. Again."

Nearby, a young woman finished her first three-strand twist. The braid maker smiled with pride.

"Yes! There! Watch how it settles. You listened."

The woman beamed—proud, exhausted, trembling.

Dravokh nodded quietly.

Small victories matter, and the forest takes notice of them.

On the eastern edge of the Quarter, Maaren Faelwind and a group of mages tested resonance alignment.

Singing Sprigs glowed softly in the early light, each leaf shimmering with gentle tone.

A girl barely 16 touched a sprig—

It chimed a perfect Life harmonic.

Maaren inhaled sharply.

"Life school. High affinity. Bring her to the healers."

Two refugees later, a tall man touched a sprig and conjured a vortex of swirling spores that exploded outward in a ring.

Maaren stepped back immediately.
"Dark school. Very strong. Keep him isolated; no Dreamwillow contact."

Then came a quiet older man with white-braided hair. He approached hesitantly, as though afraid to try.

He touched the sprig—

And the leaf rang a harmonic unlike any other that morning.

Minor key.
Low.
Cold.
C-minor.

Aafje, observing from the far circle, froze. Her breath caught.

She knew that interval.

Every ancient Anari did.

It belonged to no clan alive today.

Whispered in lost stanzas.
Mentioned in half-forgotten Song tablets.

The cadence of the Lynx.

All dead for millennia, consumed by the Greenwood curse.

She forced the thought away.

Coincidence.
A refugee with a damaged spirit.
Trauma leaves strange echoes.

Maaren, unaware of the legends, recorded the data in his slate:

"Candidate #231 — Dark-aligned resonance, outside primary twelve-clan keys.
Minor scale — C-minor irregularity.
Flag for advanced isolation and long-term monitoring."

Above them, the Dreamwillow hissed sharply, branches shivering as though it recognized the note.

Even the Singing Sprigs dimmed for a breath.

Dravokh noticed the shift, his brows drawing tight.
Something in that tone unsettled the trees.

She listened but did not press the matter.

Larger threats were approaching.

At the edge of the glen, a young woman—one of the first refugees to learn wind-step footwork—was blindfolded and led through a curtain of Whisper-Vines.

Refugees watched, whispering:

"Where is she going?"
"Who are those Sylph?"
"They looked… different."

Dravokh heard every murmur.

The female instructors stepped aside.

Three male Sylph warriors emerged from the shadows—not dramatically, but with a quiet, potent presence that froze every refugee mid-breath.

Tall.
Silent.
Armor crafted from leaf-metal that caught the light like razor slashes.
Every movement perfect in pressure, weight, and silence.

The refugees recoiled from them instinctively.

One warrior nodded once to the instructors.

The blindfolded girl was handed over.

She vanished with them into the deeper branches.

Whispers rippled:

"I thought their men were all mages."
"They weren't mages."
"What are they?"

Laeryn smirked.

"Progress," she murmured.

By noon, the strain showed on the Sylph themselves.

Bindweavers worked with twitching hands, exhausted from repairing broken threads.
Hunters limped back with minor injuries sustained while correcting missteps.
Druids rubbed their temples calming Dreamwillow lashings.
Whisper-Vines drooped, reacting to sustained turbulence.
The Singing Sprigs sounded thin with fatigue.

Dravokh felt the ache in the forest's pulse.

A deep, slow tremor.
Protest.
Distress.
Fear.

She brushed a vine — it trembled beneath her hand.

"I know," she whispered. "We are asking too much."

Maaren approached quietly, wiping residue from his palms.

"We tested over three hundred today," he said. "We identified 18 Life-magic candidates, six Light, four Animal, 37 Shadow, and ten Dark."

"Shadow and Dark are rising," Dravokh said softly. "We have no one to train dark mages. Ellendyl Felhart is the only Anari dark mage. She can't be with all 12 clans to train their dark mages."

"Trauma awakens those Songs," Maaren replied.

He almost turned away — then frowned, remembering.

"And there was one anomaly. A minor-key resonance. C-minor. Not in any current clan catalog. I've flagged it."

Dravokh said nothing.
But she felt the forest shiver again.

In the Academy archives, the Lynx chord was categorized as a myth.

Yet the sprig had recognized it.

She did not comment.

Not now.

As evening bled into the Quarter, the forest's breath sharpened.

Wind sliced unevenly through branches.
Whisper-Vines trembled.
Leaves drifted from higher boughs.
Dreamwillow hissed like cooling metal.

Laeryn approached Dravokh, face grave.

"The wind-line is wrong," she said. "The forest is angry."

Dravokh surveyed the Quarter:

- Refugees limping back to tents

- Sylph instructors exhausted

- Whisper-Vines recoiling from disrupted harmonics

- Singing Sprigs whining with discord

- The forest groaning under the weight of fifty thousand foreign footsteps

She laid her hand against a root.

It trembled.

"The forest isn't angry," Dravokh whispered. "It's afraid."

Laeryn's jaw tightened. "And when a forest fears…?"

Dravokh answered the ancient truth:

"It prepares to fight."

A shadow detached from the northern ridge and approached.

A male Sylph warrior.

Vaelkorh.

He bowed.

"We scouted the tunnels," he said.

Dravokh's pulse sharpened. "And?"

His voice was barely above a whisper:

"The Osiri have breached the third root-layer."

Laeryn inhaled sharply. "Already?!"

"And worse," Vaelkorh continued, eyes dark as obsidian. "They are carving upward with purpose. They know exactly where they are going."

Lady Dravokh felt her breath tighten.

"Then the next move is ours, husband," she said.

Vaelkorh nodded once.

"The Hidden Host awaits your command."

Dravokh looked out over the Windborne Quarter — the groaning forest, struggling refugees, exhausted instructors, and the trembling harmonic threads.

Then she turned north.

Toward the tunnels.

Toward the breach.

And her voice carried like a blade across the branches:

"Tell your warriors… the forest bleeds tonight."

Vaelkorh vanished into the upper green.

Far to the south, beneath the desert stars,
Ahsin paused mid-stride.

For a single heartbeat,
he heard it:

C-minor
whispering through memory…

as if a lost clan had just retaken its first breath in the Aeralith
Canopy.

And he walked on.

Chapter 27 - The Golden Apex

Planet: Vaelthara
Location: Approaching the Tomb of Amenemapet
Chronometric Stamp: BV 24.029

"I'm not looking down on you—well, actually I am."
— *Skylune Sharpeye (Aeryndai – a.k.a. Hawk people)*

[FIELD LOG // TDG-512B — FRAGMENT 20]
The pyramid remains intact and fully sealed, with its exterior
casing preserved. It dwarfs all known Anari structures in size.
Ahsin breached the entrance using a non-living resonance.
The interior details are unknown.
Crossing the threshold now.
— Commander Kellyn Windstream

By the fourth morning after Ra Oasis, the dunes had shifted
again.

They flattened, then straightened, then aligned.

Lines untouched by wind—razor-sharp, geometric, precise.

Froster whispered, "Sand doesn't do that."

Ahsin stopped abruptly.

His tone shifted to one more like dread. "Here. Look."

They crested the final dune.

And the world fell away.

A vast basin of gold lay below them, perfectly circular, and at its heart—

The Pyramid of Amenemapet.

Kellyn's breath vanished. Froster muttered something half-prayer, half-curse. Elowen's voice went quiet with awe.

Serithyl Dawnstep and Vaelinnae Windpetal flanked Seris Thorn, Windveil cloaks flickering as gooseflesh rippled along their arms.

"The wind does not flow here," Serithyl whispered. "It recoils."

The basin felt engineered.
Not by quarrying — by will.

White casing stones shone like honed marble, seams invisible. Angles too perfect to belong to anything mortal.

From the peak, the electrum capstone flung razors of sunlight across the bowl.

"Electrum," Harvey murmured. "Gods…"

Ahsin nodded. "Sun-priest forging. Years for a single plate. Amenemapet believed the sky itself could be bent by faith."

The closer they drew, the quieter the world became.

No wind.
No shifting grains.
No desert shimmer.

As though reality exhaled and then refused to draw breath again.

Kellyn scooped a handful of sand.

Perfect quartz spheres.

Not erosion.
Manufacture.

Khandyl stared at her own handful. "He shaped the very desert."

"Yes," Ahsin breathed. "Amenemapet rejected chaos. Even dust obeyed him."

Halfway across the basin, Froster swallowed loudly and pointed north.

A dust formation — fast, coordinated.

Through heat distortions came the silhouettes:

- Osiri bronze-masked warriors

- a jackal cavalry phalanx

- and towering above them:

A Sphinx.

Metal sinew, sigil mane, sun-fire eyes burning with divine circuitry.

"Emissary-engine," Ahsin hissed. "Pharaoh-forged."

"Are they after us?" Froster asked.

"They want the Necrodemicon," Ahsin said. "And a sealed tomb violated is a sacred offense. They will call it righteousness. They have come to kill you."

Froster muttered, "You mean us."

"Yes, yes," Ahsin gestured vaguely. "They will kill us."

Kellyn drew in a breath. "Then move."

They pushed harder, racing the Osiri shadow.

By midday, they reached the pyramid's base.
Even the Sylph — minds sharpened by years of stealth discipline — felt their breath slow with reverence.

Serithyl murmured, "Wind threads can't cross these walls."
Vaelinnae added, "Even the canopy would bend away."

Ahsin led them along the eastern face.

A perfect limestone panel, smooth as milkstone, hieroglyphic sigils like faint scars under frostlight.

"No door," Witmar muttered, "no handle—"

"It is there," Ahsin said. "Buried under death-binding."

He placed his palm to the stone.

The sigils flared like molten ivory.

Sand lifted around them.

The basin itself held its breath.

W H U M M.

Cracks lattice-worked the panel — then converged to a burning point.

The slab folded inward like softened parchment.

Cold, ancient air rushed out.

"It is open," Ahsin whispered.

No one moved.

The Sylph stepped closer with a silent formation reflex older than fear.
Their thread-cloaks fluttered — not from wind, but from memory.

"The air here remembers screams," Serithyl whispered.

"And waits for new ones," Vaelinnae added.

Ahsin raised a hand, warning. "You step into intent. Not architecture. Amenemapet shaped death through will."

Kellyn stood at the lip, voice steel. "We don't have the luxury to hesitate."

Behind them, Osiri war chants rose like a grinding storm.

Ahsin hesitated.
And for one fragile moment, the old centuries seemed to weigh on him.

Elowen spoke first, soft as breath:

"Ahsin… before he became this—what was Amenemapet? In the days when gods still walked among mortals. Before the Chamber. Before the curse."

Ahsin did not look at her.

He answered the stones instead:

"A man who learned too much of the gods and believed he could complete what they began. He walked beside creation once… and tried to command it. He also purged the Aeryndai from the Osiri people."

Then Witmar — blunt curiosity sharpened by nerves:

"What? I thought all Osiri were jackal-headed beings."

Something tight passed through Ahsin's jaw.

"No. The Osiri were more than one race in the beginning. Amenamapet led a civil war that drove out the Aeryndai."

He dragged a breath, speaking like memory hurt:

"The hawk people you call Aeryndai were once a sub-race of Osiri. They called themselves children of Osiris once."

Aafje dared one more question:

"Did you know Aelrindel, Ahsin?"

Ahsin finally turned to them — cavern-eyed, hollow with beauty and loss.

"He taught my people the Bow of First Silence. When gods walked as flesh. When they carved Songs into our bones."

Kellyn swallowed. "What were the others like?"

But Ahsin pulled away, the dread closing hard around him.

"No more questions. Not here."

His voice became stone: "Inside, the dead listen."

He stepped over the threshold.

Kellyn followed.

Then Witmar, Harvey, Elowen, Froster, Loka, Khandyl, Seris Thorn.

Serithyl Dawnstep next, then Vaelinnae Windpetal — movements so perfectly silent that even the tomb did not notice them passing.

The last to cross was Ahsin.

And for a heartbeat, the basin felt alive — watching a lost son return.

As soon as his heel passed the threshold—

SHHHK.

Stone sealed shut with a final whisper.

The world outside disappeared.

Chapter 28 - The Descent Through the Painted Halls

Location: Amenemapet's Pyramid — LEVELS 1–3
Chronometric Stamp: BV 24.030

"Other kind grow, but Osiri build." — *Hesep-Amun (Osiri)*

[FIELD LOG // TDG-512B — FRAGMENT 21]
Interior structure resembles Osiris Shaft analogs.
Decorative gallery → narrow shafts → belly-crawl → ladder
descent → final vertical drop.
Ahsin required for further access.
Air: cold, stagnant. No life.
— Commander Kellyn Windstream

The corridor swallowed them whole.

Cold stone.
Cedar resin.
Silence so dense it felt like frost in the lungs.

Lightstones reflected off walls polished smooth as river bone.

Elowen breathed the first words, almost a prayer:
"By the breathing crown of the Green Mother…"

And the walls answered.

Not with sound — but with memory.

Hieroglyphic murals spread on every surface, lit with gold
inlaid so thin it glowed like captured dawnfire.

Amenemapet was carved a thousand times:

- Leading sun-blinded phalanxes

- Commanding storms of molten glass

- Slaying beasts that dwarfed war caravans

- Opening sky-gates with geometry and blood

- Sitting enthroned while kneeling multitudes waited for judgment

Loka's fingers hovered inches from the carvings.
"No erosion. No decay. Not a single pigment lost."

Ahsin's voice echoed strangely inside the stonework.
"He demanded eternity. Even from walls. Even from death."

Aafje traced a scene: Amenemapet binding living servants with sigil-cords woven through their spirits.
"He wasn't merely a lich. He was engineered. A ritual architecture molded into flesh."

Behind them…

WHUD.

Something struck the outer seal.

Heavy. Impatient.

Khandyl whispered: "They followed us."

Another blow — closer, like a titan's knuckles tapping bone.

"Osiri war party," Harvey muttered.

"Then we move," Kellyn said.

The corridor narrowed into a long ceremonial gallery where dozens of gods from distant cultures were carved along the stone in silent procession.

Aelrindel, the Huntsman:
depicted as a silver-furred stag-man striding into dawnlight,
bow unstrung but ready.

Faelor, the Moon-Hunt:
shown as a shadow-scape wolf trailing stars from its mane.

Both surrounded by Osiri sigils — as though the priests tried
to cage even gods within their logic.

Elowen paused, eyes soft.
"They carved them as prisoners of Amenemapet's order.
Did the Osiri think the gods were his servants?"

"No." Ahsin's voice was raw.
"They feared him. And anything he feared, they tried to bind
as well."

Harvey ran a hand over the stag-runes near Aelrindel.
"Ahsin… when you walked with the gods… were they like
this?"

Ahsin did not answer at first.

His eyes were locked on a tiny sigil in the stone — a stylized
cat's eye flanked by fangs.

Lynx Clan combat mark.
Half-hidden within the murals.
A sign placed by ancient hands to say *We were here.*

He reached toward it and stopped, shaking once.

Finally:

"Aelrindel laughed more than any of us expected.
Faelor never laughed at all.
And both hunted only what could hunt them back."

He turned away.

"No more questions here. He will hear us through the stone."

They moved on, and the question died behind them like a candle starved of air.

The gallery sloped downward into a smooth, polished ramp so slick even Sylph boots slid.

Witmar skidded five paces.
"Oh good. Doom slide."

Ahsin descended effortlessly, almost hovering.

Kellyn stared. "You move like you've done this before."

He did not respond.

THUD.
Closer.

The Osiri were hammering the sealed entrance with divine lattice tools.

The ramp constricted into a coffin-height channel.

"Absolutely not," Harvey muttered.

"Absolutely yes," Kellyn replied, shoving him gently ahead.

Armor scraped stone.
Breath echoed too loudly.
Sand grated between teeth.

Serithyl's silver hair snagged on an unseen seam — then drifted loose in a pattern that defied gravity.

Even the air behaved wrongly.

Vaelinnae moved with weightless precision, every step a prayer.

The Windveil cloaked her like moon-fog.

Ahsin flowed past them like ink sliding downhill, barely touching matter.

THRUM.

A deep pulse rolled through the rock.

"They're breaking through," Khandyl whispered.

"Then crawl faster," Kellyn hissed.

The tunnel spilled into a small chamber with a single rotting ladder attached to the far wall over a vertical shaft.

Kellyn tugged a rung.

It held — grudgingly.

"One at a time."

Harvey muttered while climbing, "If I fall, I swear I'm haunting Loka."

"The fall isn't fatal," Loka said absently.

Harvey stopped mid-ladder. "How do you know that?!"

"I was trying to help."

Ahsin released his grip and fell.

He landed without sound, like paper settling.

Witmar whispered, "I hate him."

The shaft yawned below them—the bottom swallowed in endless dark.

Kellyn raised a lightstone — and its glow vanished as if consumed.

"A hundred feet," Ahsin murmured. "This descent was carved for spirits, not living feet."

Behind them…

KROOM.

Dust cascaded from the ceiling.

The Osiri had found the entrance seal.

Kellyn moved close to Ahsin.

"We don't have time. Get us down."

Something brittle and ancient passed across Ahsin's expression.

"He will know me," he whispered, "even beyond death."

Harvey put a hand on his shoulder.

"Whoever Amenemapet was… he's gone now. And you're not alone."

Ahsin's face twisted — an emotion caught between grief and denial.

Then he nodded.

"Join hands. Lose contact, and you scatter into the stone."

They linked wrists, thread, and cloak.

Serithyl clasped Vaelinnae.
Seris Thorn took Froster's arm.
Kellyn steadied Harvey and Khandyl.

Ahsin raised his hands.

Necromantic frost stung the air.

The walls thrummed like ribs around a heart.

BOOM.
BOOM.
BOOM.

Not impacts.

A heartbeat.

Amenemapet's heartbeat.

"Hold tight," Ahsin breathed.

Black resonance surged.

Gravity inverted.
Stone dissolved.
Cold flooded their bones.

And the world dropped away.

Chapter 29 - The Hall of Amenemapet

Location: Amenemapet's Pyramid — The Depths
Chronometric Stamp: BV 24.030

"Ah, the living. So dramatic about breathing."
— *Count Varis Umbershade (Veydrath)*

A tremor rolled through stone just after the teleport finished.

Then the world burst into green fire.

Torches along vast columns surged alight: pale emerald flames that made the whole chamber breathe with sickle-tinted shadows. The ceiling was so high that the light could not reach it; the heights remained pitch, as if the pyramid preferred half-truths.

The walls were worse.

Not simply carved —
venerated.

Gold-leaf hieroglyphs lined every surface:
sharp, deliberate, and chillingly precise.

A throne room built for judgment, not death.

Serithyl Dawnstep exhaled in a temple-tone whisper.
"Mother's grace…"

Before them waited row upon row of Osiri skeletal warriors.

A thousand bones welded in black-bronze armor; jackal skulls; blades meant for souls; shields bearing the sun's crowned tyrant.

Silent.
Perfect.
Awaiting command.

Vaelinnae's voice wavered, "We are not meant to stand in this place."

And yet they did.

Kellyn's lightstone skimmed a lower tier of glyph sequences. Osiri script angled into stylized Anari runes — incomplete, broken by misunderstanding.

Aelrindel's name appeared three times.

Once as

"Ael-Reh-Djal:
the Silver Stag
who is servant to Amenemapet."

Seris touched the panel, brow tight.
"They thought he could be owned."

Ahsin's jaw hardened.
"Osiri power always tried to rewrite what they feared.
Aelrindel hunted entire armies bare-handed. Amenemapet's priests carved lies instead of admitting they could not bind him."

Higher up, the mural expanded:

Aelrindel trapped within the Greenwood —
his antlered form caught in a tightening lattice of ice-sigils,
Osiri sun-geometry,
and the runic chains of the Frost Thraekers.

Amenemapet stood above, hands raised, harvesting the resonance of the imprisoned god.

Harvey stared. "He… took power from Aelrindel?"

Ahsin's voice thinned.
"No. He failed. But he tried. And part of the Greenwood curse began here."

In a darker corner of the mural, another inscription:

Eight Lynx warriors
wearing branch-plated armor,
caught in a final stand before the Greenwood's curse.
Their eyes blacked by stylized Osiri ink — as if death itself
had been edited over their memory.

Elowen whispered:
"The Last Hunt of the Lynx Clan…"

Ahsin's hand tremored.
But he only said,
"Not here. Not now."

And walked away.

The torches flickered.

Gears turned somewhere in the beyond.

And movement stirred at the dais.

The false arch-lich stepped forward:
electrum crown like captured night,
jet mantle sweeping,
blue witch-flame kindling in sockets
that once held judgment.

Its voice cracked through the air like a tomb splitting open:

"Ḥekau-netjer…
Rise, children of my silence."

Armored Osiri surged forward.

The chamber exploded into war.

Blades screeched.
Shields shuddered.
Necrotic spears slammed.
Khopesh hooks scraped bone-deep into armor.

Their formation bent.

Nearly broke.

Witmar screamed as skeletal fingers crushed his throat.

And then—

Harvey moved.

Silent.
Focused.
Eyes narrowed into something neither mortal nor Anari.

His sword fell like law.

Green fire erased the undead.

Ash drifted in spirals
like frightened insects fleeing from light.

Ahsin stared —
not with awe,
but with ancient dread.

"Elowen… Aafje… all of you… no Green Knight has ever done this."

No one answered.

They were watching Harvey burn death away.

Row after row collapsed before him, dissolved not into ruin
—

but into release.

Aafje whispered: "He is closure, like Thalorin, the God of
Death."

Kellyn glanced at Aafje, "Did you say closure? Corlyn said
the powerful being defending their escape from Sylos IV
called himself Closure. He said the Malloch feared it."

Harvey ascended the dais.

The arch-lich raised arms:
fire-script sigils,
soul-gears turning.

"Tshet-seferu! Amar-netjeru! I bind the su—"

One stroke.

Green fire brighter than dawn.

Silence.

The Osiri fell to lifeless heaps.

Kellyn's voice trembled, "You… saved us all."

Harvey said nothing.

He watched ash fall from his blade.

At the podium, the gold chest gleamed with sun-eating
moons.

Ahsin reached it with shaking hands.

"The Necrodemicon… after so long…"

He opened it.

The pages shriveled into dust.

Ancient script died.

Ritual geometry cracked to charcoal.

Ahsin dropped to his knees.
"No. NO — pages decayed! A hollow prize!"

Kellyn tried to reach him.
But something inside Ahsin shattered.

Worse than grief.

Recognition.

Fear.

He looked at Harvey —
not like a rival —
but like a prophecy.

"You are the death of my kind."

And with a single teleport whip—

CRACK.

He vanished.

A tremor rolled through the pyramid.

Metal screeches answered.

The war-sphinx repositioned in the chambers above —
constructing a descent system.

Voices chanted orders.

Stone dust drifted.

Seris whispered, "They've found the shaft…"

Witmar leaned on Harvey.
"Ahsin really just left us."

Froster snorted.
"Counts don't stay for funerals."

Vaelinnae and Serithyl searched the chamber walls.
No exits.

Elowen healed wounds at the edge of collapse.

Loka listened to the metal grinding.
"They're coming down. Soon."

Kellyn stood tall — the last pillar against collapse.

"We find answers. We learn what Amenemapet was.
And we survive until the Osiri arrive."

The torches guttered.

The gears above screamed.

Loka prayed in a whisper, "Stars help us."

The pyramid answered with cold metal hunger—patient,
methodical, descending toward them.

[FIELD LOG // TDG-512B — FRAGMENT 22]
Hostile contact: 1 arch-lich; approx. 100 animated Osiri
skeletal warriors. Necrodemicon decayed to dust.
Outcome: Destroyed (via Harvey Oakenstride).
Compromise: Teleport guide (Ahsin) abandoned team.
Current Status: Trapped in the lower chamber with no
vertical egress.
— *Commander Kellyn Windstream*

ADDENDUM: Ahsin's Sealed Memorandum

(Recovered Post-Departure)

To the Council of the Veydgrath
From: Count Ahsin Blackvein
Subject: Threat Assessment — Harvey Oakenstride

I report as one who has walked the Greenwood before its curse,
who bent knee to gods before mortals forgot their names,
and who has watched empires rot beneath their own arrogance:

Harvey Oakenstride is a danger greater than Amenemapet, Osiri necromancy, or any death discipline we wield.

I have witnessed a Green Knight before — three in all my long existence.
They were blades, nothing more: sworn to cleanse rot, never capable of extinguishing us.

Harvey is not that.

His harmonic fires unmake the dead.
Not break, not scatter — erase.

This phenomenon is unknown in all vampiric histories.
If one man carries that resonance, and if it matures,
we — the Veydgrath — may face extinction.

I recommend:

- Earliest possible study.

- No engagement without overwhelming force.

- Avoid all confrontation within forests (there, his power magnifies).

- Research counter-sigils keyed to green harmonic cycles.

He is young, uncertain, and terrified of himself.
That will not last.

When the Horn of the Wild Hunt sounds again —
if the ancient phantoms are truly tied to it —
and if the Lynx spirits answer…

I will no longer be able to oppose him.

I fear that moment.

But I fear what I will remember about myself even more.

Signed,
Count Ahsin Blackvein, Veydgrath (Lords of the Dead)

Chapter 30 - The Breaking of Outpost Four

Planet: Vael'thara
Location: Aeralith Canopy
BV 24

The forest woke screaming.

Not in sound — the Aeralith never screamed — but in the violent snapping of Whisper-Vines pulled taut, in the sudden downward shudder of branch-lines, and in the way the wind simply… died.

When the wind stops in the canopy, every Sylph knows: something terrible has happened.

Lady Dravokh the Mistshaper stood on the high branches, cloak of veined Whisperthread trailing behind her in irregular pulses — as though mirroring her heart. Her pale, tapered features — sharp Sylph cheekbones, narrow jaw, midnight-green eyes — flickered with controlled alarm. Her braids of silver-black hair, bound in wind-wefts, trembled though no breeze moved.

Laeryn reached her first, breathless, bow in hand, with shoulder muscles tense from years of hunting precision.

"Lady — Outpost Four's signal vines went dark."

All around, the Windborne Quarter vibrated in distress.

- refugees emerging from tents

- Sylph instructors stiffening in place

- Singing Sprigs pulsing discordant tones

- Dreamwillow bristling in agitation

Maaren arrived moments later, fingers stained with phosphor sap.

"Three harmonic pulses reached us before silence."

"What kind?" Dravokh asked, voice clipped.

Maaren's jaw tightened. "Draining. And then… collapse."

Silence.

Then the forest itself sounded the alarm — a violent downdraft that tore leaves upward, scattering them like an inverted snowfall of green ghosts.

There were no doubts left.
The Osiri had broken through.

The first eruption originated from the southern ridge—sand and roots bursting upward as a Khem-Duat tunnel broke into daylight. Bark shredded; roots tore apart. Three more breaches erupted nearly simultaneously.

Outpost Four was gone.

Sylph warriors surged to the ridge:

- some wind-stepping from branch to branch

- some sliding along bark-trails

- some descending on whispering threads

Female archers released spirals of Queen's Kiss arrows.
Druids forced roots to snarl and form barricades.

But the Osiri were ready.

Warriors erupted from tunnels clad in lacquered desert armor, eyes blazing with ritual sun-fire. Behind them, priests murmured low, sand-colored harmonics that made groundlines jitter and Whisper-Vines curl defensively.

The forest recoiled.

Dravokh hissed — a sound between fury and dread. "They studied us."

Laeryn's twin wind-blades flashed free. "They want our root-lines. They want an artery to the Hidden City."

"They know it exists," Maaren muttered.

"And they will not have it," Dravokh said.

The Sylph charged.

Sylph war choreography unfolded: women moved like falling leaves, sharpened to knives, silent, fluid, precise. Archers shifted position with every shot. Bindweavers reinforced cracked bark where a single talon-step could send refugees crashing below.

Maaren and the male mages raised their palms.

"Syl'phyr — lend us your breath."

Catal'ri tones wove outward — soft flute-harmonics. When the sound touched Osiri's armor, the plates vibrated violently, throwing soldiers' footing askew.

The Osiri countered with deep desert harmonics — sounds that scraped the bottom of the spine — snapping bark and lifelines. Four Sylph fell instantly, Dreamwillow around them going silent in shock.

A harsh sand-whorl flung open.
An Osiri champion — golden axe, sun-etched armor —
cleaved bark like cloth.

Laeryn intercepted him.

Their duel was vicious and close — wind versus heat, grace
versus brutality.

Before Dravokh could summon aid, she felt the air shift.
Her instincts screamed.

"Hidden Host! On the ridge!" Laeryn shouted over her
shoulder.

They stepped from shadows — not walking, not gliding —
but emerging as though the roots themselves had lifted them
into battle.

The male Sylph.

Leaf-metal armor, built to refract light, flashed like wet
razors. Half-veiled faces revealed only storm-still eyes. Their
movements were impossibly precise, every strike pre-
calculated, every step aligned with wind-geometry.

Even Osiri troops recoiled.

Shyr moved first — a perfect Ribbonfall Slice that only
became visible at the instant it lashed through a priest's torso.
Emerald light flashed — and the priest fell.

Faelen followed — wind-assisted spear-thrust piercing armor
at the seam, twisted, and released. The air finished the kill.

Osiri ranks faltered.

Dravokh saw a new kind of fear on their faces:
not fear of defeat —but fear the Sylph were no longer a
known quantity.

But for every priest felled, another took his place.

Thousands of Osiri now surged.

Dravokh pressed nails into her palms.
"We cannot hold the front. Collapse the tunnels."

Maaren paled. "Lady, the roots—"

"If they breach second-layer root-lines, they will walk the
path to the Hidden City. Collapse. Now."

Maaren signaled to five male mages.

They formed a Spiral Knel — one of the most dangerous
Sylph convergences.

Their Windveils rose in an unseen draft.

The forest pulsed in response.
Roots coiled.
Stone folded inward.
The tunnels trembled.

Dravokh's face tightened — and her voice cut like winter:
"Release it. Now."

Maaren exhaled a long breath.

The Spiral dropped.

Silence —
then a world-deep implosion.

The tunnels caved with crushing force, swallowing rock, Osiri
soldiers, priests, and war-glyph infrastructure.

Screams flickered, then were gone.

Dust geysers burst upward.
Tree roots sagged with violent exhaustion.

And then—
stillness.

Maaren staggered. Dravokh stood unmoving.
Leaves drifted in slow circles, unsure whether to rise or fall.

Laeryn — streaked with blood and earth — knelt beside her
Lady.

"We held."

"No," Dravokh whispered.
Her voice cracked like bark under frost.

"We paid."

Five elder trees — ancient, memory-bearing giants — leaned
at broken angles. Their roots, ripped by seismic force, bled
sap like amber tears.

Maaren's voice was quiet and ashamed.
"The collapse saved us. But it tore the forest's deep veins."

"And the Osiri felt it," Dravokh said.
"They will test harder now."

Vaelkorh approached — Windveil hanging like dusk.

"The Hidden Host stands ready."

Dravokh nodded slowly, but something inside her faltered.
She stepped toward a wounded root, knelt, and lay a hand
across its torn fibers. The Whisperthread of her sleeve curled
toward it as though wanting to help.

The root trembled—and for a moment the sound was almost language:

deeper
deeper
deeper

Maaren went still, listening.
"We've only destroyed the first tunnels. There are more. Far down. Past memory strata."

Laeryn inhaled sharply. "How can you tell?"

Maaren's fingers hovered over the soil, not touching — reverent.
"The resonance is old. Not wholly Osiri. Something borrowed. Something echoing techniques from… legends."

Laeryn frowned. "What legends?"

Maaren hesitated — then whispered as though speaking forbidden lore:

"From before the Chamber of Victory. When gods walked as mortals. When the lost clan — the Lynx — still shaped harmonics no forest school now remembers."

A hush fell.

One bindweaver near them murmured, "Those Songs were said to bend roots like rivers…"

Another added quietly, "And to build passageways deeper than light ever reaches…"

Then all fell silent, suddenly aware they had said too much — even with no outsiders present.

The earth pulsed again.

Not digging.
Not probing.
But signaling.

Dravokh rose, wind-tattoos glinting along her arms. Tiny white scars — marks of old oaths — semilunar and precise, shifted as her muscles readied.

"They are not testing anymore," she said.
"They are advancing. And they are learning."

Laeryn swallowed. "And us?"

Dravokh looked toward the Windborne Quarter — where refugees, exhausted and afraid, stood unknowingly on the brink of a war none of them could yet fathom.

Her eyes hardened — luminous, fierce, almost fevered.

"We accelerate everything.
Every Song.
Every training.
Every tunnel watch."

She turned to Vaelkorh: "Place shadow-knives at every breach point. They strike fast, strike unseen, and report only to me."

Vaelkorh nodded, voice like steel against flint. "They move now."

"Maaren." Her voice softened, almost fragile.
"Triple magical testing. Identify talent before the enemy does."

Maaren winced. "That will drain the sprigs dry."

"Grow more. We do not have time."

Laeryn frowned toward the ruins of Outpost Four.
"And the refugees?"

Dravokh's mantle flared faintly — like wind igniting leaves.
"We push them harder than pain wants. The longest day
cannot be tomorrow. It must be every day."

She paused — one heartbeat of weakness breaking through
— then whispered to the broken roots:

"Forgive us. We will not fail you."

The roots pulsed back:

not alone
not alone
not alone

Dravokh inhaled sharply and looked north — toward the
Hidden City, invisible under slumbering roots.

"Whatever sleeps beneath us wakes with purpose.
And next time they breach, they will not stop at Outpost
Four."

Leaves turned inward.
Sprigs sang off-key.
Dreamwillow hissed softly, as though trying to hide.

In a whisper of breath, Lady Dravokh spoke what no one
wanted to say:

"War has come to the Aeralith.
And the forest itself will fight at our side."

Chapter 31 - The Black Sun Forge

Location: Deep Desert — Sanctum of the Black Sun
Chronometric Stamp: BV 24.030 (Osiri internal calendar
offset unknown)

"If a Gravhal is late, the world is early." — *Sundrim Orecarver
(Gravhal)*

The forge didn't burn with fire, but with trapped sunlight.

Ma'at-Khenu of the Jackal Crown stood before the heart
altar, jackal visage illuminated by the harsh white glare of
condensed sunfire. Chains of gold and black iron suspended a
spherical crystal overhead. Inside that crystal, a miniature sun
writhed and wailed — its light crushed inward, corona
sharpened by etched curse-runes.

Lesser priests whispered His title only in private:

He Who Commands the Black Sun.

He always heard.
He simply did not care.

Power mattered.
Reputation was dust.

Ma'at-Khenu faced the creature on the obsidian dais.

A sphinx.

Bronze ribs arched like a lion sculpted from architecture.
Obsidian plates along its sides bore rows of binding script.
Segmented paws ended in razor-edged claw-curves. A gold

disk crowned its jackal-shaped helm — Ra-Khepra inverted, the sigil of the Black Sun.

Soul-chains chimed faintly within its ribs.

Enmeshed in that lattice, something not of Osiri lineage pulsed.

Malloch-tone.

A scraping, impossible resonance that strained the seams of reality. Even the junior priests did not dare stand close. Malloch harmonics were not merely power — they were hunger. The gods had sealed such frequencies behind twelve veils and forbidden geometry, fearing the resonance that remembers conquest. Amenemapet called that fear cowardice.

Ma'at-Khenu called it opportunity.

"The gods sealed the Malloch because they feared power," he murmured. "We do not fear it. We refine it."

"The gods built paradise once, and then hid from the world's teeth. They feared their own designs. They feared the Malloch. We do not fear what is stronger than us. We chain it. We burn it. We recite its true name and make it kneel."

The chamber behind him flickered with blue light. Silhouettes of living constructs stirred: sarcophagi humming with internal heartbeats, skull-masks wired into brass arachnids, spine-rigs twitching with instinct.

Among those shapes lay cracked tablets — fragments sealed behind quartz panes, sketched with Anari warriors in moon-lit armor, their motions annotated in harmonic glyph-math. Most bore a single label:

Specimen A-17, Pre-Dynastic Lynx Form — "breath stolen by the Greenwood curse."

Ma'at-Khenu had once attempted to recreate that form — warriors who moved like music and hunted like shadow. The subjects failed. Their bones could not hold the pattern. Their souls broke.

He had abandoned the experiment, believing the Lynx Song extinct.

But the intruders in Amenemapet's pyramid had stirred that old curiosity again.

The Lynx Song walked the desert once more.

He lowered his claw to the sphinx's neck.

"Awaken."

Glyphs ignited down its spine like desert torches. The machine hissed.

"Sun-Hierophant," croaked Smed'Lee, limping forward. His left leg was made of bronze and bone, and his body was covered with scars from experiments both endured and performed. "Breath chambers holding pressure nominal."

"Report."

"Frame integrity stable. Furnace-heart accepting siphon. Crew compartments sealed. Aim-rotation precise to half a degree."

"And the breath?"

Smed'Lee's eyes flicked toward the chained sun, then away.

"The breath renders wood into glass. Stone into slag. Flesh… to remembrance."

Not ash.

Remembrance.

As doctrine required.

"Where is my observer?"

An acolyte stepped forward — muzzle cloth bearing glyphs of silence.
"I know my purpose."

"Enter."

Two bone-priests bowed and formed the seal of the Black Sun. They and the observer entered the sphinx's interior. The ribs locked shut like divine jaws.

The sphinx inhaled — a sound like stone dragged across sand — then stood upright.

"It obeys," Smed'Lee whispered.

"It will," Ma'at-Khenu corrected, "until I tell it to stop. Or until the chains crack."

He raised his staff.
Obelisks surged.
A lattice of golden geometry unfolded.

The sphinx vanished in a ripple of scorched heat.

Smed'Lee trembled. "H-how will it reach the target? The canopy lies far—"

"It will reach."
Ma'at-Khenu did not elaborate.

The desert inclined for those who commanded deeper geometries.

A messenger stumbled in, breath ragged.

"Sun-Hierophant! Trespassers — Anari — have breached the outer seals of the Pyramid of Amenemapet. Tomb guardians pursue them below. Your war-sphinx converges upon the coordinates."

Ma'at-Khenu finally turned. "The Pyramid. Sealed for 25 centuries."
His eyes gleamed. "And opened by foreign hands."

"For now, they live," said the messenger. "The descent shaft is sealed behind them. No escape."

"Then the gods have delivered a crucible. A perfect proving ground."

"Prototypes?" Smed'Lee asked.

"No." Ma'at-Khenu smiled.
"We accelerate."

He swept his staff downward.

"Send word:
Hold position at the shaft.
Let the intruders stew.
When the tomb opens again…"

His voice thinned into the cold of the forge: "…only remembrance will remain."

The messenger fled.

The chained sun pulsed once like a black eye waking.

Ma'at-Khenu said: "Begin the second."

Deep in the forge, something enormous stirred, chains clanking like distant thunder.

Chapter 32 - The Chamber of Forgotten Paths

Location: Amenemapet's Pyramid — Hall of the Eternal
Chronometric Stamp: BV 24.030

"Any invention can work—if you define 'work' creatively
enough." — *Mipsi Frangle (Nimvrel)*

The chamber seemed to shrink a little more every hour.

They examined every stone, every seam, every carved jackal
and falcon—and found nothing.

No hidden doors.
No ladder back up the shaft.
No cracks that weren't decorative.
No Ahsin to pull them out.

Above them, the ceiling murmured with distant metal:

hammering
dragging
gears ratcheting

The Osiri were building.

Getting closer.

Kellyn swept the long, golden chamber with a weary soldier's
stare and said, steady but drained:

"Short rest. Food, water. Stay alert. We don't know how long
we have."

They settled, exhausted:

- Witmar leaning on Harvey—still pale from the soul-drain
- Froster and Khandyl wrapped in a single blanket
- Serithyl Dawnstep and Vaelinnae Windpetal staring up the shaft, hunter-still
- Aafje bandaging her leg with shaking fingers
- Elowen coaxing a soft green healing light over cuts and bruises
- Seris Thorn sitting pressed against Kellyn, Whisperthread wrapped tight

And Loka—

Unable to rest.

The necromancer paced the walls, fingers ghost-tracing sigils, lips whispering calculations.

Harvey sat apart, silent.
Haunted.

His fingers flexed occasionally—twitches that looked like muscle memory from a battle that ended in ash. He'd joked less and less since the Hall of Amenemapet, and now there wasn't a single smile left in him.

An eerie stillness settled over the group.

A Fragment of God-Lore

Witmar broke it first—staring at the ceiling and murmuring:

"Ellendyl's journals mentioned trial-constructs, right? Gods judging worth. Remind me—Faelor hunts in the dark. Who hunted everything else?"

Elowen, tired but unflinching, answered softly:

"Aelrindel. The Hunt that never ended. Before the Frost Thraekers and the Crone bound him in the Greenwood."

Harvey blinked.
"Why bind a god?"

"He chased something forbidden," Elowen whispered. "A sacred frost-spawn tied to the Thraeker pantheon. They hunted him across the world and sealed him in the Greenwood. The Crone laid the curse atop it."

Witmar shivered. "That's… bleak."

Loka didn't comment.

But he filed the names away.

Trial gods. Judgments. Forgotten paths.

He'd studied worse possibilities in Time Bureau archives— half as a linguist, half as a man afraid he'd someday need one of those patterns to survive.

And now he did.

He'd passed it twice already and dismissed it as art.

But Ellendyl's notes pressed at his mind:

"Osiri trial constructs evaluate intention more than force. Often riddled."

He leaned forward.

A heading.

Not decorative.

"FIRST: The Guardians of Dawn."

Symbols:

Jackal
Falcon

Crocodile
Lion

And the inscription:

Four who stand when kings are dust,
Each holding a gate, each keeping a trust.
Jackal hunts the dying day,
Falcon claims the rising ray.
Crocodile waits where endings sleep,
Lion guards the secrets deep.
Touch the path the sun walks first…
And hidden ways reverse the curse.

Loka murmured:

"The sun wakes in the east.
Jackal of the eastern gate.
Jackal."

He pressed the carved jackal.

CLICK.

A metallic pulse shook the chamber.

Everyone jolted upright.

Even Harvey.

Loka moved to the next heading—voice quick and sharp as he deciphered:

"SECOND: The Weight of Judgment."

Scale
Feather
Blade
Crocodile jaws

Inscription:

I weigh the living.
I drink the dead.
Feather fails, and hearts are bled.
Yet I move not, hunger not, breathe not.
Speak my name—
and judgment parts the stone.

His breath quickened.

"Ammit."

CLICK.

Sand fell from seams overhead.

Froster whispered:
"Do that again."

"THIRD: The Deceiver's Absence."

Twelve Osiri figures.
Eleven cast shadows.

One did not.

Sun gives birth to shadow.
Shadow betrays the sun.
One walks in both…
and leaves neither.
Touch him who casts none.

Loka pressed the shadowless figure.

CLICK.

The floor trembled.

Harvey rose, moving closer—eyes unreadable.

"FOURTH: The Whisper of Life."

A flute-shaped vent.

Inscription:

I am the desert's breath.
I whisper and unmake.
No blade holds me—
yet I open what stone forbids.
Give me voice.

Loka inhaled.

Blew once.

Nothing.

He frowned, steadied his breathing into the low rhythm of desert winds he'd studied back in the Bureau archives, and breathed again.

WOOOOHM—CLICK.

A deeper, mechanical groan rolled behind the walls.

Elowen whispered, "That sounded like a lock."

"FINAL: The Watchers of Night."

A ring of carved beasts—local desert wildlife.

Except one.

A fish.

"There's no fish in the desert night."

He pressed it.

CLICK—
KRRAAAANK—
THOOOM—

The eastern wall split open down a razor line.

Sand poured like bleeding sunlight.

Cold air whispered out.

A dark passage widened beyond the cracked stone.

Silence fell.

Followed by the smallest, quietest celebration.

Vaelinnae Windpetal stepped forward first.

Brushed dust from his cheek.

Kissed him softly.

Serithyl Dawnstep followed—second kiss, just as warm.

Seris Thorn pressed her lips to his forehead, Whisperthread
drifting like a blessing.

Elowen cupped his jaw and kissed once—brief, earnest,
grateful.

Loka nearly collapsed.

His knees buckled and he grabbed the wall.

Harvey met his eyes.

Not joking now.
Not smiling.

Respect.

Kellyn placed a steady hand on Loka's shoulder.

"In every timeline," she said quietly, "we're lucky you're with us."

Above them, the hammering from the shaft sharpened.

Metal cutting stone.

Gears shifting.

Closer.

Kellyn vanished into commander mode:

"Form up. We move. Now."

Loka swallowed hard and stepped into the darkness he'd unlocked:

"Please let this lead somewhere."

The torches fluttered.
The carving seams sighed shut behind them.

And the party descended into the hidden passage—

away from the dead,
toward the truth,
with steel biting stone overhead
as Osiri gears turned in the dark to meet them.

Loka Meadows deciphering the puzzle beneath the Pyramid of Amenemapet.

Chapter 33 - The Sapphire Gate

Planet: Vaelthara
Location: Amenemapet's Pyramid — Lower Descent Tunnel
Chronometric Stamp: BV 24.031

"Osiri are tall. Thraekar are taller. Minos are strong. Thraekar are stronger. Zagg'rin are cunning, Thraekar are… strong!"
— *Gorhul Skybreaker (Thraekar)*

The hidden corridor sloped downward like the throat of a stone giant.
The walls gleamed with unnatural polish—no dust, no erosion, not even the soft bite of air on mineral. Their footfalls made no sound. The pyramid swallowed it all.

High above, muffled noise continued:

hammering
chain-drag
grinding stone
measured Osiri chanting

They were building a descent rig.
Methodical.
Confident.

Kellyn led them, Whisperthread cloak mapping faint silver arcs as it skimmed unseen wind-lines. Elowen paced beside her with a sphere of life-light hovering in her palm.

Twenty paces into the dark—

The tunnel ended at a veil of blue radiance.

Not flame.
Not force.
A liquid wall of sapphire light, pulsing with the slow rhythm
of a controlled heart.

Khandyl whispered, "A barrier."

Seris narrowed her gaze. "No. A directive. The Osiri built
passageways that forbid retreat."

Even Kellyn hesitated.

She lifted a hand.

Cool. Mist-soft.
Not a defense—an invitation.

Harvey stood beside her, voice low, disturbingly calm:

"Forward."

Kellyn nodded.

She stepped through.

The blue light parted around her like silk, and released her
into the continuation tunnel beyond.

One by one, the others followed:

Elowen
Aafje
Seris Thorn
Serithyl Dawnstep
Vaelinnae Windpetal
Khandyl
Witmar
Loka
Froster—

Harvey stepped through last—

SCH-THOOM.

The blue hardened behind him like poured stone—opaque, impenetrable.

Then came grinding stone, like a final breath before burial.

A hidden door sealed shut behind the sapphire veil.
Perfect.
Absolute.

A trap disguised as mercy.

Elowen whispered, "The tomb is… guiding us."

Aafje corrected softly:
"No. It is herding us."

The blue dimmed.

They pressed on.

Less than two minutes later, another glow bloomed ahead.

Green.
Deep.
Alive.

This barrier filled the entire corridor.

Froster strode up to it, reckless as usual. "First one didn't kill us, so—"

Kellyn opened her mouth—

Too late.

Froster stepped into the green.

It parted around him like drifting smoke.

He blinked back, startled. "See? Perfectly—"

Harvey stepped forward to follow—

SHRAAACK.

The green barrier snarled with emerald thorns of force, hurling Harvey back a full stride. Kellyn caught him before he fell.

Seris breathed, almost reverently:

"This barrier weighs the living."

A beat.

"And rejects death."

Harvey stared at the wall—jaw tight, breathing slow and controlled.

Khandyl hissed, "Why him? Why Froster?"

Froster looked at his hands. "I barely passed algebra. I'm not hiding anything mystical."

Kellyn ignored that.

"Froster. What's ahead?"

He stared down the hall. The curve of a descending tunnel. A faint glow beyond it.

"I'll scout. Careful and quick."

Khandyl nearly grabbed him. "Don't you dare leave us."

He tried a smirk, but couldn't quite shape it.
"I'll come back. Promise."

And he slipped beyond the green.

The veil sealed behind him like breath on glass.

The passage spiraled down, air thinning and sharpening until every inhale felt like prayer. The deeper he went, the more reverent the atmosphere became—like walking into the lungs of a god.

Froster turned the final curve—

And froze.

The chamber was vast and silent, echoing with old judgment.

Obsidian pillars rose like frozen lightning.
Gold Osiri hieroglyphs crawled across the walls in throbbing execution-script.

Scenes:

Jackal warriors kneeling.
Priests lifting miniature suns.
Amenemapet towering beneath a halo of eclipse-light.

Black bones littered the floor—cracked, gouged, splintered.
Armor dented by claws.
Marks of desperate fingernails raked into stone.

A reflecting pool divided the chamber, perfectly still.
The mirror-surface shone like midnight ink.

And on a throne of black marble—

Amenemapet sat.

The real one.

Not the puppet.
Not the hollow construct animated by leftover ritual patterns above.

This was him.

• Golden pharaoh mask fused to ancient face
• Ruby suns burning in the crown
• Scepter capped with jackal skull
• Collar of bone and beaten gold
• And beside him—

A pedestal bearing a tome bound in cracked, human-like skin.

The true Necrodemicon.

No dust.
No fraud.
No lie.

Amenemapet stirred.

The mask tilted.

A dry click of bone on bone.

Sickly blue flame awakened in hollow sockets.

His voice rasped out—
cold, sovereign, perfect Osiri:

"Welcome, Anari."

At the mouth of the pyramid shaft far above, a war-priest slammed fist to chest.

"Send word to the Sun-Hierophant! The intruders are trapped in the Death-King's crypt. The seal is broken. They cannot escape."

A skeletal courier sprinted out.

Deep in the Black Sun Forge, the bronze sphinx stirred from chains.

And the emissary smiled.

Froster remained frozen before the throne.

And in the green veil above him, Harvey stood with Kellyn's steadying hand on his arm—green motes still fading from where the barrier had rejected him.

Elowen whispered, shaken: "The veil weighed him."

Aafje swallowed hard. "It saw him as death's opposite."

Serithyl murmured, remembering Ahsin's fear: "You are the death of my kind."

Harvey said nothing.

But somewhere in his core, where the green light grew quieter with each breath, he wondered what Amenemapet would see when *he* finally stepped into the lich-king's gaze.

Because if the barriers had judged him incompatible, then Amenemapet would not see him as prey.

He would see him as a threat.

The chamber strained with pressure, as if aware of the convergence to come.

Down below, the arch-lich's laugh slithered through the air— low, ancient, and hungry.

And above, Osiri gears and chains continued grinding downward toward the inevitable collision in the dark.

Chapter 34- The Hidden Host Awakens

Planet: Vael'thara
Location: Aeralintar
BV 24

The Hidden City of Aeralintar was not built.

It was grown.

It lay deep beneath the layered boughs of the Aeralith Canopy, a spiral of roots and luminous branchvaults shaped by centuries of druidcraft. The air here trembled faintly with harmonics—old Songs running through wood and sap, murmuring secrets known only to those permitted to walk this deep.

Most Sylph lived and died without ever seeing Aeralintar. Most believed it half-myth.

But tonight, after the devastation at Outpost Four and the rising panic in the forest's pulse, Dravokh Mistshaper descended into its shadowed heart.

The living gates parted at her touch—root-fingers uncurling like waking hands to reveal a great open glade suspended between trunks and massive, braided branches. Whisper-

Vines glowed faintly along the inner walls. Lantern-fruits grew in spirals above, casting flowing green patterns across bark and armor.

And waiting within that glow—

The Hidden Host.

Male Sylph warriors stepped from alcoves carved into the roots, not with theatrical stealth but with something worse: perfect stillness transitioning into motion. Their very presence shifted the air.

- Tall.
- Armored in leaf-metal etched with windlines and Catal'ri sigils.
- Cloaked in whisperweave that caught light and turned it into moving shadow.
- Windstep blades sheathed at their hips.
- Masks marked with fine patterning—each line a signature of their personal Song.

Dozens.
Scores.
Silent.

The living wood beneath Dravokh's boots tightened in subtle ripples, as if bracing under the concentrated harmonics of so many hunters.

Dravokh herself was all controlled storm—dark braids bound back with silver leaf-rings, mantle of muted green and black falling in clean lines, fingers unconsciously tracing tiny wind-circles against her thigh as she read the forest's mood.

Vaelkorh, Commander of the Hidden Host, stepped forward. His mask revealed only the lower half of his face; his gray eyes were visible above, sharp and patient as weathered stone.

"Lady Mistshaper," he said, bowing slightly. His voice carried like wind through narrow canyons—quiet, edged. "Aeralintar answers."

Dravokh swept her gaze across the Host.

"We are no longer dealing with probes or scouts," she said. "The Osiri have breached the third root-layer."

No one flinched.

Readiness—not fear—moved through the assembled warriors.

Maaren Faelwind joined Dravokh's side, carrying carved root-scrolls that pulsed faintly with druidic resonance. He bowed to Vaelkorh before speaking.

"The collapse at Outpost Four slowed them," Maaren said, "but secondary tunnels continue upward. The Osiri are not searching blindly."

Vaelkorh inclined his head, jaw tightening behind the mask. "Their priests wield harmonic chisels now. Crude. Effective."

Dravokh's eyes narrowed. "They're not digging simply to invade. They're trying to identify our inner breath-lines."

"Aye," Maaren murmured. "They're testing the Songs themselves—mapping where our harmonics run strongest. They seek the branches that feed Aeralintar's core."

Dravokh's pulse tightened. "If they find the Song-root…"

"They will breach our heart," Vaelkorh finished.

And Aeralintar—for all its power—could not survive a direct harmonic inversion at its center. Even a forest could be killed, if its Song were turned inside out.

Root-speakers entered the glade—druids whose skin bore swirling bark-pattern tattoos, their eyes faintly luminous with saplight. They carried living branches heavy with whispering glyphs.

Their leader bowed deeply. "Lady Mistshaper. Aeralintar stirs. The lower Singing Trees are… frightened."

Dravokh did not dismiss the phrasing.
Singing Trees did not fear lightly.

"Show me," she said.

The root-speakers spread the branches, opening a living map of the canopy's energy flows. Lines of faint light ran through wood and leaf—currents of power.

Seven resonance points glowed bright.
Four pulsed dimly, like bruised stars.

"Lady," the root-speaker whispered, "the Osiri have identified more than half of Aeralintar's heart-streams."

Maaren inhaled sharply. "They are tuning themselves to our Songs—using desert rites braided with stolen forest resonance."

Dravokh's expression darkened. Her fingers brushed a nearby vine; it twitched beneath her touch.

"They're learning too fast."

Vaelkorh's hand shifted to rest lightly on his windstep blade. The motion was casual; its intent was not.

"Then we will teach them to stop," he said. "Permanently."

Dravokh stepped into the center of the glade. Platforms and roots adjusted underfoot, subtle, as if the city itself leaned in to listen.

"Warriors of Aeralintar," she said, her voice carrying into every hollow and alcove, "the Osiri press toward us through the deep roots. They search for our heart. They must not find it."

Every masked gaze lifted to her.

"You will descend into the tunnels tonight," she continued. "Follow the harmonic trails. Track their priests. Learn where the desert's Song collides with our own."

She let a breath pass, then let the next words fall like a drawn blade.

"And when their path becomes clear—
cut it.
Quietly.
Completely."

The Host answered with a synchronized inhalation—a sound closer to a whispering storm than breath.

Vaelkorh crossed his blade over his chest. "We walk into the dark," he said.

"We return with silence," the Host breathed.

At Dravokh's signal, Sylph instructors led in a group of ten refugees—those who had mastered basic wind-step footwork and shown early harmonic awareness. They were blindfolded until they crossed Aeralintar's threshold.

When the cloth came away—

Their reactions were immediate and quiet.

One whispered, "This place is… alive."

Another, trembling: "I can hear it breathing."

A third stared at the Host, voice shaking. "They… they have men. Warriors. All this time?"

No Sylph answered him.
They didn't need to.

The silence of the Hidden Host was answer enough.

Vaelkorh approached the refugees.

"You were brought here because you listen," he said. "You do not yet understand our Songs. You do not yet understand the forest. But you can learn."

His mask shifted almost imperceptibly as he spoke.

"You will not enter the tunnels tonight," Vaelkorh continued. "But you will observe what walks them."

A refugee swallowed. "We… we watch the Hidden Host fight?"

Vaelkorh did not blink.

"You watch us disappear."

The Host assembled at the downward spiral—a colossal, ancient root descending into green shadow.

Dravokh placed her hand briefly on Vaelkorh's forearm—an intimacy rare in front of others.

"Your blades carry the forest's breath," she said quietly. "Make sure the desert feels it."

Vaelkorh bowed deeper than before. "To the last leaf, Lady Mistshaper."

He turned to his warriors.

"Wind beneath us," he whispered.

"Wind beneath us," came the near-silent reply.

And then—

They moved.

Not like soldiers.
Not like predators.
Not like ghosts.

They moved like wind given form—flowing down the root-path in a perfect, terrifying harmonic spiral, edges blurring as the Windveil took them.

The refugees stood frozen, breath shaking.

Maaren murmured at Dravokh's side, "Whatever the Osiri expected in those tunnels… it wasn't them."

Laeryn, watching from the shadow of an arching branch, crossed her arms.

"I pity the desert," she said.

Dravokh did not smile.

“The forest is done warning,” she answered. “Now it will answer.”

As the last warrior vanished into the deep tunnels, Aeralintar itself dimmed.

Vines curled inward.
Lantern-fruits lowered.
The Singing Trees fell quiet.

A hush rolled up through the canopy above, through the Windborne Quarter and the strained training fields.

Aeralintar was no longer waiting.
Aeralintar was hunting.

And somewhere far below, in the rising tunnels of the Khem-Duat, the Osiri were about to learn what it meant to anger the forest's hidden blades.

Chapter 35 - Froster's Test

Planet: Vaelthara
Location: Amenemapet's Pyramid — The True Hall of
Judgment
Chronometric Stamp: BV 24.031

"Warmbloods freeze at danger. We adjust our temperature."
— Hisskra Taloncurrent (Sza'thir)

Froster's breath misted the instant he stepped into the true
hall.

The barrier behind him sealed with a soft shimmer, then a
deep, final THOOM that shook dust from the ancient ceiling.
On the far side, muffled panic:

"FROSTER!"
"STOP—WAIT!"
"HOLD POSITION!"

None of it reached him.

He was alone.

The chamber rose like a circular execution pit carved into
obsidian by a civilization that believed judgment was a kind of
worship. Pillars speared upward—smooth, black, etched with
gold sigils that pulsed in perfect intervals like a heartbeat.

The floor was scorched in rings. Melted stone. Old impact
craters.
Bones—charred and twisted—half-buried in the onyx tiles.

Veydrath.

Froster recognized remnants of their armor: hooked pauldrons and crescent blades fused to bone. The claw marks on the obsidian walls told the rest.

They had died trying to get out.

"Great," he muttered. "Perfect ambience."

At the far dais, a relic stood—no, rose.

Amenemapet.

Not stiff.
Not decayed.
Not uncertain.

He stood as if he had merely paused for breath between victories.

A golden mask fused to desiccated flesh gleamed in cold torchlight. Jewels in his crown burned like red suns. His obsidian scepter tapped the stone once—

TOK.

The entire hall vibrated.

His voice was a tectonic shift:

"FIRST JUDGMENT — THE HUNT."

Sand spiraled into a vortex. Heat gathered. Form hardened.

A jackal-headed Osiri champion materialized:

- nine feet tall

- plated in black-bronze

- cleaver-sword radiating sun-heat

Amenemapet spoke with perfect ritual cadence:

"Break the rhythm of the prey."

The Champion charged.

Froster drew his Wolf Clan sword.
He inhaled.

And the Wolf Catal'ri rolled out of him—low, minor key, a heartbeat growl-pattern aligned not with known Anari forms, but with something older and stranger.

The rhythm of Faelor's moon-hunt.

His fear settled. His pulse synced with the cadence. His body loosened—instinct, Song, breath, blade.

The Champion's cleaver slammed down—

WHOOM

Molten stone splashed.

Froster glided sideways on the S-Curve Hunt Path, cloak bending light.
He countered:

Vael'Shar — Silver Prowl Arc.
CLANG.

Parried.

Reverse: Vael'Shar — Rising Howl Reversal.

The blow hit—
the Champion staggered—

Then roared and retaliated, faster and far heavier.

The cleaver smashed Froster's sword from his hands.
A shield slammed him.

The pillar hit his spine like a falling tree.

Stars burst behind his eyes.

"… okay," he coughed. "Ow."

The Champion advanced, cleaver flaring white-hot.

Froster slid into Pulse Gap—the predatory silence between breaths.

And his hand brushed metal.

The sonic baton.

A cheap Sylvancrest field tool.
No magic.
Just tuned vibration science.

"Sorry, Faelor," Froster whispered. "Improvising."

He flipped the dial.

High amplitude. Narrow beam.

The cleaver rose for a killing stroke.

Froster leapt, cloak snapping behind him—

Vael'Shar — Silent Pounce Draw
and fired.

THUMMMMMMMMMMM—

The sonic lance tore straight through the Champion's chest.

Bronze ruptured.
Obsidian split.
Sun-flame died.

The giant fell like a cracked obelisk.

Silence hit harder than any blow.

Amenemapet froze.

His witch-fire eyes flared in shock and fury—the first emotion Froster had seen in the lich's undead face.

"WHAT WEAPON DEFIES THE SUN'S ORDER? WHAT BLASPHEMY OF THE FUTURE IS THIS?"

Froster wheezed.

"…Science?"

The title left his lips unironically.
And sacrilegiously.

The arch-lich's rage boiled—but ritual law was older than his fury.

His scepter lowered.

"You have slain my champion.
Honor binds me.
Take your prize, huntsman."

The cleaver rose from the floor, hovering like an executioner's moon, heat rippling off the blade in molten waves.

Froster grasped the hilt. A shock of power climbed up his arms—hot, ancient, predatory, "… now that's a weapon."

Emerald energy wrapped him—roots of light, runes spiraling over his armor.

The glyph for HUNT.
The sigil of BLOODLAW.

He was lifted, weightless, sealed inside an emerald sphere.

Alive.
Frozen.
Witnessed.

Amenemapet intoned:

"The first judgment is complete.
Let the hunter be stored."

Far away in the corridor, Kellyn saw the flicker of green through stone. Walls trembled.

"Froster…?"

Witmar shook, voice breaking, "BROTHER!"

No answer.

Only silence.

Chapter 36 - Khandyl's Test

Planet: Vaelthara
Location: Amenemapet's True Hall — Chamber of Judgment
Chronometric Stamp: BV 24.031

"We do not fear the dark; we coordinate in it."
— *Vrix-Vrix (Krikk'ar – a.k.a. Insect folk)*

The green barrier pulsed once—slow and deep, like the forgotten heartbeat of an ancient god whose pulse still remembered war.

Amenemapet's voice scraped from unseen corners, carrying the weight of millennia:

"SECOND JUDGMENT — DEVOTION.
Step forth, Wolf-child."

Every nerve in Khandyl's body locked.

Behind her, Froster slammed both palms against the emerald sphere imprisoning him.

"Khandyl! Don't— we'll figure out something! Just wait!"

But the energy field that held him was the same ancient light that beckoned her—unchanging, unmarred by plea or fear.

Kellyn gripped her shoulder.
"Listen—don't let him manipulate—"

The pulse came again.

Refusal was never an option.

Khandyl inhaled once—sharp, measured—and stepped into the green light.

It swallowed her whole.

Amenemapet tapped his scepter.

Reality fractured.

Warmth.

Sunlight as gentle as breath.

A meadow glade rolling under a sky too blue to be real.

Wind whispered through tall green grasses.
Birdsong drifted.
Fire-leaf blossoms swayed.

And beside her—

Froster.

But aged:

- jawline marked with an old scar
- eyes edged with lines of laughter and grief
- posture bearing quiet strength

He turned toward her, relief unfolding across his face.

"Khandyl… you're here."

Before she could answer—

"Mama!"
"Mother!"

Three adolescents stormed across the grass and collided
with her in a storm of arms and warmth.

- The eldest—tall, holding her eyes and Froster's
  stance.
- The second—her movement, Froster's crooked grin.
- The daughter—Wolf Clan braids, freckles scattered
  like stars.

They clung to her with trembling joy.

Khandyl staggered, stunned by the impossible realness.

This wasn't an illusion—not the cold kind.
This was memory-of-what-might-be.
A life that could exist if she let it.

Her daughter's voice broke:

"Where's Papa? They told us he has to go… Mama—don't
let him!"

Khandyl turned.

Froster stood at the tree line, gloves clenched, shoulders
bowed with the weight of a choice only he could make.

"Khandyl…" His voice shredded softly. "It's time."

A rip in the air split open behind him—light, geometry,
chronal distortion.

A silver shuttle descended, sleek and advanced far beyond
their age.

Ellendyl Felhart stepped out in lattice-armor, flanked by two soldiers.
Behind them glowed a chronal ring:

FY 3553 — Malloch Warfront

Ellendyl's voice carried sorrow and authority:

"Merren Froster. The Outer Gate is failing. Sonic specialists are few. Malloch advance has accelerated."

She swallowed.

"You must come now."

The children collapsed around him in panicked sobbing.

"Papa—no!"
"You promised—"
"Don't leave us!"

Froster fell to his knees, crushing them to his chest.

"I know, my cubs… I know."
Tears streaked his face.
"But if I don't go—everything ends. Everyone."

Khandyl shook, caught in a storm of instinct:

Wolf Clan vows:

- Protect mate.
- Protect cubs.
- Protect pack.
- Protect the world.

Ellendyl looked at her gently, painfully.

"Khandyl… only Froster can pass forward without unraveling the timeline. You and the children must stay. If you cross that threshold, you erase this moment—and all who stand upon it."

Her daughter sobbed against her armor.

"Mom—please! Stop him! Make him stay!"

Froster rose, trembling so hard she thought he might break.

He faced her as if she were the axis that held his universe in alignment.

"Khandyl… tell me to stay."

One word.
Just one.

"And I stay.
Here.
With you.
With them."

Amenemapet's voice coiled beneath the scene like venom in water:

"Choose, Wolf.
Choose the heartbeat you save."

Khandyl's lungs refused to work.
Her throat locked.

The word tasted like a blade.

"…Go."

The children's screams tore the glade apart.

Froster broke—utterly. He kissed each brow, turned to her, and held her cheek with shaking fingers.

"My wife… my heart… I will find you again."

The time-ring flared—

and he vanished.

The children's sobs hollowed the meadow.

The sky dimmed.

The grass withered.

Fire-leaf blossoms turned to ash.

Darkness swallowed the world whole.

A figure stepped forward—

Ellendyl again.

Older.
Clothed in soot.
Eyes dull with unbearable loss.

"Khandyl…" Her voice trembled. "I'm sorry."

"Tell me he lived," Khandyl pleaded.
"Tell me the war was won. Tell me my children—"

Ellendyl crumbled.

"We lost everything. The Malloch devoured the Gate. Mirren fell. His squad fell. All future Anari—gone."

Khandyl collapsed.

"I… I chose right… I gave him to the war… it should have saved you…"

But Ellendyl was fading, grief echoing.

Amenemapet's laughter cracked the void.

Khandyl slammed back into her body, gasping.

She trembled so violently she could barely stand.

Froster pounded the barrier until his fists bled.

"Khandyl! Look at me! LOOK AT ME!"

She pressed her brow to the hardened light.

Her voice was a broken reed:

"I let you go."

Froster froze.

"What did they show you?"

Tears scorched her cheeks.

"…I let you go."

Amenemapet spread skeletal arms wide, delighted.

"Such agony.
Such exquisite sacrifice.
You pass, Wolf-heart."

Green force lifted her gently—cruelly—encasing her beside Froster.

He reached out, tears falling freely.

"Khandyl… gods…"

She curled inward, silent.

Amenemapet raised his scepter.

"THIRD JUDGMENT — BALANCE.
Let the healer come."

The wall pulsed.

And slowly—inevitably—

Elowen stepped forward.

Chapter 37 - Elowen's Test

Planet: Vaelthara
Location: Amenemapet's Pyramid — The Hall of the Eternal
Chronometric Stamp: BV 24.030

"The best pranks reveal themselves after you have a good head start." — *Krizzle Snaptooth (Zagg'rin)*

The green barrier pulsed once—
a slow heartbeat of ancient magic.

A hush fell across the hall.

Along one wall, three containment spheres hovered in a cold emerald row:

- Froster, unconscious but alive inside his blazing globe.

- Khandyl, curled and shaking, tear-tracks still visible on her cheeks.

- An empty third sphere, humming faintly, waiting.

Elowen stood before the barrier now, hands trembling despite her effort to hold them steady.

The others clustered behind her:

Seris Thorn, Serithyl Dawnstep, Vaelinnae Windpetal, Loka, Witmar, Aafje, Kellyn, Harvey—
every one of them drawn tight as bowstrings.

Amenemapet's voice seeped from stone and shadow alike, oil poured over old bone.

"THIRD JUDGMENT — BALANCE.
Elowen of Life and Song.
Step forward."

The barrier's surface rippled, as if something behind it drew breath.

Witmar grabbed for her sleeve. "El—don't go. We'll find another way."

Kellyn's voice came low, tight. "Elowen. Think before you commit. He wants to unmake you."

Elowen turned slightly, green life-glow limning her bronze skin.

"I have to," she whispered. "We all do."

Harvey didn't speak. He simply touched her shoulder once— a rare, quiet gesture.

A promise.

She stepped into the green— and the world shattered.

Light.

Soft, warm, impossibly gentle.

She stood in a place that felt like memory wearing future-skin:

A garden shaped like a forest,
but grown from crystal ribs that arched overhead like the inside of a living machine.

Vines of light ran through them, carrying data the way sap carried Song.

Her breath caught.

"This…" she whispered. "This isn't the past."

"No," a familiar voice said.

She spun.

Corlyn Windstream stood before her—older, sharper around the eyes, dressed in sleek geometric armor of a far future. Bronze skin. Auburn hair pulled back. A faint, crooked smile he only ever wore around her.

"Elowen," he exhaled. "I knew you'd find your way here."

Her heart forgot to beat.

"Corlyn… what is this place?"

He led her through the crystalline grove toward a vast circular construct:

- a ring of metal and crystal

- etched in chronal glyphs

- pulsing with raw harmonic energy

"The first stable time-bridge," he said softly.
"A way to bring our people from the past into the future… without tearing the threads apart."

He took her hand.

"I can't finish it alone. Your harmonic field… your life-song… is the missing component."

Her throat tightened.

"My… magic?"

"Your resonance," he said. "Your pattern."

Behind him, the time-bridge thrummed.
She felt its pull in her bones—familiar and alien at once.

A shadow lengthened over the machine.

The light dimmed.

Amenemapet stepped into the illusion, tall and crowned,
jackal skull bending reality around him like heat over stone.

Corlyn didn't see him.

Only she did.

The arch-lich circled, fingertips skimming the edge of her
aura like a surgeon testing skin before the cut.

"A choice," he crooned.
"Identity… or brilliance."

Corlyn's eyes shone with earnest trust.

"Elowen, if you help me finish this, we can save them. All of
them. The future Anari. The timeline. Your people when the
Malloch rise again. We only need your harmonic signature
aligned with the machine."

Amenemapet's whisper slid behind her ear, cold and intimate.

"Give him your magic…
and you become something else.
No life-song.
No healing.
No woven miracles of Green.
Only intellect.

Only logic.
A creature of science alone."

Elowen shook.

Her fingers trembled.

Corlyn held his hand out to her, as if offering both salvation and an execution order.

"I trust you," he said. "Whatever you choose… we face it together."

Amenemapet's teeth gleamed like carved obsidian.

"Choose."

Her pulse roared in her ears.

She saw the bridge carrying thousands safely forward.
She saw the forests burning under Malloch shadows.
She saw herself stripped of Song—no more Renewal, no more life-light—
still brilliant, still useful, but hollow.

Her voice cracked.

"…Corlyn… if I do this… I won't be me anymore."

He cupped her cheek, thumb brushing away a tear.

"Elowen. Whatever you become… I will still know you."

Her heart split along fault lines she hadn't known were there.

Her magic flared in panic—green, wild, alive.

And then—

She placed her hand in his.

"Corlyn...
I choose—
science."

White-blue light detonated through her skull.

Her knees buckled.

Her magic ripped out of her in a scream of emerald fire.

Suddenly she saw everything:

- Temporal vectors

- Quantum harmonic lattices

- Phase-gating matrices

- Resonant threshold constants

- Dimensional flux compression spirals

- Stabilizer fractal collapse patterns

Her mind became a star collapsing and exploding at the same time.

Corlyn's voice reached her through the storm.

"That's it! Elowen—by the gods, that's it! You solved it!"

She felt brilliant.
Boundless.
Terrifyingly lucid.

And hollow.

So hollow.

Amenemapet's laughter rippled through the illusion.

"Marvelous."

She turned toward him—vision fracturing.

And in that instant—

Her eyes cleared.

This wasn't her time.
Wasn't her bridge.
Wasn't her path.

This Corlyn was a what-if, not a when.

The future he offered would save many…
but at the cost of erasing the woman who had stood in the
desert, hands bloodied, promising to heal those beside her
now.

She wrenched her hand from his.

"No," she whispered. "I choose magic."

The illusion imploded.

Knowledge tore free of her mind—
entire constellations of understanding ripped back across a
sky.

Her life-song slammed into her chest like a hammer striking a
bell.

Her knees hit cold stone.

Darkness.

Stone beneath her palms.

The Hall of the Eternal around her again.

Her whole body shook—bones buzzing, nerves burning. She dragged in a ragged breath, feeling like someone had widened her soul to the size of the heavens and then forced it back into mortal bone.

Khandyl slammed her palms against the sphere wall, voice raw.

"Elowen! Talk to us!"

Froster hit his own prison with his fists. "El—was it real? What did he show you?!"

Elowen couldn't answer. Not yet.

Amenemapet loomed above her, delighted.

"You chose identity," he mused. "Not power. How very… Anari."

She forced herself to stand—swaying, but upright.

Her voice was hoarse, but it did not break:

"I choose to stand with my people now.
Not chase a future that isn't mine to walk."

The golden jaw of his mask twisted into a grin.

"A satisfying answer."

Green force wrapped around her—gently cruel—lifting her into the air. The third containment sphere condensed around her like mist turned to glass.

Khandyl pressed trembling fingers to the outside.

"Elowen," she whispered. "You passed."

Elowen closed her eyes.

Passed.
Survived.

But some part of her still echoed with equations she would never quite remember—
and a version of Corlyn who had loved a woman she had chosen not to become.

Amenemapet's scepter rose.

"The Hunt.
Devotion.
Balance.
Three truths revealed," he intoned.

The chamber trembled as he lowered the staff toward the remaining free Anari.

The green wall shimmered—
then peeled open to admit only one silhouette.

Dark.

Shadow curling at her feet like smoke learning to breathe.

Amenemapet hissed with obvious pleasure.

"Aafje."

The shadow-mage froze.

Witmar grabbed her arm. "Aafje—don't. We'll find another way, we can—"

She laid a hand over his—soft, final.

"I have to face this," she said quietly. "You all know I do."

Behind her, her shadow writhed upward—taller, sharper, like a serpent deciding which way to strike.

Chapter 38 - Aafje's Test

Planet: Vaelthara
Location: Crypt of Amenemapet
BV 24

"A warm hearth, screaming prisoners, and a fresh labyrinth to solve." — *Bronzak the Content (Minos)*

The green barrier pulsed once—
a tightening heartbeat,
a predator inhaling.

Then it opened—
a thin, vertical seam of emerald radiance.

Aafje's breath caught despite herself.

Kellyn turned sharply.
"Aafje—wait."

She shook her head.
Her voice trembled, but her stance was iron.

"No. It's my turn."

Behind her, the others stiffened instinctively.

Froster's hands pressed against the inside of his containment sphere.
Khandyl leaned forward until the bubble bowed inward.
Elowen whispered a life-prayer, voice still thin with the exhaustion of her own test.
Witmar's voice cracked, desperate.

"Aafje, if it speaks—don't listen!"

Harvey muttered, "Kind of the opposite of what she has to do, Wit."

Aafje managed a crooked smile despite the ice knotted in her stomach.

Bronze skin.
Auburn-streaked hair.
Fungal-leather armor creaking faintly.
On her shoulders, the Twilight Cloak the Sylph gifted her—liquid dusk, woven of restraint and Song.

She touched it once.

You are not alone.

She memorized their faces:
the fear,
the hope,
the helplessness.

Then she stepped through.

The green swallowed her whole.

Darkness.
Then reshaping.

Threads of dim starlight wove upward, spinning pillars, vaulted ceilings, a hall of shadow and gold. Every surface breathed with funerary reverence—like an ancient cathedral built to remember horrors no one wanted to speak aloud.

Aafje's throat tightened.

It felt like the death-chambers her ancestors built.
Places meant to house forbidden power.

A ripple ran across the far wall.

He emerged.

Tall. Jackal-headed.
Crowned in lapis and gold.
Cold blue flame staring from hollow sockets.

Amenemapet.

His voice was layered:
iron,
sand,
wind,
grave-dust.

"Aafje of the House Without Name."

Her blood iced.

No one in this era used that phrase.
Her House had been erased from Anari histories for crimes
against the Song—shadowcraft that severed the harmony of
the forest, unrooting souls from the gods' resonance.

"How do you—?" she whispered.

Amenemapet drifted nearer, delighted.

"I know all that is buried.
All that was cut away.
All that still whispers in your marrow."

Her fists closed tight.

Shadow magic wasn't forbidden.
Corrupted shadow magic was.

And her House had walked that abyss.

She had spent her entire life refusing the pull of that bloodline.

Amenemapet lifted a hand—blue flame curling like a serpent—and four constructs materialized above his palm.

Forbidden Spells.

They hovered, each held in a sigil of sickly flame:

Night-Suture Bind
Chains of shadow serpents, hungering for soul.

Dream-Command Descent
Whispers that bend sleeping thoughts and hearts.

Umbral Dominion
A glove of living dusk that overrides motion, instinct, identity.

Dusk-Eater Rift
A tear into utter void—feeding on light, Song, and life.

Aafje staggered, bile rising.

These were the arts her ancestors died for.
The reason her lineage's name was ritually struck from the Codex.

Amenemapet's grin widened.

"Or…"

A flick of his talon.

A second option appeared:

A garment of twilight—woven of restraint, clarity, and harmony.
Dusklight threads and cloud-petal lining.

A crescent moon sigil resting where heart and Song converged.

The Twilight Robe.

A focus of discipline.
Unbinding of corruption.
The promise that power serves purpose—not appetite.

"A trinket," Amenemapet sneered.
"A child's toy beside true shadow."

A ripple crawled across the black stone.

A mirror rose before her.

And within it—

herself.

But stripped of restraint.
Eyes sharp as obsidian blades.
Shadow writhing like living hunger around her limbs.
A predatory smile full of promises in the dark.

Shadow-Aafje.
The inheritance she could have embraced.
The future that still wanted her.

Amenemapet spread both skeletal arms.

"Choose, child of dusk.
Choose the hunger of your bloodline…
or the restraint of your trembling heart."

Her pulse hammered.

Shadowcraft roared in her bones.
Ancient memories she never lived whispered behind her ribs.

The forest had culled an entire House to prevent the return of what she could become.

Aafje breathed once, ragged.

Then whispered:

"I choose the robe."

Amenemapet stilled.

Then his jaw cracked into a delighted snarl.

"Fool."

The robe drifted to her shoulders, warm, cool, grounding—a harmonic counterpoint to the hunger gnawing at her blood.

She inhaled sharply.

Then the mirror struck.

A blade of compressed shadow slammed into her chest like lightning.
Magic vanished.
Snuffed utterly.

She collapsed to one knee, lungs frozen.

Amenemapet's laughter rolled through the cathedral.

"You think the choice ends the test?
No.
It begins it."

Shadow-Aafje advanced—eyes blazing like dying suns.

"You chose weakness."

Aafje tried to summon Song, a spark, a breath of magic.

Nothing.

"You chose fear."

Shadow magic rippled into a blade.

"Without your power… you are prey."

Aafje's vision blurred.
Her heart thundered.

"No," she forced out.
"Not prey."

She drew her sword.

Simple steel.
Dulled edge.
Well-used.
Human and mortal.

Hers.

Shadow-Aafje's smirk widened.

"Good.
I prefer to end you up close."

She lunged.

Impact rattled Aafje's bones.
Shadow against steel.
Predation against discipline.

Without magic, she was slower, heavier.
Her robe flickered with each near miss, absorbing what her
Song could not.

"You never deserved the Song," the mirror hissed.
"You hide from power.
You fear yourself."

Aafje rolled, parried, blocked—
her muscles screaming, breath ragged.

Shadow-Aafje knocked her sword aside, sent it skittering across the floor, and pinned her with a foot to the chest.

The shadow blade lifted.

"I am the legacy you rejected."

Aafje's vision swam.

"I am not you."

And she moved.

Not toward her weapon.

Toward her.

She twisted into a Wolf-Clan sidestep—Khandyl's old lesson—
drove her palm into the Mirror's wrist.
The shadow blade flickered.

She headbutted her reflection.
Hard.

Shadow-Aafje stumbled, startled.

Aafje rolled, seized her fallen sword, rose in a crouch.

Her voice shook but did not break.

"If I win…
I win as myself."

Shadow-Aafje lunged.

Steel met shadow.

Aafje curved into a Wolf S-path, rose in a modified Rising Howl, feinted left, cut right—

and drove her blade through her own shadow's heart.

Shadow-Aafje froze.
Eyes wide.

Then shattered.

Into black sand.

Aafje collapsed.

Her magic slammed back into her—
a tidal wave of Song and dusk-light—
so fierce she arched off the floor, teeth clenched.

The Twilight Robe pulsed like a second heartbeat.

Amenemapet's laughter slid across the hall.

"Exquisite."

Green magic lifted her gently toward the open containment sphere.

As she rose—

Something fluttered against cracked stone.

A scrap of blackened parchment.

Still smoking.
Still alive with predator-script shadow.

Aafje's heart seized.

Myr'ael Suthra — The Night-Sworn Veil.

The spell shadow-her had wielded.
A forbidden shaping to give shadow selfhood.

She almost dropped it.

Almost.

Instead—

She folded it.
Slid it into her sleeve.

For research, she told herself.

Just research.

Amenemapet's chuckle drifted upward.

"A wise scholar never destroys knowledge.
Even when it destroys her."

The bubble sealed around her, twilight starlight drifting
across her new robe.

Below, Witmar's voice cracked:

"Aafje! Are you—are you all right?!"

She nodded, shaking, breath uneven.

The spell scrap pulsed once against her skin.
Not warning.
Not hunger.

Invitation.

The green barrier flared.

Amenemapet raised his scepter.

"FOURTH TRUTH REVEALED.
Balance between shadow and self."

His gaze cut toward the surviving free Anari.

The barrier peeled wide.

A silhouette stepped forward.

Witmar Oakenstride.

His test had begun.

Chapter 39 - Witmar's Test

Planet: Vaelthara
Location: Crypt of Amenemapet — Inner Trial Chamber
Chronometric Stamp: BV 24.030

"Cowards die many times before their deaths;
the brave only once. The stupid die laughing."
— Old Anari barracks proverb

The green wall brightened again, swelling like a lung drawing breath.
A narrow slit opened down its center—thin, sharp, almost like a blade hung in midair.

It *looked* at him.

Witmar Oakenstride stared back for half a heartbeat longer than he should have.

His palms were damp. His heart hammered so hard he felt it in his teeth. His Sylph-woven, unseen cloak lay light on his shoulders—comforting, suddenly tiny in the gaze of an arch-lich.

Harvey slammed his fists against the inside of his emerald containment sphere.

"Wit," he said, voice raw, distorted by the barrier. "Don't do anything dumb."

Witmar huffed something that almost qualified as a laugh.

"That's... most of my skillset, Harv."

Aafje pressed her hands to her own bubble, eyes still red from her trial. "You don't have to prove anything. Just come back."

Khandyl's claws bit into her barrier. "Pick the path that keeps you alive, Oakenstride. Nothing else matters."

Froster tried to grin. It came out crooked. "Worst case, you haunt the Minos instead. They've earned it more than we have."

Loka swallowed. "Don't let him isolate you in your head. He twists things. He—"

Kellyn cut across the noise, voice steady, iron over strain.

"Witmar. Remember this: you are not alone. Whatever he shows you, whatever he says—your brother is right there. We are right here. That does not change."

Witmar looked at Harvey.

Harvey's jaw was clenched so hard it trembled.

Witmar lifted two fingers in a mock Griffyn salute.

"Last one to drop ten undead buys dinner," he said faintly.

Harvey opened his mouth to answer—

The green wall flared.

And swallowed Witmar whole.

Stone melted.

The cramped tunnel and containment spheres blurred and re-formed into a long vaulted hall carved in Osiri geometry—

sun-disks, jackal glyphs, rows of repeating sigils etched deep in gold.

The air was hot, dry, thick with old incense and embalmer's smoke.

Blue-green witchfire burned in sconces, throwing long, sharp shadows across the floor.

Witmar stumbled once, caught himself, squared his shoulders.

His unseen cloak whispered around him. Fungal-leather armor creaked. His hand closed around his sword hilt until his knuckles whitened.

At the far end of the hall, on a raised stone throne, Amenemapet sat—skull crowned with a cracked sun-disk, empty sockets burning with cool blue fire.

He did not need to move to dominate the room.

"You are far from the bravest," the arch-lich said. His voice was bone on stone, catacomb echo, distant storm. "Far from the strongest. Far from the most cunning."

Witmar forced a thin smile. "Finally, an honest performance review."

"You are, however," Amenemapet continued, "one who laughs in the presence of fear. Such mortals are… instructive."

A shadow shifted behind the throne.

A second figure stepped forward.

Nine feet tall.
Jackal-headed.
Armor of blackened bronze and gold.

In one hand, a staff topped with a miniature sun-disk skull. In the other, a long, narrow blade of midnight metal etched with blue sigils that seemed to move on their own.

His eyes burned with a harsher, more focused light than Amenemapet's.

"Nekharu," the lich said. "High Necromancer of the Dawn Pit. My hand across the ages. You will test this one."

The jackal-headed mage bowed, never taking his gaze off Witmar.

"As my lord wills."

Witmar swallowed.
"That's… a lot of teeth," he muttered.

Along the sides of the hall, spheres of green light hovered in shadow.

Inside them, his friends hung suspended—faces pressed to barriers, eyes wide.

He saw Harvey's mouth moving, but the sound came through like a muffled echo.

"…WIT—DON'T LET HIM—!"

Aafje's twilight robe glowed, starlight pooling at its hem.
Khandyl bristled.
Froster snarled.

They could see everything.
They could not reach him.

Amenemapet raised one skeletal hand.

"FIFTH JUDGMENT," he intoned. "Measure. Begin."

Nekharu struck his staff against the stone.

The sound was wrong.

It rang like a hollow bell and cracked like a breaking bone all at once.

Blue fire burst outward in a circle.

The floor split.

Hands clawed through stone—skeletal, desiccated, Osiri and Anari both. Golden sand poured from their eye sockets; blue flame flickered in their skulls. Some wore tattered jackal helms, some rotted Anari armor from long-forgotten battles.

Ten.
Twenty.
Thirty.

Witmar's stomach turned.

"Okay," he breathed. "Nobody mentioned the 'small undead battalion' option."

He dragged air in, forced his breathing into cadence.

Then pulled his unseen cloak tight.

"Aafje, this better work," he whispered.

He murmured a Sylph code-phrase she'd drilled into him in a dim corner of the canopy.

The air shimmered.

His outline blurred; light warped.

He vanished.

The nearest skeletons lurched forward, skulls turning, searching.

Nekharu tilted his head, amused.

"Ah. A little night-fox with borrowed Sylph tricks."

He lifted his free hand, fingers spreading.

Witmar felt it immediately.

The air thickened around him—like invisible mud. The unseen weave snagged and dragged like cloth through thorns.

Nekharu laughed softly.

"You hide from eyes," the necromancer purred. "But not from my Sun."

He slammed the staff down again.

A grid of gold sigils flashed outward across the floor.

They reached Witmar's boots.

For one instant, his entire form lit in harsh blue-white light, his "invisibility" sketched in fire.

"Found you," Nekharu said.

The skeletons turned as one.

And charged.

***

Witmar moved.

He wasn't Harvey.
Wasn't Nyssara.
He would never be the terror of a Griffyn drill yard.

But he wasn't helpless.

He ducked the first skeletal swing, slammed his shoulder into a jackal-helm's ribs, shoving it into its neighbor. He pivoted low, swinging up in a brutal, practical arc—no flourish, just steel and leverage.

The spine snapped.

He rolled past another, cut through a femur, sent it tumbling.

One.
Two.
Three.

The first wave hit the ground in clattering pieces.

Froster's hands slammed his bubble.
"…YES—WIT—!"

Khandyl's eyes widened despite herself.
Aafje whispered, "Come on, come on…"

Nekharu didn't look displeased.

If anything, his grin sharpened.

He twisted his fingers.

The fallen skeletons shuddered.

Bones dragged back together like filings to a magnet. Skulls hopped and locked onto necks. Splintered ribs knit.

Witmar stared.

"Oh, come on," he said. "That's just rude."

Nekharu's staff tip traced a lazy arc.

"First lesson," he said mildly. "Your effort means nothing if I do not permit it to matter."

The undead surged again—faster, tighter.

Witmar changed tactics.

No head-on attrition.
No straight line.

He slid sidewise, using the cloak for short misdirections, ducking a rusted blade, rolling behind a fallen column, coming up at an angle. He let them overcommit, tripping one into another, always moving, always forcing their formation to bend.

This time, when he dropped a skeleton, he didn't just cut bone.

He scuffed a sigil.

His boot ground one of Nekharu's golden glyphs into a smeared streak.

The skeleton that should have reassembled… didn't.

It flickered, spasmed, then collapsed in a heap of dead stone and dust.

Witmar's eyes widened.

"Oh," he breathed. "*That's* interesting."

He pivoted hard, target shifting from skulls to floor.

Steel slashed legs out from under one undead—

heel stomped down on the glyph under its feet.

Another sigil shattered under his boot.

Another skeleton stayed down.

Seris hissed: "He's adapting."

Kellyn's breath caught.

"He's reading the pattern," she whispered. "He's *breaking* it."

On the dais, Amenemapet's skull tilted—attention sharpening.

Nekharu's ears pricked.

"Clever," the necromancer murmured. "For the brother."

Witmar didn't hear him.

He was moving faster now, in a rhythm that felt weirdly familiar—half Griffyn drills, half Sylph hunts, half running from disasters in the Bureau halls with Harvey yelling behind him.

He slid under a spear thrust, came up inside a skeleton's guard, tore through the glyph at its base with the edge of his boot, then cut the binding mark on its chest—two motions, one thought.

The skeleton shattered and did not rise.

Four.
Seven.
Ten.

The ring around him thinned.

In the bubbles, Froster shouted, "He's doing it! He's actually—"

"Come on, Witmar," Aafje breathed. "Break the pattern. Break *him*."

Even Harvey, shaking, stared with dawning hope.

Nekharu's grin faded a fraction.

The staff dipped a few degrees.

"Enough," he said softly.

He raised his hand.

The grid of sigils flared brighter—burning away scuffs, resetting the pattern in one vicious pulse.

The remaining skeletons jerked, re-synced, then dropped into a tighter circle, shields overlapping.

But now Witmar knew what mattered.

"Second wave's never as funny," he muttered.

He feinted toward one side of the ring, baited a thrust, spun under it, and went not for the floor—this time—for the staff.

He hurled a jagged fan of shadow-knives from his free hand—Aafje's lessons, half-stolen, half-blessed.

The knives struck the staff's tip.

The gem at the sun-skull cracked.

Blue fire sputtered, just for a heartbeat.

Nekharu's eyes widened.

The skeletons stuttered mid-step.

Harvey's strangled shout punched against the field of light. "YES! *PRESS HIM!*"

Witmar dove through a gap, drove his sword up in a Griffyn-style rising cut—ugly but committed—aimed at Nekharu's ribs.

For one gloriously impossible moment, it worked.

Steel bit bronze.
Nekharu staggered half a step.

On the throne, Amenemapet leaned forward.

"Inconvenient," the lich whispered.

Witmar could hear someone screaming his name—it took a second to realize it was Harvey, hoarse and wild.

"YOU'VE GOT HIM! WIT—FINISH IT!"

Witmar planted his foot to swing again.
The skeletons were disordered.
The sigils were cracked.
Nekharu's stance was open.

For a breath, it *looked* like he might actually win.

Nekharu's gaze hardened.

"Third lesson," he said quietly. "Measure is not battle. It is decision."

He shifted his grip.

Not on the staff.

On Witmar's *shadow*.

His free hand closed in empty air.

Witmar felt something seize him at the heels—not flesh, not armor, but the darkness trailing from his boots. His own shadow jerked like a living thing, snapped taut, and in that instant he could not move.

His sword froze mid-swing.

"What—" he choked.

Nekharu's cracked staff flared once, not at full strength, but enough.

A narrow beam of concentrated necromantic light lanced from the half-broken gem—
not through Witmar's chest this time,
but straight down the line of his seized shadow.

Cold tore up from the floor, through his feet, into his bones, riding the path of his own darkness.

It didn't burn.
It *emptied*.

His knees buckled.

Harvey's scream shredded itself against his barrier.

"NO—NO—MOVE, WIT, MOVE—!"

Witmar tried.

He got his boot half a finger-width forward inside the ring. Then nothing else obeyed.

Nekharu's voice dropped to a murmur only he could hear.

"You almost ruined my pattern, Oakenstride," he said. "That deserves honesty. You were closer than most."

He squeezed his empty fist.

The beam flared white-blue along the shadow.

For one heartbeat, Witmar felt himself hollowed completely—

—and then there was nothing.

The light cut off. He hit the stone like a dropped canvas.

He could see, dimly. Hear, distantly. He could not move.

The vaulted ceiling blurred. The edges of his vision darkened.

Harvey's face hovered beyond the green wall—eyes red, knuckles bleeding, mouth shaking.

"Get up," Harvey whispered. "Please, Wit. Sit up. Make a joke. Anything."

Witmar's lips twitched.

"…Looks like…" He fought for enough air to speak. "…looks like I… owe you dinner after all."

Harvey crumpled behind the wall of light, a sound ripped from his chest that never reached the room.

Witmar's chest rose once more—a shallow, shuddering breath.

Then stopped.

The faint light in his eyes went out.

Something in the chamber shifted—like a chord snapping.

For a long moment, even the undead were utterly still.

Amenemapet leaned back a fraction on his throne.

"Acceptable," he said. "He bled more interestingly than I expected."

Nekharu exhaled once through his teeth—almost a sigh.

He stepped into the fading ring, dismissed the sigils with a flick of his staff, and rolled Witmar's limp body onto its back with one armored foot.

He slid a gauntleted arm under Witmar's shoulders and lifted him as if he weighed nothing.

The Sylph unseen boots remained where they'd fallen, set aside just outside the ring with ritual care.

Harvey's forehead struck his barrier again and again. "No… no, no, no—"

Khandyl's claws tore her own palms bloody.
Aafje shook in her twilight bubble, lips moving through silent curses and prayers.
Froster didn't speak at all, tears cutting pale tracks through the dust on his face.
Elowen pressed her hands to the green, healing Song thrashing and failing to cross the ancient field.
Kellyn's fingers tightened around her sword hilt until small crescents of blood welled where her nails bit skin.

The undead ring collapsed to dust at Nekharu's gesture; their purpose was done.

At the far end of the hall, the green wall rippled open again—a vertical wound of light leading back toward the throne and the outer chamber.

Without looking at the others, Nekharu stepped through, carrying Witmar's body like a claimed banner.

The light closed behind them.

The spheres trembled.

And in the silence following Witmar Oakenstride's last joke, the green wall began to pulse again—
searching for its next victim.

[FIELD LOG // TDG-512B — FRAGMENT 55]
Subject: Witmar Oakenstride
Trial Apparatus: Osiri necromantic proxy
Observations: The target demonstrated unexpected resilience
and humor in the face of an existential threat.
Outcome: Fatal.
— (Fragment recovered from damaged crystalline observer;
origin unclear)

Witmar Oakenstride's duel against the Osiri necromancer,
Nekharu.

Chapter 40 - Loka's Test

Location: Amenemapet's True Hall of Judgment
Chronometric Stamp: BV 24.030

"Anari Eagle Clan have aviary envy."
— *Rythalen Feathercrest (Aeryndai)*

The necromancer stepped back through the green wall of light like a shadow poured through a crack.

Sickly radiance from Amenemapet's throne flared behind him, casting his nine-foot jackal form into stark silhouette. The Anari still trapped in the outer hallway fell silent as he emerged.

Witmar's corpse dangled over one of his gauntleted arms.

Khandyl made a sound that was almost a growl. Her claws bit into the stone. Serithyl Dawnstep's breath shook with barely contained fury, Sylph camouflage shivering out of rhythm along her skin. Vaelinnae Windpetal half-raised her spear. Froster's hands went flat against the inside of his emerald sphere.

Harvey Oakenstride went completely still.

The easy warmth that usually lived around him was gone. What burned in his eyes now was something Loka had never seen there before—raw, lethal heat.

The necromancer did not care.

He let Witmar's body slide from his arm and drop beside the dais like discarded refuse. Bones clacked against ancient stone. Witmar's gray Anari robe spilled open, the skin beneath stained around the dark wound over his heart.

Aafje made a sound between a gasp and a sob and lurched forward against the containment field.

"He… he was learning so quickly," she whispered, voice breaking. "He didn't deserve—"

Nekharu bent, plucked something from Witmar's belt, and held it up: Witmar's Sylph-made unseen cloak, still faintly shimmering even in death.

A low growl ran through both the Anari and the Sylph.

Seris Thorn took a step forward. "Return that. Now."

The necromancer's gold-capped jackal teeth flashed in a grin.

Instead of answering, he reached down with his free hand and tore the matching unseen boots from Witmar's feet in a single smooth motion. Dust shook from them as he flicked them once, then slid them onto his own jackal-like paws. The enchantments strained, then surrendered, bending their weave around his massive frame.

The arrogance was breathtaking.

Aafje surged to her feet, shaking, eyes rimmed red. "Give those back, you—"

Amenemapet lifted one desiccated finger.

The necromancer bowed slightly to Amenemapet and took his place beside the throne. Witmar's stolen cloak hung from his shoulders, its flickering edge mocking the fallen Anari.

Amenemapet's hollow gaze drifted across the survivors.

"Next."

The green wall flared.

And the light swallowed Loka.

Loka Meadows stumbled as the radiance dissolved around him and the chamber opened up.

He was tall for an Anari, lean in a way that made humans assume fragility—but every tendon and muscle was wiry and trained. Deep bronze skin caught torchlight; the black scholar's robe over his fungi-leather armor fluttered around him like spilled ink. Sylph-crafted cloak and boots—unseen when he willed them—still carried faint green highlights from the arch-lich's sigils.

None of that mattered.

Before him rose the Hall of Divine Weighing.

A monumental scale towered from the floor, carved of obsidian and bone. Each bowl was easily large enough to hold a grown Anari. Suspended above it, weightless, floated a single feather of pale blue light, oscillating gently.

Beneath the scale yawned a pit.

Not empty.

Black mouths and shifting shapes moved in the dark—a suggestion of teeth, claws, and something like hunger given form.

The Devourer of the Unworthy.

Loka swallowed. "Oh… stars."

Behind him, the green wall sealed with a soft, final whisper. On the far side of the chamber, Froster and Khandyl—

already bound in spheres of green light—pounded against their barriers. Their voices reached him thin and warped, like echoes under deep water.

"LOKA! LISTEN CAREFULLY—!"

"DON'T LET HIM—"

Muted. Wrong. Distant.

Loka stood alone.

Amenemapet's voice rolled across the hall, old and resonant.

"Loka Meadows of the future.
Translator of dead tongues.
Master of no tribe.
Bearer of stolen magics.
You who walk in ignorance of the gods' balance…"

The lich pointed toward the scale.

"Your test is truth.
Not strength.
Not will.
Not courage.
Truth."

Loka wiped sweat from his brow. "I… I've studied your myths. I think I know what this is."

Amenemapet's hollow sockets brightened.

"Then you know that if your heart proves heavier than the Feather of Order—"

He gestured lazily toward the pit.

"—the Devourer will claim you."

Loka's mouth went dry. "What do I have to do?"

"Choose."

Three pedestals rose smoothly from the floor between him and the scale, each bearing an object.

On the first: a stone tablet packed with glyphs, thousands of them, crawling faintly with inner light.

On the second: a shadowy, flickering sphere of dark magic.

On the third: a small, dull stone, palm-sized, carved with a single unfamiliar glyph.

Loka stared. "I… don't understand."

Amenemapet's voice thinned into a hiss.

"One represents all the knowledge you crave.
One represents power you should never wield.
One represents your heart."

The pit growled softly, like something huge shifting in its sleep.

"You may place only one upon the scale."

Loka's stomach twisted.

This wasn't just any moral riddle.
This was engineered to hit him where he was weakest.

He stepped closer to the tablet first.

Black stone. Heavy. Edges chipped with age. Its surface crawled with glyphs that pulsed faintly: Osiri script interlaced with something older and colder, twisted into the text like barbs.

354

His heart lurched. "Those… those are demon-script integrals. The kind Ellendyl said even arch-liches refused to write."

Blue fire flickered in Amenemapet's sockets.

"The Weight of Knowledge," the lich said. "All that you could learn… if you stopped fearing what it might turn you into."

Loka's fingers hovered a breath above the stone.

He could *see* the structure in it—the way the glyphs nested, layered. Equation-like arrangements of Malloch resonance braided into harmonic song—matrices for prediction, containment, maybe even counter-song.

"We could understand them," he whispered. "We could map their incursion vectors, model their corruption frequencies, maybe even—"

The tablet vibrated faintly under his hand.

Amenemapet's grin widened.

"Yes. Please take it. Place it on the scale. Let your hunger bear its true weight."

Loka's hand curled into a fist.

He pictured Ellendyl watching him with that sharp, exhausted gaze.

We do not survive by out-sinning the monsters, Loka.

He stepped away.

The shadow sphere pulsed once, tugging his attention.

It floated over the second pedestal, a perfect orb of darkness, smooth as glass, humming at the edge of hearing like a heartbeat buried under coal.

As he drew nearer, the surface shifted.

His own face gazed back:

Older. Robe of darkness and cunning geometry. Eyes burning like twin blue suns. A staff crowned with skulls. Behind him, entire formations knelt. Armies bowed.

He flinched.

"The Weight of Self," Amenemapet crooned. "You, as you could be, if you cease pretending to be small."

The reflection leaned closer. His voice came back at him, distorted and too confident.

"Why pretend you're just a translator?" mirror-Loka whispered. "You're already dabbling in necromancy. Already wielding shadow. Do you think you're *not* tempted?"

The image shifted.

Malloch abominations lay dead in heaps, the Time Bureau standing behind Loka. Harvey. Witmar alive. Kellyn rested a hand on his shoulder.

"You could save them," the mirror said. "You could have saved *him*."

Witmar appeared behind the future-shadow of himself—laughing, alive, camera in hand.

Loka's chest hurt.

His fingers twitched toward the sphere.

If he'd been stronger, faster, less afraid—
if he had reached farther into forbidden things—

maybe Witmar wouldn't be lying cold on the stone.

The sphere pulsed again, like a heartbeat offering itself.

Behind him, through the barrier, Aafje's voice leaked through in a broken whisper:

"Loka… don't let him twist you. Please."

He closed his eyes for a heartbeat.

"I *do* want power," he admitted quietly. "I do want knowledge. I want to matter. I want to stop losing people because I wasn't enough."

He opened them again.

"But wanting isn't the same as being. And that… isn't who I am."

He stepped away from the sphere.

The third pedestal held a plain, cracked stone.

Dull gray. Unremarkable. The kind of rock a child might pick up on a walk and forget in a pocket.

Except for the glyph carved in its center.

It wasn't Osiri. Not Malloch. Not any Anari clan script.

Loka leaned in.

It was structural, almost mathematical. A root-sign more sung than written.

He whispered the translation, more to himself than to the lich:

"Myr'eth."

Memory.

His throat tightened.

"And that?" he asked.

"The Weight of Your Heart," Amenemapet said. "Not your flesh-heart. Your living one. The story you tell yourself about who you are."

Behind him, Froster's voice boomed faintly through the distortion:

"LOKA—DON'T TOUCH THE TABLET—!"

Khandyl's shout overlapped, ragged with grief:

"OR THE GLOBE! ANYTHING THAT MAKES YOU LOOK COOL IS BAD!"

Loka almost smiled.

Almost.

He rested his fingertips on the cracked stone.

Warmth spread up his arm. Not the thrill of power. Not the sharp spike of revelation.

Recognition.

It felt like the stone *knew* him—calluses, sleepless nights, the places guilt had rubbed his soul raw.

He picked it up.

The scale waited.

Above, the feather glowed with a soft, steady light.

On the dais, Nekharu—still wearing Witmar's stolen cloak and boots—watched him with cold amusement. The Sylph enchantments flickered uneasily around his massive frame, as if even the magic objected to their current wearer.

The sight made Loka's stomach twist.

He met the necromancer's gaze.

Nekharu bared his teeth.

"Place your lie upon the scale, little scribe," he said. "Let us see how heavy you truly are."

Loka stood over the empty bowl.

For one heartbeat, he hesitated.

Not because he was tempted to cheat.

Because he was tempted to flinch.

I'm afraid.
I second-guess everything.
I get people hurt.
Maybe I *am* the weak link.

He set the cracked stone down.

The scale shuddered.

The feather flared brighter.

The bowl holding the feather sank—just a fraction.

The bowl holding the stone rose.

Not much.

But unmistakably.

Amenemapet's skeletal fingers tightened on the arms of his throne.

"That… is not correct," the lich hissed.

Nekharu's ears flattened. "The scale is broken."

Below, the Devourer stirred—uncertain. Its many indistinct mouths opened, then closed again, as if denied a meal it had already tasted.

Loka stared at the stone.

His heart hammered.

He hadn't hidden anything. Hadn't twisted the mechanism. Hadn't whispered a spell.

He had simply *told the truth*.

"I'm not a hero," he said softly. "I'm not a prodigy. I'm not some destined anything. I'm afraid half the time. I overthink everything. And I never stop wondering if the next mistake I make gets someone I love killed."

His voice shook.

"But I'm done pretending I'm something else. This… is what you get. What they get. What *I* get."

The feather flared again.

The cracked stone remained lighter.

For the first time, Loka realized he might have been weighing himself harsher than any god.

Amenemapet's jaw creaked like an old hinge forced open.

"You pass," the arch-lich said bitterly. "On a technicality."

The Devourer hissed in frustration, slinking deeper into shadow.

Nekharu made a low sound of disgust. "He would have been more useful devoured."

"Yes," Amenemapet agreed. "But truth has its uses too."

Green light rose around Loka, humming softly.

It wrapped him like water, lifting him gently from the floor, drifting him sideways toward the line of suspended spheres.

The cocoon deposited him into an empty bubble beside Aafje's, opposite Khandyl's and Froster's.

The field sealed with a crystalline chime.

Khandyl exhaled, shoulders sagging with visible relief. Froster smacked his palm against the inside of his bubble in a clumsy little round of applause. Aafje's eyes were still red, but she gave him a small, tired, proud nod.

"You did it," she mouthed.

Loka let himself sink back against the inner curve of the emerald sphere. His knees finally shook now that they were allowed to.

He didn't feel victorious.

He felt... exposed.

Stripped down to the part of himself he usually buried under jokes, footnotes, and other people's brilliance.

Maybe that was the point.

Amenemapet turned his jackal skull toward the tunnel once more. His voice rolled across stone and light:

"Balance is satisfied.
Truth has spoken.
Send forth the next."

The green wall pulsed, brightening with that slow, terrible heartbeat.

And somewhere in the dim corridor beyond, another Anari shadow drew a breath—
and stepped toward the light.

The Hall stilled.

Not with sound.
With pressure.

Kellyn felt it first in her teeth, a faint ache as if the air itself had thickened. The braziers along the obsidian walls dimmed unevenly, their flames leaning away from the dais. Even the sand beneath their boots seemed to hesitate, grains suspended mid-shift.

Amenemapet did not move.

He did not raise a hand or speak a word.

He inhaled.

Slowly.

Deliberately.

The sound was soft yet carried weight, like stone settling into a deeper place. The jackal-headed figure's posture shifted almost imperceptibly, his head angling a fraction toward them, nostrils flaring.

The Hall reacted before he did.

Glyphs along the floor guttered, their gold lines thinning. The heat withdrew from the air, leaving it dry and brittle against the skin.

"You arrive," Amenemapet said at last, voice smooth as worn basalt, "bearing more than you carried when you entered this world."

His gaze moved across them, unhurried. When it passed Kellyn, she felt the distinct, uncomfortable sensation of being *weighed*—not measured, not scanned, but judged for density.

His eyes stopped.

Not on her face.

On her cloak.

On Froster's sleeve.
On the leather straps at Harvey's shoulder.

Amenemapet leaned forward slightly.

Again, he inhaled.

"That scent," he murmured, almost to himself. "Unfinished ash. Choice-bound decay."

Silence stretched. No one spoke.

"This is not the odor of the honored dead," he continued. "Nor of the condemned. It is… persistent."

Kellyn's pulse thudded in her ears.

Amenemapet's gaze sharpened.

"How long," he asked calmly, "has it walked beside you?"

Harvey opened his mouth. Closed it. Froster shifted, boots scraping faintly against the floor.

Kellyn answered, because someone had to.

"Long enough to matter," she said.

Amenemapet studied her for a long moment. Then he tilted his head.

"Did you invite it," he asked, "or did it decide you were useful?"

The words struck deeper than accusation. They implied inevitability.

Kellyn did not look away. "Neither," she said. "It chose to stay."

For the first time, something like displeasure crossed Amenemapet's expression.

"Choice," he said softly. "Then you carry responsibility, not contamination."

He leaned back, folding his hands atop the staff resting across his knees.

"Understand this before you proceed," he continued. "The Paths ahead do not cleanse what you bring. They do not forgive it. They do not strip it from you."

The glyphs beneath their feet flared once, sharp and bright.

"They reveal whether it already owns you."

The pressure lifted.

Sound returned in pieces—the faint crackle of flame, the whisper of sand shifting again underfoot. The braziers straightened, fire resuming its natural rise.

Amenemapet's attention drifted away from them, as if the matter were already concluded.

"We will continue," he said. "If you are still here when the Paths are done, then the judgment will have been sufficient."

He did not look back at them.

Kellyn became aware, suddenly, of the smell of her own travel-worn cloak—leather, smoke, iron… and beneath it, something colder. Something that did not belong in this hall.

Ahsin was not with them.

And yet, somehow, he had arrived first.

Chapter 41- Night of Falling Leaves

Planet: Vael'thara
Location: Aeralith Canopy
BV 24

Night did not arrive; it *fell*.

No gentle fade of color. No playful dusk-breeze weaving through branchvaults. One moment Aeralith breathed in low golden light—

—and the next, the canopy sank into a smothered, listening dark.

Lantern-fruits dimmed to a cautious glow.

Dreamwillow shivered, shedding silver hairs like falling sparks.

Whisper-Vines coiled tight around branch-lines until they creaked.

The forest was no longer humming. It was *listening*.

And beneath it, in tunnels carved by Osiri priests and scarred by Sylph counter-song, something vast and deliberate pushed upward.

The Windborne Quarter felt it before anyone saw it.

Birds exploded out of the lower branches in a single panicked wave.

Training platforms swayed as fifty thousand half-trained refugees paused mid-drill, instincts prickling.

Dravokh Mistshaper stepped onto the northern ridge of the Quarter just as the first harmonic pulse hit.

BOOM.

A dull, resonant shockwave rolled up through the root-net, through the trunks, through her bones. She caught herself against a branch, fingers splaying to feel the direction of the tremor.

Below, Dreamwillow groaned.

Behind her, Laeryn landed lightly, bow in hand, hair wind-tangled, face pale beneath bark-ink scars.

"That came from below," Laeryn said. "Not the old collapse line. They're pushing up again."

"Where?" Dravokh asked.

Laeryn swept a hand toward the dark, her eyes narrowed as she read the quivering vines.

"Three breaches. No—four."

Dravokh's jaw tightened. "Already? The Hidden Host hasn't returned yet."

Another pulse rippled through the forest floor.

Laeryn's fingers twitched toward her twin wind-blades. "We don't have time to—"

The ground answered for her.

The training glen convulsed.

Then it split.

Earth and sand erupted in a roar of shattered roots. A geyser of dirt and splinters punched skyward, spraying bark and sap across shrieking refugees.

Osiri soldiers poured out of the wound—
sun-hot armor, curved halberds, eyes painted with ritual lines that glowed with stolen harmonics.

Behind them, priests rose in staggered formation, chanting deep desert tones that *bent* the air-pressure around them.

Refugees screamed.

Sylph instructors went hoarse in a heartbeat shouting for formation.

Maaren and his cadre of male mages sprinted across the Quarter, cloak-hems snapping, Singing Sprigs vibrating violently as they passed.

Dravokh's eyes narrowed, shoulders rolling back. "They found a secondary vent," she snarled. "We didn't collapse them all."

Laeryn drew her blades with a predator's smile that didn't reach her eyes. "They're charging straight for the Quarter."

"They won't reach it," Dravokh said.

She flexed her fingers once, feeling the wind-lines tense around her like pulled bowstrings.

"Not while we still have branches to stand on."

And she leapt from the ridge.

The Sylph met the Osiri in a storm of motion.

Female archers on upper platforms unleashed spiraling volley patterns, each arrow curving mid-flight as wind-guides nudged their paths into exposed joints. Green-lit shafts struck with the precise cruelty of a surgeon's cut.

Hunters on the glen floor danced between halberd arcs, bare feet finding every root and knot by instinct. They used bark as launch-steps, slipping inside Osiri guard-ranges to open tendons and hamstrings before vanishing sideways on a curl of Whisper-Vine.

Bindweavers flung out strips of living bark, interlocking them into shields between the front line and the priests. Osiri harmonic blasts broke against them, turning into showers of splinters instead of pulverized bone.

Maaren slid to a halt at the glen's edge, eyes wide, fingers already tracing patterns in the air.

"Priests!" he shouted. "They're trying to *tune* to our wind-lines!"

Refugees moved in clumsy counterpoint—dragging wounded back, stacking bark-weave frames into improvised barricades, copying drills from earlier days with shaking hands.

For a moment—
just long enough to feel dangerous—
it looked like the Sylph might push them back.

Then the forest shook again.

Three more geysers of sand erupted along the Quarter's southern edge. Roots ripped apart. Platforms pitched.

More Osiri forces surged out—this wave carrying sun-casters: compact bronze devices that spun in their hands and spat rings of compressed heat.

The first wave struck the lower branches.

Sylph screamed as cloaks caught fire. Dreamwillow recoiled, hissing, its silver hairs blackening at the tips. Whisper-Vines shriveled where the rings hit, dropping in charred coils.

The forest roared in pain.

Dravokh landed on a branch just in time to feel it tremble beneath her boots.

"They're using heat magic this deep?" Maaren gasped, voice tight. "That should be *impossible*; the Song density—"

"It is not impossible," Dravokh said, eyes hard.

"It is blasphemy."

She lifted one hand.

"SYLPH! FORM THE WINDBOUND LINE!"

Warriors snapped into motion, training overriding fear. The front rank shifted shoulder-to-shoulder along a wide branch-line, blades angled just so. A low harmonic rolled from their chests, braided together by years of drill.

Wind burst outward in a spiraling arc, forming a resonant wall of moving air.

Osiri halberds slammed into it and staggered as if hitting invisible stone. Sun-caster heat-rings warped, their circles pulled out of alignment, bleeding out strength before they could chew through bark and flesh.

Desert priests hunched, straining to hold their resonance steady.

The Windbound Line held.

Barely.

Laeryn dropped back beside Dravokh, blood trickling from a cut along her jaw, one blade nicked. "We can't hold this front much longer," she panted. "They outnumber us three to one."

Before Dravokh could answer, a sound knifed through the chaos.

Not a battle cry.

Not a spell.

A tone.

High and clear, flute-like, spiraling down from above like a falling thread of silver.

Maaren's head snapped up.

"They're back," he breathed.

The windline above them *snapped*, like a string pulled too far then released.

The Hidden Host dropped from the canopy like falling stars.

Male Sylph warriors in full Windveil armor streaked downward—glimpsed only in flickers where moonlight caught leaf-metal edges or the faint shimmer of their cloaks.

To the refugees, it looked as if the darkness itself had grown blades.

Shyr hit first.

He dropped into the back line of Osiri priests without a sound, windstep blade punching through a sun-forged breastplate and into a chest in one perfect, surgical thrust. The priest's harmonic chant cut off mid-note as his body folded.

Before the corpse hit the ground, Shyr was gone—already a shadow flicker at another man's throat.

Faelen came next, spear spinning in a barbed spiral. He landed in the middle of a cluster of soldiers, the wind catching his weapon and adding teeth to every motion. Two Osiri flew backward as if struck by a charging drake.

Vaelkorh descended last.

He dropped like an executioner's axe—silent, controlled, inevitable. His cloak flared like a living shadow at the last instant as he stepped through an Osiri champion's guard and severed both arms in one fluid, ascending cut.

Refugees stared in awe, fear, and something like dawning hope.

Sylph warriors cheered hoarsely.

The Osiri faltered.

Laeryn watched, chest heaving, blades dripping, and whispered, "Gods… they're beautiful."

"They're terrifying," Dravokh said.

Both were true.

With the Hidden Host on the glen, the fight changed shape.

An Osiri sun-caster raised his device—

Vaelkorh was simply *there* behind him, one hand closing around the weapon's throat. He twisted once. Bronze

screamed. The device died in his grip, its heat spilling
uselessly into the air.

A desert priest drew breath to call a destabilizing tone—

Shyr's blade licked his throat. The note never formed.

An Osiri champion charged the Windbound Line, roaring,
halberd raised—

Faelen intercepted, spear tracing a perfect Vael'Shar curve.
Armor parted. Bone followed.

Sylph archers refocused, picking off anyone who survived the
Host's passes.

Refugees flung bark-thread snares into Osiri legs where
Vaelkorh had already weakened armor-straps.

Dreamwillow surged, roots whipping up like silver snakes to
grab ankles.

For the first time since the night had dropped, the Sylph
forced the invaders backward.

Maaren planted his staff into a root, eyes bright with equal
parts fear and exhilaration.

"Lady Dravokh—" he shouted over the chaos. "The moment
is *yours!*"

And Dravokh understood.

Wind gathered around her like a summoned storm.

Her cloak lifted in the sudden pressure. The silver wind-
marks along her arms lit, lines of power glowing beneath
bronze skin. The forest's breath funneled toward her—

branchvaults exhaling, Whisper-Vines trembling in anticipation.

She drove the butt of her staff into the root-line beneath her.

"AERALITH—" Her voice was a blade. "BREATHE."

The forest answered.

Leaves tore from branches in a sudden, wrenching exhale—
thousands, then tens of thousands—
ripped from twig and limb, drawn into a spiraling column over the glen.

They spun tighter and faster, a green cyclone forming in the night air, every leaf honed razor-sharp by compressed wind-pressure.

Refugees could only stare.

Osiri soldiers looked up—

—and terror washed across their faces.

"NIGHT OF FALLING LEAVES," Dravokh commanded.

The storm dropped.

It did not fall like gentle autumn.

It *slashed*.

Leaves scythed across Osiri ranks, opening scores of shallow cuts in exposed skin, slicing leather straps, shredding cloth, sawing through wrist-bands and glyph-charms. Sun-caster harnesses snapped. Priest-tokens scattered.

Dravokh hadn't aimed to kill.

Not with the leaves.

She aimed to *break the shape of the army*.

And chaos bloomed.

Formations shattered. Lines broke. Priests flailed, losing their harmonic focus as blood and shredded cloth stung their eyes. Soldiers dropped weapons to shield their faces. More than one misstep sent an Osiri tumbling into the mouth of a half-collapsed tunnel.

"Host—FINISH THIS," Vaelkorh murmured.

The Hidden Host surged forward.

Where the leafstorm had cut, they carved.

Minutes stretched, then snapped.

The battlefield fell suddenly, brutally quiet.

Osiri bodies littered the glen—some dead, some groaning, some dragging themselves toward the nearest tunnel breach only to find it half-collapsed or wrapped tight in strangling roots.

Sylph warriors stood in ragged lines, chests heaving, blades dripping.

Refugees slumped where they stood, shaking, some laughing a little too high, others too shocked to cry yet.

Maaren closed his eyes and pressed a hand to a trembling trunk.

"The forest is hurt," he whispered.

Dravokh joined him, laying her palm beside his. She felt the deep ache in the sap, the strain in the root-net, the scorched nerves where heat magic had bitten.

"Yes," she said.

Laeryn limped up, one blade sheathed, the other still in her hand.

"We won," she said, almost defiant. "We held the Quarter."

"No," Dravokh replied quietly.

"We *delayed.*"

She lifted her gaze past the torn glen, past the Windborne Quarter's swaying platforms, toward the south—where the canopy thinned and the desert began.

"The Osiri tested us tonight," she said. "Measured our Songs. Counted our blades. Next time, they will come with *purpose.*"

Vaelkorh wiped blood from his windstep blade and slid it home. His eyes were flint.

"Then we strike first," he said.

Dravokh considered him for a long moment, wind tugging at the edge of her cloak, leaves still drifting down around them like the last flakes of a green storm.

"Soon, Vaelkorh," she said at last.

"Very soon."

A gust whispered across the glen, stirring piles of fallen leaves around their feet.

The forest was not relieved.
Not grateful.
Not calm.

It was waiting.

And Dravokh Mistshaper knew:

The next battle would not be on the ridge.

It would be in the tunnels—

—and after that,

in the Osiri capital itself.

Chapter 42 - The Test of the Windborne Three

Location: Amenemapet's True Hall of Judgment
Chronometric Stamp: BV 24.030

"To walk beneath the sun is to walk within judgment."
— *Rakh-tel the Enlightened (Osiri)*

The green wall pulsed.

Seris Thorn stepped through first.

The light peeled off her like thin water, leaving her standing in the arch-lich's great hall—tall for an Anari woman, bronze skin gone a shade too pale under the sickly witchfire glow. Auburn hair braided tight to her scalp, ends bound in shadow-thread beads that flickered faint with life-magic. A dark green Sylph cloak draped from her shoulders, windlace threads softening every footstep.

On either side of her, two Sylph emerged in perfect sync.

Serithyl Dawnstep—willowy and lethal—silver hair drifting in slow spirals as if submerged, even in still air. Storm-gray eyes, pupils narrowed and sharp. Her Windveil cloak barely kissed the floor, Whisper-Vine sigils curling along her sleeves and collar like written wind.

Vaelinnae Windpetal—shorter, coiled, all precise economy. Bronze skin marked with the faint traceries of Catal'ri tattoos. Her stance said "relaxed"; the angle of her spear said "wrong assumption."

All three saw Witmar at the same time.

The hall seemed to tighten.

Witmar Oakenstride lay where Nekharu had dropped him—robes torn, fungi-leather dark with the wound over his heart.

Nothing could do anything about the stillness.

Seris drew a sharp breath.

Serithyl's nostrils flared. Her fingers flexed around her hilt.

Vaelinnae's jaw set, eyes going cold.

Then they saw *him*.

Nekharu stood beside Amenemapet's throne—nine feet of jackal-headed arrogance in black-and-bone armor, framed by a high collar of gold and onyx. Over that, Witmar's Sylph unseen cloak draped awkwardly, flickering as the enchantments strained to disguise a frame that large. Witmar's unseen boots hugged his jackal paws, stealth-magic warping around clawed feet.

Like seeing an unburied grave wearing a friend's skin.

Seris raised her bow without a word.

Two other strings whispered into readiness beside her.

Three Queen's Kiss arrows—silver-headed shafts humming with Sylph-bound death—nocked and drawn as one.

Amenemapet's blue fire gaze turned toward them.

Too late.

They loosed.

The first arrow streaked straight for the arch-lich's skull.

It struck an invisible shell of condensed necromantic force and detonated in a burst of green-silver light. The impact cracked across the hall like a whip. Fine fractures spidered over the unseen barrier.

The second arrow went for Nekharu's throat.

The necromancer snarled and flared a sunfire ward around his neck. Queen's Kiss hit like a needle through skin. The ward held—but the light there flickered and dimmed for a heartbeat.

The third arrow took a fallen Osiri skeleton near the dais. It pierced bronze and bone as if they were smoke. The corpse evaporated to fine ash in an instant.

The entire hall *reacted*.

Amenemapet rose from his throne.

"Sufficient," he said, voice edged with sudden cold.

Power pressed outward, a weight on the back of every neck. Seris felt her life-magic tense in her veins; Serithyl and Vaelinnae's bodies shifted infinitesimally, falling into Sylph attack posture without conscious thought.

Seris didn't lower her bow.

"You wear the cloak of the fallen," she said quietly. "His boots. Sylph gifts given in honor, not taken as spoils."

Serithyl's normal airy tone was gone; steel lived there now. "Those garments belong to Witmar Oakenstride. Not to jackal carrion."

Vaelinnae's voice came soft and deadly. "Strip them off, dog. Or we will."

Nekharu's ears flattened. Gold-capped teeth glinted in a slow, confident smile. His fingers tightened on his staff.

Before he could speak, Amenemapet's voice cut across them all.

"Enough."

The word fell like a blade.

"You fire upon us in this sanctum," the lich said.

Seris met that blazing blue gaze. "We object when our dead are defiled."

The jaw of the golden mask creaked, as though some old amusement tried to remember how to move.

"You claim trophies are not trophies," Amenemapet murmured. "Yet the necromancer slew the scribe. By right of conquest, his spoils are his."

Serithyl's hand twitched toward her hilt, but Sylph discipline held.

"Then let the rule cut both ways," Seris said. "If that is your law, we will live by it—and so will they."

Vaelinnae added, quiet venom under control, "Raise your champions. We will reclaim our dead's honor from their corpses."

Amenemapet regarded them in long, unblinking silence.

Then sank back onto his throne.

"As you wish."

His skeletal fingers traced sigils in the air—old Osiri glyphs that made stone vibrate and made Loka's teeth itch even inside his bubble. The floor before the dais cracked, fractures branching outward in intricate sunburst patterns.

Three shapes pushed up out of the stone.

Shadows first—tall, distorted outlines of warriors like smoke in the shape of men. Then detail: gold armor, bone-carved shields, jackal heads, staves and blades.

Amenemapet's voice deepened.

"Hear and heed, ancient servants.
Khemet-Ra, Windblade of the Third Dynasty.
Tuthai-Mek, Bonewall of the Southern Front.
Neshep-Ren, Sun-Tongue of the Upper Flame.

You who died in my service:
fight once more. If you prevail, you live.
If you fall, you return to dust."

The three spectral warriors bowed.

Flesh knit over hollow cheeks. Breath filled long-dead lungs. Muscle rolled beneath fur. Their eyes glowed—not witchfire cold, but bright and savage.

Khemet-Ra twirled twin khopeshes with lazy ease.

Tuthai-Mek slammed his massive bone-and-bronze shield into the floor; the impact rattled teeth.

Neshep-Ren's staff shimmered with quiet sunfire, runes along its length warming like dawn.

They turned together to face the three Anari.

Neshep-Ren smiled, teeth sharp.

"We thank you," he said in rich, resonant Osiri. "For the chance to walk under light again. We will not waste it."

Seris stepped forward, lowering her bow and drawing her curved Sylph-forged blade. On either side, Serithyl and Vaelinnae flowed outward, falling into a loose triangle.

Seris's voice dropped into Sylph battle-prayer.

"To the wind that hides us," she murmured.

Serithyl answered, "To the rhythm that misleads."

Vaelinnae finished, "To the misstep that kills."

The air around them *changed*.

The Windveil stirred.

Amenemapet lifted one hand.

"Begin."

The Osiri champions moved first.

Khemet-Ra lunged, nine feet of predatory speed, twin khopeshes scissoring in intersecting arcs of sun-metal meant to carve through bone and Song.

Tuthai-Mek thundered forward behind his shield, a moving wall with enough mass to shatter ribs on impact.

Neshep-Ren swung his staff up and forward, sun-runes flaring as a serpent of fire uncoiled from its tip and roared along the floor.

Any other warriors would have been overwhelmed.

The Sylph didn't meet the charge.

They *weren't there* when it landed.

Not from spell. Not from glamor.

From motion.

Windveil Step triggered in a shared heartbeat.

Serithyl drifted sideways, leaving a faint echo of herself where she'd stood—an afterimage Khemet-Ra slammed through, cutting only air. Vaelinnae spiraled back, Windstep arcs curving around Neshep-Ren's fire as if she'd seen the path before he cast it. Seris bent her soul-line into a tight Syl'phyr contraction and slid under the edge of Tuthai-Mek's shield like a gust under a door.

Three devastating attacks struck nothing.

Then the air sang.

A flute-not-quite-a-flute—Serithyl's Catal'ri—threaded through the hall. More suggestion than sound, a half-note that faded before becoming anything you could grab. The Osiri felt it as a prickle along spine and fur—unease with no clear source.

Serithyl stepped out of that unease behind Khemet-Ra.

Whispercut.

The swing looked almost lazy, slow enough to read. It landed before his nerves registered movement.

Blood bloomed along his ribs.

Khemet-Ra snarled and pivoted—

—through a second afterimage. Serithyl had already moved.

Vaelinnae dropped out of the canopy of air like a falling leaf on a private wind. Skydance Cut flowed from above down Tuthai-Mek's flank—she touched his shield, ran *across* it in three ghost-light steps, and carved a precise line along exposed shoulder before he could bring his weapon to bear.

The Bonewall roared, dropping to one knee.

Seris anchored them.

Root-magic burst through floor-cracks, braided with life-song and battlefield experience. Vines and roots erupted around the Osiri's boots, snaring ankles, searching for gaps in greaves.

In a breath, the champions were tangled.

Neshep-Ren's footing went from sure to treacherous; his sunfire stuttered.

Khemet-Ra stumbled mid-step, one leg yanked sideways.

Tuthai-Mek tilted dangerously, shield braced to avoid toppling completely.

The Sylph triangle tightened.

Whispercut.

Windveil Step.

Galespiral Rend.

They weren't faster than sight; they were faster than *prediction*. Their shared Gale Range expanded and snapped shut with no discernible pattern. One instant, they were within arm's reach. The next, three paces away, blades half-raised, already committing to the next rhythm-change.

Neshep-Ren tried to reset the song.

He slammed his staff into stone, sending out a sunflare detonation that should have incinerated everything within its radius.

The flare bloomed—

—through empty air.

The three women had moved clear *before* the spell reached critical resonance.

Serithyl reappeared behind him, twin blades tracing a downstroke along his spine.

Vaelinnae struck across his ribs from the opposite angle, their arcs crossing in a lethal X.

He gasped, spasmed, and folded.

Amenemapet's eyes burned a fraction brighter.

Khemet-Ra roared, ripping free of the roots in a surge of brute strength. He went straight for Serithyl in a blur of steel and fury, twin khopeshes carving murder-patterns.

She flowed between them.

He struck where she had been, never where she was.

Her blade brushed his wrist with surgical softness.

A moment later, the hand holding his left sword wasn't attached to his arm.

He bellowed.

Vaelinnae's spear met his knee in a spinning Galespiral cut from the blind angle. Ligaments parted. The joint gave. He crashed to one side.

Seris ghosted behind him, Miststep carrying her through his shadow.

Her curved blade rested at the base of his spine.

"One more misstep," she murmured.

He froze.

She drew the line of that misstep.

Khemet-Ra hit the floor and stayed there.

Only Tuthai-Mek remained.

Pinned by roots, shield dented, fur matted with blood, breath ragged—but his eyes were still warrior-clear, tracking as best they could.

Vaelinnae's voice gentled without losing edge. "Do you want a clean end?"

His jaw clenched. "I want… freedom."

"Then fight for it," Seris said.

He roared, tearing the last of the roots away in a brutal surge, and hurled himself at her, shield-first.

She vanished.

Serithyl spun inward on his left, Windstep flickering.

Vaelinnae mirrored her on his right.

Seris reappeared behind him.

All three spoke together, barely louder than the wind:

"Last Gale."

Three blades struck in a single, perfect beat.

A gale seemed to pass through the hall, though no leaf stirred.

Tuthai-Mek's body folded along three lines at once—knees, shoulder, spine. Shield slipped from numb fingers. He went down hard, breath leaving him in one long, surprised exhale.

Silence followed.

The Osiri champions crumbled—bodies collapsing into ash that drifted down like gray snow. For a moment, fallen dust tried to settle in sun-disk patterns on the stone.

A stray current of air—no, the leftover breath of the Sylph's motion—scattered it.

Serithyl sheathed her blades with a soft click. Vaelinnae's Catal'ri faded like a held note released. Seris lifted her chin, breathing controlled, weight still balanced for the next fight.

Behind the emerald wall, Froster pressed his palms to the barrier, eyes wide.

"By the First Hunt…" he whispered. "They carved them apart like they were shadows."

Khandyl stared, equal parts horror and awe. "That was… terrifying," she said. Then softer: "And beautiful."

Harvey's jaw locked. "That's Sylph combat," he muttered. "You don't fight it. You survive it—if the wind lets you."

Even Kellyn, bruised and pale, allowed herself the smallest, hungry smile.

"They're unstoppable," she murmured.

Amenemapet moved.

He stepped down one level from his dais—skeletal feet soundless on stone. Gold-framed rags of his robes drifted around him as if stirred by a private desert wind.

"You three," he rasped.

Seris, Serithyl, and Vaelinnae instinctively re-formed their triangle, blades angled low, soul-lines tuned to vanish in the instant intent shifted.

Amenemapet bowed his head.

Slightly.

"The wind favors the bold," he said. "You move as the desert once moved—before the first sun burned the dunes to glass."

His gaze slid toward Nekharu, still lurking by a pillar in his stolen cloak and boots.

"Watch, bone-witch," Amenemapet hissed. "They fight not with stolen souls, but with rhythm. Not with chains. With breath."

Nekharu's ears flattened further. His golden fangs showed, but he bowed—the obedience of something leashed.

The Sylph ignored him.

Serithyl's eyes flicked to the heap of Witmar's gear by his feet: unseen cloak, boots, hood, dagger. Loot displayed like trophies.

"Those do not belong to you," she said softly.

Nekharu smirked. "Spoils of victory are—"

Vaelinnae took one smooth step, blade-tip lifting to hover at his throat without touching skin.

"Do not finish that sentence."

Seris's voice rang quieter and more dangerous than a shout. "Those were gifts from our clan. Worn with honor. You are not worthy to touch them."

Amenemapet raised a hand.

A thin field shimmered between Sylph and necromancer.

"The necromancer looted his fallen foe," the lich said. "Such is the rule. Should you fall, your flesh and gifts may be taken. Should you prevail, you may take theirs."

He looked down at the ash where his champions had stood.

"You did not merely prevail," he added. "You dominated."

Three objects appeared at his feet with a brief flare:

Two curved blades of Osiri sun-metal, etched in desert runes. A golden staff topped with a lion-headed sun-disc.

"Their relics move to your rhythm now," Amenemapet said. "Bound to those who broke their last Song."

Serithyl and Vaelinnae both knelt briefly—not to him, but to the weapons and the battle that earned them—before picking up the twin blades.

Seris took the staff, feeling the weight of foreign power settle under her fingers.

Behind them, Nekharu muttered something guttural.

Amenemapet's gaze cut sideways.

Silence fell over the necromancer like a thrown shroud.

In that breath of distraction, Serithyl moved.

Windveil Step took her three paces sideways without a footfall. Her hand flashed down, snatching Witmar's cloak and boots from Nekharu's paws without ever crossing into his reach.

She carried them—not back to herself—but to the edge of the dais, where Kellyn could see through the barrier.

She arranged them there with the same care someone had used on Witmar's body.

"His things," she said, "belong to his own. Not to hands like yours."

A low ripple of approval moved through the trapped Anari.

Amenemapet lifted both hands.

Green light rose like a slow tide at the Sylph trio's feet.

"You three have passed," he said. "And you will watch."

The magic lifted them cleanly, no pain, no struggle, into three waiting emerald spheres beside the others.

Serithyl spun once inside her prison, testing the containment, then stilled. "Wind guide the next," she whispered.

Vaelinnae rested a hand against the inner surface. "And watch the shadows," she added, eyes narrowing toward Amenemapet. "He twists them first."

Seris found Kellyn through the distortion. Something haunted, warning, lived behind her steady gaze.

"Do not break," she said simply.

The spheres sealed.

Amenemapet turned, slow and inevitable, toward the last two still standing free.

Kellyn Windstream.

Harvey Oakenstride.

"Next," he rasped, empty sockets brightening, "the boy of the cleansing flame… or the Queen of Swords herself."

His bony hand lifted.

The green wall pulsed—

—and this time, it reached for Harvey.

Chapter 43 - Harvey Oakenstride's Test

Location: Amenemapet's Chamber of Judgment
Chronometric Stamp: BV 24.030

"Dead tired and undead tired have very different meanings."
— Lord Maelvhar (Veydrath)

Harvey Oakenstride stepped through the shimmering green wall of light.

The arch-lich's great hall unfolded around him—vaulted pillars etched in sun-disks and jackal glyphs, painted reliefs of Osiri victories, gold inlays catching witchfire glow. The air reeked of incense, dust, and very old death.

None of it mattered.

His gaze went straight to the body on the floor.

Witmar.

Harvey stopped mid-step. For a heartbeat, the tall Griffyn warrior simply froze—broad shoulders sagging under a weight no armor could carry. His Sylph cloak hung torn and dusty from the last battle. Bronze skin dulled. Bright green eyes dimmed as they locked on his brother.

He crossed the distance in three strides and dropped to one knee.

"Wit…" Harvey's voice cracked. "Brother…"

Witmar Oakenstride lay where Nekharu had dropped him—
limbs now arranged with care instead of twisted where he'd
fallen. Someone had smoothed his hair, straightened his gray
robe, folded his hands over the scorched wound in his chest.
A faint char blackened the fungi-leather beneath, the mark of
necromantic fire boring straight through his heart.

Near the dais, Witmar's unseen cloak and boots lay folded
where the Sylph had placed them after shaming Nekharu into
giving them back.

Harvey's rough hand brushed Witmar's cheek, thumb tracing
cold bronze skin.

"You weren't supposed to die here," he whispered.

He leaned forward until his forehead rested against Witmar's.

"I'm sorry I wasn't there."

Silence. Only his own breathing, ragged and uneven.

Amenemapet's cold voice echoed down from the dais.

"Sentiment," the lich observed. "Such a fragile thing."

Harvey ignored him.

For one more moment, he stayed bowed beside Witmar like a
knight mourning his fallen shield-brother.

Then he rose.

Slowly.

Like a mountain deciding to stand.

Now his full height filled the hall: taller than most Anari,
broad-chested and thick-armed, a wall of muscle wrapped in
fungi-leather reinforced with extra plates he'd stitched

himself. Sylph boots glimmered faintly, bending light. His long dark-auburn hair was tied back warrior-style. His jaw was set hard enough to crack stone.

Grief burned in his eyes.

Behind the grief, something harder.

Resolve.

He walked to the center of the arena and turned to face the throne.

Amenemapet watched him with the still focus of a predator who could afford to be patient. Nekharu stood at his side, leaning on his staff, Witmar's death-mark still metaphorically on his hands.

Harvey's grip tightened on his longsword hilt.

Amenemapet's voice rolled across the hall.

"Your brother failed," the lich said. "He was found wanting. Let us see if the same blood runs through your veins."

Harvey raised his chin.

"Summon whoever you want," he said, low and steady.

Amenemapet's jaw creaked in something like a smile.

"Then come forth," he hissed, "Setmekh, greatest Centurion of the Osiri Empire."

The air in front of Harvey thickened.

Dust swirled, gathering shape.

A tall phantom appeared—broad, jackal-headed, wrapped in ancient lacquered armor and gold. Ember-light kindled in its eyes. Step by step, it solidified into flesh, rising to its full nine-foot height.

The Osiri centurion bowed once to the throne.

Then turned his burning gaze on Harvey.

A massive two-handed sword rested across his back—a black-edged blade etched with sun-runes, faint fire simmering along its fuller. In his hand, he held a long spear, blade barbed like a scorpion sting.

Harvey felt its heat from ten paces away.

Amenemapet's voice slithered.

"If Setmekh wins, he will live again. If you win, you gain his sword. It was once wrought for a Green Knight of your people—taken when Setmekh slew its owner. Its name is Kuldemaekr."

A beat.

"But you will not win."

Setmekh moved first.

Not with theatrical flourishes or roar-of-the-crowd bravado. His advance was quiet, lethal, each step placed with terrifying economy. Spear lowered. Black-and-gold armor barely whispering. Blue funerary markings along his muzzle glowed with cold fire.

Harvey raised his longsword. The Griffyn Aelonai Descent-Line came to his body unbidden—blade angled down, ready to fall like judgment. His Sylph cloak fluttered once, catching an invisible breeze.

The centurion's spear tip hovered at his throat.

Harvey exhaled.

The duel began.

Setmekh lunged.

The speed was wrong for something that size—too sudden, too clean.

Harvey pivoted into a triangular Griffyn descent-step Nyssara had drilled into his bones—updraft to descent—letting the spear flash past his ribs, then slashed downward in a Talon'ir arc at the centurion's exposed wrist.

Sparks burst as spear shaft met steel.

Setmekh rolled the deflection effortlessly and snapped the butt of the spear around in a hook aimed at Harvey's ribs.

Harvey dropped his weight and twisted; the blow barely skimmed him, enough to numb one side.

He answered with a Rising Wingbeat reversal, blade cutting back toward the gaps in the chest armor—

—and struck only air.

Setmekh had already slid to Harvey's flank in a blur of desert-honed footwork, spear twisting for a gut-thrust.

Harvey got his blade across just in time.

The impact rattled his arm to the shoulder.

Behind the barrier, Seris hissed through her teeth. "He's already reading Harvey's rhythm."

In the other spheres, nobody argued.

Setmekh stepped back a fraction, studying him like a craftsman appraising flawed steel. The spear tip never wavered.

He spoke in deep Osiri, the grave-voice of someone long used to command.

"Nef-tukh," he rumbled. "You fight like one who fell from the sky. But you have no wings."

Harvey lifted his chin but didn't answer.

They closed again.

Harvey shifted tactics—drew deeper into Griffyn forms, letting Aelor'vyn, the Ascendant Wingbeat, carry him up in a small leap and then *drop* his blade with added force, like a falling star.

Setmekh caught it on the flat of his spear, body barely moving. The rebound shivered up Harvey's arms.

The centurion pivoted sharply and hammered the spear-butt down at Harvey's sword hand.

The blow landed.

Pain exploded across Harvey's fingers.

His longsword slipped from numb grip and skittered across the stone.

"Harvey!" Khandyl shouted from her sphere.

Setmekh stepped forward and drove a boot into Harvey's chest.

The kick hit like a battering ram.

Harvey slid backward across the polished floor, air ripped from his lungs. He rolled once, teeth gritted, clawing for breath.

He pushed to his knees and lurched upright.

Setmekh strode after him, spear angled for the kill.

Harvey reached out instinctively for his fallen blade—

—and Setmekh casually stamped a foot down on it. Then he scraped it away across the floor, blade clanging as it spun against the far wall.

The contempt in the gesture landed almost as hard as the kick.

Nekharu smirked and folded his arms.

Setmekh lowered his spear.

One more strike and it would be over.

Harvey's chest heaved. His right hand throbbed. His lungs burned.

His boot brushed something.

He glanced down.

A fallen Osiri bronze-rimmed shield lay near a shattered skeleton—thick, heavy, built for someone Setmekh's size.

Harvey snatched it up and raised it just as the spear drove forward.

CLANG—

The impact rang through the entire hall.

The spear slammed into the shield hard enough to warp the metal, dent blossoming where the tip struck. Harvey's arms screamed. His knees almost buckled.

Setmekh ripped the spear free, dropped it as if bored, and reached over his shoulder.

His gauntleted hands closed around the hilt of Kuldemaekr.

When he drew it, the hall dimmed.

The greatsword came free in one smooth motion—a blade of ancient Anari make twisted to Osiri service. Black-edged steel, sun-runes along the fuller, a line of sleeping green fire under the surface.

Harvey felt it in his bones.

Setmekh advanced.

The first vertical strike came down with ruinous force.

Harvey caught it on the shield.

The shield did what it had been made to do.

It lasted one blow.

Metal screamed, split down the middle, and folded around Kuldemaekr's edge. The force drove Harvey backward; the shield tore from his grip and crashed to the floor in two mangled halves.

He hit the stone on his back, breath knocked out again, fragments of bronze skittering around him.

Setmekh roared his victory cry and charged, both hands on the greatsword, Kuldemaekr raised high for the final, cleaving stroke.

Harvey's body moved before his mind caught up.

His hand went to the greatsword strapped across his own back—his familiar Griffyn blade, heavier than a longsword, built for his strength.

He ripped it free while rolling, planting the pommel against the stone as he twisted to bring the point toward Setmekh's chest.

From outside, it looked like a desperate brace, a last attempt to turn the centurion's own momentum against him.

On the inside, Harvey's training snapped into perfect alignment.

Beak of Judgment.
Aelion's Still Wing.

Setmekh leapt, Kuldemaekr descending in a killing arc meant to split Harvey in half—

Harvey *thrust.*

He drove upward from his legs and spine, not just arms, the pure Griffyn line of the form snapping through his body. His blade speared forward like a hawk's beak piercing prey.

The edges kissed.

For a heartbeat, both swords screamed against each other.

Then Kuldemaekr's angle slipped wide.

Harvey's greatsword punched through Setmekh's chest, under the breastplate, along the gap designed for breath.

Silence hit the hall like a dropped curtain.

Setmekh stared down at him, jackal muzzle slack, golden eyes wide in disbelief.

"Not…possible…" he rasped.

Green fire crawled along the wound from the inside out.

Cracks raced through armor and bone.

The centurion's spine buckled.

Then the greatest Osiri champion of his age fell forward—collapsing over Harvey like a burning wall.

The hall shook with the impact.

For a second, Harvey couldn't move. His arms were pinned; his lungs were sandpaper; his whole body rang.

Then the weight began to crumble.

Fire died. Armor split. Bone collapsed to ash.

Harvey shoved the remnants aside and forced himself upright, panting.

He stood alone in the center of the chamber.

The survivors in their spheres stared down at him.

Amenemapet leaned forward on his throne, blue fire narrow in his skull.

"Luck," the arch-lich hissed. "A fluke."

Harvey didn't look at him.

He bent, pried Kuldemaekr from the settling ash, and lifted the ancient greatsword in both hands. The blade was heavy, perfectly balanced, dangerous even at rest.

He carried it not to the center of the room—

—but back to his brother.

Harvey knelt beside Witmar again, setting his own Griffyn greatsword aside. He rested the flat of Kuldemaekr gently across Witmar's folded hands like a laid offering.

The blade warmed under his fingers.

Then, faintly, it glowed.

Not Osiri sun-fire.

Green light.

Sylph light.

Anari light.

Above, Khandyl wiped at silent tears.

Elowen bowed her head.

Aafje pressed her hand to her heart in a Webweaver's farewell.

In the other spheres, Froster and Loka watched with hollow, aching eyes. Serithyl and Vaelinnae murmured a soft Sylph mourning-chant, wind-breath rhythm like air through hollow reeds. Seris joined them, voice low and rough.

Harvey drew in a shuddering breath.

"I will carry this blade," he whispered to Witmar. "For both of us."

He closed Witmar's fingers more tightly around the hilt, then wrapped his own hand over them one last time.

When he finally stood, Kuldemaekr rose with him.

Its green light didn't fade.

The containment sphere formed around Harvey like liquid glass, rising from the floor to enclose him. The magic lifted him gently from the stone and drifted him up to hang beside the others.

Inside, the air felt cool—almost calm—but Harvey's chest still heaved. His muscles shook. Grief sat on his shoulders like a second weight.

He pressed his palm against the inside of the sphere. The barrier shimmered, reflecting his own face back at him— bronze skin drawn tight, eyes too dark, hair damp with sweat.

"Brother," he breathed. "I did it. But you're still gone."

Khandyl reached up and set her hand where his rested, separated by a thin layer of emerald light.

"He died fighting," she said softly. "He didn't die alone."

Harvey nodded once, barely.

Elowen, cheeks streaked with tears through dust, added, "He'd be proud of you. He always was."

Loka swallowed hard. "He told me that," he said hoarsely. "All the time. Said you were the better half of the team."

A bitter sound almost escaped Harvey's throat—too cracked to be a laugh.

Aafje bowed her head, whispering a Webweaver's blessing. In the Sylph spheres, Serithyl and Vaelinnae kept their mourning-chant going, a quiet current under the grief.

For a moment, the hall felt thick with sorrow.

Then a crackle of magic snapped through the air like lightning finding a taller tree.

Amenemapet moved.

The arch-lich descended one step from his dais, sand swirling around the rags at his feet. Blue witchfire flared in his eye sockets.

His jaws ground together.

"IT WAS LUCK," he snarled.

Nekharu, lounging by a pillar, allowed himself a thin, mocking smile. "Or perhaps the centurion grew soft in death."

Amenemapet turned on him with such sudden fury that the necromancer's smirk died mid-curve.

"Soft?" the lich hissed. He pointed a bony finger at Harvey's sphere. "That one has no wings. No divine ascent. No Song of War. No birthright. And *still* he killed my champion."

He began to pace along the edge of the arena, robes dragging twin furrows in the dust.

"Kuldemaekr should not have answered him," Amenemapet muttered. "That blade was forged for the gods' favored. Not for a mortal held together by stubbornness and grief."

Dark lightning crackled between his fingers.

For a heartbeat, it looked as if he might hurl it straight at Harvey's prison.

Elowen's hands went to her staff.

Khandyl's claws dug into her own sphere.

Kellyn pressed against the wall of light, shoulders tense, eyes locked on the lich.

But Amenemapet stopped.

The witchfire in his skull dimmed, changing from fury to something colder.

Calculation.

"One victory does not tilt the scales," he said. "Not yet."

He turned slowly toward the tunnel mouth where the green wall waited—where another silhouette stood in its glow.

Kellyn Windstream.

Swordswoman. Linguist. Queen of Swords—whether she wanted the title or not.

Amenemapet lifted his staff.

Power rippled through the chamber, vibrating the stone.

"Bring forth the final challenger," he intoned. "The would-be Queen of Swords. Let us see whether her heart breaks… as her companions' have."

In the tunnel, Kellyn lifted her chin.

The green wall pulsed once.

Twice.

Then it opened like a curtain of light, revealing her standing alone in the narrow passageway—Whisperthread cloak drifting around her ankles, eyes bright and hard.

She stepped through.

The wall sealed behind her with a ringing chime.

Every Anari in the chamber held their breath.

Kellyn didn't look at Amenemapet.

Not yet.

She went straight to Witmar's body, knelt, and brushed hair from his cooling forehead. No words came—just a thin, broken exhale.

Then she rose.

Slowly.

Deliberately.

And turned to face the arch-lich.

Her voice was soft, but it carried through the hall like a drawn blade.

"You will answer for this," she said.

Amenemapet's jaw twitched in something resembling amusement.

"A threat," he asked, "or a promise?"

"A certainty," Kellyn replied.

Torchlight flickered as if retreating.

The witchfire in Amenemapet's skull brightened.

"Come forth, Windstream," he rasped. "Your test begins now."

And the floor began to move.

Chapter 44 – Queen's Gambit

Planet: Vael'thara
Location: Crypt of Amenemapet
BV 24

"If destiny won't open the door, we'll pick the lock, kick it in, or build a new one." — *Captain Lysa Dorn (Human)*

She could feel every eye on her.

Harvey, leaning inside his emerald sphere, chest heaving, jaw clenched around words he couldn't say.
Seris pressed pale against her windlit bubble, her bow hand trembling once before she stilled it.
Aafje clutching the Twilight Robe at her throat, shadow still shivering around her.
Froster white-knuckled on his new flame-blade.
Loka hollow-eyed, shaken after being weighed and found wanting.

The Sylph trio hovered like caged storm-birds, all coiled precision and watchful silence.

But Kellyn's gaze stayed on Witmar.

He lay where the Sylph had reordered him: hair smoothed, cloak and boots returned, hands near the blackened wound in his chest.

Kellyn Windstream—tall for an Anari woman, lean-muscled rather than bulky—stood very still. Her bronze skin was smudged with ash and dried blood; the faint freckles across her nose still showed through. Her long auburn hair was braided back on one side in practical battle plaits, with the rest twisted into a low knot to keep it off her neck. Pale green eyes—normally quick with curiosity—were flat now, sharpened into something like a blade.

Her right thumb rubbed once along the guard of her sword.

One breath.

She bowed her head to Witmar, just enough that her braids brushed forward.

Then she lifted her gaze to the throne.

Amenemapet, wrapped in black-and-gold rags, lifted one withered hand. Bandages stirred in an invisible desert breeze.

"Step forth," he intoned, "Anari Queen of Swords."

The title still felt wrong in her bones. She was a linguist, a pattern-reader, a woman who'd once spent more time with inscriptions than with blades.

But her people had needed someone to stand where lines crossed.

The green wall parted.

Kellyn stepped through.

As she crossed the threshold, her hand moved almost of its own accord. She drew her blade in one clean motion.

The air *noticed*.

Pressure thickened. The subtle hum of a hundred curses and old spells in the stone shifted, aligning along an invisible axis that ran from crown to heel. The geometry of the room seemed to find a straight line and cling to it.

Her posture settled into Anar'Thyr—the Dominion axis her Dragon Clan instructors had half-jokingly called "the spine of law". Her breathing dropped into the deep, resonant cadence of the Catal'ri. Even the floor felt different under her boots, as if the pyramid braced itself.

Amenemapet's hollow voice rolled down the hall.

"Rise, O Queen of Swords. Return from the dust of ages. Your throne calls you."

Wind like a tomb's sigh swept the dais.

Golden dust swirled upward, coiling on unseen currents. Bone formed inside it. Then sinew. Then bronze-dark flesh and obsidian plate, war-gilded and cruelly elegant.

The Osiri Queen of Swords stepped into being.

She towered nine feet tall, jackal-headed, crowned in black heliolite and gold. Obsidian-and-gold warplate wrapped her frame in layered arcs; every curve of armor was both beautiful and functional, designed to turn blades and catch light. Her weapon—a long, curved sword of dark heliolite—hummed with a contained, hungry sun.

She looked down at Kellyn.

Her eyes burned like twin captive stars.

When she spoke, her voice carried echoes—many throats speaking in chorus behind the primary tone.

"Anari," she said. "The title you bear is mine."

Kellyn's throat was dry, but her mind, trained on a thousand dead languages, did what it always did: it listened to rhythm, to sentence weight, to the spaces between words.

"I didn't take it because I wanted it," she said quietly. "I took it because no one else could afford to."

The Queen tilted her head, amused.

"Then let the world decide," she said, lowering her blade, "which of us holds the name in truth."

She shifted her stance.

"Begin."

The fight didn't start.

It *arrived.*

The Osiri Queen did not advance step by step. Heat warped around her, and she was simply *there*—heliolite blade whistling toward Kellyn's throat.

Kellyn's foresight flared.

Divination wasn't sight, not exactly. It was grammar—a branching sentence of futures built in a heartbeat. Verbs of motion, clauses of impact, nested possibilities.

She stepped into Anar'Thyr and raised her sword on a pure vertical line.

CLANG—

The blades met.

The shock ripped down her arms, tried to drive her to her knees. Her boots slid an inch before her stance locked, Pillar Stand rooting her into the bones of the pyramid.

The Queen's jackal helm tilted.

A low, pleased growl rumbled out.

"Dominion-line," she said. "You carry the blood of command."

Kellyn exhaled one Catal'ri note—low, steady.

The air tightened.

The Queen vanished.

Futures exploded in Kellyn's mind—12, 20, too many:

—downward crescent to the right shoulder
—thrust from the left hip
—spinning arc at skull height
—double-beat feint hooking her knee
—killing cut aimed low at her leading ankle—

She chose the one that killed her fastest… and stepped *through* it.

Her blade snapped out in a single Edict-Strike—no flourish, no curve—a straight cut, written like a law.

The Queen reappeared exactly where the strike already was— and parried flawlessly.

The impact cracked through the hall.

Wind spiraled out. Braziers guttered. Dust sifted down from above.

Kellyn slid back a half-step, then reset, shoulders squaring.

The Osiri Queen pressed.

Her style was curved geometry—every strike an elegant, looping script, a sentence written in steel and sun where every clause promised dismemberment.

Kellyn answered with lines.

Vael'Shar forms adapted to Dominion, her motion a series of straight declarations: cuts, thrusts, and immovable guards. Curves met the pillar and broke around it.

They traded phrases of violence.

CLASH.
Whisper.
CRACK.

Futures flickered at the edges of Kellyn's awareness. She saw herself stepping left and bleeding out. She saw herself pivoting right and losing a hand. She saw one thin path: *do not move at all.*

She held her ground.

The heliolite blade passed so close across her ribs that heat kissed her armor, singing a line through the leather.

The Queen's eyes brightened.

"Your foresight is strong, Anari."

Kellyn didn't waste breath answering.

She lunged.

Vael'Shar Edict-Splitter—linear stride, severing decree. Her blade screamed a straight line across the Queen's torso.

SHRRAKK—

Warplate split. Gold and obsidian shattered in a tidy diagonal.

The Queen hissed, more pleased than angry.

"Good," she murmured. "Hold nothing back."

She vanished again.

This time, the futures didn't branch.

They *collapsed* from above.

Kellyn's divination sparked hot and brief: a downward spiral, black blade wreathed in solar fire, descending like an execution.

She stepped into Vael'Shar Breathlock.

Her sword thrust upward—not to pierce, but to impose stillness. Dominion didn't always cut. Sometimes it simply *refused.*

A cone of stillness snapped into place.

The Queen hit it like a falling meteor striking bedrock.

BOOOOOM—

Stone cracked under Kellyn's boots. The whole chamber shuddered. Dust rained.

The strike didn't stop, but its arc warped, glancing aside instead of cleaving through her skull. Kellyn no longer tried to *block* the Queen; she redirected, bleeding power sideways.

For a fraction of a heartbeat, the Osiri hung suspended in midair, eyes wide.

"Impressive…" she admitted.

She sprang back, flipped, landed lightly in a predatory crouch.

Kellyn's lungs burned. Her swordhand trembled once before she forced it steady.

Then her vision blurred.

Not from exhaustion—from interference. The Queen's enchantments rippled through the hall, subtle frequencies that tangled her foresight, turning future sentences into static.

Kellyn forced a slow inhale, grounding herself in the Song of Dominion, counting in old Anari numerals under her breath.

One—two—three—

Clarity edged back.

Too late.

The Queen's blade came low.

Kellyn saw the line only at the last possible beat.

The heliolite edge kissed her thigh, slicing through armor and flesh with a spray of scorching fire. Pain flared up her leg; her stance staggered.

She hissed through her teeth.

The next strike came in a spinning execution arc aimed at her neck.

Kellyn dropped, hauling her blade into Pillar Guard—a vertical, world-line defense—as everything narrowed to one axis:

Live / Die.

CLANG—

The blow hammered down, hard enough that her elbows went numb even through the deflection. She shifted the angle just enough to let that force slide away instead of crush her.

The Queen leaned close, blades locked.

"You fight like a law written into the world," she rasped. "But laws break."

She shoved.

Kellyn slid backward, boots scraping across stone. Her wounded leg screamed. Her divination splintered again, future paths blinking in and out like failing lights.

The Queen followed.

Measured steps. No hurry. No wasted motion. Grace and inevitability in one body.

Kellyn's heel hit the base of the dais.

Her options collapsed.

Futures:

—Step right → decapitation.
—Parry high and left → heliolite through her heart.
—Drop low → spine severed.

No surviving line.

Except one.

Not a path she knew.

A *shape* she remembered.

Sahn Moonspear's voice, somewhere in a training glade years and worlds away:

"The Final Edict is not a strike, Windstream. It is a sentence. The world either accepts it—or it breaks you for daring to write it."

She had never been allowed to complete it.

She didn't have any other choice now.

Kellyn inhaled.

The Dragon Song—the Dominion-line—rose in her chest like a stormfront. The air thickened. Stone shivered. Her blood felt too large for her veins.

The Queen's blade swung down.

Kellyn raised hers.

Straight. Unbending.

FINAL EDICT: DECLARED.

For one impossible instant, the hall refused to move.

Light stalled mid-glint on steel. Dust hung in the air like pinned stars. The Queen's descending blade froze a hair's breadth from Kellyn's skull, caught in the geometry of a word the world did not remember agreeing to obey.

The Osiri Queen's eyes widened—not in fear.

In recognition.

"You…" she whispered. "You carry the old mastery."

Kellyn exhaled the last syllable.

"Fall."

Her sword descended in a perfect pillar-line.

The Queen *tried* to twist aside—to rewrite the sentence, but Dominion had already filed the decree.

Steel cleaved obsidian, flesh, spine, and shadow.

The Osiri Queen of Swords split down the center—two clean halves sliding apart in a spray of light. Her armor and blade clattered to the floor.

The body itself didn't.

It dissolved into clouds of golden dust, drifting outward like embers from a dying star. The motes flowed toward Amenemapet's dais, spiraling around him in faint, worshipful streams before fading into nothing.

Kellyn didn't move.

Couldn't.

Her fingers slipped from her hilt.

The sword hit the stone with a dull clang.

She dropped to one knee, bracing on shaking hands. Her leg burned. Her lungs scraped. Her divination guttered like a candle left in a gale.

The Final Edict had not been meant for someone at her level.

The world pushed back.

Edges of the hall warped and wavered at the corners of her vision, the geometry she'd imposed still vibrating, trying to snap back into its old shape.

A low voice, older than the crypt itself, rolled through the chamber.

"…She commanded the world itself…"

Amenemapet had not left his throne.

But his posture had changed.

He no longer lounged as if watching a spectacle. He leaned forward now, elbows on his knees, jackal helm tilted, every line of his body attuned to her.

Beside him, Nekharu—the necromancer who'd killed Witmar—took an involuntary step back. His tall jackal ears flattened.

"Impossible," the necromancer hissed. "Not even *our* Queen perfected the editing form of the Axis-Song. She fell to the Sza'thir of the Obsidian Coast—"

Amenemapet raised one hand.

The words died in Nekharu's throat.

The arch-lich's voice dropped like a decree at noon.

"This Anari," he said, "has drunk from the breath of ancient dominion."

Kellyn forced herself upright.

Every joint argued. The world still felt slightly misaligned, like a text copied with one line offset—but she refused to show it. Her left hand twitched once toward her abandoned sword, more habit than hope.

Across the chamber, the others watched in stunned silence.

Harvey's hands were splayed against his sphere, eyes wide, torn between pride and terror.
Khandyl shook, remembering the futures she had been forced to choose between.
Froster stared like a man watching a myth walk.
Elowen whispered healing prayers under her breath, knowing they could not cross the emerald glass.
Seris and the Sylph warriors looked at Kellyn with an expression she'd rarely seen on their faces.

Not just respect.

Wariness. The way hunters looked at a storm.

Aafje clutched her staff, knuckles white. Loka's lips moved silently, cataloging what he'd seen like a scholar trying to file the impossible.

She saw a future that didn't exist yet, he thought, *and made the world agree.*

Amenemapet rose.

He didn't need to thunder or flare power; the whole hall simply *noticed* and made space. Gravity felt slightly wrong, the way it did near deep wells and great ships.

Black-and-gold robes shimmered with faint solar glyphs. Chains of carved bone fanned behind him like wings. Necrosolar energy thrummed in the air, pressing against skin and soul.

He descended from the dais until he stood a few paces before Kellyn.

"Kellyn Windstream of the Dragon Line," he said.

She met his empty gaze.

Her hand trembled, but her chin did not.

"…You stand," the Pharaoh of the Dead continued, "as one who commands breath itself."

She didn't answer.

Her silence was its own argument.

Amenemapet extended one clawed finger.

Kellyn felt power coil around her throat—not choking, not crushing, just… testing as if a hand of invisible sand measured the length of her breath.

"Your Dominion-Song," he mused, voice suddenly quieter. "Awakening early. Too early."

The words hit harder than any blow.

She could feel it. The way her power surged ahead of its proper age, how every use cut deeper than it should. How the forms came to her as recovered *grammar* more than learned technique.

Her future was outrunning her body.

His voice slipped colder.

"You are not merely a weapon," he said. "You are a fracture line. A paradox written into flesh. You will be…" He paused, savoring the word, "… the last test."

The force around her throat released.

Kellyn swayed, then caught herself.

Emerald light surged up around her like rising glass. The containment sphere formed in an instant, closing over her head with a soft, harmonic chime. It lifted her gently from the floor and swung her in line with the others.

She came to rest beside Harvey's bubble.

Inside his prison, Harvey pressed his palm to the barrier, eyes locked on her.

Pride. Fear. Rage. All of it sat on his face with nowhere to go.

Kellyn pressed her own hand against the inside of her sphere until it met his through a thin curve of green light.

Only then did her fingers shake.

Chapter 45 - The Last Stand in the Crypt of Amenemapet

Planet: Vaelthara
Location: The Tomb-Heart of the Eternal Pharaoh
BV 24.030

"Patience is a song only the old trees can teach—and only the young ever try to rush."
— *Erynthiel Shadebloom (Anari)*

Silence fell over the crypt.

Not peace.

The kind of silence that sits on a battlefield between one heartbeat and the next, deciding which side owns the breath that follows.

Kellyn Windstream lowered her blade, lungs burning, thigh still bleeding from the Osiri Queen's cut. The emerald shell of her containment sphere flickered once around her like a dying thought and collapsed into the stone.

Harvey reached her first.

Tall, broad-shouldered, plates sewn into his fungi-leather, every line of him built to hold a doorway or break a wall. The Green Knight's face—normally weathered calm—was fissured with raw grief.

Witmar lay 20 paces away.

Hands folded, hair smoothed, cloak and boots restored, staff laid beside him—the Sylph had done what they could. It still didn't make him look less dead.

Kellyn touched Harvey's forearm. Just a brush. *I see you. I see him.*

He didn't look away from his brother.

Ah'shin was gone—withdrawn into whatever shadow paths a Veydrath prince preferred. The tests were over.

Only reckoning remained.

The chamber trembled.

A dry rasp slid over the air like sand over bone.

Amenemapet the Eternal rose from his throne-dais at the far end of the hall.

Vertebrae snapped into alignment with parchment-crack sounds. The golden funerary crown caught the torchlight in fractured shards. Black and gold robes unfurled around him with a tattered majesty, dragging whispers through the dust.

In his right hand, he held a tome.

Not illusion. Not dream.

A heavy, iron-bound book wrapped in worn leather, its cover engraved with hieroglyphs that refused to sit still. The symbols crawled and twisted like small burning things.

The Necrodemicon.

The *real* one.

Loka inhaled sharply.

He felt it first as pressure behind his eyes, a whisper at the edge of thought, a cold gravity in the room that everything tried not to notice.

Amenemapet lifted the book slowly, as if presenting it to the ceiling.

A hollow laugh rattled from his skull.

"You reach," he said, "for what was never meant for your hands."

Beside the throne, the Osiri necromancer stepped into the light—tall, jackal-headed, draped in black war-silk. Witmar's cloak clung mockingly to his shoulders. Gold-capped teeth flashed in a grin.

Harvey's fingers tightened on Kuldemaekr's hilt until the leather creaked.

Amenemapet lowered the Necrodemicon, empty sockets flaring blue.

"You have passed the Tests of the Eternal Hall," he intoned. "You have shown strength… courage… sacrifice…"

A pause, thin and cruel.

"But you have not shown *worth*."

The torches guttered.

Then died.

Darkness slammed over the hall like a dropped curtain— thick, suffocating, absolute.

Something exhaled.

The dark billowed outward from the throne, carrying with it a hundred small sounds:

Fingers scraping stone.
Bone grinding in sockets.
Jawbones clattering in eager hunger.

Witmar's carefully laid body jerked as invisible hands seized it, flinging it aside like a broken toy.

"NO—!" Seris lunged, but a wall of bone-claws rose between her and his corpse, fingers lacing together into a barrier.

Kellyn's blade rose in a smooth, instinctive line.
Aafje whispered a shadow mantra under her breath.
Khandyl sank into Wolf stance, her breath dropping into the kill rhythm.
Harvey stepped in front of Kellyn without thinking.

Loka snatched Witmar's *other* staff—the one they'd recovered—into his grip. His dagger slid into his off-hand.

Around them, the dead rose.

Dozens at first. Then more.

Osiri skeletons clambered from cracks in the floor. Old warriors and priests clawed their way out of the stone. Spectral jackal-masked shades bled into flesh as they solidified, their eyes burning with borrowed sunfire.

Old foes from earlier duels.

New foes called from forgotten wars.

Behind them, the necromancer stretched out his staff-bearing hand.

"Rise," he purred, "servants of the Black Sun."

They obeyed.

Amenemapet raised his free hand.

"Know this, little sparks," he said. "No one reaches the Necrodemicon. Not while Amenemapet rules eternity."

His bony finger stabbed outward.

"Kill them all."

The emerald spheres around the party shattered into green dust.

They hit the stone on their feet.

Harvey whispered, "Witmar…"

Then he roared—a sound like a wild thing breaking free of a cage.

"FOR MY BROTHER!"

And the Green Knight charged into death.

Harvey struck the undead front like a meteor.

Kuldemaekr fell in a Griffyn Aelonai descent-line, a perfect falling-judgment arc fueled by rage and grief. An Osiri warrior detonated under the blow, spine shattered, ribs turning to splinters.

Three more lunged with spears.

Harvey ducked under the first, shoulder-slamming the wielder sideways. A spear scraped his armor, but he rolled the impact, twisting into a Rising Wingbeat reversal that ripped another skull from its spine.

The dead didn't care.

Twenty bodies surged toward him at once.

He planted his heel.

Featherfall Draw—cloak sweeping, blade carving a wide, clean arc. Limbs separated. Skulls flew. Ribcages folded. A green sheen flickered along Kuldemaekr's edge.

Not Song.

Not spell.

Just Harvey Oakenstride, grief-fed and utterly done with restraint.

Behind him, Kellyn stepped into Dragon stance, thigh wound screaming, Dominion-line humming in her bones.

Her eyes glowed faintly.

"Lýren'thal," she murmured. "Pillar Line."

Her sword fell on a ghost-warrior with the geometry of a verdict. Distance tightened around him; his breath locked. Kellyn walked through his center, blade a straight path of denial.

The corpse tried to fall in two directions and failed.

"Kellyn!" Froster shouted from the left.

Three Osiri spear-guards charged him, weapons gleaming with dark enchantments.

Froster spun his two-handed Osiri flame-blade—the one earned in his own trial. The metal flared, eager to drink its cousins.

Moonfang Descent—Wolf killing form—dropped onto the first spear, snapping it in half. The second thrust went for his face; he Windstepped sideways, stealing a Sylph cadence Khandyl had drilled into him, and smashed the pommel into the attacker's skull.

The third lunged from behind.

Froster twisted, baton snapping into his off-hand.

A narrow green kill-beam lanced out.

The skeleton's sternum blew open.

"Try ambushing someone else," he growled.

Khandyl dropped from above beside him, short crescent blades flashing.

Silver Prowl. Lungpiercer. Cuts so clean that two Osiri died with their throats open before they realized they'd been hit.

"Stay in the hunt, Froster!" she barked. "You think too much, you die."

He smirked, breathless. "Learning from the best."

"And she will gut you if you fall here."

On the right, wind became knives.

Seris, Serithyl, and Vaelinnae moved as one: Windborne Three in a tight, lethal spiral. Air bent around them. Their cloaks traced ghost-lines; their bodies flickered between seen and unseen.

Seris invoked Gale Spiral—passing an Osiri warrior in a blur, her blade whispering twice. He collapsed in pieces.

Vaelinnae slid through a Miststep between two converging spear-thrusts, body folding wrong then snapping straight, her Ribbonfall Sweep opening both undead from hip to shoulder.

Serithyl simply disappeared.

A heartbeat later, three Osiri fell with their spines severed, her Whispercut too quick to see.

"This way!" she called, Catal'ri flute-tone braided into her words.

Aafje moved to meet them, Twilight Robe glittering softly with starlight.

She raised both hands.

"Shadow Rend!"

Ten tendrils of black smoke rippled forth, skewering undead, tearing limbs and skulls free. Bones rained down in clatters.

The necromancer hissed.

"You dare wield shadow in my sight, little Anari?"

Aafje's eyes burned faint violet.

"I dare do much more."

She flicked her fingers.

An umbral bolt struck his jaw, black spider-cracks racing across the gold.

He snared three new corpses to rise at her back.

Kellyn's Dragon hum rippled outward—Dominion-flavored interference—and those corpses froze for precious seconds as if the command to rise had been overruled.

Aafje dipped her head, grief a hot coal in her chest.

"For Witmar," she whispered.

Shadow knives tore an undead priest in half.

Loka skirted the edge of the melee, unseen boots flickering at the edge of everyone's perception.

No Sylph speed.
No Wolf kill-curve.
No Dragon Dominion-line.

Just Witmar's staff in his hand, his own dagger in the other, and the desperate understanding that the Necrodemicon *would* decide whether any of this mattered.

He ducked a wild swing, smashed a skeletal knee with the staff, then drove the butt into its spine to finish it. He slid between three more, cloak flaring, boots bending light around his ankles.

He looked up.

Amenemapet was watching him.

Only him.

Blue fire burned coldly in the empty sockets.

Loka understood.

The arch-lich saw blades and claws and wind as noise.

The boy with the book was the threat.

Loka's throat tightened.

"Come on, then," he whispered. "I'm not Witmar. But I'm not leaving his work undone."

He took a step toward the dais—

—and 20 undead pivoted toward him as one.

"Ah," he said faintly. "Problem."

Harvey plowed into them before they could reach him.

"NOT TODAY!"

Kuldemaekr flashed, and an entire front rank disintegrated, blowing apart in a storm of bone dust and emerald light.

***

At the far end of the hall, Amenemapet lifted the Necrodemicon high.

The book pulsed—slow, heavy, like the heartbeat of something buried under mountains.

"Enough," he whispered.

"Let despair be *whole*."

He dropped his left hand toward the floor.

The stone cracked.

A tremor rolled through the hall. Sigils flared in the seams between flagstones. The slabs shattered outward as a dozen Osiri champions rose, fully armed, fully formed, screaming for blood.

Kellyn dragged in a breath.

"Brace!" she shouted. "Stay together! Stay breathing! We are not done!"

Amenemapet's laughter slid over them like a cold wind.

"You are."

The champions hit.

The impact shook the crypt.

Twelve Osiri champions—bronze and obsidian, helms crowned in sun-disks, weapons burning with spectral fire—slammed into the Anari line like a tidal wave of bone and metal.

Kellyn's sword met twin khopeshes in a shower of sparks.

The champion looming over her exhaled cold air; gold lacquered armor creaked with undead strength.

Kellyn's world narrowed to axes and futures.

"Vael'Shar Edict-Strike," she breathed.

She moved in a straight line, her blade punching through the curve of his guard, through armor, through the command channel that kept his body coherent.

He dissolved into dust mid-step.

The second tried to flank her.

Kellyn lifted her sword, humming a Still Wing counter-verse. The champion's body locked for half a heartbeat—long enough for Seris to step from nowhere and open his throat in a clean spiral-cut.

He fell. Seris vanished again.

Two champions barreled into the Wolf pair.

One swung a massive desert cleaver. Khandyl slammed into Froster's shoulder, shoving him under the arc.

"KEEP YOUR HEAD IN THE HUNT!"

Froster rolled, came up under the champion's guard, blocking the follow-up strike and riding its force sideways. Pulse Gap—inside the guard, baton jammed into metal ribs.

He triggered it.

A narrow beam bored a fist-sized hole through the champion's torso.

It sagged, armor collapsing around emptiness.

Khandyl fought like wild moonlight—Moonrise Hook, Rising Howl, Lungpiercer—her every strike appearing from angles that made no rational sense. She cut a knee, rolled under a cleaver, and drove a blade up through an exposed seam.

The champion toppled.

"Two down," she said, panting.

"Two to go," Froster answered.

Elowen lifted her staff.

Green life-aura burst outward, catching five undead in a radius. Vines of light wrapped arms and legs, tightening like roots around intruding stone.

Beside her, Aafje launched a storm of shadow-bolts that tore chunks from Osiri armor, shredding shoulders, ripping jaws free.

"You take the left!" Elowen shouted.

"Already on it!"

Aafje swept her hand upward. A vertical crescent of black light rose from the floor like a scythe, nearly cutting a champion in half.

The two remaining champions charged their line.

Elowen slammed her staff down.

"Nahliva—Bloom of the Life-Guard!"

Luminous vines erupted, cushioning one blow, flinging the attacker backward.

The other raised his sword—

—and froze as the air around him bent.

Kellyn's hum knotted the space around his weapon. Serithyl appeared at his back and finished the job.

The necromancer moved.

Nine feet of jackal-headed malice, draped in black and gold.

Witmar's staff rested against the dais.

He lifted his own staff, bone-glyphs crawling.

"Ankhotep."

The stone ruptured.

Hands of bone and sandstone erupted from the floor— grabbing Kellyn's legs, Froster's arms, Aafje's torso, Khandyl's ankle. Champions surged in to exploit the opening.

Kellyn wrenched free with a snarl.

Aafje sliced her restraints with jagged shadow.

Froster burned his away with a flare of blade-fire.

Khandyl twisted, severing hers with a single silver arc.

It cost them beats.

That was enough.

The necromancer's gaze locked on Harvey.

"Harvey Oakenstride," he hissed, gold teeth gleaming. "I killed your brother. Now you will kneel."

Harvey turned toward him.

His eyes burned green.

"You're already dead," he said quietly.

He charged.

Three undead guards sprang between them.

Harvey didn't slow.

Kuldemaekr traced a brutal arc. The guards ceased to exist—no bodies, no bones, just dust blown aside.

The necromancer's eyes widened.

"A Green Knight cannot—"

Harvey slammed into him shoulder-first, the impact cracking bone.

"You killed my brother," Harvey said.

The necromancer snarled. "He was weak."

Harvey's grip tightened.

"You shouldn't have said that."

He drove forward, breaking the staff with a twist of his torso. Splinters of cursed wood flew.

Harvey's left hand closed around the necromancer's throat, lifting his nine-foot frame off the ground. With his right, he drove Kuldemaekr into the arch-mage's chest.

Green light exploded.

The necromancer screamed—a long, tearing sound that dissolved into static halfway through as his body disintegrated into black dust, then into nothing at all.

Harvey stood over the spot, chest heaving, blade still glowing.

Behind him, Amenemapet watched.

And smiled.

"Magnificent," the arch-lich whispered. "You mortals and your grief. Such perfect fuel."

He opened the Necrodemicon.

Pages flapped as if caught in a wind that wasn't there. Symbols leapt from line to line, rearranging themselves in mid-air. Light and darkness warped around the book.

Blue fire blazed in his skull.

He spread his arms.

The walls obeyed.

Hieroglyphs peeled off the stone like molten gold, hovering. Carved priests stepped out of murals, half-shadow, half-flesh. Animal-headed figures dragged themselves free of bas-relief frames, eyes lighting with sick joy.

"KILL THEM ALL," Amenemapet commanded.

The crypt shook as if something colossal shifted in its sleep far below.

Kellyn shouted, "HARVEY—NOW!"

Harvey sprinted toward the dais, grinding through skeletal ranks. Dust and ash blew around him in clouds. Kuldemaekr blazed emerald, answering something in the very stone.

Amenemapet raised his left hand.

"KHERI-TEM—"

A beam of death magic slammed into Harvey's chest, hurling him into a column. Stone cracked, fragments raining down.

For a second, he didn't move.

Then green light surged around him, flaring brighter.

Harvey pushed himself upright.

Every joint screamed. His ribs felt like broken glass.

"You killed my brother," he said again.

He charged.

The impact when he hit Amenemapet's dais sounded like thunder trapped underground.

Kellyn plunged after him, carving through spectral priests as she ran.

Seris and the Sylph streaked like knives of wind, tearing gaps in the defensive line.

Aafje hurled shadow lances into the lich's back.

Elowen sent tremors of raw life-force into the floor, making undead stagger as roots-that-weren't roiled under the stone.

Froster and Khandyl carved a path of dust and flame.

Harvey reached the base of the throne.

Kuldemaekr rose.

Amenemapet caught the blade on his scepter. Heliolite met necromantic sun-metal, sparks spraying in emerald and blue.

"You are nothing," the Pharaoh hissed. "No god, no birthright, no—"

Kellyn arrived.

Her blade came down in a Pillar Line—the geometry of Final Edict without the full weight of its earlier form, riding the echo still vibrating through the hall.

Their strikes crossed.

Harvey's strength.
Kellyn's command.
Every grief, every test, every choice that had bled them to this point.

The scepter shattered.

Cracks raced along Amenemapet's ribs, up his spine, across his shoulders. Blue fire poured from the wounds.

For a heartbeat, he remained upright—arms flung wide, book still in one skeletal hand, skull thrown back.

"YOU THINK THIS IS DEATH?" he roared.

The Necrodemicon snapped shut on its own.

The shockwave blasted outward.

Every remaining undead collapsed in mid-motion, their forms disintegrating into ash that dissolved before it hit the floor.

Wall-carvings slipped back into stone. Hieroglyphs cooled and re-seated themselves like molten gold hardening.

Amenemapet's body could not hold.

It blew apart in a storm of bone chips and necrosolar flame, the blast shoving everyone back.

Harvey hit the tiles and slid. Kellyn was thrown to one knee, blade skittering away. The Sylph slammed into columns or rolled with the force. Aafje's robe flared and dimmed; Elowen's staff cracked and then steadied under her grip. Loka went flat, arms over his head, ears ringing.

Then—

Silence.

Dust hung in the air, glowing faintly blue.

Bits of bone and shredded black cloth lay scattered across the dais and down the steps.

The Necrodemicon landed with a heavy *thump* on the lowest stair, cover smoking, symbols slowly dimming.

Right beside it, something else fell.

Amenemapet's skull bounced once on the stone and rolled, rattling gently, until it came to rest against a fissure in the dais.

It was completely intact.

The golden crown sat crooked on its brow. Thin hairline cracks of light traced across the bone, but the structure held. Witchfire had vanished from the eye sockets—

—but as the dust slowly settled, a single faint spark glowed and then hid itself deep within.

No one was looking at it closely enough to see.

Kellyn pushed to her feet, ears still ringing.

"Loka," she rasped. "The book."

Harvey staggered upright and stooped to pick up the Necrodemicon. The leather burned cold under his fingers.

He turned, meeting Loka's eyes.

"For him," Harvey said.

He held it out.

Loka stepped forward on unsteady legs. For a second, his fingers hovered over the cover.

Every part of his scholarly brain screamed *danger*.

Every part of his heart whispered *Witmar*.

He took it.

The whispers pressed at his mind like a crowd against glass.

"This…" he breathed. "This is the real one."

Harvey nodded once.

"And this was his."

He retrieved Witmar's staff from where it had fallen amidst the battle and held it out as well.

Loka accepted it, throat too tight to speak.

Serithyl bent to gather Witmar's cloak and unseen boots with careful hands. She brushed dust from them, folded the cloak once, and laid both at Harvey's feet.

"These should leave with his blood," she said.

Harvey crouched and lifted his brother's body.

He did it the way he had carried injured comrades before—one arm under the legs, one supporting the back, careful of the head. Witmar weighed less than he remembered.

Kellyn turned toward the dais wall.

"Look," she said softly.

Behind the throne, stone had split open.

A tunnel yawned there now, lined with faintly glowing glyphs. At its end, humming like a held note, waited a Khem-Duat teleport platform—circles of light curling over its surface in familiar patterns.

The way forward.

The way out.

The crypt finally began to exhale.

As the last echoes of collapsing spells faded, Loka crouched near the scorched sigils where Amenemapet had stood. His pupils narrowed, focusing through the haze. He traced a fingertip over a fading mark.

Kellyn stepped up beside him, still limping. "Loka? Talk to me. What are you seeing?"

"These patterns…" he whispered. "They're not just Osiri. Ellendyl's work is woven through them."

Kellyn's pulse kicked.

"Ellendyl's?"

He nodded, wiping dust from a cluster of symbols.

"I've seen fragments like this in her early logs. Stuff she wrote before the Exodus codes were stable. Teleportation matrices—half-time, half-space. What Amenemapet was standing on wasn't just a throne dais. It was a *node*."

Kellyn's skin prickled.

"Are you saying he could—"

"Come and go," Loka said. "From anywhere in the network. And more than that—" He swallowed. "—he's been *recording* us. Every test. Every choice. Every fracture in who we are. A lich with a teleport nexus and a data pattern of a hundred races trying to reach the Necrodemicon? Ellendyl's notes warned about a construct like this."

Kellyn frowned. "Warned how?"

"That once it's fully awake," Loka said quietly, "you can't lie to it. You can't easily deceive it. It learns you as fast as you learn it." He looked back at the scattered bones, the intact skull against the dais, the faintly glowing pad. "We didn't just beat a tyrant of the past."

He closed the Necrodemicon gently, fingers lingering on the unstable glyphs.

"We just announced ourselves to a very patient problem."

Kellyn followed his gaze to the skull.

For a moment, she thought she saw a tiny blue spark flicker in one socket.

Then it was gone.

She tightened her grip on her sword.

"Then we'd better keep moving," she said. "Before the past decides to answer."

Harvey shifted Witmar's weight in his arms.

The Anari turned toward the Khem-Duat pad—their dead, their book, their wounds, and their very persistent future.

Behind them, in the quiet, Amenemapet's skull lay unbroken on the cracked stone.

Waiting.

Chapter 46 - Descent into the Khem-Duat

Planet: Vaelthara
Location: Beneath the Pyramid of Amenemapet
BV 24

"Gold is fine, silver is fair, but stone—stone is loyal."
— *Morgra Deepcleft (Gravhal)*

The last of Amenemapet's wards flickered and died.

A thin crack of darkness appeared along the stone seam, widening as the ancient door groaned aside. Dust sifted down like ash, stirred by the cold exhale of the tunnel beyond.

Kellyn felt the harmonic shift before anyone spoke.

Not a sound—
but a deep vibration in the bones of the stone,
as if something beneath the world had rolled over in its sleep.

She tightened her grip on her sword and stepped to the threshold, peering down into the stairwell that spiraled into black.

"Smells wrong," Harvey muttered behind her, settling one hand on Kuldemaekr's hilt. "Metal and old blood."

"It's worse than that," Seris said quietly. "The air down there hasn't moved in centuries."

Elowen lifted a small sphere of life-light. Green radiance blossomed in her palm and spilled down over the first few steps.

The glow hesitated—actually hesitated—at the edge of the deeper dark, as though reluctant to go farther.

Khandyl drew in a slow breath through her nose, Wolf-clan instincts sharpening her gaze. "Something's waiting below. Not alive. Just… watching."

Serithyl Dawnstep and Vaelinnae Windpetal exchanged a glance. Their Windveil cloaks stirred in faint, nervous spirals that had nothing to do with air currents.

Kellyn glanced back one more time toward the fading light of the crypt above.

The others were watching her.
Harvey with Witmar's weight still in his arms.
Loka with the Necrodemicon and Witmar's staff slung at his back.
Aafje's hand poised near shadow, Froster's fingers near his baton, Elowen's light trembling in her palm.

"We didn't come all this way to fear shadows," Kellyn murmured.

Then, louder:

"Quiet footing. Fast if we must. The Osiri built the upper Duat to funnel intruders—they'll hear us if we stomp around like Gravhal on a feast day."

A few grim smiles.

The ten of them crossed the threshold.

The stone seemed to breathe around them, the low hum deepening as they descended. Each step felt fractionally heavier, as if the Khem-Duat were weighing their presence.

The stairwell spilled into a broad gallery carved in stark Osiri geometry: rigid lines, knife-straight angles, walls inked in endless processions of gods and jackal-headed warriors. Thick dust blanketed the floor—untouched, undisturbed.

Kellyn raised a hand.

The party froze.

At first it was only an echo—
a snatch of harsh consonants in the Osiri tongue, warped by sloped passages and old stone. A voice answering another somewhere beyond the nearest intersection.

"Patrol," Froster muttered. "Definitely patrol."

Then came the second sound:

Tik-tik-tik-tik-tik.

Dry, crystalline clicking. Like glass beetle legs racing across polished stone in perfect, unnatural rhythm.

Seris's breath caught. "Scarab ward-clusters. They're awake."

Vaelinnae's eyes narrowed, gaze gone distant. "Wind recoils from them," she whispered. "That means they're close."

Elowen pinched her hand, dimming the life-light to a faint ember. Their silhouettes blurred into deeper shadow.

"They'll box us if we linger," Khandyl said, already angling toward the corridor with the most curves. "Osiri think in straight lines. We break their symmetry."

Kellyn scanned the gallery.

Four exits.

Three were clean, symmetrical, chiseled to Osiri perfection.

The fourth—on the left—bore crooked tool marks and hairline fractures, as if the stone itself had resisted being carved.

"Left," she decided. "Move."

They slipped into the uneven passage. The scarab clicks faded back along the main gallery…

… but the hum in the rock grew stronger.

The crooked corridor emptied into a five-walled chamber: four Osiri arches, and a fifth wall that felt… wrong.

Kellyn slowed.

The Osiri had tried to carve it—she could see the shallow, hesitant chisel marks—but they'd never finished. Beneath their half-hearted work, older lines clawed their way through.

Spirals cut so deep they warped the stone. Looping horns and knotwork that refused to be covered. The patterns seemed to twist slightly if she stared too long, like they lived in angles her eyes weren't meant to track.

Vaelinnae exhaled sharply. "This carving dances wrong. The wind won't touch it."

Serithyl stepped closer, pupils pin-pricks. "This place is too old for Osiri script. Too deep for their gods."

Froster brushed his gloved fingers over one of the deepest gouges. "These cuts… this isn't mason work. It's more like something forced its way *out*."

"Minos," Kellyn said softly.

The room felt colder the moment she spoke the name.

Loka, who had been quiet, took a single step closer to the spirals. The necromantic current around him—usually tight and disciplined—thrummed, like a plucked wire that wouldn't stop vibrating.

"Loka?" Kellyn asked. "What do you feel?"

"It's… singing," he whispered. "Low. Calling. Like it recognizes me."

"Then step back," Harvey said sharply. "Nothing down here calls you for a good reason."

But Loka's hand was already rising.

It hovered a breath from the spirals—

The wall caught fire.

Red-gold light raced along the grooves, flaring outward. Horns unwound, shapes distended. Stone rippled like the surface of a disturbed pond.

Elowen's life-light shrank back to a narrow thread, repelled.

Khandyl cursed, shoving Loka behind her, shield snapping up. Sylph instincts flared across the others.

Serithyl's blade came free with a hiss of air.
Vaelinnae's arrow rose, her stance a perfect windline spiral.
Harvey's sword rang from its sheath.
Aafje's shadows thickened at her shoulders like coiling smoke.

The wall pulsed once—
twice—

Then split.

A seam opened from floor to ceiling, revealing not dark stone, but whirling red-gold light—as if the labyrinth continued into angles that didn't belong to this world.

Cold, iron-scented air blasted out, smelling of old blood and sealed metal.

"That isn't Duat," Seris breathed. "That's *beneath* the Duat."

"It's keyed to death magic," Loka said, stunned. "Keyed to… what I've become."

"Then close it," Harvey barked.

The spirals answered by flaring brighter.

The floor tilted.

Gravity lurched sideways. Kellyn's boots stayed on the stone—but her balance slipped, as if the corridor had rotated 90 degrees in an instant.

Loka slid toward the opening, dragged by a force that had nothing to do with mass.

Khandyl lunged, grabbing his forearm, feet skidding.

Serithyl moved without thinking, catching Khandyl's other arm to anchor her.

Vaelinnae pivoted to brace them—

—but she was closest to the spirals.

The pull hooked her cloak first.

"NO!" Kellyn shouted.

Harvey grabbed Kellyn around the waist, hauling her back before the sideways gravity could take her too.

The Minos-door's pull intensified.

Loka, Khandyl, and Vaelinnae were yanked off their footing—
drawn sideways into the seam—
red-gold light swallowing them whole.

Vaelinnae's outstretched hand vanished last, fingers swept away like a leaf torn sideways by a gale.

SNAP.

The spirals slammed shut.

Light died.

The wall was stone again. Seamless. Cold. Unmoved.

Dust drifted lazily through the air where three people had stood.

"No…" Kellyn slammed her fist into the stone. Pain spiked up her arm. She didn't stop. "No, no—no."

Serithyl stood frozen, chest heaving, eyes fixed on the wall as if it had stolen her breath and refused to give it back.

"Vaelinnae…" she whispered. "Thrown into the storm…"

Seris pressed her palm flat against the sealed seam, eyes closing for a heartbeat. "They're alive. I feel something. But far. Too far."

Elowen knelt, pressing both hands to the floor, fingers splayed.

A thin tremor passed through her.

"I can still sense Loka's resonance," she said. "Alive. But very deep. Deeper than the Duat. In something older. Something that doesn't like being named."

Behind them, the scarab clicks echoed faintly from the gallery, sharper now.

Tik-tik-tik.

Closer.

Harvey straightened, jaw tight. "We can't be standing in an Osiri shrine when those beetles round the corner."

Kellyn rested her forehead against the stone for a single, tight breath.

Hold on. We're coming.

She turned.

"We are not leaving them there," she said. "We find another way in. Or another way *down*. But first we stay alive long enough to try."

"Kellyn," Froster called softly from one of the side arches. "You'll want to see this."

He stood at the threshold of another corridor. The stone here was different—clean fractures, straight cuts, tool marks that bit deep and true.

Gravhal work.

And recent.

Serithyl joined him, nostrils flaring. "Wind moves through this one," she said. "There's an opening deeper in. It breathes."

The scarab clicks sharpened, echoing off stone from the main gallery.

Kellyn lifted her sword in one hand, gestured with the other.

"Move."

They slipped into the Dwarven-cut passage just as Osiri boots pounded into the five-walled chamber behind them.

As they vanished into the deeper dark, the hum in the stone followed—
steady, patient, pulsing like the heartbeat of something ancient and newly aware.

Chapter 47 - The Primordial Maze

Planet: Vaelthara
Location: Khem-Duat – Somewhere between Amenemapet's
Crypt & Kheu-Duat
BV 24

"Improvisation is just long-term planning done very quickly."
— *Pipwin Jaxle (Nimvrel)*

The world snapped back into shape with a violent lurch.

Stone hammered against Loka's palms as he hit the floor, red-gold light collapsing behind him like a dying pulse. The air that greeted them was thin, motionless, and old — older than the Duat above, older than Osiri empirework — and carried a copper tang like the aftertaste of lightning over wet iron.

Khandyl landed in a half-crouch beside him, shield raised, teeth bared in Wolf instinct.
Vaelinnae Windpetal rolled to her feet, twisting mid-movement, bow half-drawn before she registered they were alone.

The chamber breathed.

Faint pulses of labyrinthine glow rippled along the walls — spirals, horns, and interlocked curves carved so deep that the stone looked stretched around them rather than chiseled. Every surface was geometric recursion: no angles, only sweeping arcs that gave the unsettling sense that the room was inhaling and exhaling in a slow, alien rhythm.

Loka pushed upright, eyes wide.

"This isn't Duat."

"No," Khandyl said, voice controlled but tight. "It's below it. And we need to find a way back before those Osiri above decide to follow the noise."

Vaelinnae drifted to the nearest spiral. She didn't touch it — Sylph intuition never did — but she studied it as though listening to a silent instrument.

"This pattern… it's moving. Not enough to see. Just enough to confuse the eye. This place wasn't quarried."
She swallowed.
"It grew."

Loka felt the tug before he registered it — the same necromantic undertow he'd sensed before the spirals swallowed them. It wasn't hostile. It was curious.

"It's answering death resonance," he breathed. "Harmonizing with it. Like a tuning fork."

Khandyl shot him a razor-sharp look.
"Which means it's answering you. Stay near us, Loka. And do not touch anything that looks older than the first sunrise."

A low tremor answered her — not through air, but stone.

A heartbeat.

Slow. Distant. Massive.

The spirals shifted. Not visibly — but Loka felt the patterns realign, like a lock clicking toward its key. Vaelinnae's ears twitched sharply. She drew an arrow, letting the bow's weight settle into the bones of her wrist.

"We're not alone."

Khandyl exhaled, tension sharpening to readiness.
"This place is reacting to something. Maybe to you. Maybe to us. Either way — pick a direction and move before it chooses one for us."

Loka closed his eyes.

Threads of resonance brushed through him — ancient, brittle, forged in pressure and time.
Death-magic threads, yes, but braided with something older: the quiet patience of stone that has survived the rise and failure of civilizations.

A single direction drew strongest.

"This way," he said, pointing deeper.

Khandyl muttered a Wolf prayer under her breath, but followed. Vaelinnae fell into silent stride behind them, arrow still nocked.

The corridors refused straight lines. Every step curved. Every view bent. Their footsteps echoed with strange delay — at times like someone walked behind them, at times like echoes came from ahead.

Vaelinnae whispered, "I do not like this wind. It sneaks sideways."

The air cooled further as they entered a hall carved in spirals that seemed to descend impossibly inward, like staring down the throat of a living thing.

Loka laid a hand near — not on — one of the spirals.
"This isn't symbolic. It's functional. It channels—"

The floor shuddered.

A low resonant pulse boomed through the stone, deep as a god knocking on the underside of the world.

Khandyl seized Loka's arm, hauling him back.
"That was an answer. From something big."

Vaelinnae's bowstring tightened.
"Wind flees the center. Something at the heart is breathing. Waking."

Loka's voice was tight, but certain.
"The center is where the resonance originates. That's where the Minos buried their power."

"That's where it'll kill us," Khandyl bit back.

The second pulse hit harder. Dust drifted from ceiling fissures. The walls flexed — not physically, but perceptually — compressing the chamber, squeezing breath from their lungs.

"We're cursed down here," Khandyl muttered. "Keep moving."

The architecture changed as they pressed deeper — spirals rising higher, knotwork tightening, the geometry sharpening into horns and angled labyrinth glyphs. The farther they went, the more the corridors resembled a throat narrowing toward its core.

Loka slowed at the mouth of a wide chamber ahead.
A red-gold radiance pulsed from somewhere unseen.
The resonance was louder — a vibration in bone and teeth, dense with age.

Khandyl flung her arm across their path to halt them.
"If this is a creature's den—"

"It's not," Loka whispered.
"It's a forge."

They stepped into a vast circular chamber, carved in descending rings. Spiraled bands sank tier by tier toward a sunken basin at the center — as though the maze's arteries led here.

The air shimmered, heatless and bright. Spiral lines glowed faintly along the stone, raw geometry threading through the walls like veins.

Khandyl's voice shook despite herself.
"What in all the gods' graves… is this?"

Loka descended two careful steps. The glow intensified around him, responding to his presence like a drawn breath.

"It's listening," he murmured.
"It recognizes necromancy. Or life stolen from death."

"That doesn't mean you go closer," Khandyl barked.

But the forge had its own will.

The moment Loka neared the basin, a deep thrum rattled the chamber.

The spirals ignited.
Stone cracked.
Light raced through the labyrinth lines like blood pumped hard after a long sleep.

Vaelinnae's bow creaked under her grip.
"Something is waking."

The basin's runes erupted.

Stone in its heart began to move — not crumble, not melt —
but rise.
Lifted by the labyrinth itself.

Fourteen feet of granite and red-gold glow took shape:
A broad torso, thick arms like carved pillars, digitigrade legs
forged for war, and a bull-skull helm fused to its shoulders.

A Minos titan.

Its labyrinth-etched body pulsed with the spirals from the
walls, as though the entire maze exhaled into it.

The first sound it made was not a voice —
but a roar of subterranean resonance that knocked all three of
them stumbling.

Khandyl tore Loka back by his collar, shield raised, stance
braced.

"Run."

Then the titan's stone eyes opened.

Red-gold light burned in their depths — old, unblinking,
aware.

And the maze itself shuddered in answer, spirals brightening,
whispering through the stone as if welcoming back an ancient
king.

Chapter 48 - Through the Gravhal Cut

Planet: Vael'thara
Location: The Khem-Duat — Southern Artery
Chronometric Stamp: BV 24.051

"Trust the river—it remembers every predator that swims it."
— *Zsathrek Scale-Mender (Sza'thir)*

The passage narrowed so tightly that the group had to fall into single file. The walls were different here—each strike of the chisel straighter and deeper than Osiri geometry ever allowed.

Kellyn brushed her fingertips across the stone as she led. The wall vibrated faintly beneath her touch—an old Gravhal signature, stone-magic embedded in every groove. The pitch and pulse of it reminded her of her training halls: how stone answered Dominion when the practitioner's posture was perfect.

"Gravhal," Froster said behind her, voice low. His winter-bright gaze tracked the scoring like a hunter decoding tracks. "They leave a heat-burned edge when they cut. These are fresh. A few months at most."

Aafje's Twilight Robe shimmered in faint motes as she leaned close, reading the cuts through arcane lens. "They shouldn't be under Osiri dominion. Not this deep. Not this far east."

Harvey—broad shouldered, dark bronze skin dusted with sand, jaw set in that familiar Green Knight grimness—

answered without slowing his heavy, measured stride. "They go where the stone calls. Gravhal don't care about borders. They listen to pressure, fault lines, bedrock memory."

A faint breath of air slid along Kellyn's cheek.

Her posture straightened instantly—Pillar reflex.
Air movement this deep was impossible unless something cavernous yawned open ahead.

Serithyl Dawnstep, hair lifting in wind that wasn't there, tilted her head. Sylph senses flashed through her wide gray-silver eyes.
"There's an opening. Large. Either natural… or carved with purpose."

Kellyn gave a short nod, though anxiety knotted between her ribs.
"We keep moving. If the Osiri patrol finds the spiral chamber, we lose every advantage we have."

The passage angled sharply downward. Loose gravel skittered under boots.

Harvey's hand touched Kellyn's elbow. Not a romantic gesture—never that—but protective instinct honed by war and near death.
"Downward grade. Gravhal shaping. They always spiral down to strike seams."

Seris pressed her palm flat to the wall. Whisper-vines wound around her wrist, sensing the stone through her Song.
"There's thinning beneath us. A natural fault… or a breach."

Another minute of descent—slow, breath counting, boots careful—

—and then the passage dropped them onto a stone lip overlooking a world far larger than anything the Khem-Duat maps dared suggest.

A massive cavern opened below.

A gulf of blackness swallowed their torchlight. Broken platforms jutted from the stone walls—collapsed Gravhal scaffolding and rusted lift mechanisms twisted into dead shapes.
At the bottom, an underground river pulsed with faint bioluminescence—blue drifting into green, with veins of ghost-white wending like starlight trapped underwater.

Serithyl inhaled, voice barely a whisper.
"The Deepwell Hollows. An old Sylph myth speaks of these places, where stone remembers its first shaping."

Elowen held up a small bloom of life-light. The glow reached only the ledge, then died against the cavern's immensity.

"This chamber spans hundreds of strides," she said softly. "Maybe thousands. The Khem-Duat record has nothing like this."

Aafje knelt, fingertips gliding over thick bronze-iron bands embedded in the floor—sigils hammered deep into the stone. "Gravhal earthbind seals. Whatever was kept here… it was meant to remain sealed."

Harvey's brow tightened, voice rough.
"And whatever they bound—broke out."

Froster scanned the darkness, his stance angled, his weight on the balls of his feet in Wolf-readiness.
"Osiri won't chase us over uneven stone. Too unpredictable. Good. That buys us time."

Kellyn swallowed. Memory stabbed fresh: Loka's eyes, shocked and terrified as the spirals devoured him. Vaelinnae's hand disappearing into red-gold light.

Her heart twisted.

"We go down," she said. "There's a spiral ramp on the right. Stonecut shape. Gravhal always leave one descent coil for engineers."

Harvey raised a brow at her certainty, his voice low. "You're sure?"

Kellyn didn't look back.
"No. But the harmonic trail is stronger here. The same resonance that swallowed them lies down there."

They descended.

The ramp circled the cavern, curving widely. Gravel and rubble tumbled from their steps and vanished into the glowing current far below.

Even the Sylph trod carefully—steps placed heel-to-ball, shoulders angled to maintain balance on treacherous stone.

Halfway down, a deep boom shook the cavern.

Not explosive.
Resonant.

A pulse.

Dust cascaded from fissures overhead.

Serithyl went still, tension locking her posture. "That sounded wrong."

"Not Osiri, not machinery," Aafje murmured. "Something deeper. Something old."

Kellyn closed her eyes, fingers tightening on Witmar's staff. The stone hummed in answer, soft and ominous.

"It came from beneath the river. Far beneath."

Harvey and Froster exchanged looks—grim, silent, warrior-to-warrior acknowledgment.

"Whatever woke down there," Froster said, jaw clenched, "wasn't small."

At the base of the cavern, their boots scraped over stone grit and tangled Gravhal debris. The glowing river wound through fractured platforms and toppled machines like a captured aurora vein.

On the far side, faint orange light burned within an archway carved into the stone—no Osiri glyph lines. This was Gravhal: sharp block scripts, layered depth runes, and pressure-shaped fault seals.

Kellyn's fingers trembled as she gripped her staff tighter.

"It's tied to the Minos resonance. Same pattern that took them. Which means we're close… either to the path they fell through or to what's powering it."

Another tremor rose from the deep.
Dust rained from above in delicate curtains.

Serithyl's voice cracked.
"If she breathes, my sister will find wind. Vaelinnae always finds wind."

Harvey rested a heavy hand on Serithyl's shoulder, his voice gentler than his battle tone ever was.
"She's tougher than any of us. She'll fight. And Loka… is a survivor. He won't fold down there."

Kellyn wished she believed it as fiercely as she once had.
Guilt scraped through her like sand under armor.
Loka shouldn't have been that close to the spirals.
Vaelinnae shouldn't have been nearest the wall.

Her mistake. Her burden.

At the archway, the harmonic hum in Witmar's staff surged through her grip—stronger, sharper, like the low rumble of distant horns.

"We're near the Minos core," she said. "Whatever opened that spiral doorway is deeper and active."

One breath.
One step.

They crossed into the archway—

—and the light of the cavern died behind them.

Into the deeper dark they went.

Chapter 49 - The Soul-Furnace Awakens

Planet: Vael'thara
Location: Beneath the Great Desert, somewhere within the Great Maze
Chronometric Stamp: BV 24

The Minos titan tore itself from the basin like a mountain shrugging off sleep.

Stone ground against stone as colossal limbs unfurled—spiraled musculature carved as if the rock had grown those shapes rather than being forced into them.

Red-gold light pulsed through seams in the stone, threaded like molten lifeblood beneath its bull-shaped head and wide-planed shoulders.

Each movement sent tremors through the chamber.
Dust drifted from the ceiling in long, slow ribbons.

Loka staggered back until his spine pressed against the spiraled wall, breath sharp and panicked. His necromancer's senses rang like struck bronze.
"It heard me," he whispered. "It recognized my magic."

Khandyl pulled him behind her, shield rising in an instinctive Wolf-guard. Her stance widened, feet already finding kill line geometry.

"No. It recognized your blood," she growled. "Whatever your future line fell into, whatever experiments or curses you carry—this place was built to answer it."

Vaelinnae Windpetal slid along the titan's flank, moving with Sylph's drifting cadence—light, angled, breath measured. Her bow was drawn, yet her fingers shook on the string. "Wind recoils from it," she murmured. "When wind refuses—its spirit is old. Not a guardian. A hunger."

The titan lowered its head, nostrils flaring.
The sound was like boulders grinding underwater—deep, slow, ancient thought waking.

If stone could stare, it stared.

Its eyes weren't eyes at all—just twin spirals of layered glow, tightening inward as they fixed on the trio.

"It's looking straight at us," Loka said, heart shaking.

Khandyl didn't blink.
"No. It's looking at you."

The titan stepped forward.

Spiral runes ignited beneath its feet—red-gold circles rippling outward with every footfall.

Vaelinnae released her arrow, not to kill—Sylph never wasted a shot they hadn't read the wind for—but to shock, to redirect attention.

The shaft struck stone and bounced away with a tinny clack.

The titan paused.

Turned.

Its internal glow dimmed—evaluating, tasting threat or insignificance.

"Bad idea," Khandyl muttered out of the corner of her mouth.

"Worse idea," Vaelinnae whispered back, silver eyes steady, "is letting it think we're prey."

Then—
A deeper pulse.

Not from the titan.
From beneath it.

A resonant tremor rolled up through the floor, as if something enormous were knocking on the underside of the world.

Loka swallowed hard. "Something else is waking. The Soul-Furnace didn't just stir the titan. It activated whatever sleeps below."

Khandyl grabbed his cloak and forced him toward the only exit tunnel. Her scarred knuckles were white, her grip iron. "Then we move. Now."

The titan roared.

But no breath moved.
No sound carried through air.

The roar traveled through stone—vibrating marrow, teeth, shields, and nerve endings.

Dust poured from above in choking curtains.

Vaelinnae broke into motion—a flicker of wind-spun footwork, steps cutting tight arcs, drawing the titan's spiral-eyes off the others.
"Go!" she yelled. "Its gaze follows movement! I'll keep it confused!"

"Not alone you won't." Khandyl's voice was a knife's edge.

The titan's arm swung.
Five colossal stone fingers, each as thick as Khandyl's forearm, carved a semicircle of death.

Vaelinnae slid beneath it—perfect Sylph drop-angle—but the shockwave of displaced force hit her like a wall.
She slammed into a spiral pillar and fell to her knees. Her bow clattered across the floor, sliding out of reach.

"Vaelinnae!"

Loka lunged—but Khandyl hauled him backward again.

"You go that direction, you die," she snapped.

"She needs help—!"

"She needs us alive," Khandyl bit back. "We pull her out one heartbeat at a time, not in a suicide dash."

The titan lumbered toward the fallen Sylph.
Its shoulders cracked open with glowing fissures, and spirals along its torso twisted like veins carrying magma.

Vaelinnae forced herself up, but pain shot through her leg; it buckled again.
"Go—" she gasped. "Lead it away!"

Loka stepped forward despite Khandyl's braced stance and shield blocking him.
"It listens to necromancy. It reacted to me. So maybe—"

"Loka, don't—"

"—maybe I can redirect it."

No spells.
No commands.

He simply raised both hands—open, fingers spread—like a necromancer greeting a Shade at the edge of its grave.

His aura flickered.

Thin threads of shadow-resonance seeped from his pores—barely visible, but alive.

The titan froze mid-stride.

Its glow intensified.
Spiral whorls in its limbs contracted; chest-carvings constricted like lungs bracing to breathe.

Vaelinnae stared, stunned.
"You have its attention."

"Good," Loka said—though terror quavered behind the word.

"Good," Khandyl repeated, voice dry as bone, "is not the word I'd pick."

The titan bent at the knee.
It lowered its head toward Loka as if scenting him across millennia—like a beast recognizing distant kin.

Loka felt something brush his mind:
Not speech.
Not language.

Recognition.
Old as death, cold as stone.

A tether.

Not dominance.

More like… inheritance.

"The Minos necromancers practiced the same discipline I do," Loka whispered. "This forge was theirs. The titan is keyed to their bloodlines. To mine."

Khandyl's eyes widened. "If you try to control it, you'll die."

"I'm not trying to control it."

He inhaled, his pulse sharp.

"I'm trying to mislead it."

He sent a thin pulse of necromantic resonance outward—just enough to create a phantom signal, tugging toward the opposite spiraled wall.

The titan jerked.

It turned sharply toward the direction Loka indicated, as though newly awakened resonance flared from that point instead.

"Move," Khandyl hissed.

Vaelinnae limped toward them, half-supported by Khandyl's arm, teeth bared in pain.

"Don't stop. It'll shake off the confusion."

They sprinted for the tunnel entrance—

Boots pounding spiraled floor, breath harsh, shoulders

brushing cold stone as they squeezed through the narrow mouth.

Behind them, the titan twisted to re-acquire them.
Stone scraped, spirals lit, the roar-through-stone surged again.

At the tunnel's threshold, Loka looked back.

The titan stood at the heart of the Soul-Furnace—
Spirals glowing brighter beneath its feet.
Veins of light pulsed like arteries.

A throne without a throne.
A king without a crown.
But the posture said everything.

This was not a guardian.

This was royalty awakened.

And the labyrinth shook as though greeting its sovereign.

"Another one is waking," Loka whispered—voice small against the enormity.

Khandyl shoved him harder into the passage. "Then we outrun the coronation."

They plunged into the twisting dark as the titan's heavy steps shook the forge behind them—
and the Soul-Furnace roared to life for the first time in thousands of years.

Chapter 50 - The Osiri Containment Patrol

Planet: Vael'thara
Location: Khem-Duat near the Great Labyrinth
BV 24

Far above the spiral chamber that had swallowed Loka, the listening chamber awoke violently.

The scarab wards—glass-bodied constructs threaded with gold filaments—shuddered as they clung to the walls and ceiling. Their legs clicked in rapid, panicked rhythms against polished granite.

Blue runes beneath their mounting discs flickered erratically—then flared in a single, shared pulse.

The ward tone deepened, vibrating through the hall like a subterranean heartbeat.

The listening-priest halted mid-stride. His breath turned to ice.

He clutched a ceremonial staff carved with Anubis-sigils, its obsidian jackal-head gleaming at the crown.

A faint light crawled beneath the floor tiles—then died, as if unwilling to touch what stirred below.

The priest whispered, voice gone papery and thin:

"…No. Not again."

A war-mage strode into the chamber—robes edged in red from desert dye, jackal helm polished to a mirror-black sheen. Irritation sharpened every word.

"What now? The wards have screamed all week. The Duat shifts. It is nothing."

The priest jabbed a trembling finger at the scarab clusters, which were now rattling like bones in a jar.

"This is not tremor. This is resonance. The old kind. The forbidden kind."

The mage's annoyance vanished like breath on frost.

"You mean—"

"Yes."

The priest's jaw clenched. "A labyrinth pulse. From beneath the sealed levels."

A glass scarab cracked—collapsing into powder.

Another followed.

Scarabs only shattered when exposed to ancient power older than the Duat.

The mage reacted instantly.

"Arm the containment squad. All of them. Now."

Within moments, eight Osiri guards assembled—towering nine-foot soldiers in overlapping plates of desert-black steel. Their blades—long, crescent-shaped khopesh forged with solar rites—gleamed with a faint heat, as though hungry.

The war-mage forced power into the listening ward, seeking clarity.

The runes shrieked instead—patterns warping into spirals that echoed the geometry of the Dead Empire, unseen for centuries.

The priest swallowed hard. "Minos awakening."

All eight guards stiffened.

Every Osiri city knew the warnings—whispered over cups of spiced ash-wine.

Caverns where spirals birthed horned giants.

Forges that sang to necromancers.

Labyrinths that devoured entire regiments, leaving no bones.

Myths.

Until this moment.

"Form ranks," the mage commanded. His voice was harder than the steel in his fist.

"Eyes sharp. Irons ready. If the labyrinth is bleeding into the lower Duat, we hold it there."

The guards exchanged looks.

They knew "hold" really meant **die**.

The patrol advanced down the access corridor.

With each dozen paces, another scarab ward shattered behind them, spewing powder and charged dust that hissed along the floor.

The air thickened.

Static crawled over armor plates.

The stone felt like it was bracing against impact.

One guard drifted close to the priest, whispering, "Why here? Why now?"

The priest did not look at him. His eyes were fixed ahead, unreadable.

"Because someone opened a door that remembers our blood."

They reached the spiral-seam—the exact threshold Loka had triggered.

The stone still held a faint internal glow, red-gold like dried blood reflecting torchlight. The war-mage crouched, brushing gauntleted fingertips along the seam.

"These lines… Osiri geometry sits atop something older. These spirals weren't carved by us."

"They were grown," the priest murmured. "Shaped by Minos rites and reinforced with necromancer latticework."

He spoke a low sun-charm, palm against stone.

The seam did not answer him.

It rejected his voice.

"Only chosen blood opens this path," he said.

"Then whoever passed through carries Minos necromancer lineage," the mage muttered. "That explains the resonance."

Another tremor rolled through the walls—harder this time.

The spirals in the stone twisted like serpents waking beneath the sand.

Somewhere ahead, a roar shook the corridor.

It was too deep to be a beast's throat and too vast to belong to anything with lungs.

One guard stumbled back, armor grinding against the wall.

"What—what was that?"

The priest spoke softly, as if admitting guilt.

"A titan. One of the primordial Minos. Stone-born. War-bound."

The war-mage rose straight and cold.

"Into the labyrinth. If it reaches the upper Duat before command is warned, our lower city will be erased."

A guard hesitated.

"Entering Minos territory is forbidden… even to us. The traps—"

"This is not a council debate," the mage snapped. "This is burial protocol. We stall the titan or die proving our worth."

Fear hardened the air.

Obedience followed.

They stepped through the spiraled break.

The temperature plunged immediately—an abrupt silence and cold that felt like stepping into a tomb filled with ritual memory.

The labyrinthine corridor was angled and curving, every stone etched with interlocking spirals. The floor formed concentric rings, resonant geometry pulling everything downward.

The next tremor nearly threw them off their feet.

Then they saw it.

A colossal silhouette at the bend of the spiral hall.

Fourteen feet tall.

Horn-crowned head.

Red-gold light pulsing through spiraled seams.

Stone flesh cracking as it flexed, each movement heavy enough to warp the air.

The Minos titan turned.

Its eyes—those twin spirals of molten depth—locked onto them.

For a heartbeat, no one breathed.

The war-mage whispered, almost reverently:

"If the gods are kind… our deaths will be quick."

The titan roared.

The stone itself roared back.

And the labyrinth trembled in answer.

Chapter 51 – Predator in the Maze

Planet: Vael'thara
Location: Khem-Duat, somewhere near the Great Labyrinth
Chronometric Stamp: BV 24

The tunnel swallowed them whole.

Sound chased them first—a seismic roar rolling down the spiraled passages like a collapsing mountain.

It rattled teeth, shook lungs, and dislodged dust in long gray veils.

The walls themselves pulsed, spirals beating like a second heart.

Khandyl ran point, one arm locked around Vaelinnae's waist, half-carrying the Sylph's weight. Sweat streaked the Wolf-clan warrior's temples, and her breath came in short, disciplined bursts.

"Keep moving," she growled. "Slow feet get eaten."

"It doesn't eat," Vaelinnae hissed, her teeth clenched. Pain spasmed in her leg, but she kept her bow hand free. "It crushes."

"That's not remotely an improvement."

Behind them, Loka stayed close, glancing over his shoulder every few strides, his pallor stark against the dust. He could almost feel the titan's attention on his skin—like static on fur.

"Step lighter," he gasped. "It's following my resonance. Every pulse I give off—necromancy, breath, fear—resonates with it."

"Then shut the resonance off," Khandyl snapped.

"I don't know how!"

Boom.

Boom.

Boom.

Each titan step pressed deeper than the last—impact tremors rippling through the floor and up their bones.

The passage bent sharply left. The air grew colder, metallic. Each step angled them farther downward, as if the maze itself wanted to fold them into its lungs.

Stone cracked somewhere behind them—massive, structural, final.

Khandyl braced against the wall to keep Vaelinnae upright as the floor rolled. "Something just collapsed up there. Probably half the Soul-Furnace."

"We need a ceiling lower than its horns," Vaelinnae said between breaths. "Or this hunt is done."

They pressed on, the tunnel disgorging them into a vast, high-browed passage, its stone carved with endless Minos reliefs—bull-headed warriors in spiraled armor, their horn motifs repeating like echoing nightmares.

Loka's eyes darted up.

Deep grooves marred the ceiling—gouges cut by something

enormous dragging stone horns along the corridor over centuries.

"It's used this route before," he whispered. "Many times."

"Wonderful," Khandyl muttered. "Means the maze is home field advantage. Not ours."

The titan roared again, much closer.

The wall to their right vibrated once, twice—

And then blew inward.

A massive arm tore through the stone, its spiraled musculature glimmering with inner red-gold light. Fingers as large as columns scraped the tiles, pulverizing stone into jagged furrows exactly where Loka had stood two heartbeats earlier.

Khandyl slammed into him, driving them both clear. Shards of slate rained down around them in deadly spatters.

"Run!" she barked. "Before it claws the entire hall open!"

Vaelinnae limped forward in a lurching sprint, jaw set, refusing to let Khandyl carry her any farther than she already was. Her Windveil cloak dragged behind like a frayed pennant, her bow clutched tight despite the pain.

Behind them, the titan drew its arm back, stone cascading from its shoulders. Its roar shook the entire passage, spirals on its chest tightening like molten gears.

Loka risked a glance—

And nearly stopped.

Two Osiri guards burst into the hall from a perpendicular passage, armor gleaming, curved blades raised. Their steps faltered at the full sight of the titan.

The titan turned.

"Don't—" Loka breathed.

But duty outran reason.

The Osiri charged.

For a heartbeat, courage was enough.

In the next heartbeat, it meant nothing.

The titan seized the first guard with both hands. The armor shrieked as he was crushed against the opposite wall, spirals beneath the impact flaring violently red before fading to dull ash.

The second guard tried to retreat—too late.

The titan's horned head swung sideways like a siege ram, lifting the Osiri clean off the floor and hurling him into a pillar. The guard struck stone and hung limp, broken.

Silence swallowed the aftermath.

Vaelinnae exhaled a thin, shaking breath. "We cannot outrun that thing."

"We don't outrun it," Khandyl said grimly. "We outsmart the maze."

The corridor forked ahead—three spiraling paths, each carved with near-identical Minos geometry. All sloped at odd angles, and all were carved with seamless spirals that blurred the eye.

"What now?" Vaelinnae murmured.

Loka closed his eyes. Sweat beaded on his brow, and the spiraled wall nearest him pulsed faintly in sympathy.

He stretched threads of necromantic sense ahead—grazing each passage like testing harp strings.

The titan's pulse-beacon inside him flickered.

His eyes snapped open.

"That one," he said, pointing to the left path. "It bends resonance. It masks signatures. It's the only route that feels like it's trying to hide me."

"That's not remotely comforting," Khandyl muttered.

"Nothing here is comforting," Loka replied. "But this is the only tunnel that doesn't broadcast our breath."

Khandyl made the decision.

"Move."

She hauled Vaelinnae into the chosen passage. Loka followed, her boots whispering over spiraled stone—the three vanishing into the bend just as the titan thundered into the forked hall behind them, its horns gouging the ceiling in frustration.

It paused.

Turned its massive head.

The spirals along its torso dimmed, confused.

Their chosen path curled its own geometry, redirecting the resonance they left behind—masking trails, distorting echoes.

The labyrinth itself concealed them, as if protecting a familiar bloodline.

The titan roared, enraged.

Then stormed the wrong corridor, with stone raining from the ceiling under its weight.

They didn't slow until the passage narrowed brutally—ceiling dropping, walls compressing. No titan, no matter how ancient, could fit through that shrinking throat.

They pressed flat to the wall, lungs burning.

Vaelinnae pressed her fingers against her ribs, wincing. "I think that last impact cracked something. Feels like lightning with every step."

Khandyl crouched, checking for a break, breathing through clenched teeth. "We bind it when we're sure it won't break us first."

Then her eyes cut to Loka.

"What did that thing see when it looked at you?"

The spiral wall beside them pulsed faintly—listening.

Loka swallowed, voice low and tight.

"It saw what I am. A necromancer whose lineage runs through whatever Minos rites shaped the future. Not full-blood—but enough echo for the labyrinth to recognize it."

Khandyl's tone dropped to a soft, dangerous rumble.

"And if it recognizes you… others will too."

Vaelinnae nodded, breath still ragged. "We need out before more of these things wake."

A faint breeze curled down the narrow corridor—cool,
carrying mineral scent, iron tang, and faint Khem-Duat draft.
Khandyl rose, supporting Vaelinnae.
"That wind means open passage. We take it."
Loka looked back once into the spiraled dark where red-gold
light flickered.
The titan roared in the distance—furious, denied.
Stone shuddered with its rage.
But the corridor held.
For now.
They moved deeper, toward the promise of air and
distance—
leaving the predator behind them in its ancient maze.

Chapter 52 – The Deepwell Chasm

Planet: Vael'thara
Location: Beneath the Great Desert
Chronometric Stamp: BV 24

The stone underfoot was colder here—leeching warmth through boots and bone, slick with thin ribbons of condensation that glimmered faintly in the blue haze. Kellyn tightened her grip on Witmar's staff, its weight grounding her as the group stepped onto the chasm floor.

Broken gravhal machinery lay toppled in silent ruin: collapsed scaffolds of rune-etched iron, shattered lift platforms, and skeletal supports twisted and half-buried in centuries of sediment. Not relics, but remnants. Tools abandoned mid-use, as if a tragedy had struck in one shuddering instant.

Elowen conjured a sphere of life-light the size of a cupped hand. Its green radiance pushed only a few strides before the fog swallowed it, reflected in the river winding through the cavern.

The water glowed from within: slow-moving bioluminescence in blue, green, and pale silver.

Mist drifted off it like breath.

Serithyl Dawnstep's posture shifted—shoulders angled, head tilted, eyes half-lidded. There was no wind here, not truly, but

Sylph's senses still traced subtle pressure changes, shifts in temperature, and the memory of currents that once moved. "Something breathes in this rock," she murmured. "Slow, and old."

Aafje crouched, fingertips brushing the rusted spine of a Gravhal runic machine. Rune-stamps dented the metal, sigils blackened at the seams.

"These earthbinds failed," she whispered. "Whatever they were binding… broke free. Or broke loose."

"Something heavy did that," Froster countered, scanning the shadows with a hunter's precision. His brow furrowed beneath ash-smudged hair. "And whatever did—wasn't Gravhal."

Harvey Oakenstride's jaw tightened. He kept one hand hovering near the pommel of Kuldemaekr, fingers flexing unconsciously—a tell Kellyn had recognized since childhood. Tension, ready to ignite.

"We're following something we don't understand," he muttered. "And it didn't move quiet."

Kellyn inhaled deeply, pretending calm. But her heartbeat pattered like trapped wings.

"We don't need to understand it yet," she said. "Just trace the resonance. Loka's trail is still on the harmonic lines."

Seris adjusted her pack straps, eyes still tracking the fog. "You feel anything clearer? Any direction?"

Kellyn closed hers.

Through Witmar's staff, she reached down—into the substrata where harmonic currents flowed like fault lines beneath the world. There was a faint pull, distant yet undeniable.

The same pulse she'd felt when the spiral wall devoured Loka.

"Ahead," she whispered. "And down. Farther down than this."

Elowen went pale. "There's no 'down' here but the river."

Serithyl raised an arm, pointing across the chasm floor.

A rocky outcrop hugged the cavern's far wall. Beneath its lip: a narrow, half-collapsed tunnel choked with mineral crust.

"The air moves from there," she said softly. "Slow draw. That's a way deeper."

"Which is the opposite of comforting," Harvey muttered.

A faint tremor rippled through the floor.

Stone dust drifted down from overhead in a soft rain.

Seris's breath caught. "That wasn't an earthquake."

"No," Froster said, his features tightening. "That was footsteps. Distant… but heavy."

Kellyn felt the harmonic rebound—a pressure echoing through the stone, followed by a roar too deep to be sound at all.

Her eyes widened. "That's Loka's titan."

Harvey blinked, baffled. "His what?"

"Something woke in the labyrinth beneath us," Aafje said grimly. "And it resonated with him. It reacted to his magic… and to what made him."

Froster grimaced. "And if the Osiri heard that, they—"

A metallic cadence echoed from above.

Bootsteps.

Precise. Disciplined.

Osiri patrol.

Seris seized Kellyn's wrist. "Up top."

"Down!" Froster hissed, pulling them into the shadow of a fallen grav-pillar.

Half a dozen Osiri silhouettes materialized along the upper causeway—a dark procession against the glowing fog. Black geometric plates. Curved jackal helms. Scarab wards flickered in their hands like tiny, dying lanterns.

Kellyn held perfectly still.

Even from yards away, she felt them:

rigid posture, shallow, controlled breathing, predator stillness.

One guard leaned forward, sniffing the air.

The mage beside him lifted a palm, sensing vibrations through the stone.

"The labyrinth trembles," the mage said, his voice hollow in the echo. "If Minos awakens beneath the Duat, we send word to Khem-Duat City immediately."

Another answered:

"Or we kill it before it rises."

Kellyn's pulse hammered.

They weren't here for her.

They were tracking the titan.

But the titan was tracking Loka.

Harvey crouched low, his lips near her ear. "If they hunt the tremors, they might walk straight into him."

"We can't let that happen," Kellyn breathed. "Move now. Before they sweep the floor."

The patrol descended toward the opposite ramp. Kellyn signaled—quick two-finger curl—and they slunk from cover, weaving among the rusted carcasses of Gravhal machinery. Soft steps. Hushed breaths.

Every boot placement chosen: edges of stone, never puddles, never loose shale.

Another tremor rolled beneath them—longer, deeper, closer.

Elowen steadied herself against a column. "Whatever woke… it moves faster than before."

Serithyl paused at the rocky outcrop opposite the river. Wind-senses flared; silver hair lifted.

"The air bends here. Something passed recently. Large track. Wide shoulders."

"Or Loka," Harvey said. "Trying to stay ahead of it."

"We go now," Kellyn said. "Before the Osiri triangulate."

They crossed the final stretch of luminous vapor and reached the tunnel mouth. The entrance yawned like a wound—half-collapsed, barely wide enough for single file. Mineral grit coated the stone, crunching softly underfoot.

Harmonic resonance thrummed through the darkness. Kellyn felt it in the wood of Witmar's staff, faint yet sure.

"It's here," she whispered. "This is the path the spiral wall created. Loka descended this path."

Aafje stared into the dark, eyes narrowed. "And something is coming up it."

Kellyn tasted fear—iron and cold—but nodded. "Then we reach him first."

Froster nocked an arrow. "Lead. We guard your wake."

Kellyn stepped into the dark, sloping shadows, shoulders squared, her silhouette faintly outlined in green. The others followed close, ordered and silent, as the chasm's light faded behind them.

Above, Osiri voices echoed in pursuit.

Below, tremors answered them.

The deep places of Vael'thara were waking—

and the path bent sharply downward into the heart of the ancient labyrinth.

Chapter 53 – The Second Door

Planet: Vael'thara
Location: Khem-Duat
Chronometric Stamp: BV 24

The passage pinched, twisted—and then widened abruptly into a long, slanted hall. Here, the walls broke from the spiral perfection of the Minos labyrinth. The carved grooves were shallower and inconsistent, as though ancient spirals had been scraped away and overwritten. Darker stone dominated— rough and matte, without the hypnotic symmetry of Minos craftsmanship.

Khandyl slowed, shifting Vaelinnae's weight carefully along her shoulder. Her lupine features—sharp cheekbones, silvered eyes, the faint fur shadow along her jaw—tightened with each soft grunt from the archer's bruised ribs.

"This part feels different," she whispered. "Clean lines. Straight angles. No spiral tricks."

Vaelinnae's breath stuttered as she nodded, pain pulling her posture forward. "Wind travels honestly here. Nothing coils it back on itself."

Loka moved beside them, one hand trailing along the wall. His necromantic aura—the faint blue flicker beneath his skin, the dark resonance ever-present in his voice—shimmered less here.

"The maze doesn't extend its will into this hall," he murmured. "This stone isn't Minos. Might be newer... might be older. But the labyrinth isn't riding it."

A sound drifted up the slanted corridor behind them.

Metal on stone.

Heavy boots walking with measured discipline.

Voices bitten with harsh Osiri consonants.

Khandyl froze, ears sharp.

"Osiri," she breathed.

Vaelinnae straightened, her bow pressed tightly against her leg, even as her pain knifed fresh. "Patrol or hunt-squad?"

"A containment unit," Loka said. His face had gone bloodless. "They felt the titan. They'll try to box it in."

"And we're standing right in the middle," Khandyl muttered.

A tremor rolled beneath their boots—slow, deep, as though some enormous lung inhaled from the heart of the world. Dust sifted down. The stone hummed.

The Minos titan was moving again.

Khandyl's grip on her shield tightened until her knuckles whitened. "Quiet. Quick."

They advanced deeper, boots whispering over uneven flagstone. The slanted hall widened and rose into a vaulted space. Two massive Gravhal buttresses reinforced the triangular arch overhead, their block geometry stark against the curved Minos spirals half-erased on the walls.

Dim magefire flickered from crystal sconces along the ceiling—cold blue flames trapped in calcified shells. The light cast rigid shadows across the chamber, illuminating the far wall:

A relief panel.

Not Minos. Gravhal.

Sharper angles.

Symmetrical gridwork.

Runes cut deep and straight.

At its center stood a massive rectangular stone slab, fitted with metal bands hammered deep into the frame. Not decorative. Structural.

Vaelinnae studied it with narrowed eyes. "A door."

"And sealed," Loka confirmed.

Khandyl pivoted toward the corridor they'd left—her Wolf-clan hearing catching the faint scrape of Osiri boots now entering the passage. "We need to go through it. Now."

Loka stepped to the slab, tracing the rune-lines. His brow knitted as he muttered fragments of Minos and Gravhal spellcraft under his breath.

"It's not a hinge mechanism," he said. "It's harmonic architecture. A keystone array. Something you open with sound, not strength."

Khandyl scowled. "So… a password."

"Closer to a chord." His fingers trembled against the stone. "A resonance only a Gravhal earth-shaper would know. Something tied to these runes."

Vaelinnae hissed at the pain in her side, but urgency sharpened her voice. "Can you mimic it?"

Loka's reply was flat. "No."

The titan roared through the stone. The entire hall vibrated— stray dust falling in thin silver rain.

Khandyl grabbed Loka's collar, dragging him back from indecision. "Osiri are behind us. Titan behind them. Door in front. We need a miracle."

Loka scanned the chamber—floor anchors, cracks, the wall relief—until his eyes snagged on five rusted metal rods mounted beside a support pillar. They descended in length like descending notes—thickest at shoulder height, smallest near his hip.

He touched the top rod.

A faint tone hummed.

"Khandyl," he said softly. "Dagger."

She handed it over instantly, Wolf-clan trust absolute in a crisis.

Loka struck the first rod lightly.

A low rumble rolled through the hall.

Second rod—

A higher note, sharply resonant.

Vaelinnae's eyes widened. "A chime-key. Gravhal miners used them to unlock sealed tunnels."

Behind them, Osiri voices sharpened. Curved blades hissed from sheaths.

Khandyl bared sharp canines. "Loka, faster, or I'll throw you at the door until something cracks."

He tested sequences—single notes, paired strikes, ascending harmonics. Tone echoes brushed the stone slab, resonant waves pulsing along its seams.

The titan roared again, close enough that its breath seemed to push at the backs of their necks.

Loka hit the final combination.

The slab vibrated.

Metal bands hummed.

Stone cracked down the middle—slow, grinding movement, dust billowing as the chamber trembled.

"It's working!" Khandyl barked.

But the split halted halfway.

"No—no!" Loka slammed both palms against the stone. "Secondary key. Gravhal never keyed with only one."

Before panic could spiral, a soft mechanical click echoed deep within the wall.

The slab jerked…

and fully parted.

Cold air spilled through.

Khandyl blinked. "Who opened it?"

Not Loka.

Not the rods.

A figure stood in the darkened space beyond, framed by the angular stone threshold. Broad shoulders. Human height.

Heavy gray coat cinched at the waist by a toolbelt of rune-tongs and stone hammers. A short beard, braided with bits of crystal, glinted in the blue light.

In one scarred hand, he lifted a glowing rune-sphere—pale azure, etched in layered sigils.

His voice was low, gravel-sanded.

"Step through. Quickly. The titan's coming."

Khandyl pushed Vaelinnae first, shield braced.

Loka followed, still clutching the dagger.

The stranger slapped the rune-sphere against the door frame.

THUD

The slab slammed shut with such violent force that the hall shivered. Fissures spiked across the door, but it held.

Silence dropped thick as stone.

The stranger turned to face them fully.

Close now, they saw the rune-scars carved along both his forearms—Gravhal engineer-marks: circles, triangles, harmonic frequency notation. His eyes were storm-gray, sharp with discipline, hardened by things that lived beneath mountains.

"I've been listening to that cursed maze pulse for months," he said. "Figured sooner or later it would spit someone back out."

Khandyl raised her shield, combat stance instinctive—feet apart, shoulders angled, chin tucked. "Name."

A ghost of humor touched his mouth.

"Ilaric Stoneweave. Gravhal-trained earth-shaper." His eyes slid toward the slab. "And if you're running from what I think you're running from…"

He pressed one ear to the stone.

A muffled roar detonated behind the door.

Something massive struck it—the slab jumped in its frame, cracks widening like lightning.

"…then you'll want to follow me very, very quietly."

The titan roared again—closer, furious—and the ancient Gravhal door shuddered under the strain.

Chapter 54 – Return to the Canopy

Planet: Vael'thara
Location: Great Chasm
Chronometric Stamp: BV 24

The stone passage quaked with each distant blow. Fine dust drifted like pale smoke through the narrow air. Ilaric Stoneweave — compact, broad-shouldered, his braided beard glittering with embedded crystal flecks — led the way, his rune-sphere casting a muted sapphire glow through the tight, slanted shaft. The light grazed the carved edges of old Gravhal chiselwork, their strokes angular and blunt.

"Quiet as loose grains," he muttered, his voice gruff as gravel. "If the titan breaches that door, it'll shake these tunnels apart."

Vaelinnae limped behind him, wrapped in Khandyl's steady arm. The archer's long auburn braid hung limp over her shoulder, strands stuck to her sweat-streaked cheek. Pain tightened her jaw, but her bow hand never strayed far from the quiver at her back.

Khandyl — tall, Wolf-lean, shoulders built for shields, silver eyes alert for threats — held Vaelinnae's weight as if it cost her nothing. Her mannerisms were all economy: a tap of fingers against the shield's rim, chin angled to catch faint echoes, breath measured and silent.

Loka stayed close, pale-eyed and tense, every tremor making him look over his shoulder. Necromantic resonance shimmered faintly beneath his skin — thin threads of blue-white light pulsing at his throat and wrists — but even that glow was shaky, starved down here.

"How far to the surface?" Khandyl asked, voice kept low by instinct.

"Close enough to smell dirt," Ilaric said. "Far enough you'll curse every step."

They ascended another steep cut — cramped, shoulders brushing the carved stone — the passage angling sharply to skirt a collapsed section. The air cooled noticeably, threaded now with the scents of damp soil, bark, and deep roots.

Loka exhaled. "Forest air."

Ilaric flicked a glance back. "Forest air. Not necessarily your forest. Roots don't tell you whose world you're on."

Behind them, stone groaned — a long, shuddering vibration.

Loka swallowed. "That's the titan. Still moving."

"Then the Osiri found something worth dying over," Ilaric grunted without slowing.

The shaft widened into a Gravhal antechamber, supported by thick pillars. The pillars were carved with layered runes — cube-shaped script interlocked with triangular lattice marks older than any living mason. As Ilaric brushed his fingertips across one, the runes pulsed faintly in dusty amber.

A second corridor slanted downward — the same direction Kellyn's resonance pulled.

And then voices drifted from below.

Kellyn first — brisk, exhausted, issuing clipped instructions. Harvey's deep burr. Serithyl's quiet breath. The cadence of their movement slid through the stone like the echo of home.

Loka froze. "That's them—"

Khandyl jerked him back behind a pillar. "Then stop standing like a perfect silhouette."

Ilaric lifted his free hand, palm open: silence. The voices grew clearer — boots scraping stone, careful footfalls, someone whispering prayer lines.

Light shimmered around the bend — a soft green glow.

Ilaric's gray eyes sharpened. "Friends of yours?"

"Family," Loka whispered. "Clan."

"Good," Ilaric said. "Makes what comes next simpler."

He tapped the wall with two knuckles, then pressed his palm flat. The stone softened beneath his hand — warping like wet clay — and split along a fine seam. A narrow escape tunnel yawned open, carved long ago by Gravhal hands.

Loka stepped through first — and shapes materialized opposite them.

Kellyn at the front, dark hair braided tightly over one shoulder, Witmar's slender staff raised in a two-handed guard. Her posture was straight, balanced on the balls of her feet, weight shifting through practiced Dominion stances. Her gaze — sharp, analytical — widened the instant she recognized them.

Harvey stood just behind her, tall and hawk-still, his sword half-drawn. Froster's bowstring was already drawn to the cheek.

A heartbeat of tension held.

Then Kellyn broke — rushing forward, her staff clattering as she threw her arms around Loka. Relief shuddered through her muscles, her chin pressing into his shoulder as if to verify he was real and solid.

"Loka." She breathed the name as release.

Harvey's expression cracked into fierce relief. "By all twelve gods… you're alive."

"Resoundingly debatable," Khandyl muttered, but her sharp grin underscored the humor.

Serithyl Dawnstep swept forward, her long white braids floating like silk as she knelt beside Vaelinnae — her hands already glowing with faint windlight. Tear-bright eyes widened at the bruising spreading across her sister's ribs.

"You stubborn sky-breaker," Serithyl whispered, her forehead pressed to Vaelinnae's. "You held wind where none exists."

"I held enough," Vaelinnae rasped.

Ilaric cleared his throat — polite, firm, the sound of a man aware that time had teeth.

"Reunions later. Osiri are almost on you. Titan's still trying to shred my barricade. And your scent trail isn't cold anymore."

Kellyn forced her body back into readiness, nodding once. "Where do we go?"

Ilaric pointed upward into a side passage. "Toward a root that touches the surface. Veinwood. Ancient. Your tree-walker knows what to do with it."

Elowen — calm and reed-lean, freckles dusting her bronze skin, pale green life-light flickering beneath her eyes — stiffened. "A Veinwood root?" Awe crept into her voice. "Those are sacred."

"S'why I didn't hack it apart for ore," Ilaric said flatly. "Now move before whatever's behind us changes priorities."

They followed — single file through a narrow stone throat, its walls etched with ancient pick scars. Roots intruded from the ceiling in thick, sinewed bundles, some as wide as Loka's torso, others as delicate as hair strands.

Elowen touched one with careful reverence. "This is Sylph-grown, vein-tied. It comes from a great canopy tree."

"One big enough to shade a city," Ilaric muttered.

The tremors behind them changed in nature — now punctuated by shouts, the clash of steel, and commands in the Osiri tongue.

Khandyl's ears pricked. "They engaged it."

"Doesn't mean they'll live long," Harvey said grimly. "But chaos buys time."

The passage finally widened into a cavern — larger, airier, and held aloft by Gravhal masonry. Pillars stood at intervals, carved with axes, pickheads, and lattice patterns of ancient ore channels.

At the center rose the root.

It erupted from the ground like a frozen thunderbolt — thick as the base of a siege tower, its bark gleaming silver-green beneath the rune-light. Faint inner light pulsed through it, rhythmic as breathing.

Elowen drew a sharp breath. "A true Rootway."

Ilaric blinked. "A what?"

But Elowen was already at it — palms flat, breath trembling with connection. Light rippled beneath her fingers, warm and bioluminescent.

"It touches the Aeralith Canopy," she murmured. "It drank from our forest before our ancestors spoke in words."

Kellyn joined her, features softening with hope. "Can you take us home?"

Elowen nodded slowly, though fear pinched her voice. "Guiding one or two through the roots is instinct. Guiding this many takes… far more strength. But yes."

The tremors grew louder — Osiri boots in formation, scarab wards clicking like glass teeth.

Then the titan's roar folded through the stone — furious, thunderous, echoing through every root fiber.

Khandyl lifted her shield higher. "Now is good."

Elowen braced both hands against the Rootway. Her breath steadied — one long inhale, one resonant hum.

Silver-green light spiraled from her palms.

The root split open — not cracked, but parted, like wood recognizing the sun. Warm sylvan radiance flooded the cavern, and the scent of leaf and life poured through.

Harvey exhaled faintly. "By every wandering god…"

"I'm stone-bound," Ilaric said, stepping back. "Trees don't take my kind. I stay."

Kellyn clasped his forearm briefly. "You gave us a chance. That matters."

"Make it count," he said.

"Elowen," Seris whispered. "We're ready."

"Then go," Elowen breathed. "I can't hold this for more than a few heartbeats."

They moved:

Froster first, boots silent.
Serithyl supporting Vaelinnae.
Harvey.
Aafje.
Khandyl, guarding the flank.
Loka.
Kellyn last, touching Elowen's shoulder as she passed.

The radiant fissure swallowed them one by one.

Loka reached back, pulling Kellyn through as Elowen guided the root closed. Before sealing, she met Ilaric's eyes.

"Stone keep you."

"And leaves shelter you," he answered softly.

The seam vanished.

They stepped into a world of green light.

High forest air filled their lungs — sap-rich, warm, threaded with the singing hush of wind through impossible heights. They stood in the heartwood chamber beneath the Aeralith Canopy's central platform: pale roots spiraling upward like cathedral ribs, branches braided in vaulting arcs overhead.

Sylph guardians rushed in — long twin-braids, wind-kissed cloaks, silver-tipped spears flashing — their formation breaking only when they saw Serithyl and Vaelinnae alive.

Relief flooded the chamber like rain after drought.

Elowen slumped unconscious, knees buckling. Kellyn caught her, sweeping arms under her shoulders before she could fall completely. Elowen's hair — white-gold, feather-soft — spilled over Kellyn's arm.

"We're home," Kellyn whispered, voice almost breaking.

But through the deepwood roots, reverberating faintly from far below, came a final distant roar.

The titan was awake.

And the world had not yet understood what that meant.

Chapter 55 – The Forest Holds Its Breath

Planet: Vael'thara
Location: Aeralith Canopy, City of Aeralinth (The Hidden City of the Sylph Clan)
Chronometric Stamp: BV 24

"Purpose is nourishment; hesitation is hunger."
— *Ral'kir Quickwing (Krikk'ar)*

The forest should have celebrated their return — boughs shaking with silver pollen, treetop lanterns flaring in welcome.

Instead, the Aeralith canopy stiffened as if in a single held breath.

Elowen's Rootway cracked open at the edge of the Hidden Glades, a rippling seam of green-gold radiance. One by one, the travelers stepped out. Their bodies told their story: clothing dust-grayed from labyrinth stone, skins scraped raw, veins still remembering the titanic roars in marrow-deep tremors.

Harvey Oakenstride stepped first, his towering frame hunched slightly under the burden of grief, Kuldemaekr laid across his shoulder. The bronze filigree of the ancestral blade pulsed with a predatory green fire, and the runes along its edge shifted like breathing scales.

Loka followed, Necrodemicon strapped to his belt. The tome hung like a chained predator, wrapped in runic bands and quiet as a held scream. Necromantic filament traced faint blue lines under his skin — sharp beneath the eyes, along the collarbones — as though the maze still clung to him.

Wind, that sacred messenger of the Sylph, recoiled in a sudden shift. Leaves turned the wrong direction, whispering warning.

Serithyl Dawnstep appeared behind them, expression unreadable but voice steady:
"Much is heavy. Prepare a hall of silence."

The guardians obeyed at once.

They were guided along vine-woven bridges lit by living glowmoss and moon-pear lanterns hanging like moons. The Sylph city unfurled through the canopy like constellations stitched in green and silver:

• suspended platforms,
• winding root-ramps,
• crystalline water channels winding soundlessly through carved bark conduits.

As the group passed, more guardians joined the silent escort, sleek silhouettes in wind-woven armor that shimmered between visibility and nothing. Eyes lingered longest on the Necrodemicon — and the leaves hissed their disapproval.

At the Citadel — a great spiral hollowed in a trunk as large as a castle tower — six Sylph scholars waited in a ring. They wore leaf-silk half-masks, their hair braided in sweeping patterns denoting archivist rank, and silver-green eye ink traced elegant lines down their cheeks.

At their gesture, Loka set the Necrodemicon upon the braided floor.

The moment it touched:
• vines recoiled like struck serpents,
• torches faltered into cold blue flame,
• a pressure rippled outward, ancient as root-bed stone.

One scholar whispered, "… it remembers us."

Another: "… and we remember it too well."

She removed thin parchment sheets — reinforced with
aether-ink and hardened bark. The only medium capable of
copying a cursed record.

Elowen placed a hand on Loka's arm. "Be careful. Its mind
speaks louder than most voices."

The eldest scholar — hair silver as dawn frost, age lines
graceful and unhurried — bowed slightly.
"You will rest. We begin the transcription of the First Seal.
Understand: this tome predates the Osiri, predates mortals,
and predates sunrise on this world."

She touched the cover.

The book flinched like a muscle.

"Do not disturb us until the first seal is inked."

Kellyn inclined her head. "We will give you silence."

Ritual began —
moon-sap ink,
quills dipped in life-essence, Sylph-binding hymns whispered
so thin they barely existed.

Fatigue hit like surf.

Hammocks of cloud-vine were lowered.
Warm mosswater broth was pressed into hands.

Herbal tinctures steadied muscles still shaking with adrenaline.

But silence was louder than rest.

Harvey sat beneath a lantern tree — light rippling over armor plates and old scars. He sharpened Kuldemaekr again and again, though the edge already glimmered razor-fine. His gaze always slid to the space at his right.

Where Witmar had once sat.

Khandyl joined him slowly — Wolf-still, her shield leaned against her knee, silver eyes shadowed. Their shared silence was full of jagged edges, needing no words.

Froster paced a high branch-bridge, one hand always resting on the Osiri flame-khopesh he'd claimed. His lips moved in muttered counts — tunnel lengths, choke points, fallback corridors — hunting for a pattern in the labyrinth's madness.

Elowen slept under a broad whorl-leaf, her face pale, her lashes trembling — the strain of dragging so many souls through a rootway still draining her.

Serithyl, Vaelinnae, and Seris perched like carved spirits in a high canopy fork, meditating with wind-sense open. Their breathing slowed to match leaf movement. Through them, the forest listened — and spoke.

Aafje sat at Loka's side.
Loka had collapsed at a low bark-desk, a quill still in hand, spell notes scattered like fallen feathers. Aafje traced the hilt of her twilight-forged dagger in slow arcs, jaw set, gaze soft.

"He sleeps with the weight of three worlds on his shoulders," she breathed.

Wind stirred — then recoiled.

Not a breeze.
Not breath.
A displacement.

Leaves twisted upward against gravity. Lantern lights flickered. Birds exploded from the upper branches in swirls of feathered panic.

Deep beneath the roots — a tremor. Wrong.
Like distant drilling.
Or tunneling teeth.

Seris's eyes snapped open.
Serithyl's followed a heartbeat later.
Vaelinnae rose despite her bandaged ribs.

All three spoke at once:
"Kellyn."

Kellyn woke instantly, blade in hand before her feet touched wood.
A low hum vibrated through the platform — not harmonic, not natural:

Osiri machinery.

Her stomach dropped. "They found the exit point?"

Froster stopped pacing — shoulders tightening.
"If they tracked the breach at Nenet-Kheru… followed the residual trail through dormant roots… they could emerge anywhere the Veinwood breaks the soil."

Harvey stood, Kuldemaekr in a ready guard. "Where?"

Serithyl pointed toward the north.
"The tunnels beneath Windveil Outpost."

Kellyn swore quietly. "Inside our territory. They're already through the first root barriers."

A scholar stumbled from the transcription hall — hand pressed to her brow, mask askew, fear stark as moonlight on snow.

"Commander Windstream—" Her voice shook.
"The ground trembles… the book reacts. Necrotic signatures are approaching. Many of them."

"How many?" Kellyn demanded.

The reply was ghost-thin:
"Hundreds. Perhaps more. A host tunneling upward."

Sylph war-horns sounded before Kellyn could answer — three ascending notes, then a downward spiral. Alarm. Mobilization. Wind-call.

Warriors materialized like storms taking shape:
armor flickering in and out of visibility,
cloaks woven from wind-thread,
bows strung with resonance fiber,
eyes bright as starlight on snow.

The party drew together with instinctive finality:

• Kellyn — Dragon stance forming in her limbs, emerald eyes cold as battle.
• Harvey — Kuldemaekr drawn, runes flaring.
• Froster — Osiri blade swept over his shoulder, stance coiled and ready.
• Loka — spell-sheets unfurled, necromantic ink across his knuckles.
• Aafje — blade drawn, whispering a shadow-ward.
• Elowen — hands glowing with life-fire and green song.

• The Sylph sisters — dissolving into wind, becoming swift silhouettes poised between branch-spines.

The tremor became a violent quake.

Roots split.
Earth buckled.

A fist-sized crack ripped through the grove floor — expanding with a scream of stone. Soil geysered. Broken bark flew. Hot, dry air from the deep tunnels blasted upward, reeking of tomb-dust and ancient metal.

Then came the shapes:
Curved obsidian helms.
Jackal visors.
Osiri war-armor, slick black, etched in desert glyphs.

They climbed out in formation — blades raised, sun-sigils gleaming gold against dark steel.

And far beneath them came a roar:

not human,
not Osiri,
something vast, horned, and furious.

Loka's breath turned to ice. "The titan… it's still coming."

Froster bared his teeth. "They've broken the Duat and tunneled into the Aeralith. They mean to drag their war into the forest."

Kellyn raised her blade, voice carrying through leaves and branches alike.

"Form ranks!"

The Sylph vanished into wind — spears nesting in high cover, bowstrings ready to release a storm of silent arrows.

The party advanced to the breach point, shoulder to shoulder.

Osiri soldiers emerged.
The titan stirred.
The Aeralith itself shivered.

Leaves went motionless, as if forest lungs refused to breathe.

Kellyn exhaled once, slow and steady.

"Let's finish what we started."

Chapter 56 - Where the Wind Revealed Its Hidden Blade

Planet: Vael'thara
Location: Aeralith Canopy
Chronometric Stamp: BV 24

The forest wasn't supposed to sound this way.

Kellyn knew the Aeralith's true music by heart: vinewater dripping from moss-shadowed ledges, the flute-breath of high leaves, insect song braided with the soft, shifting wind. Tonight, those sounds were drowned out by a foreign cadence.

Metal.
Chanting.
Rhythmic footfalls.

And beneath it all—threaded through the root-veins like a buried scream—a low, unbroken roar, as if sunlight itself had been forced through a narrow tunnel.

An Osiri army, on the move.

Kellyn ran harder.

Windveil threads in her Sylph-forged armor bent light around her as she sprinted along the high branchway, her boots finding each knotted curve without looking. Her braid slapped lightly against her back, her green eyes narrowed, her breath steady and measured despite the urgency.

Behind her came the staggered thunder of her companions:

Harvey's heavy, grounded stride, broad shoulders rolling with each step, Kuldemaekr strapped across his back like captured thunder.

Froster's long, predatory lope, cloak flaring, fingers flicking near the hilt of his Osiri blade whenever shadows shifted. Khandyl's shorter, compact run, bow bouncing against her hip, jaw clenched, Wolf eyes scanning every side path. Aafje's Twilight Robe snapped in her wake, shadow-ribbons curling at her wrists each time she vaulted a knotwood ridge.

Elowen kept pace at Kellyn's side, her green cloak alive with motion, auburn hair damp with sweat, silver-green eyes sharp and wide with dread. Loka ran just behind, her black robe streaming, one hand always hooked around the warded satchel of the Necrodemicon as if restraining a coiled beast.

Seris, Serithyl, and Vaelinnae were little more than suggestions of shape—flickers of wind and moonlight gliding along the branches, their armor and cloaks fading in and out of sight as they shifted through Sylph footwork.

"Closer," Serithyl murmured, not winded, her voice a calm thread over the pounding of boots. "The harmonic shift is strong. Too many heavy feet ahead."

"How many?" Harvey called, breath steady but fingers tightening on Kuldemaekr's strap.

"Hundreds," Vaelinnae whispered. Her eyes were half-closed, lashes trembling as she listened through the canopy. "And I feel three sun-priest choirs. Their chains… tear the air."

Froster spat a curse over his shoulder. "We're late."

Kellyn didn't answer. Dragon-trained divination flared behind her eyes—possible futures snapping like frayed threads. With each stride, she saw jagged glimpses: Sylph women bound in golden chains, Osiri helms glinting amid shattered trunks, sunfire burrowing into bark until whole branches shattered from within.

"Dravokh won't break," Aafje said, shadow-smoke twisting lazily around her fingers. "But she can be broken."

"Not while we breathe," Khandyl growled.

The branchway dipped, then rose toward a broad junction where six skybridges converged like spokes. Late-afternoon light speared down through the canopy in tall shafts of gold.

A fallen Sylph lay at the junction's heart.

Kellyn dropped into a slide, boots screeching lightly against bark as she knelt beside the warrior. Bronze skin, scorched at the collar. Windveil cloak burned at the edges. Her harmonic blade lay across her lap, its resonance barely audible, like a dying heartbeat.

Seris knelt opposite, hands already glowing green-gold. "Stay with me, sister…"

The woman's eyes fluttered open, pupils blown wide with shock.

"South…" she rasped. "They broke… the lower ward-grove… Dravokh holds the last line…"

"How many?" Kellyn asked, voice low and even.

"Too many… sun-masks… chains… burning without flame…"

Her head started to sag.

Seris hissed and pushed more life-essence into her chest. Vaelinnae slid in, palms hovering over the woman's ribs to catch and smooth the flow so the heart wouldn't tear itself apart.

Kellyn stood. "Aafje—shadow the bridge. I don't want Osiri track-sign on this angle."

Aafje flicked her wrist. Velvet-black darkness spilled outward, coating railings and knotwood in a thin veil and swallowing footprints into nothing.

Harvey knelt just long enough to touch two fingers to the warrior's brow. "What's her name?"

"Taeril… Windsway…" Seris whispered.

"You fought well, Taeril," Harvey murmured. The great Green Knight's voice turned strangely gentle. "Rest. We'll take it from here."

Taeril's lips twitched into the hint of a smile before she slumped into a healing sleep.

They ran on.

The southern rim of the Aeralith rose ahead like a cathedral built of living things—towering trunks braided together, with hanging root-bridges swaying between them. The air changed first: sharp ozone, hot metal, the acrid tang of sunfire residue.

Kellyn slowed at the last ridge, dropped to a crouch, and peered over.

Her stomach tightened.

Below, on the cracked root-soil, 60 Sylph women formed a crescent line. Windveil cloaks snapped around them. Their blades shimmered with harmonic light as they moved in the

Windstep Spiral—an elegant, deadly dance passed down for centuries.

But the crescent was thin. There were gaps where sisters should have stood.

Advancing toward them was a tide of obsidian and gold.

Nine-foot Osiri warriors marched in disciplined blocks, black jackal-helms gleaming, shields locked edge to edge. Bone-etched khopeshes rose and fell in perfect rhythm. Sand clung to their armor as if alive, grinding with each step.

Behind them, standard-bearers carried banners of flayed hide, scorched with sun-runes that still smoked faintly.

Behind them—

The sun-priests.

Trios of robed figures in hammered gold masks, each with chains of mirrored discs hanging from their staves. With every few breaths, they lifted their staves and cast spears of caged daylight into the trees.

The forest did not burn.

Instead, the struck trunks blackened from within. Sap boiled into steam. Bark bulged, cracked, and split with soft, terrible sounds. Branches sagged and fell without flame.

"No wonder Dravokh hasn't answered our calls," Elowen whispered, her voice shaking. "They're killing her forest around her."

Kellyn scanned the Sylph line, letting her eyes follow the rhythm of their defense until she found the center.

"There," Serithyl breathed.

Vaelwyn Dravokh stood at the heart of the crescent. Her Windveil cloak was torn, and the once-perfect braid of her dark hair had come undone into wild strands, but her blade arcs remained textbook-perfect—even slowed by blood loss. Kellyn caught the subtle hitch in her left turns, the half-step of compensation where too many sisters had fallen from her flanks.

"We can't break that army," Froster said quietly. All bravado had drained from his tone; only calculation remained.

"We don't need the army," Kellyn replied. Her voice had grown very calm. "We just need its spine."

Her gaze locked onto the Osiri commander—a towering jackal-helmed figure behind the front ranks, skull-topped staff in hand, molten runes crawling along its length.

"Assuming Dravokh survives until we cut it," Loka muttered, dark eyes tracking the weakening Sylph line.

As if summoned by his doubt, the Osiri line surged.

A wedge of shield-bearing warriors thundered forward, boots striking the root-soil like drumbeats in a sacrifice ritual.

The Sylph moved to meet them—wind made flesh.
They blurred sideways, light bending around them. Blades flashed at impossible angles, leaving silver-green afterimages that only became bodies again when they cut through Osiri's throats and joints.

For a heartbeat, the maneuver worked.

Then the second wedge hit.

Then the third.

A Stormleaf mage broke from the crescent, her bare arms
lifted, her hair whipping as she summoned a spiraling gale.
Wind screamed through the Osiri front ranks, tearing shields
loose and hurling warriors backward into tangled roots.

A sun-priest choir lifted their staves in unison.

Golden chains lashed across the clearing—
wrapped around the mage's throat and wrists—
seared burning rings into her bronze skin.

Her song cut short.

She dropped, limbs slack, wind dissolving into ragged
breaths.

Dravokh pivoted toward her—

A chain-whip whistled across the clearing and cracked against
Dravokh's ribs.

Kellyn winced at the sound.

Dravokh staggered, dropped to one knee, and her blade
dimmed as her breath hitched.

"Chain the females!" the Osiri commander roared, his voice
booming across the roots. "Kill the rest!"

Dravokh bowed her head.

Kellyn saw her lips form a single word.
"Vaelkorh…"

A final plea.
A goodbye.
An invocation.

Kellyn surged forward, fingers tightening on her sword hilt.
"We're out of time. We—"

The forest changed.

It began as a vibration in Kellyn's teeth, a deep hum that made her molars ache. The air compressed; roots beneath her feet thrummed with something older than clan or empire.

Then—

A low tone.
A deeper one.
Then a third—lowest of all, like the sound of mountains remembering how to move.

Three tones braided in perfect harmony.

The Deep Harmony.

Osiri stumbled mid-step.
Sun-priest halos flickered.
Chains of daylight jittered and sagged as their anchors faltered.

The Sylph crescent gasped—spines straightening, eyes widening. Every warrior felt it in the marrow.

They knew that sound.

"What is this?" Loka whispered, sarcasm stripped clean away by awe.

Seris pressed a trembling hand to her chest. Her eyes brimmed, not with fear, but fierce, incredulous joy.

"They answered," she breathed. "They actually answered."

"Who?" Froster demanded, already lifting his blade.

The air thickened—
color bending, light warping, leaves shivering inward as if making room for something unseen.

The Osiri commander snarled behind his jackal helm. "What trick is this!?"

The Aeralith exhaled.

Shapes stepped out of nothing.

Tall, wind-carved silhouettes unfolded from between leaves and roots, emerging as if descending from an invisible branch-world parallel to their own. Cloaks of woven sky-thread fluttered around them, and armor of pale bark and storm-metal glinted, their faces painted with Sylph war-ink in sharp spirals and linework.

Sylph men.

They moved like the echo of the Deep Harmony itself—silent, precise, and inevitable. Blades of condensed air and living wood slid free of their scabbards with a whisper that sounded like a storm drawing its first breath.

The forest wind, long thought only a shield and a whisper, had come bearing its hidden edge.

And at last, the Aeralith was no longer holding its breath.

Chapter 57 - The Men of the Windstep

Planet: Vael'thara
Location: The Aeralith Canopy, Southern Verge
BV 24.092

"Wisdom is strength that learned to think first."
— *Marnok Hearthshield (Minos)*

They stepped out of the Aeralith's breath like returning ghosts—figures distilled from wind and memory, tall as stories and silent as mourning bells.

The Sylph men.

Bare torsos marked with spiral-etched armguards.
Hair bound in long wind-knots, some braided with silver thread, others with shed feathers.
Eyes pale as distant storms.
Blades shaped from music-made metal—curved steel flecked with silver, edges humming faintly in the cadence of the Deep Harmony.

For a heartbeat, even the Osiri paused mid-march.

Sylph men had not walked the Aeralith in living memory.
For centuries, they were rumors—
storm-spirits, wind-brides, sacred lovers whispered into children's dreams.
But there they stood, breathing, solid, their arrival as quiet as the hush before thunder.

Dravokh lifted her head from where she knelt on cracked root-soil, blood trailing down her arm, breath thin.

"Vaelkorh…?" she whispered.
The name carried awe, grief, and disbelief in one single breath.

The foremost man stepped forward.
His hair shone silver as moonwater, his face seamed with age not of flesh but of remembrance.
A soft gale curled around him, bending the leaves in a spiral that matched the rhythm of his breathing.

"You held the line, Dravokh," he said—his voice borne on the wind, as if the canopy itself spoke it.

Dravokh blinked tears. "I thought you were dead."

"Not dead," he answered. "Waiting."

Then he raised his blade—
and the wind answered like a choir.

Sun-priests jerked their staves upward in alarm, voices rising in tortured counterchants.

The Sylph men moved.

Not charging.
Not sprinting.

Stepping.

A single unified step—left foot forward—
but in that movement the Deep Harmony rippled through the clearing like a low, rolling drum.
The vibration raced into Kellyn's boots, up her bones, through her lungs until she felt hollowed—re-made in rhythm. Her breath caught as every rib hummed.

The Windstep.

"Stay close!" Seris barked. "Fight with the cadence—if you resist, it will throw you off balance!"

Kellyn surrendered to it willingly.
Harvey's boots fell perfectly in time, steps like stone anchoring storm.
Froster found the beat instinctively, his shoulders loose, motion fluid.
Aafje dissolved into darkness, shadow trailing in streaks that curved with the harmonics.

The Sylph women recognized it immediately—every stance adjusted, every spin guided by the same pulse.

The Osiri commander roared, voice echoing off trunks:

"Shields! Ready! Break their spirits!"

He rammed his skull-topped staff into the earth.

Chains of sunfire burst outward—dozens:
lances of molten light, hungry for flesh.

Vaelkorh stepped forward.

He did not raise his guard.
He did not block.

He drew in a breath—
and the wind bent sideways.

The golden chains shattered midair—
sunfire breaking into cold sparks that died against soil.

A murmur rippled through the Osiri ranks.
Fear.
Recognition.

"Wind answers wind," Vaelkorh said.

Four Sylph men aligned behind him, blades glowing in spiral harmonics.
They raised their weapons—nothing else—
and then vanished.

A gust ripped across the battlefield.
Not a storm.
Not shrieking air.

A razor-wind—silent, clean, certain.

The next heartbeat:

Five Osiri fell.
Armor cleaved in perfect diagonal cuts from shoulder to hip.
Their bodies hung weightless in the air before gravity
remembered them.

Panic spread.
Sun-priests screamed orders.

"Bind-lines! Chain the air itself!"

Three choirs lifted staves.
Golden latticeworks sprang outward, forming blazing force-
nets.

But the Sylph men were smoke.
They stepped out of one spiral and into another, appearing
behind the nearest choir before priests even turned.

One helm folded inward with sickening precision.
Another priest choked as the wind condensed into a needle
and pierced him through.
A third screamed a counter-hymn—
but a Sylph caught his staff, whispered wind into the sigils—
and the chain of light inverted.

The priest vanished in a flash of his own power.

Kellyn swallowed hard.

"These are the warriors Sylvia painted in the scrolls."

"Not painted," Serithyl corrected softly. "Remembered."

Dravokh pushed herself shakily to her feet.

"Kellyn! Take our left flank. Drive for the commander!"

Kellyn nodded, body already flowing into motion.

"Harvey, Froster, Khandyl—on me!"

They surged down the ridge.

The battle detonated.

Sylph women spun in spirals of discipline—
blades singing, tearing through chain sigils before they could
form.
The men were a tempest—ageless faces, no laughter, no
hesitation—executing technique older than carved history.

Harvey raised Kuldemaekr.
Green fire flooded the blade.
He crashed into an Osiri shock-trooper nearly twice his
height. Their shield shattered under the blow as if made of
ice. Griffyn's strength—magnified by Dragon-forged steel—
sent a shockwave thumping the soil.

Khandyl fired three arrows in one breath.
Each twisted mid-flight, bending with the air-harmonic until
they struck throats cleanly.

Aafje materialized behind a sun-priest, shadow-blade slipping
through heart and sigil both. Her whispered ward
extinguished his stored sunfire with a hiss.

Froster fought like avalanche—weight, momentum,
inevitability. The stolen Osiri greatsword smashed armor
plate as if bone.

Loka held back, both hands glowing with emerald necro-
harmonics.
He severed chain constructs mid-air.
Unmade sigils with a touch.
And collapsed priest-focus with flicks of two fingers.

Kellyn moved like nothing the Osiri had ever trained to counter.
Dragon Clan geometry—curved vectors, predictive timing, harmonic resonance—all bent into razor grace. Her blade spun arcs of violet and gold, cutting khopesh, cutting armor, cutting resolve.

The Osiri line wavered.

The commander bellowed, "To me! Eternal Crescent! NOW!"

Soldiers converged, shields grinding together until they formed a jagged half-circle. Priests knelt behind them, staves locked into a single coordinate.

Vaelkorh's jaw tightened.

"This formation slaughtered the old clans," he murmured.

Kellyn's eyes narrowed. "Can you break it?"

"We have not stepped outside the Deep Wind in four centuries."

Gasps drew from the Sylph women.

Seris trembled.
Elowen paled.
Serithyl whispered, "Vaelkorh—no. The toll—"

"We will not lose this grove," he said simply.

The Sylph men shifted formation, blades angled downward, feet placed as though the world itself required that stance.

The Osiri commander understood.
His voice cracked with genuine fear.

"Break them! BREAK THEM BEFORE—!"

Too late.

Vaelkorh inhaled.

A long, trembling breath—
and the wind inhaled with him.

Leaves froze.
Roots heaved.
Sound collapsed into one crystalline instant.

The Deep Harmony detonated.

The Sylph men took three steps.

Only three.

But those steps were cataclysm.

Wind tore up roots and soil, shattered shields, bent armor inward, and hurled Osiri bodies through the trees like discarded dolls. The crescent broke in a single heartbeat— ranks shredded, formation undone, morale obliterated.

Silence fell.

Even the sun-priests faltered, staves dimming as their chanting died.

Kellyn stared, breath trembling.
No words came.

"That," Froster whispered, voice hoarse, "was a god's strike."

"No," Vaelkorh replied quietly. "Only what the wind meant us to be."

He lifted his blade toward the reeling Osiri commander.

"And now," he said, stepping forward with the storm at his back, "we finish this."

Male Sylph Warrior

Chapter 58 – The Sun-Mask Breaks

Planet: Vael'thara
Location: Aeralith Canopy
Chronometric Stamp: BV 24

Smoke crawled low across the clearing—
thin, pale, almost unreal—
as if the forest itself were trying to exhale the invaders.

The Osiri commander stood amid the wreckage of his broken formation. His sun-gold armor was cracked and scorched, the sand-layer that had once reinforced it now flaking away in dull, glassy sheets. The jackal helm he wore glowed faintly around the eyes, two coals burning behind an expressionless mask. The skull mounted atop his staff flickered with stuttering light, its sockets dimming as if the soul bound within were growing tired.

But the man inside the armor was not tired.
He was furious.

Vaelkorh strode toward him.

The Windstep master moved in measured grace, but Kellyn could see the cost of the Deep Wind strike settling into his body. His breath hitched once. His fingers trembled ever so slightly when he lowered his blade. The other Sylph men hid their exhaustion with warrior calm, yet their shoulders hung heavier, their stances more grounded than before.

That last technique hadn't been a flourish.
It had been a sacrifice.

The Osiri commander looked from one Sylph man to the next, and his lips twisted beneath the mask.

"Your wind fails," he growled, voice echoing inside the jackal visage. "But my sun never dies."

He drove the butt of his staff into the earth.

A shockwave of heat ripped outward—
a ring of gold-white radiance that scorched the ground in a perfect circle.

Harvey shoved Kellyn back with one arm, planting himself between her and the blast. The heat slammed across his armor, igniting green tongues of fire along Kuldemaekr's etched runes. Froster threw himself in front of Aafje, teeth bared; the blast burned the fur trimming his leathers and blackened the bark behind him.

Elowen gasped as the wave hit her, her life-fire flaring wildly before she wrestled it back under control.

Even Vaelkorh staggered, teeth clenched.

The commander lifted his staff again, shoulders rolling as he pulled more power from the fading skull-totem.

"Fall before the will of Amun-Netjer!" he roared.

A column of sunlight crashed down from above—
so bright it carved a glowing trench into the soil where it
struck.

Vaelkorh threw himself aside.
He was fast.
But not as fast as before.

The edge of the beam skinned his shoulder.
Silver-blue armor vaporized in a wash of light. Flesh beneath
seared. He dropped to one knee, breath hissing between his
teeth, wind around him faltering.

The Osiri commander advanced, each step thudding like a
hammer blow into the roots.

Kellyn ran.

Harvey matched her, Kuldemaekr's light blazing.
Khandyl pounded along the branch's edge, two arrows
already nocked between calloused fingers.
Froster lowered his stolen Osiri greatsword, jaw set.
Aafje vanished into a ribbon of shadow that slid along the
roots.
Seris rode a cushion of wind, boots barely touching bark.
Serithyl and Vaelinnae blurred along the treeline, silhouettes
flickering in and out of sight.
Loka came last, black robe snapping around his legs, one
hand clamped around the satchel that held the Necrodemicon
as if holding back a beast.

"Vaelkorh!" Kellyn shouted. "Fall back—we've got him!"

Vaelkorh spat a thin line of blood into the dirt and pushed
himself upright, one hand pressed to his burned shoulder.

"No," he said, voice rough but steady. "This ends with me."

The Osiri commander roared and swung his staff like a hammer. The skull's jaws opened, gathering a new flare of sunfire.

Kellyn's world narrowed.
Threads of possibility snapped into clarity—
Harvey burned through the ribs.
Froster thrown, neck broken against a root.
Aafje hit mid-shadow-step and torn out of the air.
Loka crushed beneath a falling branch.
Vaelkorh's chest split, wind-song silenced.

Too many futures.
Too many dead.

"Scatter!" she screamed.

The party exploded outward.

The commander unleashed his attack—
a horizontal arc of sunlight that shaved through three ancient trunks, sending their upper sections collapsing in slow, horrifying grace. Elowen dove aside, cloak catching fire along one edge. Aafje reappeared in a puff of shadow near a root cluster, cloak smoking. Froster rolled under a falling tree, then burst up with a snarl, splinters in his hair.

Vaelkorh vanished into a spiral of leaves—
and reappeared behind the Osiri commander—
but the movement left his knees threatening to buckle.

Kellyn's instincts screamed.

The commander twisted with brutal speed, bringing the staff around toward Vaelkorh's ribs—a killing blow fired point-blank.

Kellyn wasn't close enough.

Loka was.

Emerald sigils spiraled out from his palms—a hastily formed necro-barrier, condensed from raw harmonic entropy.

The staff smashed into it.

The barrier shattered like glass—
but the blast kicked sideways, gouging a molten trench across the ground instead of through Vaelkorh's chest.

Loka staggered, coughing red into his sleeve, face drained.

"Don't… kill him yet," he gasped. "He knows where they took the others. The Osiri aren't acting alone. They have plans—layers. We need—"

"Silence, corpse-witch!" the commander snarled.

He charged.

Harvey met him first, Kuldemaekr whistling down in a brutal arc. The Osiri caught the blow on his staff, sunfire surging along the haft. The impact sent a shockwave through the clearing. Harvey's feet slid back, boots carving furrows in the torn earth.

Froster slammed in from the side, greatsword angled for a killing cut. The commander turned his shoulder, sun-blessing flaring. Froster's strike hit a burst of heat and force that flung him backward like a thrown doll.

Aafje's shadow-blade swept upward, aimed for the gap under the ribs. A ripple of heated air lifted her just enough that the edge scraped harmlessly off sun-hardened plating, sending her tumbling.

Khandyl's double-shot spiraled toward the commander's thigh, arrows humming with Sylph wind. They struck true—
then burned to ash on contact.

"He's wrapped in a sun-blessing!" Seris shouted over the chaos. "His armor's alive!"

Kellyn darted in low, blade a streak of Dragon light.

Her cut bit under a damaged plate, punching a gouge through sand-metal. Blackened grit spilled like blood. The commander roared, spinning, and slammed his staff straight down.

Kellyn crossed her blade and Witmar's staff, braced along the pillar-line stance Sahn had drilled into her. The blow still hurled her backward. She hit the ground on one knee, teeth rattling, arms numb.

Serithyl and Vaelinnae appeared behind the commander in a mirrored flash, Windstep arcs slicing inward toward the seams in his armor. Sparks burst. The plating held.

"Blessing's anchored at the chest!" Vaelinnae shouted. "We need to break the source!"

Kellyn narrowed her eyes. "Then we kill the blessing."

Loka understood before she finished the sentence.

His hand tightened on the Necrodemicon's satchel.

"No," Kellyn snapped. "Loka—don't—"

"It will only be a whisper," he said, voice thin but resolute. "Not a summoning. Not a breach. Just… silence."

He opened the book.

Not wide.
Barely two finger-widths.

The clearing screamed.

Not in sound, but in pressure—
a sucking absence, like the world's breath being dragged sideways. Color dimmed at the edges of vision. Kellyn felt the

hair along her arms lift, every instinct shrieking to run, to close, to flee.

The sun-blessing flickered.

The glow around the commander's armor guttered. The flowing sigils that had crawled along his breastplate stuttered as if something had bitten into their power source.

Vaelkorh saw the opening.

He stepped forward—only once.

Raised his blade.

And called the wind.
Not the catastrophic Deep Wind, not the grove-breaking power that had nearly shattered him—but a single, perfectly tuned ribbon of harmonized breath.

He whispered, "Fall."

The wind struck the Osiri as if gravity had turned sideways.

The commander's staff ripped from his hand. His jackal mask cracked down the snout, a thin line of fracture running between the burning eyes. His knees smashed into the earth, armor grinding.

Harvey was there before he could rise.

Kuldemaekr burned bright emerald, answering grief and fury alike.

The Osiri commander looked up, helm fracturing, face shadowed—but there was no fear there. Only fanatic triumph.

"You have delayed nothing," he rasped. "The desert rises. The chains of Ra ascend. The gods sleep beneath the dunes, and we—"

Harvey brought Kuldemaekr down.

The blade split mask, bone, and soil in a single, merciless stroke. Green fire flared, then died.

Silence fell over the clearing.

Real silence—
no chanting, no clash of steel, only the soft creak of wounded trees and the ragged breathing of those still standing.

Kellyn lowered her blade slowly, chest heaving.

Vaelkorh stood with his weight leaned slightly to one side, fingers clenched white around his sword's hilt. The other Sylph men were still as carved statues, chests rising and falling in narrow, disciplined breaths.

Then the ground trembled.

Once.

Then again—deeper, slower, like something colossal rolling over in its sleep.

Elowen stepped closer to Kellyn, eyes wide, pupils blown. "Kellyn… the roots are vibrating. This isn't just battle echo. Something is coming."

The Osiri's dying words echoed through Kellyn's mind:

The chains of Ra ascend.

She turned her gaze downward, as though she could see through bark and earth and stone to whatever lay beneath.

Far below the Aeralith—
below root and rock and the buried veins of the Khem-Duat—
a new sound began to rise.

A grinding.
A distant clatter of links.
A rhythm like an enormous heartbeat wrapped in iron.

Something old was waking.
Something hungry.

The battle was won.

But beneath their feet, the war was beginning.

Chapter 59 - The Counting of the Dead

Planet: Vaelthara
Location: Aeralith Canopy
Chronometric Stamp: BV 24.092

"Patience is the mortar of empire."
— *Senmet the Architect (Osiri)*

The Aeralith no longer shimmered in green-gold light.

It smoldered.

Branches glowed faintly with dying ember-lines where sunfire had chewed through the bark. Splintered roots lay torn open like cracked ribs. The air smelled of burned sap and iron. A pall of ash moved with the wind, as if the forest exhaled grief with each breath.

Kellyn and her companions walked through the ruin in exhausted silence.

Harvey, Khandyl, Froster, Aafje, Elowen, Loka, Seris, Serithyl, and Vaelinnae followed behind her—each wearing fatigue like it had weight. They were all bruised, bloodstained, hollow-eyed. The Deepwell fog that had clung to them in the tunnels seemed to have followed to the surface, hanging about their steps like ghosts.

Above, Myrrathis and Sylthara circled low, bronze and silver wings beating slow aerial currents. Their shadows rippled like war banners over the ravaged canopy before both dragons landed on the broken lattice of branches—silent, watchful.

The forest never felt so quiet.

No cicada-buzz.

No rustle of animals.

Only the soft keening of wind threading through charred wood.

The survivors gathered in uneven clusters.

Some simply collapsed where they stood.

Female Sylph warriors embraced one another, their arms shaking. Their Windveil cloaks hung in singed ribbons; blood streaked their bronzed skin. They pressed their foreheads together, breath hitching in disbelief that the other still lived.

Others knelt beside fallen sisters, silent but unbroken, fingers combing gently through hair as if memorizing them by touch alone.

And some wept openly into the arms of Sylph men—men who appeared only long enough to see if their beloved drew breath…

to touch brow to brow…

to share a whispered vow…

—and then stepped backward into the wind and vanished like dew at dawn.

Kellyn stood at the edge of the devastation and understood.

This was the Sylph truth.

Not the Windstep.

Not their near-ghost invisibility.

Not even the Deep Harmony.

But this:

their bonds.

Every leaf, every breath, every pulse of life one stitched
thread.

The forest did not grow them.

They were the forest.

Vaelwyn Dravokh approached.

Her ribs were wrapped in sap-hardened bark-bandings, her
long hair clotted with dirt and drying blood. The Windveil
cloak she wore hung in shreds, but her spine was straight,
shoulders squared, gaze unbowed.

She had lost sisters today—yet walked like a banner that
refused to lower.

"Queen of Swords," Dravokh said, voice hushed with dignity.

"Thou camest in our darkest hour."

Kellyn shook her head. "You held long before we arrived."

A flicker of a smile tugged at Dravokh's lips.

"Aye. But we had begun to wane.

Thy coming restored the line."

Her silver-green gaze swept Kellyn's companions:

Harvey and Froster carrying wounded Sylph toward healers,
boots dragging from exhaustion but hands steady.

Khandyl kneeling beside a young archer, murmuring encouragement as she wrapped trembling fingers around a fresh bowstring.

Aafje whispering shadow-serenities to calm a panicking warrior.

Elowen binding roots into splints, palms glowing with soft life-fire, touch gentle even through her own shaking.

Loka standing apart, eyes lowered, hands still quivering from necro-harmonic backlash—too afraid to hold anyone, too ashamed to step away.

"And thy companions fight with honor," Dravokh whispered.

Her gaze lingered on Harvey.

"Thy Green Knight fights like doom given flesh."

Harvey was too focused on lifting another wounded warrior to hear.

Elowen knelt beside a fallen apprentice—barely 14 summers old. The girl's breath came sharp and wet, like cracked reeds in a winter wind. Vines curled around her ribs as Elowen poured life-magic gently into her chest.

But the glow fluttered.

Then faltered.

Her eyes clouded like frost across glass.

Khandyl covered her mouth, choking back a sob.

Seris knelt beside the child, fingers twining with hers.

"Easy," she whispered. "The wind carries you home."

The girl's cracked smile trembled.

"My... mother will be proud. I saw our men return..."

Her final breath slipped past her lips like a floating leaf.

Elowen bowed until her forehead touched the girl's brow, tears falling through her hair and onto the girl's cheek.

Loka stepped forward hesitantly—as if unsure if he even belonged here. He drew three thin bone glyphs from his pouch and placed them around the girl's body in a small, perfect triangle.

"Protection charm," he murmured. "So the Osiri can't mark her spirit."

Serithyl blinked.

"That is... kind."

"It's practical," Loka muttered

—but his voice betrayed him.

It cracked at the edges.

Kellyn's heart tightened.

Even in grief, kindness found a shape.

She later found Harvey at the southern edge of the clearing, staring up at Myrrathis. The bronze dragon crouched like a cathedral statue, resting her horned head upon one colossal foreleg. Green fire hummed faintly along Kuldemaekr at Harvey's hip.

His voice broke when he finally spoke.

"I thought I saw Witmar," he whispered. "In the smoke. In the flames. Just… standing there."

Kellyn stayed beside him, silent.

Harvey swallowed.

"I keep expecting him to walk out from behind a tree. Grin at me. Ask if I got the shot."

Kellyn set a hand on his arm.

"You avenged him."

"It doesn't feel like enough."

"It never does," she said softly.

"My brother is still dead, Kellyn. Nothing I do changes that."

"No. But what you do from here honors him."

Harvey let out one hollow breath.

Then another.

Finally, he nodded—slow, tired, but resolute.

"Wit would want me to see this through."

Kellyn squeezed his arm.

"You won't see it alone."

He leaned his shoulder against hers for half a heartbeat—just long enough to ground himself—then pushed away, spine straightening as the Green Knight returned.

"Then let's finish it."

Loka jogged toward them, arms full of carved obsidian plates, glyph-sand still clinging to his hair. He dropped to one knee at a scorched grove where Aafje, Seris, and Elowen waited

beside runed fragments fused into a single map.

Kellyn crouched, studying.

A chained sun-circle dominated the etched pathways.

Again.

And again.

Aafje tapped one engraving. "Khem-Duat sigils."

Seris spoke softly, eyes wide.

"There are so many. Under forests. Under dunes. Under

every homeland."

Loka nodded grimly.

"Wells. Doors. Transport rings. Barracks. Storage tunnels.

They run beneath the whole continent. The Osiri dug

centuries before we even noticed."

Kellyn traced the lines.

North, west, southeast.

Each tunnel passed beneath an entire people:

Sylph.

Wolf.

Unicorn.

Drakkenwyld.

Gravhal strongholds.

And the ancient Minos domains.

"Their conquest wouldn't be armies at our borders," she

whispered. "It would begin under our feet."

Elowen shuddered.

"That is how they reached the Aeralith so deep…"

"And how they would have hollowed the clans from the roots up," Aafje finished.

Dravokh approached—leaning subtly against Vaelkorh's arm for balance. He stayed only long enough to steady her before dissolving into wind once more.

"Our scholars will read this," Dravokh said. "But hear me, Queen of Swords: the Osiri will not cease. For every wedge we cut down in daylight, another marches in darkness."

Kellyn's voice lowered, sharpened by resolve.

"Then we go into the darkness. And into the sand."

Dravokh met her eyes—equal parts pride and dread.

"The Aeralith will arm thee. We owe thee more than leaf and breath."

From the shadows, Vaelkorh whispered a single phrase in Old Sylphic. Kellyn did not know its meaning, but its weight settled on her bones like storm-oath steel.

The sun dipped low, stained amber through the smoke-stripped canopy.

Kellyn looked at her companions:

Harvey—grieving but unbroken, hand resting on Kuldemaekr like a vow.

Elowen—eyes distant, lost in thoughts of Corlyn and home.

Khandyl—red-eyed, but bowstring steady.

Froster—silent as winter stone at her shoulder.

Aafje—cloak rippling with shadow-tension, ready for the next kill.

Loka—arms full of glyphs and doom-script, walking with shoulders hunched from too much knowledge.

Seris, Serithyl, and Vaelinnae—alive by thread and miracle, but alive.

Around them, the Sylph tended their dead.

They laid bodies on woven root-platforms, washed wounds with leaf-water, braided hair with strands of mistlight, then sang the Windfare Hymn—a thin, spiraling harmony that rose through the branches like a farewell whispered by the world itself.

Kellyn inhaled slowly.

The weight of command settled across her shoulders like wet stone.

"We rest tonight," she said quietly.

"Tomorrow…

the sand."

A wind stirred the ruined clearing—

cold, uncertain, tasting of distant dunes.

Whether it arrived as an omen or blessing, Kellyn could not say.

But she would.

Soon.

Chapter 60 – The Will of Sylveron

Planet: Vaelthara
Location: High Druid's Grove, Draknest — Drakkenwyld Highlands
Chronometric Stamp: BV 24.093

"Magic bends reality. But people—ordinary people—bend fate."
— *Adric Vance (Human)*

Word of the Anari victory spread across Vaelthara like wildfire through dry autumn forests.

From the storm-lashed cliffs of the Eagle aeries…

to the frost-bitten Wolf Holt in the far northwest…

to the whispering Unicorn groves and the Moon Clan's mirrored pools…

even to the distant Dragon Isles where drake-song flew faster than wind…

The impossible had happened.

Not a city taken.

Not a treaty forced.

Something far greater:

They had broken the finest and largest army the Osiri could muster in open battle—and lived.

And in the smoking aftermath, beneath shattered sands and fallen jackal-helms, the Anari uncovered something older and far more dangerous:

The Khem-Duat—an underground road spanning the continent, carved by Osiri hands over eons.
A hidden artery of conquest.
The path from which every incursion into every clan had been launched.

Its revelation shook every forest, every clan, every ancient root of Vaelthara.

So the Great Tree summoned the Twelve to the High Druid's Grove.

Night was falling when Kellyn stepped into the vast clearing.

The Grove rose around her like a living cathedral.
Massive roots arched overhead in rib-vault curves.
Saplight pulsed through bark in silver veins, casting drifting constellations across terraces of living wood.

Ancient druids tended the roots with low melodic chants.
Lantern-fruit glowed warm gold from hanging boughs.
Feasting platforms braided themselves up from the soil in slow spirals, forming tables and seats from living branches.

It smelled of cedar and wet moss and distant rain, undercut by the deep harmonic hum of a world that knew it was being watched.

Kellyn Windstream—bronze skin, auburn hair tied back in a Dragon fighter's knot—felt the Tree's vibration through the soles of her boots—a heartbeat made of root and memory.

Harvey Oakenstride walked beside her, longbow over one shoulder, Griffyn-blue cloak trailing behind, Kuldemaekr balanced across his back. His eyes kept drifting, always returning to her.

At the Grove's center, atop a root-dais, stood Brun:

Nine years old.

Barefoot.

Golden-eyed.

A child of the forest—and the High Druid.

His amberwood staff pulsed with gentle light. When he lifted one hand, the entire Grove exhaled and fell still.

Families hushed.

Warriors lowered weapons.

Even the dragons perched in the high branches quieted their breath.

The Great Tree inhaled with him.

Twelve great root-seats rose from the soil, unfurling in a perfect circle.

One for each clan.

Dragon Clan

Lady Nadja stood in red-gold armor, fire-scarred gauntlets gleaming, dark eyes old and fierce. Dragon warriors lined the roots behind her; children traced invisible blade-forms in the air.

Griffyn Clan

Lord Sylveron Windstream entered beneath a mantle of storm-feathers. Storm-singers stood behind him with war-flutes and lightning-thread cloaks. Nyssara Windstream—tall, poised, auburn hair braided with silver plumes—took her place just behind her father. Her gaze flicked once toward Harvey, then away.

Sylph Clan

Lady Vaelwyn Dravokh stood half-in, half-between the world—her form shimmering at the edges like wind given flesh. The faint outline of Vaelkorh drifted behind her like a ghost of air. Sylph women stood serene as moonlit clouds; their men were unseen but brushed perception like a change in pressure.

Wyvern Clan

Lord Maerwyn Wyvernaeg stood marked by ash and resolve. His warriors waited behind him like obsidian shadows.

Bear Clan

Lord Tans Bjorn, massive and pine-scented, stood bare-chested beneath a fur mantle. Bear children wrestled around his boots, cheered on by warriors who called it "training."

Wolf Clan

Lady Vyrna Faelorwyn wore a mourning-thorn cloak. Her warrior's eyes were feral-keen; grief hung about them like cold fog.

Eagle Clan

Lord Kalmir Aeralion descended with wings rimed in frost. His pale blue cloak rustled like glacier wind, every step precise.

Owl Clan

Lord Lowsm Thalosmyr wore dusk-shades and moved like deliberate silence. His clan watched everything with unblinking calm.

Unicorn Clan

Lord Corbys Elaryaen stood poised and geometric, children arrayed behind him in precise formation. Their discipline was a kind of living mathematics.

White Hart Clan

Lord Thaloryn Hart'Thorne gleamed serene and winter-still. White-antler helms shimmered behind him.

Felhart Clan

Lord Flans Felhart stood stone-still, stern, his warriors echoing his quiet, relentless focus.

Moon Clan

Lord Perris Moon'Sael shimmered in tide-silver radiance. His clan's Songs shifted like water under moonlight.

Kellyn scanned the circle.

Most future-born were absent—vanished into forests for their Six-Month Trials of Discovery. Even Corlyn's fate was uncertain—alive, or swallowed by roots.

Not knowing gnawed at her more sharply than any wound.

When all twelve seats were filled, Brun stepped forward.

The Great Tree's heart beat once—a deep, resonant boom that trembled through bark and bone.

"Anari," Brun said, his small frame carrying a voice older than any clan, "tonight we celebrate the first victory in the War of the Twelve Races."

The Grove erupted.

Dragons roared.
Wolves howled at the rising stars.

Sylph Songs shimmered like woven light.

Bear Clan hammered shields.

Unicorn spears rose in perfect unity.

Eagle wings snapped open with frost-bright thunder.

Brun lifted his hand again.

Silence fell like a held breath.

"Feast, children of the forests," he said.

"Tonight, the world remembers we are not prey."

The Grove exploded into motion—
longleaf tables unfurling,
lantern-fruit deepening to molten amber,
dragons spiraling to new perches,
Sylph dancers flickering between roots like living starlight.

Kellyn's chest tightened.

This was home.

This was the world the future had lost.

This was what all their suffering was meant to save.

And yet, beneath the warmth of celebration, the Tree's deeper harmonics thrummed with tension.

The feast was only prelude.

The real storm was political.

Roots shifted.

Saplight dimmed.

Sylveron Windstream rose.

And the Grove went utterly still.

Stormlight glimmered across his mantle of wind-feathers. Every motion was precise, measured—a man certain history already belonged to him.

Kellyn felt Harvey stiffen beside her.

Sylveron raised the ceremonial Sword of Breath. The blade hummed with storm-harmonics as the Grove waited in a mix of anticipation and dread.

"High Druid. Clan Lords. Children of Anarion," Sylveron said, voice rolling like distant thunder. "Tonight we mark our first victory in an age. But victory must be secured. A fractured people cannot withstand a world of enemies."

Griffyn warriors murmured approval.
Other clans shifted uneasily.

He lifted the sword.

"Thus, as Clan Lord, I bind oath with blood and Song."

Stormlight brightened.

He turned toward Harvey.

"Harvey Oakenstride," Sylveron intoned,

"who has taken Griffyn Song into his marrow,

who fought with storm-courage before the very jaws of the

Osiri—

I declare you pledged…

to my daughter, Nyssara Windstream."

Shock rolled through the Grove like a thunderclap.

Griffyn:

Spears thumped in approval from some; others winced at

Nyssara's rigid posture.

Dragon:

Uneasy murmurs—this smelled of overreach.

Sylph:

Silent as still air, tension rippling like high-altitude currents.

Bear:

Low, impressed grunts—boldness appealed to them.

Wolf:

A line of growls—heartless bonds offended their instincts.

Eagle:

Eyes narrowed—already calculating the angles.

Moon and White Hart:

Serene but unsettled.

Wyvern:

Their death-sense stirred. Ambition was a herald of blood.

Harvey's voice stayed calm, but Kellyn felt the anger under it.

"Lord Sylveron… I respect the honor, but this is—"

"I am not finished," Sylveron cut in, slicing the air with his hand.

He turned toward Kellyn.

The air thinned.

"Kellyn Windstream," he said,
"Dragon-trained, future-born, spark of our deliverance—
for your deeds in Amenemapet's crypt and at the Osiri breach,
I bind you as well."

Kellyn's breath went cold.

"You shall be pledged to Torval of Draknest, son of the Dragon Isles—
that Griffyn and Dragon may stand united as we enter a new age of war."

Torval, standing behind the Dragon seat, blanched. This had not been his design. But he bowed anyway—refusing a Clan Lord in the Grove was unthinkable.

Kellyn's lungs locked.

Harvey's jaw clenched so hard she heard his teeth grind.

Nyssara's face cracked—not in weakness, but as if the mask she'd worn her whole life had finally grown too heavy.

The Grove erupted.

"Too soon!"

"He cannot bind her!"

"This unites two clans—"

"—or destroys them."

"He oversteps!"

"It is wisdom!"

"It is madness!"

Brun lifted his staff, but even the High Druid's authority strained against the uproar.

Before Kellyn fully realized she'd chosen, she stepped forward.

Her voice cut through the noise like a blade.

"You have no right to bind my life."

Sylveron's eyes narrowed.

"I have every right. You stand among us as Anari. Anari follow the ancient ways."

Kellyn's voice dropped to something colder than steel.

"I follow the way of choice."

Nyssara flinched as if struck. Hurt, anger, shame—all tangled behind her eyes.

Kellyn stepped deeper into the lanternlight.

"I invoke the Rite of Binding-Reversal."

The Grove detonated.

Gasps.

Shouts.

Prayers.

Half a dozen clans arguing at once.

Nyssara stepped forward, lifting her spear, knuckles white.

"I answer the Rite," she said, voice steady.

Silence fell like snow.

She met Kellyn's gaze, wounded and resolute.

"You have made this necessary," she murmured.

Kellyn shook her head.

"No. Your father did."

Nyssara's jaw hardened.

She raised her spear.

Kellyn drew her sword.

Brun spoke softly, and the Grove obeyed.

"The Circle must be drawn."

He touched his staff to the earth.

Roots withdrew from the Grove's center, coiling back like patient serpents. A smooth ring of earth appeared, veined with glowing sigils representing each clan:

Dragon — red-gold

Griffyn — storm-gray

Sylph — pale green

Wyvern — bone-white

Bear — deep umber

Wolf — icy blue

Eagle — frost-silver

Unicorn — white-gold

White Hart — leaf-white

Owl — dusk-purple

Felhart — ember-red

Moon — silver-blue

The Circle of Twelve.

Kellyn stepped in first—
weight centered, sword low, Dominion Song coiled around her in red-gold arcs. Divination hum vibrated in her bones, Sahn's training alive in every breath.

Nyssara entered opposite—
a storm condensed into one woman. Spear raised, eyes bright with fury and humiliation and something like desperate pride.

Brun raised his staff.

"You stand in the Circle of Twelve," he said. "Where Song meets Song. Where will presses against fate."

He lowered it.

"Begin."

Nyssara moved first.

Griffyn warriors did not stalk.
They struck.

She leapt, spiraling downward in a killing arc that would have split stone.

Kellyn was not there.

Divination pulled her half a step aside before thought. The spear cracked the earth where she'd stood.

Gasps rippled around the Circle.

Nyssara slid back, feathers along her braids lifting as she drew in breath. Her Song shifted—storm-harmonics rolling out like pressure before a hurricane.

Griffyn Form VII: Drag of the Tempest.

The air thickened. Kellyn's limbs dragged. Breath turned to syrup.

Nyssara lunged.

Kellyn parried once. Twice. Each motion grew heavier, slowed by the clinging Song.

Griffyn ranks murmured in fierce approval.

Kellyn stepped back—just enough to break her own rhythm—and changed her Song.

Dragon Form III: Cleansing Breath.

A red-gold counter-harmonic flared through her veins. The slowing Song tore away from her like rags in a gale.

The Grove cried out as one.

Nyssara's eyes widened.

She pivoted mid-stride into Form IX: Sky-Breaking Spiral, vanishing into a corkscrew blur, descending in a chain of precise, lethal strikes—

—and Kellyn moved through them like she'd already seen them.

Because she had.

Divination sang each line a heartbeat ahead.

A slip.

A pivot.

A low turn.

Nyssara's spear cut only light.

"How?" Nyssara gasped.

Kellyn's answer was soft.

"I see the next step before I take it."

Nyssara thrust again.

Kellyn twisted, caught the haft with her blade, and stripped the spear from Nyssara's hands. It clattered across the Circle.

Silence crashed over the Grove.

Kellyn lowered her sword.

"Pick it up."

Nyssara's cheeks flushed scarlet. She retrieved the spear and launched herself again—brilliant, angry, desperate to salvage honor.

Kellyn disarmed her a second time with a tap to the wrist.

"Pick. It. Up," Kellyn said, voice low.

Shame flickered through Griffyn ranks.

Nyssara called the last of her strength, body blurring into Form XII: Sky-Shattering Coil—vanishing into wind and reappearing behind Kellyn with a final killing strike.

Divination sang the angle before it began.

Kellyn stepped aside, touched Nyssara's elbow, and the spear skidded far from them.

Nyssara froze.

Song faltered.

Then she dropped to her knees, throat bared.

Harvey let out a long, shaking breath.

Sylveron went ashen.

Brun's voice rang soft and absolute.

"The duel is decided."

Kellyn walked forward, lifted her sword, let its point rest against Nyssara's collarbone…

…and lowered it.

"I claim no life," she said. "But I claim my freedom from your father's decree."

The Circle recognized the ruling. Bonds unraveled like old rope.

Nyssara remained kneeling, shoulders tight, eyes burning. Not broken—but cracked where pride could not hide the wound.

The glowing clan-sigils faded. Roots eased back into the earth.

The Circle of Twelve closed.

The Griffyn council surged to their feet.

Sylveron still stood in the roots of his seat, face bloodless, gaze fixed on the ground where his will had been broken twice in one night.

Vhailos Stormcrest, senior war-councilor, stepped forward. His voice cut like sleet.

"Clan Lord, the Circle has judged you twice. Your decree overturned. Your heir defeated. Griffyn honor demands action."

Murmurs stirred among Griffyn ranks.

"You hesitated in the Khem-Duat," another councilor hissed.
"You let the Sylph mock you in counsel."
"You let a future-born bend the Circle."

Sylveron closed his eyes.

He did not argue.
He did not beg.
He did not rise.

"So be it," he whispered.

Four Griffyn lords drew steel.

But they did not turn on Sylveron.
They turned on Dravokh.

Gasps rippled through the Grove.

Dravokh did not move until the last possible moment. Then her form bent like wind striking stone.

She parried Vhailos with one smooth, economical motion. His sword flew; he hit the roots hard.

The other three closed in.

The air shimmered.

Someone stepped out of it.

Not half-faded.

Not ghostlike.

Fully anchored. Fully real.

A man.

Tall, bronze-skinned, shoulders relaxed, hands empty. He moved like drifting dusk, every shift of weight precise. Presence poured off him like pressure before a storm.

He struck once.

Three Griffyn lords collapsed—disarmed so cleanly their blades hadn't yet hit the ground.

The Grove froze.

A male Sylph.

Visible.

Powerful.

Whispers shot like sparks:

"They're real…"
"He moved like the Windstep itself…"
"How would he fare against Sahn?"
"How would he fare against Kellyn?"

Nyssara stared, stunned.

Sylveron stared, horrified.

Kellyn felt another truth of the world tilt and slot into place.

Dravokh rested a calm hand on the man's forearm.

"Vaelkorh," she said.

Recognition crashed through the clans like a shockwave.

Her husband.
A living Sylph lord.
Hidden for generations.

Standing openly in the Grove.

"You dare strike my council?!" Sylveron roared. He snatched the Sword of Breath and charged.

Vaelkorh turned—not vanishing, not slipping into half-existence, but meeting him fully, grounded.

Steel flashed in storm-lit arcs. For several breaths, two masters collided: Sylveron's precision against Vaelkorh's unhurried, unforced grace.

Then Vaelkorh pivoted, drew in a single measured breath, and moved.

Sylveron's sword spun from his hand and embedded in the roots. Two of Vaelkorh's fingers pressed lightly to Sylveron's chest.

Sylveron flew backwards and skidded across the earth.

Energy exploded through the Grove.

Bear shoulders squared.

Wolf teeth bared.

Unicorn staffs blazed.

Wyvern hands fell toward hilts.

Eagle wings flared.

Moon robes rippled.

Dragon warriors shifted stances, ready.

The Grove stepped to the brink of clan war.

Dravokh's voice sliced the tension in half.

"Stand. Down."

The words carried a command that lived in the wind itself.

"That man is Lord Vaelkorh Dravokh," she said, eyes blazing.

"My husband. My equal. My shadow in storm and Song."

Silence swallowed the clearing.

A male Sylph lord.

A myth—alive.

Here.

Sahn Moonspear stepped forward, calm as ever.

"You have defended your lady," he said. "But this Grove stands under the High Druid's protection. Here, only his word governs."

Vaelkorh studied him and nodded once—a warrior's respect, not submission.

Dravokh stepped forward into full lanternlight.

And spoke the words that set the world on fire.

"You are wrong, Sahn," she said.
"The Sylph answer to the High Druid…

but from this day forth, we also answer to Kellyn Windstream—Queen of the Unveiled Path."

The Grove exploded.

"Impossible!"
"No clan rules another!"
"Queen?!"
"She's future-born!"
"This is blasphemy!"
"Sylph arrogance!"
"Sylveron has lost control!"
"The Tree will not allow this!"

Songs flared into threats.
Weapons lifted halfway.
Old wounds and new ambitions howled to life.

Brun struck the root with his staff.

The Great Tree shuddered.

Bark rippled like disturbed water.

Dryads stepped from the trunk—six of them, eyes glowing green-gold, hair flowing like submerged moss.

They began to hum.

Low.

Resonant.

Ancient.

A charm-song in the first language of forests.

It rolled across the clans.

Anger softened into unease.

Blades sagged.

Wings lowered.

Wolves turned snarls into rough exhalations.

Even Sylveron's clenched fists loosened against his will.

The song did not command obedience.

It compelled clarity.

"The first to draw a weapon again," Brun said quietly, "will spend a year in heartwood with the dryads… to remember why anger has no place in this Grove."

One dryad turned her gaze on a Wolf warrior. He immediately stepped back behind his kin.

"This ground is sacred," Brun continued, staff bright with saplight. "No blood will stain it tonight."

One by one, heads lowered.

Even Sylveron.

Even Vaelkorh.

Even Sahn.

From that moment on, no one spoke to Brun without the title:

High Druid.

Brun lifted his staff once more.

"Tonight is not for fighting," he said. "Tonight is for remembrance."

He turned, young face lit with ancient certainty.

"We celebrate victory over the Osiri.
We celebrate the recovery of the Necrodemicon.
We celebrate new trade roads and the discovery of the Khem-Duat.
We celebrate the revelation that Sylph men walk among us.

And yes…"

His gaze found Kellyn.

"…we celebrate the unveiling of a new path."

He lifted the staff high.

"Let five years of peace be granted to the clans of the forests," Brun said. "A breath before the storm returns."

The dryads hummed a final chord.

It settled into every Anari heart like a seed.

Lanterns brightened.

Music unfurled.

Dragons rumbled low Songs that shook the branches.

Children danced between roots.

Clans mingled—carefully, curiously.

The Festival of Victory began in earnest.

Within a single song's length, Sylveron was quietly removed from leadership. Griffyn elders gathered around him, voices low and relentless. Vhailos's words carried to nearby listeners:

"The Circle judged you. The Grove watched you fall. Griffyn honor demands change."

Sylveron did not argue.

A new future for Griffyn Clan began—without him.

At the edge of the Grove, Nyssara sat beneath the outer roots where lanternlight faded into shadow. Her spear lay across her knees. Her fingers trembled despite her iron posture; her eyes were rimmed red, not from battle smoke, but from humiliation she refused to show.

She had lost twice tonight—once in the Circle, once in her clan.

Torval found her first.

He approached slowly, then knelt beside her.

"Nyssara," he said, voice gentle. "You fought with heart. You stood in front of the whole world and refused to bow small. I've always admired that."

"I have never failed like this," she whispered. "Not in drills. Not in war. Not in anything."

Torval shook his head.

"You showed them what courage looks like when pride has nothing left to stand on," he said. "That's rarer than victory."

Her breath hitched—just once.

For the first time that night, she leaned, just slightly, into someone who wanted nothing from her except the truth of who she was.

Something small and fragile took root there.
A seed in the dark.

Kellyn stood at the edge of the dance-terrace, scanning the crowd until she found Harvey.

He caught her searching and smiled—tired, but real. He crossed to her in quick, sure strides, as if pulled by something older than either of them.

"You shouldn't have had to fight that duel," he murmured.

Kellyn managed a wry, worn smile.

"You didn't have to worry," she said. "I knew her forms. And…"

She reached for his hand.

"…I knew you were watching."

His fingers closed around hers—warm, solid, anchoring.

"I'm here," Harvey whispered.

"And I'm free," she whispered back.

Nearby Dragon, Wolf, and Sylph warriors pretended very badly not to watch. Their small nods carried something like blessing.

Up in the branches, Froster sat beside Khandyl of the Wolf Clan.

He had survived Osiri chains, haunted sea, the Khem-Duat's horrors… and still he fidgeted.

"You survived Osiri," Khandyl murmured, nudging him with a shoulder. "You survived crypts and tunnels and titans—and you're still afraid of me?"

Froster flushed.

"You're… very confident."

"That's why you like me," she said, looping her arm through his.

He went crimson but did not move away.

Khandyl tilted her head back and gave a quiet, satisfied howl.

Froster smiled—a real, unguarded thing.

Loka lingered near a ring of Sylph dancers, Necrodemicon finally out of sight, shoulders still tense with the memory of its weight.

Ellendyl sat nearby with a Felhart elder who carved spirals into driftwood. She watched her clan cautiously, as if too near might break something fragile inside her.

"Still not speaking to them?" Loka asked softly.

Ellendyl flinched.

"It is… difficult," she admitted. "They're my people—and my past. I'm afraid that if I walk back into their circle, I'll break something that can't be mended."

"They won't break," Loka said. "They'll bend. And they will embrace you. Maybe not tonight. Maybe not all at once. But they will."

Her tension eased—barely—but enough.

"Maybe soon," she whispered. "Not tonight."

Their hands stayed lightly touching far longer than either of them noticed.

As music deepened into twilight, Lady Dravokh approached Kellyn. Vaelkorh walked at her side—hands clasped behind his back, presence like the calm center of a storm.

Dravokh inclined her head.

"Kellyn Windstream," she said softly, "Queen of the Unveiled Path. The night was nearly lost. You turned it."

Kellyn shook her head. "It wasn't just me."

"Everything is paths," Dravokh replied. "You see the ones others cannot. Because of that, my clan stands with you."

She gestured.

Two Sylph stepped from the edges of perception—tall, elegant, half-faded at the edges, but very real. In lanternlight they looked like moonlit wind given form.

"From this day," Dravokh said, "these two stand at your side. Until peace fails, or your path ends."

"I don't need guards," Kellyn protested.

Vaelkorh smiled faintly—a dusk-soft curve of the lips.

"Everyone who walks ahead of the Song does," he said. "Especially queens who unveil truths others fear to see."

The two Sylph bowed, hand to heart.

Whispers stirred through the Grove.

Protector-wind, standing behind a future-born queen.

Kellyn's breath caught.

Queen of the Unveiled Path.

Not a title she had sought.
A mantle the world had quietly woven around her.

Near the central root, Brun climbed onto a low rise. The dryads stood behind him, eyes like molten leaves.

"For five years," Brun said, his child's voice bearing an ageless tone, "let there be peace."

A hush rippled through the Grove.

"The world will not hand us peace," he continued. "So we will carve it from the years ourselves."

The dryads hummed—a soft, warm chord, rich as deep soil.

The Great Tree dimmed its saplight in gentle approval.

Music swelled once more.
Dragons rumbled lullaby-Songs.
Children spun between roots.
Clans—Dragon and Wolf, Sylph and Bear, Unicorn and

Wyvern and all the rest—found one another amid shared food, shared scars, shared wary hope.

The Festival of Victory unfurled into the night.

Kellyn stood beneath drifting lanterns, Harvey at her side, the two Sylph guardians a quiet presence behind her.

She watched clans dance.
She watched peace form itself in fragile, shimmering threads.
She watched the world she'd been born too late to know.

Queen of the Unveiled Path.

Not a throne.
A direction.

For the first time since stepping into the past, Kellyn did not feel like a refugee from a dead future.

She felt like someone who might actually change it.

Chapter 61 – Death of a Pharaoh

Planet: Vael'thara
Location: Kheu-Duat (Osiri Capital)
BV 24

The Khem-Duat beneath Kheu-Duat, capital of the Osiri Empire, had never known fear.

It was a place of stone certainty—
vaulted sandstone halls carved with jackal-headed gods,
incense braziers burning an eternal flame,
and the deep, humming resonance of the sun-glyphs that lined the walls.

Priests moved through the corridors with quiet confidence.
Warriors patrolled the upper chambers without caution.
The Pharaoh's council debated treaties, sacrifices, and war without imagining interruption.

No one in the empire had ever thought the Sylph could reach this far south.

No one believed the Aeralith forest could cross the desert.

No one had envisioned that the forest would walk into their capital.

That changed tonight.

Deep beneath the capital, in a long-forgotten chamber whose walls bore symbols older even than the Osiri, a faint shimmer rippled across the teleportation pad.

A breeze stirred.

But no air should have existed here.

The braziers flickered.

The engraved glyphs pulsed.

Then—

Wind.

Shadow.

Movement.

The Hidden Host stepped through in perfect silence.

Vaelkorh emerged first, blade drawn, cloak whispering like a memory.

Behind him came Shyr, Faelen, and 20 more Windveil warriors.

They spread through the chamber with choreographed precision, each man slipping into a different angle of shadow.

Vaelkorh lifted two fingers.

The Host vanished.

Only the soft dimming of the torchlight marked their passage.

The Osiri council chamber was a masterpiece of desert artistry:

- a vast oval hall of obsidian and sun-gold,

- a giant map-table depicting the desert kingdoms,

- glyph-columns rising like petrified flame,

- the Pharaoh seated upon a raised dais of sandstone lions.

He was flanked by advisors—four priests, three generals, and a single terrified scribe who had been trying, for the last hour, to warn them that something had gone wrong underground.

"…the harmonic readings have shifted, Great Pharaoh," the scribe stammered. "Something is—"

A general scoffed.

"Their forest magic cannot reach here. Speak sense."

Another added, "Our priests assure us the forest cannot cross sand. This is our domain."

The Pharaoh waved lazily. "Enough. The Sylph are cornered. They bleed. Their canopy burns. Soon we will turn their forest into timber—"

He stopped.

Something in the air changed.

A faint swirl.

A whisper.

A breeze where no breeze should be.

The nearest torch sputtered.

The generals looked up.

The priests frowned.

The scribe's eyes widened in horror.

"Great Pharaoh… someone is here."

A single leaf drifted down from nowhere.

An Osiri priest reached for it—
and Shyr appeared behind him, blade flashing once.

The man fell before he realized he'd been touched.

Chaos erupted.

The second priest screamed—
And Faelen's spear ripped him from behind, dragging him
into the shadows.

A general raised his halberd—
and Vaelkorh materialized mid-step, slicing clean through the
weapon's shaft before severing the general's throat.

The remaining priests tried to chant, but the Hidden Host
knew their rhythms.

They counter-sang in silence—
a harmonic null-field built from their own breathlines.

The Osiri priests' voices choked off instantly.

Not a spell miscast.

Not a prayer interrupted.

A Song stolen.

The priests collapsed.

Two guards grabbed the Pharaoh and pulled him behind the map-table, but Vaelkorh stepped between them, a blur of wind and shadow.

One heartbeat—
both guards fell, their armor sliced apart.

The Pharaoh staggered backward, eyes wide, sand-magic crackling along his arms.

"You cannot be here," he whispered.
"This is the heart of the desert. No tree grows here. No forest breathes."

Vaelkorh stepped closer.

"We came through your tunnels," he said quietly.
"Your own Khem-Duat guided us."

The Pharaoh raised a sunstrike—the desert's most lethal close-range spell.

Vaelkorh didn't flinch.

Shyr struck first, knocking the Pharaoh's arm aside.

Faelen stepped in from the left, blade angled.

A third warrior blocked the exit.

Vaelkorh raised his windstep blade.

"For the forest you burned," he said.

"For the roots you carved.

For the Songs you tried to silence."

The Pharaoh's last breath trembled.

"Impossible…"

Vaelkorh cut him down.

He fell across the giant desert map—

blood spilling across the etched dunes.

The council chamber was silent.

No alarms.

No cries.

Just stillness.

Vaelkorh looked to the corner of the room where a shriveled ornamental desert-tree stood—a ceremonial offering brought from a distant oasis.

Its roots trembled.

"Faelen," Vaelkorh said. "Grow it."

Faelen stepped forward, pressed his palm to the withered bark, and whispered a Sylph spell:

"Lun'thar syl'ari—awaken."

Roots burst outward.

Branches spiraled upward.

Leaves unfurled in shimmering green.

In seconds, a full-grown tree filled the chamber—
alive, vibrant, swaying with impossible life.

Vaelkorh bowed to it in silent gratitude.

Then he stepped inside.

One by one, the Hidden Host followed, vanishing into the bark.

Shyr entered last, whispering the ritual phrase:

"By leaf and breath, let home remember us."

The tree sealed behind him.

Then collapsed into dust.

Osiri guards burst into the chamber seconds too late.

They found:

- the council dead,

- the generals slain,

- the Pharaoh's body lying across the map-table,

- blood dripping from dunes and city glyphs,

- and a pile of leaves on the floor that should not—
  could not—exist in the desert.

There were no windows.

No exits.

No broken doors.

The guards stared at the impossible scene.

One finally whispered:

"The forest came here…
and it killed our king."

In the heart of Aeralintar, Dravokh opened her eyes.

Wind stirred her cloak.
Whisper-Vines trembled with relief.

The forest pulsed—
not in fear,

not in anger,

but in release.

Vaelkorh stepped from a great-root transport tree, lowering his hood.

"It is done," he said.

Dravokh bowed her head.

"The desert's head is severed," she replied.
"The war shifts now."

Vaelkorh's eyes darkened. "Yes," he said.

"And the forest is not finished."

Epilogue

Planet: Vaelthara
Location: Talos Eyrie
BV 24

Later, as the songs quieted and lantern-light drifted like slow-burning embers, Harvey stepped away from the feast and found stillness beneath the outer boughs.

The night was calm—**too** calm—and memory crept in where celebration left space.

He saw the crypt again:

the air choked with dust,

the emerald roar of Kuldemaekr's flames,

the clean, final stroke he'd sworn ended a tyrant.

Amenemapet's form had shattered under the blade—

bone, flesh, and spell-work dissolving into ash.

Except for one thing.

The skull.

It had remained.

Smooth.

Untouched.

Whole.

Back then—stunned, wounded, poisoned by grief—the sight barely registered.

But here, beneath the whisper of frost-laden branches and the soft rumble of dragons nesting in the heights, that detail struck him hard.

Nothing shaped by necrotic harmonic reaction should have survived Kuldemaekr's fire.

Not bone.

Not spellbound carbon.

Nothing.

Harvey's breath rose faint white in the cold air.

A knot tightened in his chest.

"Something isn't finished," he murmured.

He didn't tell Kellyn.

He didn't tell anyone.

Some truths didn't belong to a night of peace.

But unease stayed with him—

a shape in the dark,

patient and waiting.

Far to the south, beneath Pahentum—a city of sandstone monoliths and obsidian spires—

a concealed Osiri sanctum pulsed with amber glyph-light.

An acolyte knelt in the glow, voice shaking.

"Sun-Hierophant… Amenemapet has awakened.

His echo has reached the deepest chambers."

The emissary did not lift his gaze from the tablet.

His eyes flicked once over the runes.

He exhaled—

quiet,

measured,

almost reverent.

"Then the reckoning begins."

Appendix 1: Pantheon of the Anari with Clan Affiliations

1. Anaridin — The Creator
Domain: Origin, unity, sovereignty
Clan Affiliation: Dragon Clan (ancestral, ruling line; tied to
creation and leadership)

2. Elaria — Mother of All
Domain: Fertility, nurturing, beginnings
Clan Affiliation: Unicorn Clan (purity, life-giving)
Secondary: White Hart Clan (renewal, rebirth)

3. Aelion — God of War
Domain: Valor, conquest, defense
Clan Affiliation: Griffyn Clan (courage, aerial mastery in battle)
Secondary: Bear Clan (strength, frontline defense)

4. Faelor — Nocturnal Hunt
Domain: Hunter god with respect for life
Clan Affiliation: Wolf Clan (moonlit hunters, loyalty, primal instinct)

5. Elandor — The Killing Huntress
Domain: Predator, bloodhunt, merciless killing
Clan Affiliation: Wyvern Clan (fierce, darker hunting traditions)
Rivalry: Wolf Clan (whose hunt honors life)

6. Valkryss — Goddess of Magic
Domain: Sorcery, mystical knowledge
Clan Affiliation: Moon Clan (arcane mystery, nocturnal spellcraft)
Secondary: Sylph Clan (air, illusion, glamours)

7. Thalorin — God of Death
Domain: Endings, passage of souls
Clan Affiliation: Owl Clan (wisdom of death, silent watchers of mortality)

8. Sylvara — Goddess of Creatures of the Forest
Domain: Beasts, fae, wild companions
Clan Affiliation: Sylph Clan (connection to spirits, faerie)
Secondary: Felhart Clan (guardianship of small but fierce creatures)

9. Thorne — God of Forest Trees & Plants
Domain: Roots, growth, plantlife
Clan Affiliation: White Hart Clan (sacred groves, renewal)

10. Lireal — God of Justice
Domain: Balance, fairness, judgment
Clan Affiliation: Eagle Clan (judges from above, impartiality, high vision)

11. Lyrianne — Goddess of Vengeance
Domain: Wrath, retribution
Clan Affiliation: Bear Clan (unyielding vengeance, strength of retribution)

12. Tha — God of Luck
Domain: Fortune, chance
Clan Affiliation: Felhart Clan (bold risk-taking,
unpredictability)

13. Fyran — Goddess of Dance & Music
Domain: Celebration, rhythm, joy
Clan Affiliation: Unicorn Clan (beauty, harmony)
Secondary: Sylph Clan (song, performance, air-born arts)

14. Varethor — God of Weather
Domain: Skies, storms, shifting climate
Clan Affiliation: Eagle Clan (lords of the skies, bringers of storm)

15. Nyrielle — Goddess of the Stars & Heavens
Domain: Night sky, constellations
Clan Affiliation: Moon Clan (celestial wisdom, navigation by night)

16. Vaelyndra — Goddess of Seas & Storms
Domain: Tides, ocean's wrath
Clan Affiliation: Wyvern Clan (deep connection to sea storms, ferocity)

17. Selvaria — Goddess of the Ocean & Travel
Domain: Journeys across water
Clan Affiliation: Griffyn Clan (travelers, messengers, far-fliers)

18. Vaelthas — God of Shadows
Domain: Secrets, concealment
Clan Affiliation: Owl Clan (guardians of shadowed wisdom, stealth)
Secondary clan: Sylph Clan

19. Galather — God of Light
Domain: Illumination, hope, truth
Clan Affiliation: Dragon Clan (radiance of kingship, unifying light)

20. Caelrin — God of Rangers & Tracking
Domain: Woodcraft, survival, pursuit
Clan Affiliation: Wolf Clan (masters of tracking and wildcraft)

21. Aelrindel — The Imprisoned Huntsman
Domain: Wild Hunt, primal pursuit
Clan Affiliation: Eagle Clan (once the horn's bearer, taken from him)
Status: Bound long ago, his cult was suppressed

22. Burk – God of the Tree folk.
Domain: Dryads, tree folk, trees.
Clan Affiliation: None. Tree folk revere Burk.

23. Vecha-los – The Crone.
Domain: Fate, Destiny, Glamours
Clan Affiliation: None, but feared by all.

24. Daryana – Goddess of Fertility

Domain: Birth, Fertility, Family

Clan Affiliation: Unicorn Clan

Appendix 2: The Twelve Races of Vaelthara

1. Anari (Wood-elf–like people)

Core Traits: Tall, lithe, long-lived, deeply tied to forests and magic.

Culture: Clan-based society (Dragon, Griffyn, Wolf, Unicorn, etc.), with a Confederation in the future. Forest protectors.

Strengths: Magic, song, archery, linguistic gifts, and a strong oral tradition. Fay beings and the forest itself are their allies. Long life span (average is 1,500 years).

Weaknesses: Pride, internal rivalries, and proven only within forests.

—Thaliryn Leafstride, Sylph Clan scout
"We don't get lost. We discover better paths than the one everyone else insisted on."

2. Gravhal (dwarf like people)

Core Traits: Short, stocky, endurance unmatched.

Culture: Stone citadels and underground halls, strong guild traditions.

Strengths: Master smiths, rune magic, resilience in battle. Long lifespan avg. (about 740 years).

Weaknesses: Stubborn, conservative, poor adaptability outside mountain/stone environments.

—Bromdur Ironshoulder, Gravhal mason
"Aye, I'll change my mind… once the mountain does."

3. Nimvrels (Gnome like people)

Core Traits: Small, clever, endlessly curious.

Culture: Tinkerers, inventors, alchemists.

Strengths: Ingenious inventors, illusions, clockwork devices, cunning diplomacy. Long lifespan average (900 years).

Weaknesses: Physically weak, lacks military power, and overreaches through curiosity.

—Tinkletop Gearwisp, Nimvrel inventor
"Relax! I tested this device thoroughly. Only exploded twice, and I wasn't even in the room either time!"

4. Thraekars (various giant races)

Core Traits: Towering, immense physical strength, semi-nomadic.

Culture: Tribal, honor-based; keep oral histories.

Strengths: Physical might, endurance, and some storm magic. Very long lifespans (Frost giants about 15,000 years, Fire giants 12,000 years, Fomorians about 900 years, Ogres about 200 years).

Weaknesses: Slow to adapt, often manipulated by smaller races, and rare in number.

—Urmak Storm-Walker, Thraekar wanderer
"Patience is the calm before the stomp."

5. Sza'thir (Reptile bipedal race)

Core Traits: Reptilian humanoids, scaled, cold-blooded.

Culture: Marsh and river dwellers; pragmatic and survival-oriented.

Strengths: Amphibious, resilient, natural warriors, cunning hunters. Long lifespans (400 years).

Weaknesses: Distrusted by others, seen as "alien," cold pragmatism limits empathy.

—Ssilvar Yex, Sza'thir hunter
"Warmbloods panic too easily. If the water bubbles, it means lunch is coming."

6. Krikk'ar (Insect like race)

Core Traits: Carapace exoskeletons, varied insectoid forms (mantis, beetle, wasp types).

Culture: Hive societies with queens and castes.

Strengths: Numbers, coordination, tireless workers, venom or flight depending on type. Racial memory.

Weaknesses: Rigid caste system, lack of individuality, fragile diplomacy with others. Short lifespan (80 years).

—Kritt-Kritt, Krikk'ar worker drone
"Individuality is overrated. I tried it once. Terrible experience. Much confusion."

7. Zagg'rin (Goblinoid race)

Core Traits: Small, wiry, sharp-featured, cunning.

Culture: Scavengers, opportunists, live in marginal lands.

Strengths: Adaptable, tricksters, alchemy, and sabotage specialists. Rapid breeding (large birth counts).

Weaknesses: Poor unity, susceptibility to corruption, and cowardice in battle without numbers. Short lifespan (60 years).

—Zibbit the Untrustworthy (self-given title)
"Look, if I'm holding it, I definitely didn't steal it. Yet."

8. Minos (Minotaur-like)

Core Traits: Bull-headed humanoids, muscular, labyrinthine instincts.

Culture: Warrior clans, honor duels, blood oaths.

Strengths: Fierce warriors, strong seafaring tradition, labyrinth memory, infectious bite turns victims to Minos.

Weaknesses: Hot-tempered, divided into warring tribes, easily baited.

—Thalgar Redhorn, Minos war-leader
"I do not have anger issues. I have anger solutions."

9. Aeryndai (Avian people)

Core Traits: Winged humanoids, hollow-boned but strong.

Culture: Sky citadels, keen hunters, and scouts.

Strengths: Flight, sharp eyesight, aerial combat dominance. Long lifespan (about 500 years).

Weaknesses: Frail bones, isolationist, disdain for ground-dwellers.

—Skylune Sharpeye, Aeryndai sky-scout
"I'm not looking down on you. Well… I mean I am, but only because I'm literally above you."

10. Osiri

Core Traits: Tall, bronze-skinned, desert-dwelling humans with mystical lineage.

Culture: Ancient cities, sun cults, pyramids, and preservation of old magics.

Strengths: Strong in ritual magic, desert survival, and prophetic traditions. Long lifespan (about 500 years).

Weaknesses: Arrogance, bound by strict hierarchy, and insularity.

—Hesep-Amun, Osiri ritualist
"If the sun wanted you to question me, it would have blinded you sooner."

11. Veydrath (Undead)

Core Traits: Tall, pale, necrotic aura, often cloaked in shadows. Undead of various forms led by vampire counts.

Culture: Masters of necromancy, rule over undead thralls.

Strengths: Command over death, raising armies, and the feared lore of the grave.

Weaknesses: Shunned by all other races, tied to necrotic energies, fragile when cut off from their dark magic.

—Count Varis Umbershade, Veydrath noble
"Ah, the living. So dramatic about the whole 'breathing' thing."

12. Humans

Core Traits: Versatile, numerous, short-lived.

Culture: Expansive, adaptable to all lands, and empire-builders.

Strengths: Flexibility, innovation, rapid technology advancement, adaptability, sheer numbers, and quick breeding cycles.

Weaknesses: Lack of specialization, short-sightedness, hunger for expansion. No special abilities. Short lifespan (70 years).

—Captain Jalen Ward, human mercenary
"We don't need magic. We've got optimism and bad ideas in equal measure."

Appendix 3: The Twelve Known Clans of the Anari

- Dragon Clan — High-warrior lineage; keepers of martial traditions, draconic banners, and flame-sigils.

- Griffyn Clan — Proud knightly houses, aerial cavalry, chivalric codes.

- Eagle Clan — Scouts, skyward seers, farsight traditions.

- Wolf Clan — Stoic defenders, cold-weather legions, survivalists. Superb scouts and group tactics.

- Bear Clan — Heavy infantry, guardians of taiga strongholds, craftsmen.

- Unicorn Clan — Mystics and healers, linked to Verdantis and ancient rites.

- White Hart Clan — Rangers and wanderers; lore of forests and liminal places.

- Wyvern Clan — Fierce but more mercantile; pragmatists who balance tradition and trade.

- Felhart Clan — Resilient survivalists, famed for stubbornness and unconventional tactics.

- Moon Clan — Dream-seers, diviners, tied to lunar cycles and prophecy.

- Owl Clan — Scholars, archivists, keepers of the Old Tongue; often allied with Kellyn's work.

- Sylph Clan — Graceful wind-kin, aerial combat specialists, poets, and diplomats.

Appendix 4: The Sylph Clan

 — Vael'Shar Codex Fragments

A classified entry of the Time Bureau Files, TDG-512B.

THE AERALITH CANOPY — DOMAIN OF THE SYLPH

The Aeralith Canopy is a tri-layered rainforest suspended above the world like a living sky. The Sylph dwell between the Second and Third Canopy layers, where leaf-light, wind-paths, and shadowed walkways form the hidden city of Lunethryn.

- First Canopy — Root-light and shifting sunbeams.
- Second Canopy — Traveler's Edge, home to whisper-bridges.
- Third Canopy — The Hidden Heart, domain of the Sylph city.

Male Sylph become unseen after completing the Ritual of Discovery, living six months alone in the canopy. Within the forest, the canopy itself hides them; outside it, their invisibility weakens to a radius of roughly ten feet.

WHISPER-VINE (Vespertillis silens arborum)

A sacred vine native only to the Aeralith Canopy. Its fibers dampen vibration, shift light, and hum in harmony with forest frequencies. Woven into Sylph fungal armor, it creates the Windveil Field — the biological heart of Sylph stealth.

Properties:
- Vibration-damping lattice fibers
- Canopy-resonance mimicry
- Photoadaptive leaf-cell camouflaging

CODEX HARMONICA — ENTRY IX: SYLPH CLAN

"The world moves in straight lines because it does not know how to dance." — Sylph blade-teaching.

The Sylph fight as wind dances: never where expected, always moving, always singing.

Seichūsen (Soul-Line): Syl'phyr — the Dancing Line.

Lýren'thal (Path): Windstep Spiral — shifting arcs like sudden gusts.

Veyl'Ashar (Distance): Gale Range — unpredictable flow of near and far.

Catal'ri (Tone): Fading flute-breath, mistaken for wind or laughter.

THE EIGHT VAEL'SHAR — WINDSTEP DANCES OF DEATH

1. Vael'Shar Windveil Step — "Step Beneath the Windveil"
Whisper-Vine enhances lateral drift, erasing sound and making the Sylph appear to glide.

2. Vael'Shar Whispercut — "Cut of the Whispering Wind"
Masks timing shifts; enemies parry too early or too late.

3. Vael'Shar Gale Spiral — "Galespiral Rend"
Photoadaptive shimmer dissolves the spiraling silhouette.

4. Vael'Shar Skydance Cut — "Cut of the Skydancer"
Reduces drag, enhances weightless aerial movement.

5. Vael'Shar Miststep — "Miststep Through the Blade"
Vine contracts under pressure, shrinking the body profile.

6. Vael'Shar Ribbonfall — "Ribbonfall Sweep"
Wave-resonance creates flowing, silk-like lethal arcs.

7. Vael'Shar Breath of Two Winds — "Twinwind Turn"
Dual-tone resonance creates mirrored false images.

8. Vael'Shar Last Gale — "Last Gale of Sylvara"
Full Windveil activation makes the fighter move like
storm-torn leaves.

RITUALS, OATHS, AND LANGUAGE FRAGMENTS OF THE SYLPH

ᚠᛁᛐᛏᚯ'ᛋᛗᚱ — *The Whispering Oath of Sylvara*

"By leaf, by breath, by wind unseen — I walk the paths
between the worlds. Let no shadow claim me, let no storm
unmake me. I am Sylph, child of the Aeralith."

ᚦᚠᛖᛚ'ᛋᛁᛚᚹᛁᛗᚱ — *Whisper-Vine Harvest Rite*

Performed before gathering Whisper-Vine:
• A single breath offered to Sylvara.
• A whispered petition: "Luneth syl'ari, fael'tharyn."
• No more than an arm's length taken from any one vine.

Language Fragment: Sylph Windscript

Syl'phyr — soul-line
Vael — wind-dance
Lunethryn — veiled city
Fael'tharyn — sacred permission
Arath — divine breath

Fighting Styles of the Anari

Cultural Martial Terms of the Anari (Applied to Griffyn
Style)

Concept	Japanese Equivalent	Anari Canon Term	Meaning
Form	Kata	*Vael'Shar* ("Form of the Blade")	The physical technique pattern
Seichūsen	Line of Center	*Ael'thyr* ("Line of the Soul / Divine Axis")	Alignment of spirit and blade
Embusen	Movement Path	*Lýren'thal* ("Sung Path")	The rhythm-path traced through space
Maai	Combat Distance	*Veyl'Ashar* ("Breath-Distance")	Ideal harmonic distance of engagement
Kiai (battle cry)	Voice Focus	*Catal'ri* ("Verse Cry")	The vocal harmonic that empowers a movement
Complete Technique Name Format	—	*Vael'Shar [Name], sung along Lýren'thal, aligned to Ael'thyr, at Veyl'Ashar*	Full codex description

ENGRAVING THE CODEX — CEREMONIAL RELIC FORMAT

This is not just a list. This is the Anari sacred war-script as it would appear in a temple archive or master-blade chamber, carved in silverglyph or sung onto crystal vellum.

Appendix 5: Core Dragon Commands

- "Sythra!" — *Fly / Take wing*
- "Vorenn!" — *Strike with flame / acid / breath weapon*
- "Kraal!" — *Claw / rend / tear*
- "Druuk!" — *Descend / land / come down*
- "Veyth!" — *Ascend / climb higher*
- "Throsk!" — *Hold / hover in place*
- "Nekra!" — *Circle / prowl overhead*
- "Grath!" — *Charge / dive*
- "Shal!" — *Withdraw / retreat / fall back*
- "Orryn!" — *Guard / protect this one*
- "Keryn!" — *Sleep / rest / stillness*

Battlefield Variants

- "Feydra!" — *Scatter foes / spread terror* (roar, wing-buffet, intimidation)
- "Aelthos!" — *Burn the earth* (sustained ground attack)
- "Draven!" — *Strike mount or rider* (target cavalry/airborne foes)
- "Skarros!" — *Break the line* (slam or smash into infantry)

Bonded / Ritual Commands

(used by tamers like Sahn Moonspear)

- "Velthir." — *Bind / obey / submit to my will*
- "Ilyara." — *Peace / calm / soothe frenzy*
- "Druvien." — *Summon / come to me, wherever you are*
- "Thaloré." — *Oath / blood-pact reaffirmed*

Appendix 6: Calendars of the Anari

The Anari keep two principal reckonings of time. In ancient times, time was measured from the Sealing of the Chamber of Victory and expressed in divine years and animal months. In the future age, after the War of Twelve Races, time is recorded as BV (Before Victory) and FY (Future Year).

The Sealing Calendar (Ancient Anari)

Epoch: The placement of the Chamber of Victory. Dates are written as '<Divine Year> — <Animal Month>, <X> years since the Sealing.' The divine year names reflect the gods' patronage; the months honor clan totems.

Divine Cycle (Years of the Gods)

Representative entries from the divine cycle include:

- • Lireal — God of Justice, Law, and Oath.
- • Vaelthas — God of Shadows and Secrets.
- • Nyrielle — Goddess of Stars and Fate.
- • Lyrianne — Goddess of Vengeance and Redress.
- • Varethor — God of Storms and Weather.
- • Caelrin — God of Rangers and Tracking.
- • Burk — God of Treefolk and Deep Root.
- • Aelrindel — The Imprisoned Huntsman.
- • Tha — God of Luck and Turning Tides.
- • Fyran — Goddess of Dance and Song.
- • Vecha-los — The Crone, Fate and Ending.
- • Sylvara — Goddess of Forest Creatures and Growth.

Totemic Cycle (Months of the Animals)

The twelve animal months are:

- - • Wolf — strength, loyalty, ferocity
- - • Griffyn — guardianship, vision, courage
- - • Dragon — majesty, fire, destruction
- - • Owl — wisdom, silence, foresight
- - • Unicorn — purity, healing, grace
- - • Wyvern — cunning, exile, resilience
- - • Eagle — swiftness, vigilance, honor
- - • Serpent — knowledge, transformation, peril
- - • Stag — fertility, pride, wilderness
- - • Bear — endurance, patience, wrath
- - • Hawk — precision, freedom, the hunt
- - • Boar — stubbornness, battle, sacrifice

The BV/FY Calendar (Future Confederation)

After the War of Twelve Races, the futurists abandoned sacred cycles. Years are counted as BV (Before Victory), leading up to the war's end, and FY (Future Year) after. Example: BV 24; FY 3553.

Conversion Notes

Anchor points differ. By Bureau estimation, FY 3553 ≈ 25,000 years since the Sealing.
Examples:
- BV 24 ≈ Year of the Jackal, 21,423 since the Sealing.
- FY 3553 ≈ Year of Lireal, ~25,000 since the Sealing.

Appendix 7: The Osiri Sun-Chain Pantheon — *"The Solar Court and the Black Chains"*

Cultural Name of Religion: The Obsidian Covenant or The Sun-Chain Doctrine

Osiri Divine Creed: *"All power flows from the Sun. All shadow is only its servant. The weak banish demons. The strong command them."*

Tone: Regal, ritualistic, terrifyingly orderly, mixing Egyptian solar majesty with demon-binding arrogance.

Only pantheon that openly integrates Malloch energy under the claim of "righteous bondage."

☼ 1. RA-KHEPRA, THE SUN IN CHAINS — *High God of Dominion and Radiant Control*

- Dominion: Solar ascendance, rule through ritual law, dominion over lesser gods

- Symbol: A blazing sun encircled by golden chains

- Role: Supreme deity of Osiri, believed to bind gods, demons, even fate under solar law.
  Osiri priests say: *"The sun does not plead. It commands."*

- Echo of Anari: Galather (light) + Anaridin (sovereignty), but purity replaced by imperial doctrine — light as subjugation, not hope.

- Time Bureau Note:

"Harmonic resonance aligns with Galather but warp-distorted by control frequencies. Classified: Domination Light."

🌑 2. ANUB-HET, LORD OF THE SHADOW SEAL —
Binder of Demons, Warden of the Second Sun

- Dominion: Midnight rites, demon-binding, shadow under solar law

- Symbol: A jackal-headed god gripping a Malloch chain that bleeds black fire

- Role: Patron of Osiri demon-mages. Believed to chain Malloch shards to solar pillars beneath temples. Osiri believe shadow is only holy when it kneels before light.

- Echo of Anari: Thalorin (death) fused with Vaelthas (shadow) — but instead of passage, he enforces eternal captivity.

- Time Bureau Note:

"Binding rituals match Malloch interference patterns. Risk: Osiri pantheon partially compromised by controlled Malloch harmonics."

3. MA'AT-KETRA, THE JUDGE OF SUN-DUST —
Lady of Law, Scales, and Eternal Record

- Dominion: Judgment, balance under heaven, legal binding rituals

- Symbol: Scales held aloft by a chained sun emblem

- Role: Patron of scribes and solar judges. Belief: All souls weighed not for goodness, but for obedience to Sun Law.

- Echo of Anari: Lireal (justice) but made absolute —
  no mercy clause.
  Mercy is considered divine inefficiency in Osiri
  doctrine.

- Time Bureau Note:

"Faith-scales resonate sharply with Eastern Human Mandate-court harmonics — possible doctrinal crossover."

---

4. SEKHTAR THE FLAME-JACKAL — *Hunter of the Unbound*

- Dominion: Purge-fire, holy burnings, execution of
  unchained heretics

- Symbol: A roaring jackal-headed figure wreathed in
  golden-black fire

- Role: Enforcer god, invoked when Osiri burn shrines
  of other races or chain rebels in blazing pits.
  Fire here is not life — it is purification by destruction.

- Echo of Anari: Lyrianne (vengeance) + Elandor
  (predation) but ritualized under solar discipline.

- Time Bureau Note:

"Flame-harmonic shows strong potential to counter Malloch… but only if unbound from chain-runes. Currently tethered, not free."

---

5. NEFRA-SU'R, THE DESERT VEIL — *Mistress of Mirage and Withering*

- Dominion: Desert illusion, slow death by thirst, mind-
  mirage trials

- Symbol: A golden mask half-buried in sand with jackal eyes

- Role: Patron of Osiri seers who use mirages to break the minds of invading armies, showing false oases, false hope.

- Echo of Anari: Sylvara (fae illusions) + Nyrielle (celestial signs) but without beauty — only withering clarity.

- Time Bureau Note:

"Nefra-Su'r illusions strip memory of water — similar to Malloch consumption but executed through lawful ritual, not chaos."

🎭 Pantheon Tone Summary — Osiri

Aspect	Hawk-Kin	Osiri
Justice	Clear sight, duty to truth	Enforced hierarchy — truth is defined by the Sun
Shadow	Silence and precision	Shadow bound, enslaved to light
Magic	Harmonized wind-song	Commanded flame and chained demoncraft
Relationship to Malloch	Avoid direct corruption	Harnesses corruption as chained weapon

Time Bureau Verdict: *"Osiri pantheon is the only one to incorporate Malloch harmonic deliberately. If chains break during final convergence — Osiri gods may fall first... or ascend furthest."*

Appendix 8: The World Atlas of Vaelthara

Era of Harmony Year Zero — Compiled from Bureau Reconstructions and the Codex Harmonica

"The land dreamed itself awake, and the gods wrote their names across its forests." — Lireal the Just

I. The Continent of Vaelthara — "The Land That Dreamed Itself Awake"

Vaelthara is the cradle-world of the Anari, a single vast supercontinent encircled by the Seven Seas. Its terrain forms a natural lyre-shape: mountains as frets, rivers as strings, forests as notes. Twelve Sacred Forests mark the harmonic pillars of creation, each tied to a god, a clan, and a divine Song within the Codex Harmonica.

II. The Seven Seas of Vaelthara

Sea Name	Meaning / Domain	Location	Divine Association
Sea of Vael'mura	Waters of Forgotten Dawn	Between Amadin Jungle & Selunar Grove	Sylvara – Life & Memory
Bay of Thir'saal	Bay of Mirrors	Between Selunar Grove & the Great Desert	Lireal – Justice & Reflection

626

Lythar Reach	High Wind Waters	East of Skyrend Mountains	Arion High-Wing – Judgment
Narthan Deep	The Sleeping Sea	North of Frostcrag Mountains	Thalorin – Death & Endurance
Ael'tharyn Sea	Sea of Echoing Peaks	North of Toluscpatn Mountains	Valkryss – War & Courage
Fenlath Ocean	The Wolf's Mouth	West of Faelwyn Holt	Faelor – The Hunt
Dracoryn Sea	Sea of the Crowned Fire	Between the Dragon Isles & the Lavaridge Mountains	Anaridin – Creation Flame

III. The Twelve Sacred Forests of Vaelthara

Each forest is tied to a clan, a god, and a divine Song, embodying a single note in the Twelvefold Harmony.

IV. Harmonic Structure

The twelve keys form the base Song of Twelve, the harmonic counterpoint to the Seven Null Gods of the Malloch. When sung together, the forests form a resonance field sustaining Vaelthara's life-song.

V. Cartographer's Final Annotation

"To read this map is to hear the world breathe. Each sea is an echo, each mountain a pulse, each forest a note in the long memory of the gods. And if ever the Song falls silent, so too shall Vaelthara dream no more." — Inscription on the Aetherholt Tablets.

Forest / Region	Clan	God / Goddess	Domain
Drakkenwyld	Dragon Clan	Anaridin / Galather	Creation, Unity, Light
Ursathor Taiga	Bear Clan	Aelion / Lyrianne	War, Valor, Vengeance
Faelwyn Holt	Wolf Clan	Faelor / Caelrin	Hunt, Tracking, Instinct
Verdantis Glade	Unicorn Clan	Elaria / Fyran / Daryana	Life, Fertility, Harmony
Liminalis Forest	White Hart Clan	Thorne / Elaria	Renewal, Growth, Rebirth
Aetherholt	Griffyn Clan	Aelion / Selvaria	War, Travel, Honor
Wyvernwood	Wyvern Clan	Elandor / Vaelyndra	Predation, Storm, Cunning
Atheryn Holt	Owl Clan	Thalorin / Vaelthas	Death, Shadow, Wisdom

Aeralith Canopy	Sylph Clan	Fyran / Sylvara / Valkryss	Wind, Freedom, Illusion
Selunar Grove	Moon Clan	Valkryss / Nyrielle	Magic, Stars, Prophecy
Stonespire Thicket	Felhart Clan	Vyrna / Tha / Sylvara	Resilience, Luck, Guardianship
Skyrend Reach	Eagle Clan	Lireal / Varethor / Aelrindel	Justice, Weather, Vision

Appendix 9: Atlas of the Aeralith Canopy & the Great Desert

Era of Harmony Year Zero — Compiled from Bureau Reconstructions and the Codex Harmonica
"Where the winds falter and the sands remember, the world holds its breath." — Aetherholt Tablets, Fragment 44

I. Invocation & Sacred Geography of the Southern Frontier
"The Border Where Harmony Meets Silence"
The southern frontier of Vaelthara is not a boundary of land alone,
but a rift in the Twelvefold Harmony,
where the Song of the forests weakens
and the Null Echo of the desert begins.
Here, the Aeralith Canopy rises as the last green note of the gods—
a vast and wind-woven sanctuary shaped by the hands of Fyran of Dance,
Sylvara of Memory, and Valkryss of Storm and Vision.
Its leaves shimmer with the breath of ancient melodies,
a living testament that light may yet triumph over silence.
But beyond the canopy's southern descent lies the Great Desert,
known in old harmonic texts as
"Itharos Fen'Gaath — The Wound of Song."
It is a realm where:

- wind sings without harmony,
- mirages echo without source,
- and the dunes drift like sleeping beasts
  remembering an age before the gods carved the
  forests into being.

The Anari claim the desert was once touched by Sylvara's
shadow, but fell into dissonance when the Seven Null Gods
first slithered across the world in forgotten ages before the
Twelve Clans.
Thus, this place became the border of all borders—
the edge where harmony falters and silence hungers.
The Liminal Threshold
The southern frontier is a threshold of three truths:

1. To the North, the canopy holds its breath in green
    resilience.
2. To the South, dunes whisper Null Songs beneath an
    unblinking sun.
3. Between them, the wind remembers both—
    and belongs to neither.

Scholars of Aetherholt call this strip of land
"The Thin Breath,"
for even the Song itself grows wary there.
The Sacred Duty of the Sylph
To stand upon this threshold is the ancient charge of the
Sylph Clan, whose lightfooted warriors guard the border
between harmony and silence.
Their cities cling to the canopy's upper vaults,
their songs carried on wind
that refuses to surrender to the desert's stillness.
They keep the world in balance—
a duty older than their recorded memory.
The Southern Harmonic Divergence
The Codex Harmonica teaches:
"Where the Canopy meets the Desert,
the Song fractures into its two primal truths:
Wind that carries, and Sand that consumes."
This Atlas concerns that place of fracture—
the land where the Twelvefold Harmony
fought its oldest battle

and where, in the era of refugees and rising entropy,
its echoes stir once more.

II. The Aeralith Canopy — "The Last Green Note Before Silence"
"Where the wind learns its first song, and the leaves remember every footstep." — *Sylphan Archives, Verse 19*
The Aeralith Canopy rises like a suspended eternity—
a cathedral of living branches woven by the breath of the gods.
It is the southernmost of the Twelve Sacred Forests,
yet its nature is unique among them:
For the Aeralith does not grow upon the earth.
It ascends above it,
a layered horizon of wind, leaf, and shimmering light
that rides the sky as if held aloft by memory alone.
Those who first beheld it wrote:
"Here the world becomes weightless,
and even the shadows dream of flight."

---

1. Sacred Essence of the Aeralith
While other forests root themselves in soil and stone,
the Aeralith roots itself in air.
Its trees stretch not upward,
but *outward*,
creating endless vaulted terraces where countless lives may
walk without ever touching the ground.
Divine Associations
The canopy is the shared hymn of:
- Fyran, Goddess of Dance and Song
- Sylvara, Spirit of Memory and Renewal
- Valkryss, Lord of Storm, Vision, and Destiny
Thus, the forest expresses three harmonies at once:
1. The Song of Motion — the wind that dances

2. The Song of Remembrance — the leaves that whisper
3. The Song of Vision — the light that reveals truth
No other place in Vaelthara bears such triple resonance.
For this reason, the canopy is called:
"The Airborne Sanctuary."

---

2. The Living Architecture
The Aeralith is not built.
It is *grown.*
Vines bend to the will of song.
Branches twist to cradle platforms and bridges.
Lantern-pods glow with soft bioluminescence,
lit by the breath of the forest itself.
Bridges of the Wind
The bridges woven across the high canopy are alive.
When touched by breeze, they hum faintly,
creating a gentle chorus that shifts with the seasons.
Vaults of Light
Some vaults are so high that sunlight falls through them in
pillars,
transforming the forest floor into shifting mosaics of gold
and green.
The Sylph say:
"A traveler need not sing in the Aeralith—
the forest sings for them."

---

3. The Cities of the Aeralith
The Sylph construct no walls of stone,
for the canopy itself is their fortress.
Their cities cling to branches suspended hundreds of feet
above the world,
hidden from any who walk among the ground-born races.
Aeralintar — The City of Sky-Hold Light

The capital and highest of the canopy cities.
Its bridges ripple in the wind like woven banners,
and the entire city glows at twilight
as if lit from within by ancestral memory.
Ancient commentary claims:
"If the gods ever return, they shall descend first upon
Aeralintar,
for it alone remembers their footsteps."
Lenthrys A'erel — The Shrouded Verge
A city where fog gathers and refuses to leave.
Here the canopy thins,
and the desert winds sometimes rise to meet the forest
breath.
The mist is said to be alive:
a guardian spirit born from the first Sylph songs.
Siral — The Wind's Listening Post
Siral watches the northern curve of the desert frontier.
It hears threats carried on wind
long before eyes may see them.
Its archers stand silent for days,
listening to the shifting tones of the air,
reading warnings from patterns that others would call mere
breeze.

---

4. The Sylph — Children of Breath and Illusion
No clan is more intimately bound to the wind than the Sylph.
Their movements are light and deliberate,
guided by a lifetime of harmonic discipline.
The Unseen Rites
At age eight,
Sylph boys undergo The Ritual of the Vanishing Path,
after which they become nearly undetectable within the
forest.
Only the canopy itself sees them clearly.

To outsiders, Sylph culture appears dreamlike and elusive.
To the Sylph, it is simply harmony lived.
Sacred Thread: Selythra Vine
Their armor is woven from
Selythra vine-thread,
a plant that resonates with the wind
and disperses light around the wearer.
To the untrained eye,
a Sylph warrior appears as a shimmer in the leaves—
a shadow briefly misplaced.

5. Purpose and Vigilance
The Aeralith Canopy stands as the final bulwark
against the encroaching sands of the Osiri Empire.
It is a fortress not of stone,
but of Song.
Every leaf a sentinel.
Every branch a memory.
Every platform a vow.
As ancient Aetherholt tablets record:
"When the desert rises,
the wind must stand alone.
Thus the Sylph hold vigil,
and the gods' breath endures."

III. The Three Vigil-Notes of the Southern Canopy
"Where harmony grows thin, vigilance becomes the Song." — Lenthrys Codices, Leaf 12
Along the southern descent of the Aeralith Canopy,
where the last green breath meets the first rising dunes,
stand the Three Vigil-Notes —
Outposts 3, 4, and 5.
They are not fortresses of stone or iron.
They are living echoes of the forest's will:

raised from shaped branches, braided roots, and Song-woven platforms
that bow neither to desert wind nor to the Null Echo sleeping beneath the sands.
Ancient Sylph texts call them:
"The Notes That Hold the Line."
"For when the Wind must stand, it stands through us."

---

1. Outpost 3 — The First Breath of Warning
"Where the dune's whisper first reaches the leaf."
Outpost 3 rests upon the highest stable rise of the southern canopy,
its woven platforms facing the desert's northernmost tide.
It is the first to hear the shifting sands' dissonant murmur,
and the first to sense when the Osiri stir beneath the surface.
The winds near Outpost 3 change tone abruptly—
a subtle, trembling resonance that Sylph scouts learn to read
as one reads the changing rhythm of a heartbeat.
To stand here at dusk is to feel the world hold its breath.
Sacred Function:
- Detecting desert wind-tone changes
- Reading mirage-shift patterns
- Listening for tremors from the Khem-Duat beneath
- Relaying harmonic warnings deeper into the canopy

A Sylph watcher once wrote:
"The forest listens through me here.
I am its ear against the sand."

---

2. Outpost 4 — The Cliff-Edge Canticle
"Where leaf and dune behold each other without fear."
Perched upon a steep natural escarpment where forest height drops into rolling dunes,
Outpost 4 gazes directly into the desert's shimmering veil.

Its platforms are suspended like harp strings
between living trunks and anchored root-spires.
When the desert winds rise, the entire outpost hums softly,
producing a low, resonant chord that echoes for miles.
This is a place of vigilance and vision—
the strongest point of sight into Osiri territory
before the sands twist distance into illusion.
Sacred Function:

- Watching far-desert heat patterns
- Reading long-range mirage arcs
- Tracking caravan dust trails
- Seeing Osiri banners days before approach

Those who serve here say:
"Outpost 4 does not sleep.
Even in silence, it sings the truth of the horizon."

---

3. Outpost 5 — The Edge-Watch of Fading Green
"Where the forest gives its final vow to the world."
Outpost 5 stands at the southeastern border of the Aeralith,
where the canopy thins into the early sands
and the world feels neither entirely living nor entirely silent.
It is not a distant desert station.
It is the last rooted sentinel before the dunes take full
dominion.
From its platforms, scouts can see:

- The golden rise of the first dune belts
- Dust plumes along the road to Ankhuriset
- Faint surface vibrations when Khem-Duat tunnels
  shift
- The "breathing sands" that pulse during mirage-
  season

Outpost 5 is considered the most spiritually demanding of the
three,
for it stands closest to the Null Echo of the desert.

Sacred Function:

- Guarding the eastern approach
- Monitoring Osiri activity from Ankhuriset
- Watching for surface-level Khem-Duat anomalies
- Maintaining the forest's final harmonic resonance against the sands

The Aetherholt Tablets describe it thus:

"To stand at Outpost Five is to feel the Harmony thin,
yet refuse to break."

The Three Vigil-Notes Together
When the winds shift in unison across Outposts 3, 4, and 5,
the Sylph know that the desert is moving
—whether by weather, mirage, or marching army.
Together, these outposts form a living triptych of vigilance:

- 3 — The Ear
- 4 — The Eye
- 5 — The Heart

And they are said to embody the Three Aspects of Wind:

- Hearing (the listening breath)
- Seeing (the clear gust)
- Enduring (the steady gale)

Thus the Sylph maintain the southern harmony—
not through walls or armies,
but through awareness so deep
that the forest itself listens through them.

IV. The Great Desert — "The Wound of Song"
"Where silence learns to speak in mirrors, and the sun remembers what
the gods have forgotten." — Skyrend Hymnal, Line 807
South of the Aeralith Canopy,
where the last green syllable of wind falters,
lies the Great Desert —
a realm older than forests,

older than mountains,
and older, some say, than the Twelvefold Harmony itself.
The ancients called it
Itharos Fen'Gaath — The Wound of Song,
for here the resonance of creation fades
and the world's forgotten voices
gather like shadows beneath an eternal sun.
It is a land at once empty and overflowing,
silent yet never still,
a paradox written in sand and sky.

---

1. The Silence That Breathes
Unlike the forests, where the Song is warm and layered,
the desert carries the Null Echo —
a thin, brittle resonance
that neither nurtures nor destroys
but simply *remembers*.
Here the wind speaks without harmony,
and the air shivers with dissonant memories.
Scholars claim that the Null Echo is the desert's attempt
to sing without a god.
The Sylph whisper:
"The dunes are the grave of an abandoned Song."

---

2. The Mirage Belt — Veil of Forgotten Truths
Near the canopy's southern fall lies the Mirage Belt,
a shifting region where heat, memory, and resonance collide.
Mirages here are not mere illusions.
Some are:

- echoes of past wars,
- reflections of future threads,
- fragments of lives never lived,
- or memories the world itself tries to forget.

Travelers have reported:

- processions of Osiri priests walking into the sun and vanishing,
- wolves of wind chasing shadows that leave no tracks,
- a woman in green robes crossing the dunes without touching them,
- a city of glass rising at dawn and dissolving by dusk.

Aetherholt's Seers teach that the Mirage Belt is a
"thin place between Song and Null."

---

3. Singing Dunes — The Chord of Dust
Some dunes in the deep desert are said to "sing"—
vibrating beneath the shifting sands
and producing low, resonant tones
that echo across miles.
These tones change with seasons, storms,
and the burrowing movements of creatures below.
The Osiri claim the dunes sing
when the under-sands awaken.
The Sylph respond:
"If the desert sings, we should fear its hymn."

---

4. The Breathing Sands
In the regions closest to Ankhuriset and Sutekh'Kher,
the ground sometimes rises and falls subtly,
as if the desert itself were inhaling.
Scholars once believed this to be heat fluctuation.
Now, with the rediscovery of the Khem-Duat,
it is known that such movements often indicate
shifting tunnels below
or the passage of entities
that do not walk upon the surface.
To stand upon breathing sand is to feel the desert alive
beneath you—
and to know you are not alone.

5. Storms of the Sun-Scarred Sky
The desert gives birth to storms unlike any other place in
Vaelthara:

- Glassstorms — when lightning fuses sand into black shards
- Ashwinds — carrying dust that tastes metallic
- Echo-tempests — storms that repeat distant sounds, sometimes hours old, sometimes not yet spoken

In rare moments, these storms align with the Null Echo,
creating dissonance strong enough to disrupt magical
resonance
as far north as the canopy's edge.

6. Sacred and Cursed Zones
The Glass Fields
Where sand melts into smooth plains of mirrored black.
Some are natural.
Some… are not.
The Sun-Tombs
Ancient burial vaults whose outer stones glow faintly at night.
The Osiri claim their kings still whisper there.
The Shadowed Corridors
Rifts between dunes where sunlight never reaches,
even at midday.
Some say these corridors drink light,
leaving travelers cold even in the heat.
The Dune Lakes
Rare pools of still water reflecting stars even at noon,
as if the desert holds its own sky beneath the surface.

7. The Desert as a Harmonic Being

The Codex Harmonica classifies the desert as
"a Null Song entity"
—neither alive nor dead,
neither hostile nor passive,
but a vast, slumbering echo
of what Vaelthara once was
before the gods carved harmony into its bones.
The desert does not merely surround the Osiri Empire.
It *defines* it.
And it remembers everything.
As written in the oldest Aeralith scrolls:
"Beware the sands that dream.
For they dream of days when gods did not yet rule the world."

V. The Osiri Empire — "Stone, Shadow, and the Echo of
Forgotten Kings"
"Where the sun kneels to death, and memory takes the shape of a
jackal." — *Fragment of the Sutekh Tablets*
South of the Aeralith frontier,
beyond the first rising breath of the dunes,
the Osiri Empire endures like a scar upon the world.
It is a civilization carved from stone, shadow, and the
relentless will
to master both life and death.
The Osiri do not build forests or songs.
They build monuments—
places where silence has shape
and memory has teeth.
In harmonic lore, the Osiri realm is classified not as a
sanctuary or a Song-spire,
but as a Dissonant Dominion,
a counter-harmony aligned not with the gods of the
Twelvefold Song,
but with the Seven Null Gods,

ancient beings whose whispers cling to the desert's deepest
shadows.
To walk among Osiri cities
is to tread on the boundary between the living and the
unbound.

---

1. Amen'Kharethis — The Crescent Gate of the Black Sun
"Where kings ascend, though their hearts no longer beat."
Carved into a crescent cliff overlooking the western sea,
Amen'Kharethis stands like a scythe raised against the
horizon.
Its stone terraces drink sunlight and return it as shimmering
heat,
making the entire city glow like red-gold embers at dusk.
Hieroglyphs line the cliff walls—
etched with a precision so ancient
that even Osiri priests debate their meaning.
Some claim they are prayers.
Others insist they are warnings.
To the Sylph, the city is known as:
"The Western Fang."
For from here the Osiri launch their sea-bound raids
and begin their marches northward toward the Aeralith
frontier.

---

2. Sutekh'Kher — The City of Painted Kings
"The murals watch. The murals breathe. The murals remember."
Sutekh'Kher rises from the central desert like a colossal tomb
left standing
after its occupant refused to die.
The city's walls are covered in murals
depicting jackal-headed kings,
priests carrying soul-jars,

and serpents of ink winding around the pillars of forgotten
dynasties.
At dusk, these murals change color—
and sometimes form entirely new scenes.
Scholars call this phenomenon
"the shifting of the painted veil."
The Osiri call it
"the memory of kings."
None agree on what it means,
yet all fear to look away lest the murals show them something
meant only for the dead.

---

3. Mara-Sakhet — The Arid Redoubt
"In this city, the dead learn discipline."
Located south of Sutekh'Kher,
where the dunes turn a faint shade of blood-red at sunset,
Mara-Sakhet is the stronghold of the embalmer-priests.
Its halls are lined with jars sealed by gold-threaded resin.
Its streets echo with ritual marches
performed in absolute silence.
The air here carries the scent of resin and stone,
as though the entire city is preparing for an unending funeral.
In harmonic texts, Mara-Sakhet is named:
"The House of Stillness."
And stillness is both its burden and its blade.

---

4. Kheu-Duat — The Mouth of the Undersands
"All tunnels begin here. All shadows return here."
Kheu-Duat is the grand gateway
into the sprawling Khem-Duat beneath the world.
A cavernous sinkhole lies at its heart,
descending into blackstone stairways
lit by pale blue flames that burn without fuel.

Osiri armies vanish into this underworld
and reemerge days later across the desert frontier,
as if the sands themselves had carried them.
Above ground, Kheu-Duat appears muted—
a city of stone-faced priests and watchful statues.
Below ground,
its tunnels pulse with a cold, ancient rhythm
that echoes through the bones of any who dare descend.
The Sylph believe this city is a wound the earth has not
healed.

5. Ankhuriset — The Eastern Watch of the Golden Horizon
"From its spires, death looks northward."
Rising near the eastern boundaries of the desert,
Ankhuriset is a citadel of gold-tipped towers
that catch the sunrise like sharpened blades.
Here, the Osiri train their horizon-watchers—
priests and soldiers alike who study mirage behavior
and chart harmonic distortions caused by the Aeralith.
From Ankhuriset,
scouts monitor the Wind-Clan forests,
the border outposts,
and the quiet shifts of the dunes.
To the Sylph, this city is known in whispered fear as:
"The Eye That Does Not Close."
For it watches the Aeralith without rest,
as though waiting for the forest's courage to falter.

6. The Empire's Harmonic Nature
The Osiri Empire is a civilization out of step with the Song,
yet not entirely devoid of it.
Their resonance is inverted—
a mirror-Song shaped by death, memory, and the binding of
spirits.

Harmonic scholars classify Osiri resonance as:
- The Song of Preservation (binding)
- The Song of Dominion (commanding)
- The Song of Null Reflection (mirroring the living)

Thus, the Osiri are not enemies of harmony—
they are its shadow.
As the Codex warns:
"Where the forest grows, the desert remembers.
Where the gods sing, the dead reply."

VI. The Khem-Duat — "The Under-Sand Empire"

"Beneath the dunes lies the realm that breathes without air, and
remembers without light." — Aetherholt Subharmonic Tablet

South of the Aeralith frontier, beneath the shifting sands and
sun-scarred ridges of the Great Desert,
dwells a realm as old as sorrow and as patient as stone.
The Khem-Duat is not a mere tunnel system.
It is an underworld woven beneath the world,
a labyrinth of blackstone arteries through which the Osiri
Empire moves like a shadow with a thousand silent feet.
To the Sylph, the Khem-Duat is a horror.
To the Osiri, it is destiny.
To the Codex Harmonica, it is defined simply as:
"The Negative Harmony."
For where the forests sing,
the Khem-Duat consumes.
Where light reveals,
the Khem-Duat remembers.
Where life breathes,
the Khem-Duat waits.

---

1. The Nature of the Under-Sand World

The Khem-Duat breathes,
though no lungs fill its caverns.

Its walls pulse with a faint, cold resonance—
a rhythmic thrum felt in bones rather than heard by ears.
Some tunnels hum a single low note,
others whisper in shifting tones like restless spirits.
Scholars describe this phenomenon as
"Null Echo Resonance."
The Sylph prefer a simpler term:
"The Dissonance Below."

---

2. The Arteries of Stone and Shadow
The Khem-Duat is structured in three great layers:
The Upper Veins
Just beneath the desert surface—
a tangle of transport corridors used for troop movement
and sudden emergence beneath enemy borders.
These are the tunnels that cause the breathing sands above.
The Deep Roads
Massive blackstone halls carved in geometric precision,
lit by blue-white witchflame that burns without heat.
These are wide enough for entire battalions.
Here, murals shift like living ink.
Here, echoes walk behind you.
The Abyssal Wards
The deepest and oldest sections—
a cold empire unto themselves.
Even Osiri priests tread lightly there.
Some passages descend into darkness so complete
it smothers flame.
Legends claim the Seven Null Gods
whisper from these depths.
The Codex Harmonica cautions:
*"Where the world's Song does not reach,
the forgotten gods make their home."*

---

3. Gates and Entry Wells

Every major Osiri city rests atop at least one
Duat Gate,
though most are sealed with ritual wards.
The greatest entrances include:

- Kheu-Duat's Black Descent
  The grand gate to the entire under-empire.
- Amen'Kharethis' Echo Cavern
  A coastal tunnel that speaks in two voices.
- Sutekh'Kher's Painted Maw
  Where murals shift in time with Null resonance.
- Ankhuriset's Golden Shaft
  A precise stairwell descending in counter-spiral—
  the exact inversion of sacred Anari architecture.

Some entrances were once natural caverns.
Others were carved long before Anari memory began.

---

4. The Magic of the Khem-Duat

Magical principles behave differently here:

- Light bends and weakens
- Sound repeats or delays unpredictably
- Spells of detection are muffled
- Resonance-based magic loses clarity
- Illusion and necromancy grow stronger

Some tunnels warp distance,
allowing armies to march for minutes
and emerge miles—or days—away.
Aetherholt theorists call this
"Harmonic Inversion Geometry."
The Sylph call it
"the desert's lie made stone."

---

5. The Khem-Duat's Purpose

Though the Osiri cloak their underworld in mystery,
its true purposes are fivefold:
1. Military Conduit
Armies travel through it unseen,
striking far from their cities
and retreating without a trace.
2. Necromantic Laboratory
Silent chambers amplify spells
that bind spirits, preserve bodies,
and command shadows.
3. Tomb-Vaults
Burial halls that allow the Osiri to speak
with those long dead—
or return them to service.
4. Resonance Forge
A place where Null Echo power is harnessed
and woven into glyphs, wands, and soul-stones.
5. Memory Repository
The deepest murals depict events
older than the Twelve Gods—
events even the forests cannot recall.
Some show cities that never existed.
Some show futures that have not occurred.
Some show the Malloch.
And some show nothing at all.

6. The Sylph Interpretation
The Sylph view the Khem-Duat as
a violation of the world's breath,
for it stifles wind,
smothers harmony,
and replaces natural resonance
with the dissonant echo of death and dominion.
Sylphan seers teach:

"The forest sings.
The desert remembers.
But the Duat hungers."

---

7. The Khem-Duat in the Era of the Refugees
With the arrival of Kellyn Windstream and her companions
from the far future,
the rediscovery of the Khem-Duat
has altered the fate of the southern frontier.
The tunnels are awakening.
The Null Echo is strengthening.
Amenemapet's power grows.
And the wind no longer feels safe
beneath the sand.

VII. Paths of the Southern War — "Stanzas of Conflict in the
Wind"
"Every journey is a verse. Every battle, a chord. Every loss, a silence the
Song must learn to bear." — *Codex Harmonica, War Leaf VII*
The struggle that unfolds along the Aeralith frontier
is not merely a series of marches and clashes.
To the Sacred Cartographers of Aetherholt,
it is a harmonic event—
a disturbance in the Twelvefold Song
whose echoes will shape both past and future.
Thus the travels of Kellyn Windstream and her companions
are recorded not as routes or engagements,
but as Stanzas of the Southern Harmony,
each step a note resonating across the border
between forest and desert,
between life and Null,
between destiny remembered and destiny undone.

---

1. The Stanza of Falling Leaves

The Wolf's Cry in Faelwyn Holt
The first verse of this southern war
was not written in the desert,
nor in the canopy,
but in the lonely forests of the northwest
where the Wolf Clan stood against the rising flood
of human expansion.
Here, the Harmony trembled
as Corlyn's band of refugees fled through the frost-dark trees.
The Wolf Clan rallied,
facing siege and sorrow in equal measure.
When Kellyn arrived,
the resonance shifted—
a sharp upward sweep in the Song
marking the first turn of destiny.
The Codex records:
"From fallen leaves the first cry rose,
and the forest answered."

---

2. The Stanza of Hidden Roots
Crossing Aetherholt and the Vaelen Path
The company's journey eastward
toward Aetherholt and the sheltered Vaelen
was a verse of swift breath and gathering tension.
Through ancient ruins,
between river-chants,
and beneath Griffyn archways heavy with memory,
the world's Song darkened.
Each step carried them closer
to the parting of green and gold,
toward the forest that did not welcome outsiders
and the desert that welcomed no one.

---

3. The Stanza of the Wind's Descent

Entering the Aeralith Canopy
The Aeralith received them like a whispered question.
Sylph eyes watched from branches,
barely glimpsed.
Songs moved through the air in threads so fine
they were felt more than heard.
Here Kellyn's presence became a point of divergence—
a new chord woven into an ancient melody.
Sylph seers later wrote:
"The wind shifted that day,
for it carried the breath of those out of time."

---

4. The Stanza of the Three Vigil-Notes
Outposts 3, 4, and 5
The crossing between forest and desert
was a descent through vigilance.

- At Outpost 3,
  the company learned the language of the dunes—
  a whispering tongue spoken through shifting sand.
- At Outpost 4,
  they beheld the desert's horizon
  and felt the first dissonant pull of the Null Echo.
- At Outpost 5,
  the green world gave its final vow of protection,
  and silence pressed in like unseen fingers.

Each outpost marked a thinning of harmony,
a step closer to the dissonant void beyond.

---

5. The Stanza of the Breathing Sands
Crossing into the Great Desert
The desert greeted them with mirages
that showed truths and untruths in equal measure.
The sands breathed.
The dunes sang.

Storms whispered memories
that may never have been real.
Travelers of later ages called this passage
"The Walk of Unbound Steps."
For here,
no path is ever truly the same twice.

---

6. The Stanza of the Black Sun
The Pyramid and the Arch-Lich
At the pyramid buried beneath sun-scorched sky,
the Harmony fractured.
Amenemapet, Lord of the Undying,
stirred the Null Echo into a swirling dirge,
raising legions from the sands
as though calling up the desert's own grief.
The earth shook with dissonance.
The forest's Song strained across miles
to hold its boundary.
And beneath the blinding sun,
Kellyn and her companions faced the ancient truth
that memory, once awakened,
does not sleep again.

---

7. The Stanza of the Under-Sand Escape
Flight through the Khem-Duat
When the Null Song rose too sharply upon the dunes,
the company plunged downward—
into the cold, dead arteries of the Khem-Duat.
Here the world's music inverted.
Here echoes walked.
Here walls remembered.
The under-sands swallowed their footfalls
as though tasting the resonance of those who should not exist
in this time.

Yet they escaped.
And the Song, though shaken, endured.

---

8. The Final Stanza — "The Breath Before Battle"
The company's return to the Aeralith
carried with it the weight of new knowledge
and the tremor of greater wars yet to come.
The forest received them,
but the Harmony did not settle.
It vibrated like a bowstring
drawn toward the future.
As the Aeralith Tablets record:
"The wind returned laden with prophecy,
and the leaves trembled,
knowing the world's next verse
would be written in blood."

VIII. Final Invocation — "The Wind Remembers"
"When the frontier trembles, the world listens." — *Aeralith Closing*
Tablet, Fragment 9
Thus ends the atlas of the southern frontier:
the canopy of living wind,
the desert of silent memory,
the Vigil-Notes that stand against dissonance,
and the underworld that hungers beneath the sand.
These lands are not passive terrain
upon which stories are written.
They are participants in the Harmony—
listening, responding, and shaping the fates
of those who dare walk the border
between Song and Null.
The Aeralith breathes with vigilance.
The Great Desert whispers in forgotten tongues.

The Khem-Duat coils beneath both,
waiting for the shape of coming wars.
And northward, in the cold forests of Faelwyn Holt,
a new verse stirs.
The winds of prophecy gather,
carrying the scent of the hunt,
the shadow of storms,
and the distant tolling of a horn
long thought lost.
As the Codex Harmonica concludes:
"The Song endures,
even when broken.
Even when burdened.
Even when whispered beneath the tread of time.
For every silence the world suffers,
the Harmony will answer."
The world stands now upon the threshold
of deeper truths and darker melodies.
What emerges from forest, desert, and under-sand
will shape not only the fate of Vaelthara,
but of all who remember the gods—
and all who have forgotten them.
And so the atlas closes,
but the Song does not.
Its next verse waits in the shadows of Faelwyn Holt,
where the Hunt prepares to rise.

Appendix 10: The Anari Confederation of Planets

(Sixteen-Point Mandate and Expanding Frontier)

Core World

1. Vaelthara (Homeworld)
Capital: Sylvara Prime
Population: ~1.6 billion
Traits: Birthplace of the Anari; vast forests and cities where nature merges with civilization. The gods' touch lingers in its soil.
Governance: Confederation Assembly and planetary council with colony representation.
Role: Minimal government. Free citizenry.

Inner Arc Worlds — The Confederation's Heart (High Population Zones)

2. Calenwynd — Second Sylvara
Population: ~600 million
Traits: Endless forest world of life-healing and deep herbal lore.
Governance: Republic of forest councils.
Role: Healer's world and botanical supplier.

3. Eloweth — The Singing Vale
Population: ~400 million
Traits: Verdant valleys and amphitheaters beneath living glass.
Governance: Monarchy of the Song-Queens.
Role: Cultural and artistic capital of the Confederation.

4. Veylthar — The Breadworld
Population: ~700 million
Traits: Rolling plains and rivers sustaining vast farmlands.
Governance: Agrarian senate of land-stewards.
Role: Agricultural heart; feeds both homeworld and colonies.

Forge Belt — Industrial and Naval Worlds (Middle Population Zones)

5. Draventhis — The Forge-Heart
Population: ~300 million
Traits: Jagged mountains, forge-cities glowing red against eternal dusk.
Governance: Oligarchy of forge-houses and refineries.
Role: Arms and armor production, heavy manufacturing.

6. Korrin's Reach — Shipwright's Crown
Population: ~250 million
Traits: Volcanic archipelagos and orbital dry-docks.
Governance: Industrial Directorate under Wyvern Fleet command.
Role: Primary shipbuilding and fleet engineering world.

7. Torvalis — Sea of Blades
Population: ~180 million
Traits: Oceanic world of perpetual storms and naval fortresses.
Governance: Admiralty Council.
Role: Confederation's fleet training and coastal defense hub.

Shard Realms — Research Worlds (Moderate Population Zones)

8. Sylvaranth — The Crystal Gardens
Population: ~210 million
Traits: Forests veined with living crystal resonating to
harmonic song.
Governance: Confederation of Communes. Call themselves
"Mage Council"
Role: Nature research and ley-energy regulation. No "magic"
demonstrable, just belief.

9. Lirien — The Aetherholt
Population: ~170 million
Traits: Auroral mesas and desert laboratories.
Governance: Academy of Aetherholt.
Role: Thaumic research and energy innovation.

10. Thaloryn — The Veiled World
Population: ~120 million
Traits: Fog-shrouded necropolises and alabaster cathedrals.
Governance: Oligarchy of bone-priests and healers.
Role: Controversial center of necromantic medicine.

Outer Rim — Frontier, Refuge, and Intelligence Worlds
(Low Population Zones)

11. Caeranthys — The Frost March
Population: ~90 million
Traits: Boreal tundra, auroras above glacier cities.
Governance: Clan-based council.
Role: Survivalist world-breeding explorers and soldiers.

12. Faelwyn — The Hunter's World
Population: ~80 million
Traits: Deep predator-forests and moonlit canopies. Timber
resource.

Governance: Ranger councils.
Role: Scout-training and field-reconnaissance hub. Hunting and Tracking.

13. Vaelthar Secundus — World of Shadows
Population: ~60 million (classified)
Traits: Mist-jungles and subterranean citadels.
Governance: Hidden councils of the Shadow Lords.
Role: Espionage and data-intelligence headquarters.

14. Hearthfall — The Haven World
Population: ~250 million
Traits: Valley sanctuaries and eternal hearth-lights.
Governance: Council of Hearth-Keepers.
Role: Refugee and resettlement world for displaced clans.

15. Aegros — The Borealis Frontier
Population: ~40 million
Traits: Polar ice shelves and geothermal rift arrays.
Governance: Frontier Directorate under the Confederation charter.
Role: Outer-rim research and monitoring station.
Status (FY 3553): Contact lost after polar anomaly.

Expanding Colonies and New Frontiers

16 – 19. The Spiral Reaches (Provisional Worlds)
Locations: Selen Rift, Carinth III, Sylos IV, and Eryndor Beta.
Population: ~100 million combined and growing.
Governance: Confederation Colonial Directorate.
Role: New settlement arc, maintaining population balance; each new world lowers pressure on the Core.

"When one world grows crowded, we seed another. The
Confederation does not expand for conquest but for
equilibrium—so that every child may walk beneath open
sky."
— Excerpt, Charter of the Second Expansion, FY 3512

✧ Demographic Summary ✧

Total Confederation Population (FY 3553): ≈ 5 billion Anari
Population Distribution:

Core + Inner Arc = ~3 billion

Forge + Shard = ~1.2 billion

Outer Rim + Frontier = ~0.8 billion
Trend: Stable growth at +0.7% annual; controlled expansion
through migratory accords and off-world incentives.

📖 Cartographer's Note — "The Living Constellation"

"The Confederation does not stand still. Each world is a note
in a chord, ever-expanding—new planets join the harmony as
older ones rest.
The pattern of the Mandate is not fixed in stone, but sung in
motion."
— Atlas Anaridica, 4th Confederation Edition

Author's Note

Across the worlds where the Anari once called home, their history is broken and scattered through time—buried in collapsing timelines, preserved in drifting star archives, and encoded in fragments never meant to last. What you just read is one such fragment. It is a record, a warning, a hero's testament, and—like all surviving Anari histories—an incomplete truth.

Book Two reveals a crucial truth about the Anari: they were never a single empire.

They consisted of fiercely independent clans—each guided by a deity, a homeland, a song, and a unique way of warfare. The Sylph Clan, in particular, embodies a paradox: unseen but constantly observing, fragile to outsiders but lethal when the wind summons its members. Their lives and combat style—crafted from blade, wind, and triple-harmonic song—underscore the duality at the heart of the Anari race: beauty and ferocity, mysticism and discipline, devotion and independence.

This book was also written to cast a wider shadow over the Osiri, a civilization known only through ruins and dust in the distant future. Their sorcery, their living-weapon genetics, and their ghost-roads beneath the sands—these were barely whispered myths in Kellyn's era. This volume brings their empire into the light, only to reveal how deep its darkness runs.

Kellyn's journey is only just beginning. She's a warrior — but also something more: a leader not yet crowned, a unifier still striving for acceptance, a woman who can see a path others cannot.

Her divination isn't just foresight. It's a revelation.

It's the gift—and burden—of the Unveiled Path.

The events in this book serve as the first real test of whether Kellyn and her friends can survive the ancient world they once thought was only a myth. But the journey ahead will require more than just survival.

It will require decisions that unite clans, challenge gods, and alter the War of Twelve Races itself.
Book Three awaits—and with it, revelations older than the Anari and dangers even the future couldn't foresee.
Thank you for walking the Unveiled Path with Kellyn and her companions.

—K. J. Hausheer

Drakkenwyld Archives, Compiled from recovered fragments of the Aelthrys Temporal Directorate Spire